# Chasing Angels

ISBN: 0-9857-9541-7
ISBN-13: 9780985795412

# Chasing Angels

## Polly D. Boyette

2012

# Dedication

To my sister, Robin for her love, prayers and encouragement. Without your support, Chasing Angels would have never been written.

# I

"Watch out! The dragon is right behind me! I can feel his breath on my neck. Run for your lives before he destroys us all."

Nathan was just a young boy who had not seen much of the world outside the small town of Fairhaven, and yet, he was wise beyond his 11 years. He spent a lot of time on his own these days. His mother was often too busy to pay attention to him. Nathan didn't mind though. He used his imagination to stay occupied. Right now there was a fire-breathing dragon lurking at the edge of the woods. If he kept low to the ground, perhaps he'd be invisible to the monster's yellow eyes. He hid for what seemed like forever, until the sky was clear with only a few motionless clouds drifting above him.

Cautiously, he left his hiding place and walked along the banks of the Black River. The trees were amber and gold today, much brighter than they had appeared yesterday. The wind sent a chill through him. Kicking at the leaves, he picked up a stick that could have easily passed as an ancient sword of a warrior who walked this same path centuries ago along the old Black River. Nathan paused to think how the river had been there since he could remember. He thought of it more as a trusted friend than just simply a river. No matter what happened, he could always come there and find the comfort and warmth that was missing at home.

The sun was radiant today. So he took advantage of it and used his powerful sword to ward off evil and invisible enemies. He felt strong with the sun shining on his back. It was different from the night, when everything was colorless and cold. He turned quickly to make sure no one had followed him with a surprise attack from behind.

Nathan jumped and rolled in the crisp leaves on the soft ground. What a day! No mere human could make a day like this, even if they tried. He leaned up against a tree and listened for a while. The birds were rehearsing a new symphony that would be debuted tomorrow morning for lucky early risers. They didn't seem to mind him eavesdropping. As a matter of fact, they seemed to sing even louder now. Nathan closed his eyes and he could almost hear a piano and a distant flute. His imagination was perfect today. He paused a little longer, and then, as if something or someone had called him, he took off running down the edge of the river's bank, skipping and dragging his sword closely by his side. "Wait, was that the dreaded dragon hiding behind that tree?" he wondered to himself. Even a dragon couldn't conquer the magical sword he possessed. He posed himself like a brave knight about to do battle with his worst enemy.

"This will surely make me famous," he thought. "Why, I bet there hasn't been a dragon slain in these parts in hundreds of years." The dragon was breathing heavily now. Nathan could see smoke rising from his nostrils. "Be brave," he whispered to himself. "You have your sword. Nothing can harm you as long as you swing it with all your might." He steadied his hand and placed one arm behind his back. He ran at the tree with the sword outstretched and leapt on the other side to greet his opponent with surprise.

The fire-breathing dragon had disappeared. Apparently, too frightened to stay and fight. But something had been left behind. As Nathan bent to push some of the leaves away for a better view, he saw what looked like a human hand. He fell backwards, landing awkwardly on his sword. Could it be? Should he look again? He was trembling inside and suddenly felt afraid. But his curiosity was greater than his fear. He stepped closer and bent down again to search for what he thought he had seen. Yes, there it was, a small pale hand, like that of a child. He carefully removed more of the leaves until he could clearly see that it was a child, a boy, with dark hair and smooth skin. The small body was motionless and cold and his lips were a bluish color. Off in the distance, he heard someone calling his name.

"Nathan, where are you? Are you playing out there? Nathan, answer me!"

He quickly covered the body with leaves again and ran toward the voice. He thought it was the voice of his mother, calling him for dinner, but as he ran, it grew more faint. "Wait," he yelled back. "I'm coming." He ran as fast as he could. "Please, wait Mom, I'm here," he gasped, as he continued to run. Suddenly, he didn't know where he was. The woods had turned dark and confusing. Yet, he continued to run, listening for the voice in the distance to guide him.

The voice called him again, "Nathan! I'm here. Nathan, over here."

He stopped and listened. Was that his mother?

"Nathan, where you going?"

That wasn't his mother's voice, but who was calling him? He decided to run in the opposite direction, back to where he started. But an old man with thin white hair appeared right behind him, blocking his escape. His eyes were bright and open wide. He wore a white shirt and what looked like a wide blue sash running from shoulder to waist, almost like some kind of angel. His face seemed strangely hidden.

"Nathan, where you going?" the old man asked in an odd broken English. "Why you running away?"

Nathan was too terrified to answer, so he just stood and stared. The old man reached out to touch Nathan's hair.

"You young," he said softly. "You strong, but you look scared," the old man said calmly.

Nathan wasn't sure if he was afraid, or just numb. "Who are you?" He asked in a quivering voice.

"Friend, Nathan," he answered.

Nathan couldn't believe what he was hearing. "My friend?"

"Yes," the old man spoke as though he knew him well.

Nathan backed away, "I've got to go home. My mom will be looking for me."

"Okay," said the old man. "I wait for you here, okay? Then we play."

Nathan turned and ran until he reached home. Too afraid to stop, he slammed the door and ran past his mother as she stood in the front room.

"Where have you been, Nathan? I can't hold dinner for you forever you know. I have to be at work at seven tonight."

He raced up the stairs and slammed the door behind him with his mother still yelling up to him.

"Nathan, get down here and eat your supper so I can go to work without feeling guilty that you haven't eaten."

Nathan lay frozen on his bed. Dare he tell his mother what he had seen? Would she ever believe him? What if the old man he saw in the woods killed the young boy he found in the leaves? Maybe he would be next. He should tell someone.

His mother stormed up the stairs. "Nathan, are you deaf? I said your supper is getting cold. Why are you lying there like a mummy? Get moving."

He slowly made his way past his mother, but he didn't utter a sound. She would never understand. She always said his imagination ran wild. This was a story he would have to keep to himself. Maybe it was his imagination. After all, the woods had always been full of games and wonders for him. His imagination, yeah, that's all it was.

That night in bed he was tired, but he was too afraid to close his eyes. He stared up at the ceiling counting the cracks that ran through the paint. The house was old, but it was the only thing his father had left him and his mother. His father died in an accident on a construction job. He could still remember his mother crying when he walked into the house from school that day. He could barely understand her through the sobbing, but he knew his father had died. Three men from the job site brought the news and they were still standing in the front room. They had those "we're-sorry, but-what-do-we-do-now?" looks on their faces. They stood shifting awkwardly from one foot to the other until his mother told them it was all right for them to leave. He remembered his grandmother coming to stay with them that night. Both his mother and grandmother had cried way into the night, but for some reason, he couldn't cry. Nathan loved his father, but he still couldn't bring himself to cry. Maybe it would come later. As he studied the cracks in the paint, there seemed to be more than before, or was it just that he hadn't counted them in a long time?

A howling wind woke him at 3:15 in the morning. The window shade was flapping loudly against the woodwork. As he turned to face the other way, he thought he caught a glimpse of a face in the window. He turned to look again, but there was no one there. As he turned over, he heard a child's voice calling his name.

"Nathan," it called softly. "Come play with me."

Nathan sat up in bed. Did he hear his name?

"Nathan, please come play with me," the voice called again. "I've got nobody to play with me. The woods are great at night. The moon is shining full. Can't you come out?"

He slipped out of bed and cautiously walked toward the window. He couldn't see a thing. Was it the wind? Was it his imagination again?

"Nathan," the child called again. He seemed farther away this time. Yes, he clearly heard someone calling his name.

Nathan pulled on his coat and slippers and grabbed his flashlight from a drawer, testing it against the bedroom wall. Climbing carefully out of the window, he dropped quietly down to the ground and followed the voice toward the woods. The trees always drew him to the woods in the daytime, but at night they seemed scary and threatening. Everything seems different at night.

The child's voice was laughing now. "Nathan, I'm over here. Hurry, up!"

He walked quickly now to catch up to the voice. The wind seemed to blow him in the direction of the child's constant calling. He found himself at the river's edge, but he couldn't see anyone there.

"Little boy," Nathan called out. "Where are you? Why do you keep calling me?" There was no answer. Nathan shined his flashlight toward the water, running the light up and down the Black River. At night the rocks looked like backs of crocodiles resting in the water. He stood very still, listening to the sound of the river rushing by him.

"Nathan!"

He turned his light in the direction of the voice. There he was, a young boy, maybe Nathan's age, with dark hair. He stood in the middle of the river, perched on one of the crocodile backs, or rocks or whatever they were.

Suddenly, the boy started jumping from rock to rock. "Nathan, can you do this?"

"Of course I can," he answered, "but it's the middle of the night." The child seemed weightless and unafraid of the dangers of the river. "Hey, what's your name?" Nathan asked.

"Robert," the child answered.

Then just as quickly as the child had appeared, he was gone. Nathan stood alone in the night with just his flashlight shining on the rock where Robert had been standing. "Where'd he go?" Robert was gone with no trace.

The woods were quiet. Nathan backed away, and then walked back toward home. He kept looking over his shoulder to see if Robert was behind him, but there was no one there. It was as though he had just vanished. Nathan began to wonder if he had just imagined him again. What was happening to him? He had a strong urge to look back once more as he was walking. As he slowly turned around once again, there, at the edge of the woods, stood an old man with white hair, waving at Nathan.

"Goodnight," the strange man said in a low raspy voice. "Goodnight, Nathan."

# 2

Nathan pushed the memories of Robert deep inside him and they weren't recalled again. However, he vividly remembered the dark, rich river that flowed near his home when he was a boy. He'd often sit in a trance thinking about that place. His Mother was gone now and he was a grown man. He had become a successful writer, having left the small quaint town of Fairhaven behind. He had outgrown a lot of his awkwardness, but not his ever-changing imagination. Inside, he still felt like the same young boy running along the Black River. Sometimes his writing would be interrupted by long pauses as his mind wandered back over that period of time again and again.

For now, he had decided it was time for a break from his busy life. He was heading back to Fairhaven for a return visit. He didn't know for sure exactly what was drawing him back home since his family was all gone now, but there were thousands of memories in that old town that somehow made him relax and feel at peace with himself. He decided he would just take some time off, do some fishing, see old friends again, and see whether there might even be some new stories there worth writing.

Driving back home, he stopped along the way to pause at a stream that emptied into the Black River. It wound its way through the woods, like a snake twists and turns over everything in its pathway. "Funny," he thought. "Everything seems to change except this old river. It seems determined to rush past, no matter what's going on around it. Nothing can stop it." Just hearing the rushing sounds of the water moving over the rocks and fallen tree branches made him feel at home. He felt as though he could stand and listen with his eyes closed for the remainder of his time off, but he finally tore himself away and drove on to town. The river paid no attention.

When he reached town, he took a room in one of the beautiful bed and breakfasts available, The Raven Inn, which was run by an old friend of Nathan's mother, Maggie Sanding, and her daughter, Marcie. It was as beautiful as ever, like an old friend welcoming him home.

"Nathan, Nathan, get yourself over here and give me a hug."

Nathan turned to see Maggie walking as quickly as she could at her age with arms open wide and a big grin on her face.

"Maggie, how are you doing old girl?"

"Well, as good as a person my age can, I expect," she said. "Where's your wife?" she asked, trying to see around behind him.

"My wife? Maggie, I'm not married. You know that. Don't you think I would have invited you to my wedding if I were getting married?" Nathan asked looking puzzled.

"Well, I guess you are going to die single, Nathan. I declare you ought to be married with nine children all around you by now."

"Speaking of married, where's that daughter of yours, Marcie?" Nathan asked anxiously. "I heard a rumor she took the plunge herself."

Maggie leaned closer to Nathan, "Well now, aren't we behind the times. That wedding knot never did get tied, honey. I reckon at the last minute Marcie panicked. If you ask me, she's still carrying something warm in her heart for you."

Nathan looked down at the ground silently celebrating that Marcie hadn't married after all. "Where's she living nowadays anyway?"

Maggie pointed in an upward general direction. "Oh they bought a nice house up on the ridge there, thinking that's where they would live after the wedding. When they parted ways, David, that's who she was marrying, David Moore, decided to let her keep the house. I think he just wanted out as much as she did. It has more room than she needs, but I think she loves that house so much she just had to keep it. "Maggie looked past Nathan in the direction of the house up on the ridge. "I just want her to be happy." Maggie walked back inside and slowly sat on the worn, antique couch in the living room. She looked tired, but peaceful.

"I'm sure she's happy, Maggie," said Nathan softly. "She's got a lot going for her, always has. I've always been a little jealous of her myself," he teased.

"Jealous? Why, what on earth of?" Maggie asked.

"Well, for one thing you're the best cook in the state and she gets to eat your cooking every day," Nathan laughed. "Speaking of food, when's dinner?"

"Oh, you always did manage to change the subject to food when you were around me. Get up to your room and clean up a bit before you eat. Dinner is at six o'clock sharp. So don't be late." Maggie started picking up and fluffing the pillows from the chairs.

"I'll be there," said Nathan. He grabbed his bags and headed up the stairs, turning to watch Maggie shuffle off toward the kitchen. He knew she would prepare something special tonight.

That night, after a wonderful dinner, Nathan decided to go for a walk to enjoy the evening air. As he walked along an old dirt path that wound around the property of the Raven Inn, he couldn't help staring up at the house where Marcie lived. Did he really want to see her again after all this time? Deep down inside Nathan knew that he did, but his head wouldn't allow his heart to even dream about being with her again. She was so beautiful. He could remember her movements and her soft dark hair that always hid a little bit of her face. How would it be if they met again? Would it be like it was back then? Would he still feel at ease with her like when he was younger? They used to talk forever until her mother would start calling out her name in the quiet night. Nathan had left her and this town to pursue an unknown future, not knowing where he would finally end up. He only knew that it was something he had to do.

He stood in the dark and thought about the night he said goodbye to her. She sobbed quietly. The tears streamed down her cheeks as she looked deeply into his eyes. She seemed to be looking for something that he wasn't telling her. He didn't even understand at the time why he had to go away; just that he desperately needed a change.

The world always seems so much bigger when you're born and raised in a small town like Fairhaven. It almost calls you away, beckoning you to explore the unknown. At least, that's what he felt at the time, and so he left. But just as he had heard something calling him away, he now felt called to return for a while and he didn't know how he would even begin to explain that to Marcie. Would she even let him explain? Maybe tomorrow he would see her and it would be like old times again.

As he turned to walk back to the house he heard someone walking around in the woods near him. "Hello," he called into the darkness. He continued to walk and again he heard the noise in the woods. It sounded like the cracking of twigs under someone's feet. Nathan stood very still and listened, but he didn't hear anything. "Probably a rabbit," he thought. But just as he started walking again, he heard the noise. This time it was going away from him and with quick steps. Nathan's curiosity got the best of him, so he walked toward the wooded area and the footsteps. "Hello, is somebody there?" he shouted. But no answer came.

It was pitch black and Nathan couldn't see anything at all, so he decided to just give up and head back to The Raven. It was too late to be chasing things through the woods anyway. As he turned to head back, the noise started again, except this time it seemed to be coming toward him. Nathan kept walking but turned to see if he could see anything behind him, nothing but complete darkness. However, the steps seemed faster now and even sounded as if something was running toward him. He quickened his pace, but the steps sounded closer now and faster. Nathan could hear heavy breathing now, almost directly behind him. He stopped and turned to face his mystery stalker, but as he turned, the steps sounded as though they were right behind him. The steps continued closer and closer until suddenly, Nathan felt a heavy breath on his face and the steps seemed to run right through him. He closed his eyes, shocked that it just ran past him, through him or around him. He wasn't sure. His head bounced back and then forward as though something had actually passed through him. Then, it was gone. Nathan was gripped with overwhelming fear, making it impossible for him to move. He just stood still while the steps and the panting breath rushed by him. And then it was quiet again.

Nathan opened his eyes, but there was nothing to see. Only darkness surrounded him in the woods. Finally, he got the courage to look around him, but again, there was nothing there. Nathan backed out of the woods and out into the open. There was nothing as far as he could see. "Was it an animal just running scared? It must have been," he reassured himself. "What else could it be?"

Nathan made his way back to his room still shaken. As he crawled back into his bed and closed his eyes he thought, "This is great. You get scared the first night back by some animal in the woods." As he dismissed the whole thing and tried to put it out of his mind, he started to drift off to sleep. There was something very strange, but at the same time, very familiar about what had happened to him tonight. He didn't understand it, and he was too tired to try to figure it out now. He reached for the light by his bed and turned it off. Everything felt familiar to him here.

# 3

The next morning Maggie treated Nathan to a big country breakfast like he hadn't tasted since he left home. It was a beautiful day and he was eager to go check out the town and see what changes had taken place.

"Maggie, that was the best meal I've had in ages. You're still the best cook around," he bragged loudly.

"Oh, hush. It's been so long since you had a good home-cooked meal you're just bound to compliment my cooking," Maggie said in a modest tone.

"Well, I still know a good meal when I eat one. Sorry to eat and run," he said standing up from the table. "But, I really want to go exploring today."

"Not too much has changed around here since you left us. Maybe a new store or two and a few different folks living here, but not much else."

"Well, I still want to see—" Nathan was interrupted by a call from the hallway.

"Mom, could you please give me a hand? I've brought you some things from the store and I need some help carrying them in," a familiar voice called from out front.

Just then Nathan looked up to see Marcie standing in the doorway. At first they just stared at one another without saying a word.

"I'm a little tied up, but I'm sure Nathan here will be glad to give you a hand with the things. Right Nathan?" Maggie teased, as she waited for Marcie's reaction.

"Nathan, it's you. I can't believe it," Marcie said looking shocked. "When did you get into town?"

"Yesterday. You look absolutely, good. I mean, great. You look great." Again there was silence.

"Of course, if you're not going to help her I could carry in the things myself, even though I'm just an old woman with small, thin arms," Maggie said in an amused tone.

"No, no I've got it," Nathan replied, his eyes still fixed on Marcie.

"This way," Marcie said pointing to the car outside, never taking her eyes off of him.

They both walked outside without speaking, totally unprepared for this moment.

"Well, I hear you almost got married." Nathan didn't know how to even begin a conversation with Marcie. Already, he wished he hadn't mentioned her failed attempt to marry.

"Yeah, almost. I guess it was for the best that it didn't work out though. He was a busy man, always on the go. He didn't really know anything else except his work." Marcie paused. "Well, look at me. We see each other after all these years and within moments I'm sharing my personal life with you."

"Sorry, I didn't mean to pry. I was just trying to think of something to say to you after all this time. I picked the wrong subject."

"Never mind, it's all right. It was over before it started. I think Mom's glad it never happened. She never cared for him much. Maybe she was right. Maybe it's best that the marriage didn't work out." Marcie looked down at the ground and Nathan could see that it was a hard subject for her to discuss.

"Come on, let's get these things in the house before Maggie comes out here and starts carrying them in herself." Nathan grabbed the bags and started toward the house.

Marcie lingered at the car a few moments to collect herself. Then she grabbed the last couple of bags and followed him inside.

"Nathan was just about to go into town, Marcie," Maggie said, as she began browsing through the bags. "Why don't you go along and show him the changes around here?"

"Oh, where are you off to?" Marcie asked.

"I just wanted to take a drive around the town and maybe drop in and say hello to a few folks. But if you're busy—"

"Well, I was going to help Mom put these things away." Marcie started to quickly go through the bags and sort out everything.

"I've got this darlin'," Maggie said, grabbing the things out of her hands. "You two run along. I can handle it from here."

"Oh, all right then." Marcie picked up her purse. "Well, ready then?"

Nathan and Marcie drove into town with only polite conversation between them. It was really awkward being together after all these years with nothing to say to each other.

"Any particular place you wanted to go?" Marcie asked.

"How about a walk through the park?" Nathan suggested. "It's a beautiful day and I used to love going there as a kid."

Walking along the brick-paved paths in the park brought back a lot of memories for Nathan, the smells, the sounds and the gorgeous gardens. He wanted very much to get to know Marcie again. Why did it have to be so hard? "Uh, let's sit for a while," suggested Nathan.

Walking over to a nearby bench, they took a seat underneath an old maple tree. Marcie looked the same, just as Nathan had remembered her, with her hair hiding parts of her lovely face and a smile that always put him at ease.

"Marcie," Nathan began.

"Nathan, please. You don't owe me an explanation. You did what you felt you had to do. I don't have any ill feelings about us, if that's what you're worried about. You did what you thought you had to do at the time and that's it. Maybe it was the right thing to happen for both of us. Anyway, look at you, a writer. Do you think that would have ever come about if we had gotten married and tried to raise a family? Would you have just gotten a job, any job, just to make ends meet? Your writing would have never taken off." Marcie softly touched Nathan's shoulder and smiled, "But I do hope we can be friends again."

Nathan didn't know what to feel at this point. He couldn't think of how to respond to her right now. His world was turned upside down. Just looking at her took his breath away, but he tried hard to disguise his true feelings.

"We can always be friends, Marcie. I've known you since I was a boy. You and your mother are like family to me." Nathan gave a quick smile and looked away. "Family," he thought. He knew it was much more than a family feeling that made his heart beat twice as fast each time they looked at each other. Maybe it was best left alone. What if she was right? Nathan loved writing and he also liked his life right now. Was there room in his life for anyone else?

They just sat for a while saying nothing, stealing looks without the other noticing and then staring down at their feet. "This visit was a big mistake," Nathan thought.

Marcie took Nathan around the town of Fairhaven and pointed out some of the changes that had taken place. Old favorite stores had gone out of business and had been replaced by more modern buildings. Some of the familiar faces were still around, but working in different occupations now. Little by little Nathan placed the names and faces together in his mind, drawing on his past memories. Sometimes his memory failed him, but he still smiled as though he had known them for years. He probably had, but he somehow misplaced more information than he could remember. It was almost like he was coming out of amnesia. Different faces jogged memory after memory, like various short frames of film running through his mind, until he was able to find their proper place in his boyhood.

"What about Mark?" Nathan asked. "I know he's bound to be still kicking around here someplace. What's he doing nowadays?"

"You won't believe this, but he's the sheriff now." Marcie watched as Nathan's face drained of color.

"Sheriff? He stayed in more trouble with the police than anybody else in this town!" Nathan laughed out loud. "This I've got to see. Where is he now?"

"Probably in Jordan's Diner having lunch this time of day."

"Jordan's, man it's been ages since I was inside that place. You want to go and grab something to eat? If I remember correctly, they had the best hamburgers I ever tasted. Even since I moved away I haven't tasted any better."

"You go ahead," Marcie replied. "I can't spend all day parading you around town. I have to go and help Mom. We're running an inn you know. I'll catch up to you later." Marcie pointed the way to Jordan's for Nathan.

"Maybe we can have dinner." Nathan said as Marcie was walking away.

"I've got to help Mom serve the evening meal."

"That's right, I forget you're a working girl. Tell Maggie to hold my table for dinner tonight."

Marcie smiled, "Maybe we'll have dessert together." She waved goodbye and headed back to The Raven.

Nathan stood for a moment and watched her walk away wondering how or if Marcie would ever allow him back in her life again. He only knew one thing for sure. He had never stopped loving her.

# 4

"Hey stranger! What brings you back home?"

Nathan turned to see a familiar face. "Gracey? Gracey Davis, is that you?" Nathan couldn't believe his eyes. Gracey Davis was a vision from the past. She had a crush on every boy in town when he was growing up. "Wow, Gracey, you look great."

"I can't believe it's you walking around town again," Gracey said as she hugged Nathan. "Let's go and have lunch. I'm starving."

Gracey was always available for a free meal and anything else that she could get from whoever had it to give. She dressed like a movie star that was well past her fame. She'd do anything to attract attention. Nathan couldn't believe that she was still in town. He figured she'd be in Hollywood by now doing B movies and riding on the coattails of some rich, well-to-do man.

"Lunch, yeah, that's fine," Nathan fumbled.

Gracey was already locked on to his arm, so there wasn't a lot he could do or say at this point.

As they walked into Jordan's, Nathan spotted Mark right away. There he was, wearing a sheriff's uniform along with a bright shiny badge. It was hard to imagine Mark as a lawman of any kind. As a kid he was always bucking authority of any sort.

"Now look at him. He is the authority," Nathan laughed to himself.

"Mark, looky over here, honey," Gracey yelled out.

Everyone looked at this point, including Mark. Nathan smiled, a bit embarrassed by her introduction. "It's Nathan. He's here for a visit."

Mark slowly stood up from his table. He had always thought of Nathan as a good friend when they were younger. Without saying a word, Mark ran over and grabbed Nathan in a big bear hug. "Hey, you old buzzard. When'd you get into town?"

"I haven't been here long. I'm just trying to get around to all of the places I remember. I've seen a lot of changes, but I think this is the biggest one yet. You're, a sheriff. I would have never dreamed it." Nathan stepped back and walked around Mark looking him over. "It's really true, isn't it?"

"I'm afraid so son," Mark said laughing.

"Isn't this exciting, having the two of you together again?" Gracey announced. "You both look as handsome as ever."

Nathan leaned over to Mark and whispered in his ear, "I ran into Gracey Davis on the way over here. She kind of locked arms on me and I didn't have a choice. She's still the same, huh?"

Mark looked down and grinned. Then he stepped over near Gracey and put his arm around her. "Well, she's not quite the same. You see, her name isn't Gracey Davis anymore. It's Temple now." Mark stared back at Nathan waiting for his reaction.

"Gracey Temple? You mean, as in Mark Temple? You two are married? When? How? I mean, I didn't know." Nathan didn't know what to say, he was so rattled. "Congratulations!" Nathan shook Mark's hand until Mark finally pulled it away from him.

"All right, Nathan. I know you're surprised. We've been married for a few years now. I always had eyes for Gracey, you know that." He kissed her on the cheek and then they sat down at the table.

Nathan found himself still standing in a daze.

"Would you like to join us?" Gracey asked.

"Oh, right. Lunch, I need some lunch. Are the hamburgers still good here, or has that changed too?" Nathan asked with a near frantic look on his face.

"The hamburgers are still the best anywhere," Mark replied.

The three enjoyed lunch together, catching up on old times. However, Nathan mostly chewed and stared at Mark and Gracey. He would never have put these two together but there they were, Mark, a sheriff and Gracey, his bride.

"I can't take many more changes," Nathan thought to himself as he watched Gracey hanging all over Mark and giggling with delight. "Never in my wildest dreams could I make up anything as strange as this. Never in my wildest dreams."

After lunch, Mark dropped Gracey off at their home. Nathan rode with Mark, but he couldn't believe the beautiful house they owned. It had lots of land, some horses and lots of trees. Mark noticed that Nathan was staring with his mouth open. "We'll have to have you over one night for dinner. How long are you going to be in town?"

"Uh, I'm not sure, probably a couple of weeks." Nathan said looking around. "You've really done well for yourself, haven't you, Mark? The sheriff's business must pay better than I thought."

"No, I came into a bit of money along the way. Not a fortune mind you, but enough to help me buy this place and to keep Gracey in the style she's always wanted." Mark got back into the car. "Want to ride along with me while I go and take care of some business back at the office?"

"Sure, I'm free until dinner." Nathan got back into the car and put his hand on his head. "I'm starting to get a headache from all of the sights I've seen today. You say you came into some money? I didn't know you had any rich relatives."

"Do you remember old lady Radcliff? She lives outside of town. Her first name is Betsy. Well she doesn't have any family and she's always calling on me to come over and fix things for her, or paint, or something like that. I always liked her a little, even though others didn't care for her. She has her ways and I understand them enough not to make a big fuss over everything she says or does. Anyway, I always try to help her out whenever I can and she's very grateful. It turns out she has a pretty good chunk of money stashed away and then she up and decided to give me some of it as a gift, you know, for helping her. She said she didn't have anybody else to leave it to and she didn't want to wait until she died. Heck, I wasn't about to turn it down. She still gives me money occasionally, although I don't often get to do much for her these days. I reckon it makes her feel better if she pays for my services. At first I felt funny accepting money from an old woman, but she's not using it for herself. She still lives in an old run down shack when she could live some place decent. I might as well get some use of her money. "

"I remember her. She used to throw rocks at us kids if we even got near her yard. She was a mean and cranky woman. How in the world did you ever even get close enough to fix anything?"

"Like I said, I understand her ways. In a way, I feel sorry for the woman. Nobody in town ever pays any attention to her. I carried some groceries once for her when she was in town and her back was bothering her. From there we hit it off. Anyway, she didn't give me a fortune, but it was a nice surprise. Maybe kindness does pay after all." Mark turned into his office. "Come on in for a minute. I'd like you to meet my deputy."

As they went into his small, cluttered office, Mark introduced his deputy, Jerry to Nathan and then excused himself to use the telephone. Nathan sat down and closed his eyes for a minute. He must have been tired because he drifted off briefly only to be awakened again by Mark's loud voice.

"Nathan, how about riding along with me? We've got ourselves a dead body in the woods."

Nathan's eyes opened wide. For a brief moment he froze, unable to move. In just a flash of light he could see himself again as a boy running in the woods and playing. As he tumbled to the ground, there, sticking out of the colored leaves, he saw a hand. It looked like it was reaching, except this hand wasn't moving. It was still and lifeless.

"Nathan, are you coming? Let's go!" Mark called from the door.

Nathan blinked his eyes a few times and jumped up from his chair.

"Are you all right?" Mark asked, seeing that Nathan seemed a bit dazed.

"Yeah, I'm fine. Let's go." Nathan headed for the car, fearful of what they were about to find.

As they pulled into the wooded area, several cars were there already. Mark hopped out quickly, but Nathan stayed put.

"You want to wait in the car for this?" Mark asked, as he stuck his hand through the window and put it on Nathan's shoulder.

"No, I want to come if it's all right." Nathan slowly got out of the car and walked behind Mark. He felt as though he was moving in slow motion as they walked through the woods to where the body was discovered. With every step his muscles seemed to tighten until his legs and arms began to ache.

Nathan could see people standing in a circle up ahead. As they approached and pushed past the people, Nathan looked down to see the body of a young boy, partially covered by leaves and sticks. His dark hair was matted with patches of blood and debris. Nathan knelt down beside Mark who was carefully examining the body and the ground around him. He couldn't speak a word as he stared at the small lifeless body.

"What do you think happened here, Mark?" asked Jerry. "How was he killed?"

"I'm not sure, but it looks like he was hit on the head with something heavy. Maybe a rock or something made of metal." Mark looked closer at the boy's face. "I think I know this boy. I believe his name is Todd Harper. He lives just outside of town." Mark stood up and wiped the sweat from his face with his handkerchief. "Jerry, go and pick up his parents and bring them down to the morgue. We'll have to get them to identify him to be sure."

"Okay, sheriff. I'm on my way."

Nathan was still kneeling beside the boy. He couldn't speak. He could only stare. Not too far off, in the background, Nathan could hear the running water of one of the many streams that empties into the Black River. The sound seemed to drown out the voices of the people around him. He felt as though he was alone with the boy and the river.

"Nathan, can you come and play with me?" he heard a familiar voice calling from the water. He slowly looked up at the faces standing over the body, but none of them acted like they heard the voice that had suddenly paralyzed him.

"Nathan, can you hear me? Come and play with me. It's a beautiful day," the voice called again.

Nathan forced himself to stand up and pushing past the people, he started walking toward the sound of the river. As he got closer, he saw a young boy standing on one of the rocks in the water.

"Over here, Nathan," the young boy waved and shouted to him.

Nathan rubbed his eyes and looked closer. "Robert? Robert is that you there?"

"Yes, come and play with me. Why are you wasting your time just standing there?" Robert started jumping from rock to rock. Nathan felt a cold breeze blowing all around him. There was a rattling sound as the wind picked up the crisp leaves and twirled them around and around. He jumped on one of the rocks and tried to follow Robert across the stream, but he was way ahead of him, his image in the sunlight and then shadows, leaping from rock to rock with his arms waving.

"Nathan, follow me," Robert called. The sound of his voice echoed all around him.

"Robert, wait up. Wait for me. I'm trying to follow you. Don't go so fast." Nathan was fiercely trying to keep up. "Wait a minute, Robert. Hold up."

"I'm over here, Nathan. Can't you see me?" Robert shouted back.

A loud roaring sound could be heard now. As he looked up, there was Robert, standing at the top of a thunderous waterfall.

"Look over here, Nathan. Isn't this great? Wow, listen to that. Come over and stand up here with me." Robert danced back and forth with excitement.

Nathan jumped quickly from one slippery rock to another trying to keep his balance. As he approached the roaring sound of the waterfall, he looked to see where Robert was standing. Nathan could feel the spray from the water rushing over the edge of the rocks, blowing back into his face. He turned all the way around searching for Robert, but he had disappeared.

"Nathan, Nathan where are you?"

"I'm right here, Robert," he said waving his arms. "Look over here."

Nathan stood still waiting to hear the sound of Robert's voice, but there was no answer. He knelt down to look over the edge of the waterfall. There was Robert, jumping on the rocks down below. His arms were straight out to help him keep his balance. He kept going until he was out of sight. He started to call after him, but he knew it wouldn't do any good. Robert was too far down now. Staring down at the rocks below, Nathan saw something moving alongside the trees. As he strained to look, he held on to one of the tree branches. Suddenly, there appeared to be a man stepping out onto the rocks. The man stopped and looked up at Nathan. Then he lifted his arm and waved up at him. It was the old man with thin white hair.

"Hi, Nathan," the man shouted up to him.

"Do you see anything?"

Nathan fell backwards, startled from the voice. He looked up to see Mark standing behind him.

"Didn't mean to scare you. Any signs of anything down there?" Mark asked again.

Nathan peered back over the waterfall, but all he could see was the trees, rocks and water. Nathan paused for a while. "No, there's nothing down there."

"Let's head back then. I've got a lot of questions to get answered." Mark turned to go back to the car.

Nathan stood for a while. He slowly turned and walked back along the stream, glancing back over his shoulder. As he crossed the water, he stopped on the other side to look back. The river continued to rush past him, throwing itself over the edge of the rocks as though nothing had happened that day.

# 5

Nathan sat in his room at the Raven, trying to make sense of everything that had happened. Why was Robert skipping through his memory again, now, after all these years? When he was younger, he used to think that Robert was only a product of his active imagination and nothing more. He was mysterious, but yet, real. Why would he reappear in his mind now? Was he just a childhood fantasy? The dead boy he had seen in the woods had brought back his vision of Robert skipping from stone to stone.

Nathan rested his head on some pillows and tried to put it all out of his mind. Just as he started to drift off, he heard a knock on his door.

"Nathan? Is it all right if I come in?"

Nathan really wanted to sleep, but he slowly made his way to the door. As he opened it, there stood Maggie with a tray of food.

"You missed dinner, so I thought I'd bring you up something. You need to eat, Nathan. Don't go to bed on an empty stomach." Maggie sat the tray down on an old oak table beside the bed.

"You sound just like my mother, Maggie," Nathan said smiling. "I'd really rather sleep right now than eat though."

"Sit down," Maggie demanded without even blinking. "You'll sleep better with some of my roasted chicken in you. Besides, I want to talk to you for a minute." Maggie pulled up a chair and sat across from him. "Mark called after you came home and he said he wanted to make sure you were all right. He told me about the young boy they found today. That poor, dear, sweet boy, I didn't know him very well, but he never caused any trouble for anybody. It's hard to believe someone would want to kill him. Anyway, I told Mark that he shouldn't have dragged you along with him. Finding dead bodies in the woods is not my idea of a vacation." Maggie watched as Nathan played with his food. "Let Mark handle this. You don't need to be involved."

"I'm okay, Maggie," Nathan said, as he gently touched her hand. "The boy was so young, it just really got to me. This town is not a place where you'd expect to find a kid lying dead in the woods." He leaned back in his chair and noticed Maggie had a strange look on her face. "Are you okay, dear?"

Maggie's eyes dropped down to the floor for a brief moment. "You still don't remember, do you?"

"Remember what?" Nathan asked hesitantly. "This isn't the first time this has happened here is it?"

Maggie paused and stared at him. "Let's not discuss this now. You're tired and you need to get some sleep." Maggie began picking up the dishes and the tray.

"Maggie, please talk to me about this now," Nathan begged as he took the tray from her hands.

Maggie sat back down and stared down at the floor, fumbling with her apron. "Yes, there was another young boy found dead in the woods many years ago." Tears began to swell in her eyes. She took out a small handkerchief and began nervously twisting it around in her fingers.

"How old was I when it happened?"

"You were about ten years old then, I believe, very young. That's why you can't recall much about it. But mostly you can't remember because it was so shocking. The doctors said you might not ever fully remember everything." Maggie smiled softly at Nathan. "As a child, you were always playing in and around the streams and running through the woods. Your mother could never find you, because you were always outside chasing after something or, you know, just childhood games. Oh, you were such a bright and lovely boy. You would play outside all day if you were allowed, rain or shine."

Maggie paused for a moment as she stared at Nathan. "It was one of your adventures into the woods that led to your discovery of the dead boy. I remember you told the police that you found him when you accidentally fell while you were playing." Maggie got up and walked over to the window and looked out behind the curtains. "You really couldn't remember much except where you found him. The sheriff, his men and even the police from other counties launched a big manhunt, but they never turned up anything that could help."

Maggie closed her eyes for a moment. "Oh, the people in this town were terrified. But after so much time passed, and no one was ever found to blame for the boy's death, folks just assumed whoever did it must have moved on and things gradually got back to normal." Maggie turned to look at Nathan, "You used to cry yourself to sleep every night your mother told me, thinking about that young boy all alone out there in the woods. For the longest time your mother wouldn't allow you anywhere near that place, but that was like trying to tie down the wind. Eventually you were right back out there, jumping and running just like before." Maggie hung her head and wiped her face with her handkerchief. "Children heal the fastest I suppose."

Nathan sighed and put his head in his hands. Maggie walked over and began rubbing his head, as a mother comforting her child. "That was an awful thing for a boy to have to experience, darlin'. It robbed you of some of your innocence I reckon." Maggie started picking up the dishes and placing them on the tray. "Nathan, you don't think there's any connection between this boy found today and the boy you found back then do you? I mean, you still don't remember anything about that day do you? Anything at all?"

Nathan didn't answer.

"Well, I guess there really couldn't be any connection. It was so long ago. Why don't you go to bed now? You look exhausted. You're supposed to be here to rest, not to wear yourself out."

"Maggie, do you recall the name of the boy that I found?" Nathan asked.

Maggie paused at the doorway with the tray for quite a while. Finally, she cleared her throat and answered with her voice shaking, "His name was Robert. Folks called him Robby sometimes." Maggie paused again, but then quickly turned around toward Nathan, "Now don't think about it any more tonight, darlin'. Try and get some rest now. Goodnight dear." Maggie quietly closed the door behind her.

"Robert?" Nathan mumbled to himself. "The same boy I've seen running in the woods? How can that be? Am I purposely suppressing the memory of something because it's too awful to remember? Maybe this is the reason I felt the urge to return to Fairhaven; to fill in the gaps, gaps I didn't even realize I had."

Nathan got up and walked around the room. "Maybe the man with the white hair killed Robert and I just don't want to remember," Nathan said to himself. Then he had a frightening thought, "Maybe the same man who killed Robert killed Todd Harper too. Is that what this is all about? Why can't I remember everything? It's just bits and pieces from my past floating around in my head."

Nathan knew he had to find the answers for himself. "I don't want to reveal too much to Mark just yet, because it doesn't all make sense right now," Nathan reasoned. "But how can I explain it to anyone else? Somehow I've got to find a way to force myself to remember what happened that day, the day Robert was killed. I must have been with Robert playing in the woods the day he was killed."

Nathan wasn't the least bit sleepy now. So he decided to go downstairs just to try and find something else to occupy his mind. He felt tired and restless all at the same time. He wandered into the library where Maggie kept a collection of old books, magazines and pictures. There in the corner was an old black desk and Nathan found himself rummaging through it just out of curiosity. He wasn't even sure what he was looking for, but he just had to look.

He carefully pulled open the bottom drawer to the desk where he found a large envelope filled with old family photos. As Nathan flipped through each one his memory seemed to be in a fog. The faces were familiar, but not well known to him. Then his eyes came to rest on a tattered and faded old photo of a young boy with dark eyes and dark hair. It was the boy in the woods. It was Robert.

He quickly turned over the photograph and there, on the back in small, smeared writing it said, "Robert Sanding, Age 7." Nathan leaned back in his chair. "Robert was Marcie's brother." Nathan stared back at the photograph in disbelief. He began to recall the good times they had growing up, playing in the woods most days along side the Black River. Robert could skip stones better than anyone else. He was always running everywhere and Nathan was always running behind him, trying to keep up. "How could I have forgotten Robert? He was Marcie's brother and my best friend."

Nathan remembered running and running until he was completely out of breath. "Wait for me," Nathan heard himself calling. "Don't run so fast."

"Hey, try and catch me, Nathan," Robert would call back. "You'll never catch me."

Nathan would desperately try to keep up and follow Robert's voice because he could no longer see him.

"Robert," Nathan called out. "Robert, where are you?"

There was no answer. Nathan tightly closed his eyes trying to force himself to remember more, but all he could see was Robert running, jumping and playing along the river.

Finally, Nathan returned the envelope to the drawer, but kept Robert's photo. He crept back to his room. The urge to sleep was overwhelming now. He fell across his bed, staring at Robert's picture once more. As he drifted off to sleep the picture slipped from his hand and landed on the floor beside the bed. It was all he had for now.

# 6

The next day Nathan got up early and headed down to Mark's office. He felt he somehow had to be involved in the investigation into the young boy's murder. Maybe he could be of some help. He didn't know anything for sure right now, but he knew he had to be a part of solving this case if he could.

When he arrived, Nathan found Mark busy answering questions on the telephone. Jerry was just as tied up with trying to explain what their next step would be. Mark finally looked up and acknowledged Nathan, motioning for him to sit down. Nathan strolled over to the bulletin board and looked at some of the posters of wanted criminals hanging there. They all seemed to look and sound alike after reading a few. He finally took a seat over in a corner and started to read the morning edition of The Fairhaven Daily Newspaper. There was Todd, the dead boy, on the front page. His smiling school picture stared back at Nathan. Under his picture it read, "No leads found in Todd Harper's murder." Nathan looked again at the boy's picture. Suddenly, the shape of Todd's face began to change. Nathan blinked a few times, trying to focus on the picture again. He stared at it for a few moments before noticing that the picture of Todd faded as it was replaced by another photo. Nathan rubbed his eyes. This time the picture looked familiar to him. As he read the caption again, his hands began to tremble. "Still no clues in the death of Robert Sanding."

"Nathan, what are you doing here so early?" asked Mark from his desk.

Nathan didn't answer right away. He just kept staring at the newspaper.

"Oh, I see you've discovered the front page. It's still hard to believe isn't it? Who would want to do such a thing? I must have gotten a hundred phone calls this morning from panicked folks wanting to know what we're going to do about this mess. We have a dead boy in a quiet little town with very few clues to help us." Mark leaned back in his chair and noticed that Nathan wasn't paying much attention to what he was saying. "Did you come down here this morning for any particular reason?"

Still staring at the photograph in the newspaper, Nathan thought the picture seemed to fade back and forth between Todd and Robert.

Mark leaned forward across his desk, "Nathan, did you hear what I said?"

Nathan jumped a little as he looked up from the newspaper. "Do you think there's any connection between this boy's death and what happened to Robert?" he asked.

"Robert? Robert who? What are you talking about?"

"Robert Sanding, you know the boy I found in the woods when I was a kid? Do you think there's a connection?"

"You mean, you remember his name? After all these years you finally remember his name?" Mark came over and sat in front of Nathan. "I thought you couldn't remember anything about that day? The police must have asked you a thousand questions, but you would only say you found him in the woods while you were playing. Then after that you never said another word about it. The doctors said you must have blocked it out of your mind. When did you suddenly remember his name?"

"Just now, I mean, I haven't thought about it for years, but the name just popped in my brain while I was looking at Todd's photograph. Strange, huh?"

"Yeah, really strange, but are you thinking that Todd's death is somehow connected to Robert's? That was a long time ago, man. I don't see how they could be related. Maybe it's just because they were both young and it's making you recall some things you've long forgotten." Mark took the newspaper out of Nathan's hands," Why don't you go back to the Raven and take it easy for a while? I can tell this is all starting to get to you, man."

"No, Mark. Please, let me help you with this. I'm not sure what I can do, but I want to be involved. If nothing else, maybe I can gather some material for my next book." Nathan smiled awkwardly. "I promise not to get in your way. You're right, this whole thing has brought back a few memories, but I can handle that. Just let me hang out with you for a while. I promise not to get in your way."

"Okay then, if you really want to, but, you can really pick odd ways to spend your vacation," Mark teased, trying to lighten the air a little. "Well, I've got to go and talk to the boy's parents. You can come along if you like, but it's going to be heavy duty."

Nathan glanced back at the newspaper, "I'd like to come anyway."

# 7

Back at the Raven Inn, Maggie and Marcie were both busy cleaning up after the morning breakfast.

"Where was Nathan this morning? I didn't see him," Marcie asked.

"I guess he took off early 'cause he wasn't in his room when I checked on him before breakfast," Maggie answered, looking for Marcie's reaction.

"You checked on him? Why would you be checking on him? Are you worried about him for some reason?"

"Well, we had a little talk last night and I felt a little uneasy about it, so I just wanted to make sure he was all right this morning." Maggie continued putting the dishes away.

"What did you talk about that would have upset him? You weren't discussing us were you?" Marcie came over and sat at one of the tables closer to Maggie.

"No dear, we weren't discussing you two. Although, I think that's a subject that you both need to get to real soon before he goes away again. No, we were discussing the boy that was recently found dead, Todd Harper. Nathan seemed really disturbed, so I asked him if he was all right. Somehow or another he ended up asking me about the name of the boy he found dead in the woods when he was growing up."

Marcie looked up at Maggie from her coffee cup. "He still doesn't remember, does he? Did you answer him?"

"Of course I answered him. I told him it was Robert."

"You did? You told him? How did he react?" asked Marcie. "Did it seem to jog anything in him?"

"I don't know. After I told him the name, he didn't really say anything else. I didn't want to pressure him, so I just closed the door behind me and left him alone." Maggie dropped her head and walked into the next room.

Marcie folded her arms tightly and walked over to the window. "Maybe it wasn't good for Nathan to come back here. He probably should have just stayed away." But Marcie knew in her heart that she didn't mean that. She was glad he was back, but she didn't know where to begin with him again. Should she keep her distance or get closer? He was almost like a stranger to her now. Marcie wasn't sure what she wanted at this point, but it was nice just knowing he was around for a while. She felt safe when he was close to her and was beginning to realize how much she had missed him. Maybe things could be different now.

Marcie took off her apron and went upstairs to help clean some of the rooms. As she started cleaning in Nathan's room, she saw something sticking out from underneath the bed. She reached down and picked it up. As she turned it over she saw a photograph. Tears filled her eyes as she sat on the bed. It was a tattered picture of Robert. Marcie slumped back on the bed and began to weep. As her tears fell on Robert's picture, she could feel her heart pounding. How much did Nathan remember about the death of her brother, Robert? It was a mystery that had never been unlocked. She had never gotten over her brother's death, especially, the fact that the killer was never found, and now, it was starting all over again.

# 8

It was late when Nathan arrived back at the Raven. He spent the day with Mark going from the Harper's home to other houses in the vicinity. They hoped to find someone who had seen or heard anything that could be helpful to them, but they had no luck. It was as though Todd had been invisible the day he was killed. Nathan was tired as he quietly climbed the stairs to his room. All of the questions they had asked kept churning over and over again in his mind. As he unlocked his door and flipped on the lights, there sat Marcie in a chair by his bed.

"Marcie, what are you doing in my room? It's after midnight. Is something wrong?" Nathan stood in the doorway, almost afraid to go inside.

"No, nothing's wrong. I was just cleaning your room today and found something I wanted to ask you about," she said, handing Nathan the old photograph of Robert. "I found it lying under your bed. She paused for a moment as Nathan stared at the picture. "Nathan, where did you get it?"

Nathan sat on the bed still staring at the picture. "Maggie told me that the boy found dead years ago was named Robert. Something froze inside of me, because that name had been spinning around in my head since we discovered Todd Harper dead. I hadn't thought of Robert in years and all of a sudden, it was like he was the one we found instead of Todd. I couldn't sleep, so I went downstairs and ended up in the library. I found an old envelope and started leafing through it. I saw this picture of Robert." Nathan was choking back tears as he held the picture tightly in his hands. "How could I not remember him? He was your brother and my best friend."

Marcie put her arms around Nathan and tried not to burst into tears. "Nathan, it was a terrible shock for you, finding him like that. It just blocked out everything you remembered about him. It was so painful you couldn't handle it. Your brain just erased it all, as though it had never happened."

"No, not all of it," Nathan said. "I remember after he died, I would see him running through the woods and skipping stones in the river, just like when he was alive. It was so clear in my mind, I thought it was real. I was always running behind, trying to catch up to him, but I never could. He would call out my name late at night or early in the morning, pleading with me to come and play with him, but then, for some reason, it left as I got older. Maybe I tried too hard to block it all out, because it was so horrible."

"Anyway, I didn't understand what was going on and didn't even tell my mother about the dreams. Sometimes she would see me, sitting with my hands trembling, and she'd ask what was wrong, but I couldn't tell her. I only wanted Robert to be alive again, instead of lying dead in the wet leaves. Over and over again, I kept seeing him. How can a little boy live with a memory like that in his head? Eventually, I could only see him running and laughing at me. But, even that became too much for me to carry around. So, I guess I just wiped out his memory altogether, until the first day I arrived here. I went walking around the grounds that evening. I know this sounds crazy, but I felt as though someone was following me and, as I turned to look, something rushed right through me. It was as though someone was running because I could hear this heavy breathing and then it rushed right past me, or through me, I'm not sure."

"Marcie, I know these are all just memories trying to resurface inside of me, but there's more that I need to remember. Something happened that day that I can't see clearly. I just get bits and pieces of it in my head and then it's gone. I want to remember." Nathan started pacing back and forth, as though he had gone into a trance.

"Nathan!" Marcie cried out as she reached to hold him still. "Stop, you're going to make yourself crazy. Please, stop. It's all right. You don't have to torture yourself like this. It happened a long time ago. It's over. Just let it go for now. It's going to be all right." Marcie held on to Nathan with all of her strength.

Nathan could feel Marcie's arms holding him tightly and the panic he felt slowly melted into a feeling of calm all around him.

Marcie kept holding him tightly, afraid to let go. Nathan dropped his head on her shoulder, letting his tears run down the back of her blouse. They stood in the middle of the room and rocked back and forth, holding on to one another as though there was no one else in the world.

"Don't ever leave me again," Marcie whispered in his ear. "Please don't ever leave me. Take me with you this time."

Nathan raised his head and looked into Marcie's eyes, mesmerized, as all of his fears seemed to be washed away in her tears. They held each other and stared into each other's faces, not speaking a word for a while. For the first time, he felt he was home.

Marcie rested her head on his chest and began to hum a soft, but familiar tune. Nathan closed his eyes and they swayed back and forth to the song. He knew tonight he would never leave her arms again. As they held on to each other, time didn't seem to exist. If a moment could be frozen in time, Nathan would have captured this one for his own. He gently touched Marcie's cheek and held her face in his hands. "I'm never letting you go," he said softly, and as they kissed, Nathan felt as though the whole world and all of its confusion had briefly faded away.

As Marcie was leaving his room, he wondered whether he would wake up in the morning and find that none of this had taken place. "I'll drive you home," said Nathan picking up his jacket. "I don't want you on the road alone at night."

"No, you don't have to do that. I'll be fine. It's a short drive home and you need to get some sleep. You look exhausted. I'll come by and fix you a special breakfast in the morning." Marcie kissed him once more and ran down the stairs and out to her car.

Nathan watched her from his window, waving at her as she drove off into the night. Nathan found himself humming their song as he fell into bed. As he drifted off to sleep, he could still hear the song, pleasantly floating in and out of his head.

# 9

The next morning as Nathan got dressed, he felt a spark of excitement come over him. Had last night really happened to him? He could hardly wait to see Marcie again. Maybe he would forget about the Todd Harper case for now and just concentrate on his relationship with Marcie. He wanted to have a fresh start with her and he wanted them to spend as much time as possible together. There were so many things he wanted to tell her.

As he made his way downstairs for breakfast, he heard mumbling in the foyer. At the bottom of the stairs he could see Mark talking with another man. "Morning, guys. What's going on? Did something break in the Harper case?" Nathan asked anxiously.

"No, but something has happened," Mark said as he looked down at the floor and shuffled his feet. Nathan could see Maggie sitting in a corner chair with her face in her handkerchief.

"Mark, what's wrong? Where's Marcie?" Nathan turned and ran into the breakfast room where she was always working in the morning. "Marcie, are you in here?" He frantically searched while surprised guests whispered politely.

"Nathan," Mark called as he tried to grab him by the arm. "Please, come with me in the other room. I need to talk to you." Mark led him away and shut the door behind them quietly.

"Mark, what's going on here?" Nathan's heart was pounding harder and harder as he waited for Mark to answer.

"We don't know for sure right now, but Marcie didn't come to work this morning and she's not at her house. Maggie called me when she couldn't reach her at home, half crazed out of her mind with panic. There may be a good explanation for all of this, but for right now, we don't know where she is." Mark let go of Nathan's arm and sat down. Nathan looked at him in shock, unable to say anything.

"Were you with her last night, Nathan?" Mark asked.

"Yes, we talked for a while in my room. She was there when I got in last night."

"What time did she leave?"

"I'm not sure. I think it was around two in the morning. Look, are you sure she didn't just go for a drive or something instead of coming into work this morning or maybe she slept in since she was so late getting home last night."

Mark shook his head.

Nathan headed for the door, "I'm going over to her house to make sure."

Mark jumped to his feet and spun Nathan around and away from the door. "Look, we've already searched her house from top to bottom. She's not there."

Nathan felt weak and leaned back against the wall to steady himself.

"Did you two argue last night about anything that would have made her take off like this?" Mark asked, sounding more like a sheriff than a friend.

"No, there was no argument. As a matter of fact, we had a great night. It felt like old times again. She was happy when she left. I offered to drive her home, but she insisted on driving herself. You know how independent she can be. I waved goodnight to her from the window of my room. That's the last I saw of her." Nathan put his hands over his face hoping that this would all disappear in a minute or two.

"You're not forgetting anything are you?" Mark asked in an almost sarcastic tone.

Nathan glared back at him, but didn't bother answering.

"Stick close by. I may need to talk to you again."

"Let me go with you to search for her. I can't just sit here and wait to hear from her." Nathan said, following Mark back into the foyer.

"No, I want you to stay here in case she shows up. The doctor gave Maggie something to help her rest, so she should go upstairs to her room. Some help will be sent over from one of the other inns to take care of the guests. You just wait here and maybe she'll call." Mark motioned for the other men to leave.

Nathan stood helplessly and watched them drive out of sight, desperately wanting to help. He knew that something was wrong, because Marcie would never abandon Maggie and the Raven Inn. She loved them both too much to just run off with no word. "Could she have gone somewhere to be alone to think about last night?" Nathan wondered. "Maybe she just took a day and went for a drive." He decided he couldn't just stand around doing nothing, so he jumped in his car and decided to drive out to her house to see for himself.

Beacon Hill Road, leading to Marcie's house, was an old winding mountain road that had as many twists and turns as the Black River. Nathan's mind was racing as he drove up higher and higher to the top of the ridge. With each turn he pushed the car to go a little faster. The sharp curves kept coming and Nathan was taking each one at top speed. He began to drift into the other lane as he tried to negotiate each turn at high speed. As he took the next curve, he tried to hug the side of the mountain to keep from going too far into the other lane.

Suddenly, he thought he saw someone. As he came closer, he could see a boy standing in the center of the road. He slammed on brakes and skidded sideways onto a grassy area. When the car finally stopped moving, Nathan looked back over his shoulder, but there was no one there. He climbed out of the car and walked back along the road to make sure he didn't hit anyone. As he walked, he could only hear the rushing sounds of the river and the wind rustling the leaves in the trees. There was no one there. He was still shaking, so he sat on a fallen tree lying next to the water. "Calm down, just calm down," he kept repeating to himself. "You're just upset. Just take it easy." He pulled his knees up close to him and rested his head for a minute.

"Be careful. You're going to kill him!"

Nathan raised his head and looked around.

"Watch out. Oh no, what have you done?"

He put his hands over his ears to try to stop the sounds.

"Nathan, help me. Please, help me."

"Robert, where are you? I can't see you." Nathan climbed to his feet and turned in every direction.

"You've killed him! Oh my God!"

Nathan ran toward the voice. "Robert, where are you?"

Nathan started running through the woods, pushing back tree branches and vines as he went. He ran faster and faster reaching for his sword to kill the monster in the woods. Suddenly, his foot hit something and he tumbled to the ground. Nathan pushed his hair out of his eyes and sat straight up. In front of him was a small white hand sticking up out of the leaves. "Robert! Robert!" Nathan shouted, but Robert didn't move.

Just then, out of the corner of his eye, he saw something moving through the trees. He jumped up to follow it, but it was too dark to see through the thick trees and brush. Suddenly, he could hear heavy breathing right behind him. As he turned, he felt something rush past him and he lost his balance and hit the ground once more. He lay there for what seemed like forever before he was brave enough to get back up. Brushing himself off, he managed to get to his feet, but he appeared to be all alone. Listening to the sound of the river running through the woods, Nathan suddenly realized that he had been chasing a memory that seemed set on torturing him for the rest of his life. Slowly, he walked back to where he had left his car, trying to see through the tears swelling in his eyes. When he reached his car, he opened the door and fell in. This was like one long nightmare. He started his car and slowly turned toward Marcie's house.

As he pulled away, he thought he heard someone say, "Goodbye, Nathan." He quickly stopped the car and looked back out into the woods. Off in the distance, he could see a man with white hair walking in the opposite direction. Before he could get out of the car, he had disappeared. Nathan quickly blinked his eyes and looked again, but there was nothing there. He waited for a while before driving on, still looking in the direction where he thought he had seen the image of the old man, but he couldn't see a thing. Finally, he gave up and slowly drove away.

Wishing Marcie was there for him to hold, Nathan would stay until he found her and until all of the jumbled pieces of his memory could all be put back together again.

# 10

The tree-lined Beacon Hill Road that led up to Marcie's house was beautiful. As Nathan rounded the curve of the long driveway entrance, her house came into sight. The house overlooked a stunning view of the endless mountains and trees. It was quiet, with only the faint sound of birds singing in the high treetops that surrounded the house. Nathan decided to take a peek inside the windows, just to be sure that Marcie wasn't there. Cautiously looking in through the large picture window in front, he could see a rustic great room with a huge fireplace in the center. The room looked cozy and warm, but empty. He tried the front door, only to find it securely locked. Cautiously, he walked around to the back of the house to take a look around. Peering into one of the back windows, he could see what appeared to be Marcie's bedroom. There were clothes lying on the bed, but the bed was made. He could also see clothes hanging in her closet. Something must have happened to her. She apparently didn't willfully leave all of her things behind just to take off for some other place.

Nathan was getting scared now. He knew someone was holding Marcie against her will or she was lying someplace hurt and unable to get help. He continued to walk around the house in a panicked state until he noticed a small bathroom window that was slightly open. Looking around, he carefully removed the screen and pushed up the window. Cautiously, he stuck his head in to look around and then lifted himself up and climbed into the bathroom, lowering the window behind him. Slowly, Nathan crept through the house. The rooms were large and beautifully decorated with a mixture of antiques and contemporary furnishings.

As Nathan walked into the great room, he could see a newspaper lying on the sofa and Marcie's robe thrown across the arm of one of the chairs. It certainly didn't look as though Marcie had planned to leave. Maybe she never made it home that night from his room at all. He sat down to think for a moment. He wondered whether he and Marcie would ever get to spend time here together. Now he realized how much he loved her and wanted to be with her. Why had she just suddenly disappeared? Where could she be?

Suddenly the phone rang. Nathan wasn't sure if he should answer it. No one knew he was there. Maybe he should just let it ring. It rang again. "What if it's Marcie trying to get help," Nathan thought. "No, she wouldn't call her own house. But maybe she called the Raven and didn't get an answer. Maggie was probably sleeping. Marcie might be checking to see if someone is here." The phone rang again and Nathan picked it up without speaking, waiting to see who was on the other end.

"Hello? Who's there?" a voice on the phone asked.

Nathan didn't answer. He placed his hand over the mouthpiece because he was nervous and breathing heavily.

"Hello," the voice spoke again.

Nathan's hands were sweating now. He stood silently holding the phone, but he could only hear breathing on the other end.

Then the voice spoke again in a familiar tone, "Nathan, is that you?"

Nathan's heart felt as though it would pound right out of his chest, but he still didn't answer. "I know you're there, Nathan. You don't have to speak if you don't want to. Oh, by the way, I saw you today in the woods. Were you chasing someone, or was someone chasing you?"

Nathan held the phone with both hands. He couldn't speak. He just stood frozen. The voice sounded familiar to him, but he couldn't place where he had heard it before. His whole body trembled with fear.

"You should stay out of the woods from now on, boy. If I were you, I would head back to where I came from," the voice laughed.

"Who is this?" Nathan finally screamed out. "How do you know my name?" He waited for an answer, but there was none. "Where's Marcie? Do you have her with you? What have you done to her?" Nathan waited for an answer from the voice on the other end.

"Goodbye Nathan." The voice said hanging up the phone.

Nathan could only hear a dial tone ringing in his ear, but fear gripped him so he couldn't hang up the phone. "The old man," Nathan mumbled to himself. "Maybe it was the old man's voice." Nathan dropped the phone and backed away from it.

He felt like falling to the floor, but instead, he ran to the front door, unlocked it and swung it open. There was no one around. He stepped outside, locked the door from the inside and slammed the door shut. Jumping into his car, Nathan started the engine, but then he just sat, gripping the steering wheel. What was happening to him? Was he having flashbacks from his past? Nathan put his head back for a moment and put both hands over his face. "Wake up, Nathan," he said to himself thinking he must be dreaming, but as he slowly lowered his hands, he could see he was wide awake and sitting in front of Marcie's house. A chill ran down his back and he quickly turned to look behind him in the back seat, but there was no one there. He felt as though someone was watching him, but he didn't know who it was. He finally put the car in gear and drove away, looking back over his shoulder to make sure no one was there.

# II

Nathan spent all day searching everywhere for Marcie. His mind was a hundred miles away as he wound down the twisting road through the mountains. The scenery passed in a vague blur through his windshield while his eyes were fixed straight ahead in a glazed stare. But as he rounded one of the sharp curves, something caught his attention. Curiously, one of the wooden guardrails beside the road was damaged. Driving past, he began to get curious and pulled over to the side of the road as far as he could. He walked back the short distance to the damaged area and noticed that there were skid marks leading up to the break in the rail.

It was just beginning to get dark as Nathan peered over the side of the cliff to see if anything was there. The smaller trees and bushes were bent and broken for a long way down, as though something had gone over the side. It was a steep drop, but he had to go down to see what he could find. Remembering he had a rope in his trunk, he ran back to get it, along with an old pair of gloves and a flashlight.

Nathan tied one end of the rope to part of the remaining wooden rail and the other end around his waist. He put on the gloves to protect his hands and tested his grip on the rope. Painstakingly, he began lowering himself down the side of the mountain, slipping and sliding down farther and farther until he came to the end of the rope. Looking down, all he could see were trees and bushes. He could also see strong limbs and rocks that he might be able to hold on to climb down a little farther.

Nathan untied the rope from his waist and continued to make his way down by testing his footing little by little and holding on to anything he could find. Reaching out for a branch, he lost his balance and slid down feet first for what seemed like forever. A sharp branch jutting out from the rocks caught on his jacket and stopped his slide to the bottom. Hanging on for dear life, Nathan was able to pull himself onto a ledge with barely enough room for his feet. This was one adventure he almost wished he had never started, but he had to continue.

"How will I ever climb back up the side of the mountain now?" he wondered. The daylight was quickly disappearing and he knew he would have to either start trying to make his way back up or continue his journey down. Taking a deep breath, Nathan slowly bent down and gripped the ledge with both hands and began lowering himself down into a thick area of bushes. At a snail-like pace, he worked his way down the mountain, suffering scratches, scrapes and stabs all along the way.

Finally he reached the bottom and jumped to the ground. He landed flat on his back, exhausted and sore, trying to catch his breath. After a while, he was able to get to his feet and started to stumble around in the darkness trying to get his bearings. He reached for his flashlight and turned it on. Luckily it actually worked. "How will I explain this little trek in the woods to Maggie or Mark?" he asked himself. "They'll really think I'm crazy now."

As he walked along, he thought he could see something off in the distance. As he got closer, he could see that it was a car turned over on its side. Nathan's heart was beating fast as he quickened his limp and ran to the car.

"Is anybody in here? Hello, can you hear me?" Nathan yelled as he ran around the car trying to see inside. He climbed up onto the side of the car, shining the light into the window. There was someone in the car, but they weren't moving.

"If you can hear me, I'm going to try to help you." There was no answer. Nathan attempted to kick in the window, but to no avail. He jumped down, found a big rock, lifted it up onto the car and climbed back up. He shattered the window, grabbed his flashlight and looked into the car again. The person still wasn't moving. He lowered himself slowly into the car. Breathing heavily, he picked up his flashlight and clicked it on. It was Marcie. She was unconscious, but breathing.

"Marcie, can you hear me? It's Nathan. I'm here baby. Can you hear me?" He could see that she was bleeding from her head and cuts covered her arms and neck. Nathan unbuckled her seat belt and began pulling her from the car. She moaned in pain as he pulled her through the broken car window. He lowered her to the ground and began wiping the blood from her face. "Marcie, you're going to be all right. I'll get you to a hospital somehow. Just hold on. Please, hold on, don't leave me." Nathan covered her with his jacket and tried not to cry.

He knew he had to try to find the road to get help, so he lifted her limp body into his arms and began making his way through the trees using only his flashlight to find his way out. The sounds of a speeding truck led him to a nearby road.

As he walked cradling Marcie in his arms, a car finally pulled up behind him. Nathan stepped out into the road to get the car to stop. It sped by and then suddenly stopped by the side of the road, slowly backing up. When Nathan reached the car, a man jumped out to help.

"What happened, mister?" the driver asked.

"She's been in an accident. I need to get her to a hospital. Can you help us?" Nathan was exhausted and his arms were trembling. He didn't think he could carry her one step farther.

"Sure, get in. Here, you can put her in the back seat so she can stretch out."

The man opened the back door and Nathan got in and laid Marcie down in the seat, resting her head in his lap. "Please, hurry. I don't know how badly she's hurt."

The man jumped in and took off at top speed. As they headed to the hospital, Nathan rubbed Marcie's head and kissed her forehead. "I love you," he whispered. Then his eyes filled with tears, dropping onto her face. She was lifeless in his arms, barely breathing. Nathan began humming the song that Marcie had sung to him just before she disappeared. "Come on, don't leave me, baby. I need you and I promise never to leave you again." Marcie didn't respond, but Nathan kept humming the song in her ear.

# 12

When Nathan and Marcie arrived at the hospital, the man ran inside to get help. Nathan was met by a doctor who helped him lift her onto the waiting stretcher and quickly whisked her down the hallway of the emergency room.

"What happened to her?" the doctor asked.

"She was in a car that went over the side of a cliff, up on Beacon Hill Road."

"What's her name?"

"Marcie, Marcie Sanding," Nathan replied, staring at her pale, lifeless body lying on the stretcher.

"Are you a relative?"

"No, I'm a friend."

"Wait here. We'll let you know as soon as we determine her condition," the doctor yelled back to Nathan as they pushed her through the double doors.

He stood helplessly in the hallway, watching through the glass windows in the doors as they pushed her out of sight.

"You can wait over there if you like," a nurse said, directing Nathan to a waiting room. "Is there someone we can call for you?"

"Yes, Maggie Sanding at the Raven Inn. I'm sorry, but I don't know the phone number," he said as he searched his wallet.

"Don't worry. We can look it up for you. Why don't you go in and have a seat and we'll make the call."

Collapsing in a chair, Nathan felt as though his life was upside down and was slowly draining out of him, but he was relieved to know Marcie was alive. He put his head back against the wall, closed his eyes, and began to pray.

Nathan anxiously waited without news of Marcie. He was worried, but exhausted. He tried his best to fight the urge to sleep but finally gave in and closed his eyes.

"Where is she? I want to see her?" Maggie cried to the nurse who was trying to calm her. "Is she all right?"

"Mrs. Sanding, the doctor hasn't come out yet. I'm sure as soon as he can, he will answer all of your questions. Please, wait in here and I'll get you a cup of coffee." The nurse led Maggie into the waiting room.

Nathan was awakened by their voices, and ran over to comfort Maggie.

"Don't worry, dear. I'm right here with you." He put his arm around her and held her close.

"They said you were the one who brought her to the hospital. Was she awake when you found her?" Maggie asked, clinging to his arm.

"She was unconscious, but breathing. Marcie's a fighter, Maggie. She can pull through this." Nathan held her tightly.

"I'm so thankful that you found her when you did, otherwise—" Maggie's voice broke and she began to cry.

Handing her his handkerchief, he continued to hold her close. "Nathan, is she going to be okay?" He looked up to see Mark standing in the doorway of the waiting room. "How on earth did you manage to find her? You must be part bloodhound, man."

"Not really," Nathan snapped back. "Part of the guard rail was busted out on Beacon Hill Road, so it looked like an obvious place to begin searching. I'm surprised you didn't see it."

"I did see it," Mark began explaining. "A truck ran off the road there last week, so I assumed the damage was from that accident, but it appears that we should have paid more attention. Good work, Nathan. You'd make a fine sheriff."

Nathan let go of Maggie and walked over to Mark. "Her car was torn up pretty badly. I can't believe she survived that crash."

"What do you think happened? Did she just lose control of the car?" Mark asked.

"I don't know. I haven't been able to talk with her yet. The doctor hasn't even told us how she is, or whether she's going to make it. We're just waiting." Nathan nervously shifted his feet, growing more impatient.

"Are you sure you two didn't have some kind of a spat that night, and maybe she was crying on her way home and lost control of the car?" Mark stared at Nathan suspiciously.

"I told you we didn't argue that night. As a matter of fact, I fell in love with her all over again and I think the same thing happened for her. We danced and held each other. There was no fight. Why do you keep trying to accuse me, Mark? If you've got something to say, just come out with it, but don't keep asking me questions like I'm on trial here!"

Nathan quickly left the room. He couldn't breathe and he needed some fresh air.

A few minutes later, Mark came out as well. "I'm sorry. I guess I got a little carried away. It's just that I've known Marcie for a long time and nothing like this has ever happened before. I didn't mean to accuse you of anything. I just want to find out what's going on around here. First the dead boy's body is found in the woods and now this. This is a quiet town. These kinds of things don't happen every day like they do in some places." Mark lit a cigarette and turned away from Nathan.

"Are you thinking that my being here has something to do with Todd Harper being found dead and now Marcie getting in an accident?" Nathan asked, stepping in front of him. "Well, are you?"

"I don't know what I'm saying right now. But I have to tell you, it looks pretty weird that these things just started to happen when you showed up." Mark threw down his cigarette and went back inside.

Nathan couldn't believe he really felt that way, but then again, he couldn't really blame him. "He's right. Everything started when I came back home," Nathan thought. "But why? How could my being here possibly cause these things to happen?"

He walked around the hospital grounds, down to a pretty fountain lit up against the night and sat on one of the benches. "This is stupid. Now I'm starting to believe what Mark is thinking. My visit home can't have anything to do with Todd Harper's death. How could it? Marcie's accident couldn't be related to anything I've done."

Nathan wanted to tell Mark about the old man he's been seeing and the telephone call he received at Marcie's, but he was so exhausted that he couldn't even think clearly anymore. Did he really see someone or was his mind playing games again? What about the phone call? Did that really happen? Nothing was clear right now. He didn't know much for sure, but he did know he loved Marcie. That was the only thing he was sure of at this point. "Marcie, you've got to be all right. You're the only one that can tell what happened to you that night. Please, dear God, let her get through this. I want to spend the rest of my life with her, and make up for the pain I caused her when I left."

Nathan looked up at the stars, but they all seemed to run together into one big blur through the tears in his eyes. "I need answers. I've got to find out what's going on here." Nathan lowered his head for a while and then wiped his face. Shoving his hands in his pockets, he walked back inside the hospital, praying that Marcie would soon be able to speak to him.

# 13

As Nathan stepped back inside, he could see the doctor coming out through glass doors. "Doc, how is she?" Nathan asked, as he ran to catch up to him.

"Let's go in here and talk," the doctor said, motioning toward the waiting room.

As they entered, Mark helped Maggie stand to her feet. She was wringing the handkerchief Nathan had given her nervously in her hands. "How's my baby, doctor?" she asked, choking back tears.

"Marcie's a lucky girl, Maggie. For anyone to come through that kind of an accident at all is a miracle, but she's not home free. We'll know more about her condition in the morning. She has a very bad head injury, a broken leg and some internal bleeding that we've been able to get under control for now, and various cuts and bruises all over her body. The main concern for now is the head injury. We want to monitor her very closely tonight. She slips in and out of consciousness, but she did manage to ask for you, Maggie. She also keeps mumbling the name, Nathan." The doctor glanced over at Nathan, "Would that be you?"

"Yeah, can I see her?"

"In a little while, Nathan. The nurse is with her right now. We'll send for you when it's okay for you to go in," the doctor replied.

"I need to ask her some questions, doc," Mark said, pulling out a note tablet.

"Not tonight, Mark. She doesn't need any stress right now. Perhaps tomorrow would be better." The doctor touched Maggie's hand to reassure her.

"I'll be back tomorrow to talk with her," Mark said to Maggie. He kissed her on the cheek and then paused in front of Nathan. "I'm sorry about what I said outside."

"Forget it, man. You're just doing your job," said Nathan.

Mark briefly put his hand on Nathan's shoulder before leaving. It was an awkward moment for both of them.

The nurse led Nathan and Maggie to Marcie's room, but warned them, "She may fade in and out, so don't be surprised. Don't let her talk too much. It's important that she stay quiet and rest." Maggie slowly walked over to the bedside and pushed Marcie's hair back from her face. She started to cry right away until Nathan came up beside her and put his arm around her. "Don't let her see you crying, Maggie. It'll upset her too much. Let's be brave for her sake." Maggie nodded and tried her best to control her tears.

Marcie's face was covered with cuts and bruises and her eyes were swollen. She didn't even look like herself. Her head was bandaged, hiding most of her auburn hair and her entire leg was in a cast.

Maggie felt weak as she stood by the bed, stumbling a bit, as though she might faint.

"Sit over here, dear. You've had a busy day," Nathan said as he pulled up a chair for Maggie. "Do you want me to call the doctor to see if he can give you something?"

"No, I'm fine. I just had a little spell. It's not easy to stand and look at your only daughter bandaged and covered in cuts." Maggie sat back in the chair and closed her eyes for a moment.

Nathan sat on the bed beside Marcie and stared at her. He took her hand, trying not to disturb her. After a few minutes, Marcie's head moved and Nathan could feel her squeezing his hand. "Marcie, it's Nathan. I'm right beside you. Maggie's here too."

Marcie finally opened her eyes, blinking several times, as if she was trying to focus them. Nathan touched her cheek softly and kept repeating her name, "Marcie, Marcie." A faint smile came over her face and she reached to touch Nathan's face. "How are you feeling, Marcie?"

Marcie just groaned and smiled again as tears rolled down her face. "How's Maggie?" she asked in a hoarse voice.

"She's worried, but doing as well as you could expect. She's sitting right here beside you," Nathan said, keeping his voice low, so as not to wake Maggie.

Marcie looked relieved to see her, but then winced in pain.

"Try not to move around too much. Your leg's broken. The doctor said you're bruised and cut all over. You've also got a head injury that's bound to give you a pounding headache you won't soon forget." Nathan bent down and kissed her on the cheek. "I love you," he said. "I want you to know, I'm going to take care of you."

Marcie could only smile up at him and squeeze his hand. "I love you too," she whispered.

He kissed her again and wiped the tears away from her face. "Can you remember what happened to you?" He didn't want to cause Marcie any stress, but he was also curious about the accident. "If it's too painful to talk right now, you don't have to try."

Marcie didn't answer right away, but Nathan could see she was trying to tell him something. He moved closer so she wouldn't have to strain her voice.

"I was driving home, up Beacon Hill Road, thinking about us. I was so happy, but then, out of nowhere it seemed, this car appeared right in front of me. It blinded me with its bright lights. The car was on my side of the road. I tried to swerve to miss it. I guess that's when I drove over the side." Marcie closed her eyes and shook her head as if she was seeing the accident again.

"It's okay, baby. Don't say anything else." Nathan put his fingers on her lips. "We'll talk some more tomorrow. Why don't you try to rest now?"

Marcie pulled Nathan close to her and whispered, "Why would someone try to kill me?"

Nathan's eyes opened wide as he stared at Marcie. He could see the terror in her eyes. "What makes you think it wasn't an accident?"

"The car came out from the bushes on the side of the road," Marcie said with her lips trembling. It didn't come straight at me. It was like they were waiting for me to come along. Nathan, it was deliberate."

"Marcie, is that you? Are you awake?" Maggie asked, pushing up to see her.

Nathan backed away to let Maggie spend some time with her. He sat in a chair in the corner of the room and tried to collect his thoughts, unable to believe that someone would deliberately try to kill her. "Why?" he thought. "Could it be the same person that killed Todd Harper or maybe even Robert Sanding?" Nathan put his head back and stared at the ceiling. "This is insane," he kept saying to himself. "None of this makes any sense." He knew Mark would be questioning Marcie tomorrow. "What will he think? Will he still be suspicious of me?" Nathan knew he would need to try to find some answers on his own, but he didn't know where to even start.

"I'm going to have to ask you to leave now," the nurse said. "You can come back in the morning."

"Can I please stay with her tonight?" Nathan asked. "I promise I'll just sit with her. I won't disturb her."

"Well, I guess it would be fine, as long as you let her rest."

"Maggie, I'll drive you home and then I'll come back to sit with her. That way, you can get some rest." Nathan reached for Maggie's arm and she reluctantly agreed. He kissed Marcie again and walked Maggie to his car.

Driving home, there was little conversation between Nathan and Maggie. He didn't want her to know Marcie thought someone had deliberately tried to kill her. He didn't even know if he believed it himself. It was just too bizarre to explain. Marcie had lived here all of her life. She didn't have any enemies that Nathan knew of, so he figured it had to be a stranger in town that was causing all of these unexplainable events. A smile came across his face as he realized that he was a stranger in Fairhaven. He had just made a case for someone to accuse him.

"I'm glad you're going to stay with Marcie tonight," Maggie said, interrupting Nathan's analysis. "I know you care about her. She cares about you too. I'll rest much easier knowing that you're with her."

"Don't worry. I won't leave her side all night." Nathan touched Maggie's shoulder.

"You're a good man, Nathan," Maggie said sweetly. "You'll be good for Marcie. She needs someone to look out for her. She would never admit that, but she does. Living all alone in that great big house, I worry about her all the time. I wish she would just move into the Raven Inn with me, but she's too independent for that." Maggie paused for a while and then looked at Nathan. "But now she's going to need someone to help her get well again. She's going to have to let someone take care of her for a change."

"I plan to stay as long as it takes, Maggie. I'm not going anywhere until she's well and on her feet again." Nathan could see she was relieved to hear him say he was staying on a while longer.

"Of course Mark looks in on her now and again. I declare, for a while there, I thought he really had something for Marcie, until he up and married Gracey. He used to come around quite often to see her, but she never really seemed interested. They were never meant to be together anyway, not like the two of you. I believe Marcie thinks of Mark as a good friend, or maybe even a brother. Then when Marcie was planning on marrying David Moore, Mark suddenly married Gracey. You just can't predict life, Nathan. Just when you think you have it figured out, it changes on you." Maggie pulled her coat on around her shoulders as they pulled up to the Raven Inn. Nathan started to go in with her.

"I'll be fine. You go on back to the hospital." Maggie got out and headed up the walk to the front of the inn. A neighbor and good friend met her at the door and waved to Nathan to let him know that Maggie was in good hands.

Nathan sat in the driveway for a while thinking about the things Maggie had talked about. He never realized before now, that Mark had ever been interested in Marcie.

# 14

The next morning's light found Nathan asleep in a chair next to Marcie's bed. She had slept quietly through the night and Nathan had managed to catch up on some sleep himself. A nurse, who was there to take Marcie's blood pressure and temperature, woke him up.

"Good morning," she whispered to Nathan.

"Morning," Nathan said, stretching his arms and legs from the cramped chair. He walked over to pull back the curtains. It was a beautiful day. Marcie squinted her eyes as the sunlight poured from the window. When she saw Nathan standing there, she smiled and held out her hand for him.

"How are we feeling this lovely morning?" Nathan asked.

"I'm not sure, but I'm glad you're here."

"Do you feel like you could eat something for breakfast?" The nurse's aid asked, standing at the door with a tray of oatmeal, milk, coffee and juice. Nathan raised her bed so she could try to eat.

"Mind if I join you for coffee?" he asked, pouring some for the two of them. Marcie was weak, but she tried her best to get some of the oatmeal down. She wanted to get well and back home as soon as possible.

With the doctor arriving, the room was suddenly busy with nurses rushing about to help him. "Well, how's my patient doing this morning?" He asked, examining Marcie's head and eyes. "I see you made it through the night without a lot of problems." He looked closely at her head injury and the stitches they had sewn in the night before. "It looks like you're going to be all right Marcie, but you're going to have to take it very slow," he said, replacing the bandage. "These things take time to heal and you're going to need to take it easy for a while."

"But my mother needs my help at the Raven Inn. I can't just lie around in bed while she struggles to run that place." Marcie looked distraught at the thought of not being able to get right back to her life as it was before.

"Marcie, you're going to have to do what the doctor says. You want to get well don't you?" Nathan brushed her cheek with his hand. "Besides, you have me to take care of you. I can help Maggie run the Raven until you get back on your feet again."

"You're going to stay and take care of me and the inn?"

"Yes. Why? Don't you think I'm capable of taking care of you? I'm sure you won't be a good patient, but I think I can handle you."

"Marcie, you'd better listen to this man. You're going to need all of the help you can get. If you try to go too fast, you're going to end up right back here in the hospital. Do you understand?" The doctor, nurse and Nathan all stood staring at Marcie, creating a united front against her.

"I guess I don't have a choice in this matter," she relented.

"You've still got a lot of swelling and bruises. So you're going to be very sore for a while. You'll also have an occasional headache, for which I will prescribe some pills. If you move about too fast, you may experience some fainting until your head completely heals. There's some swelling there as well. I want you to stay here for the next couple of days and then we'll discuss your going home. I'll check in on you again tomorrow." The doctor turned to leave, but stopped when he reached the doorway. "Oh, I almost forgot. Mark is waiting out here to ask you some questions. I told him it would be okay if he kept them brief. Do you feel up to it?"

"Does he have to bother her right now? Why can't he wait?" Nathan asked in a frustrated tone.

"It's fine," said Marcie. "I'll talk to him." She looked at Nathan reassuringly. He leaned back in the chair, nervously clenching his teeth.

Mark entered the room with a small basket of flowers for Marcie. He smiled awkwardly at Nathan as he placed them on her bedside table. "I thought these might cheer you up a bit. I'm sorry to have to bombard you with questions right off the bat, but I have to do my job."

"I understand," replied Marcie. "Ask me whatever you like."

Mark glanced over at Nathan who had leaned forward in his chair to listen. "Would you like me to ask you these questions in private?"

"No, I'd like Nathan to stay," she said, smiling in his direction. "You can ask your questions in front of him."

"Okay then, what do you remember about the night of your accident?"

"I just remember driving home just like I always do, up Beacon Hill Road."

"Well, how were you feeling? Were you upset about anything or maybe crying and couldn't see very well?"

"No, I wasn't upset at all. I had just left Nathan, and I was feeling very happy."

"What were you feeling so happy about?"

"I don't see what that has to do with anything," Nathan interrupted.

"I don't mind answering," Marcie responded, sensing the tension between the two. "Nathan and I had a wonderful night just talking, and even dancing in his room that night. We rediscovered feelings we had for one another that I thought died a long time ago. I was glad we were able to start over again after all these years. So, yes, I was happy when I left to drive home. Does that answer your question?"

"Yes, that answers it fine." Mark looked over at Nathan, who was smiling back at him. "So tell me what happened to make you drive your car off the side of the mountain. Did something, an animal maybe, dart out in front of you? Maybe you were driving too fast? What happened?"

"Someone pulled out in front of me and I lost control of the car. It was on a sharp curve in the road. The car just seemed to come out of nowhere, right in front of me." Marcie closed her eyes for a moment, trying to forget the horrible accident.

"Do you mean that someone turned too wide coming around the curve and accidentally came onto your side of the road?" Mark asked.

"Maybe, I don't remember very clearly exactly what happened. I guess it could have happened that way." Marcie squeezed Nathan's hand when she saw he was about to speak. Nathan was confused, but he kept quiet.

"So you feel it was just an accident then?"

"Well, what else could have happened?"

"Did you see what kind of car it was that pulled into your lane?"

"No, it was so dark and it happened so quickly, I couldn't tell."

"That's all for now, I guess. It's not much to go on, but it appears to be a case of someone else's sloppy driving. They ran you off the road, but apparently, didn't bother to stop or call the police. You know, Beacon Hill Road does connect to the next town, Reed's Gorge. I'll put out some feelers to see whether they stopped along the way to report the accident." Mark put his notebook in his pocket and touched Marcie's hand. "I'm just glad to see you're going to be fine and back on your feet. Let me know if you need anything, or if there's something I can do for you."

Nathan wanted to tell Mark about the phone call and the old man he saw on Beacon Hill Road, but all he could say was, "I'll be taking care of her. She'll be fine," said Nathan in a protective manner. "But we'll call you if we need you."

Mark nodded at Nathan and then said goodbye. After Mark left, Nathan sat beside Marcie. "Why didn't you tell him you thought someone deliberately ran you off the road?"

"Because, it could have been an accident, I just can't remember all of the details," Marcie said. "I can't be sure."

"But you were sure the night they brought you in here. You made a point of telling me that it was deliberate." Nathan got up and stood at the foot of Marcie's bed. "You don't really believe it was an accident, do you?"

Marcie turned her head to look the other way without responding. Then she slowly looked back at him with a curious look on her face. "Nathan, the night you found me, were you alone?" she asked.

"Of course I was alone. I almost killed myself trying to get down the side of that mountain and then I carried you to the road to flag down a car. Why? What difference does it make?" Nathan walked over closer to Marcie. "Did you see someone else?"

"Before you came, I might have been dreaming, but I remember someone looking in the car window sometime after I crashed. They kept asking me if I was all right, but I couldn't answer them. I couldn't even move. They must have thought I was dead, but I don't understand why they didn't tell someone about the accident."

"Do you remember what the person looked like at all?"

"I could barely open my eyes, but I saw him briefly. He had a flashlight and he kept shining it in my face. But I remember thinking that he would never be able to get me out." Marcie was tired and started to drift off to sleep in the middle of their conversation.

"Marcie, what do you mean?" Nathan shook her slightly to keep her awake long enough for her to finish. She started to mumble as sleep over powered her. Nathan leaned in close to try to understand what she was saying.

"Old man," she mumbled. "He was an old man with white hair."

Nathan let go of her and fell back in his chair. "An old man?" he thought. "She saw the old man?"

# 15

After a few more days in the hospital, Marcie was allowed to go home by ambulance and Nathan was anxiously waiting at her house to begin nursing her back to health. Maggie was with Marcie, helping her to get her things together. She decided it wouldn't be proper for Nathan to be staying there alone with Marcie, so she insisted on staying with her. She would come in the evenings after she was finished at the Raven Inn. With the help of her good friend to help out at the inn she'd be able to spend more time with Marcie.

Nathan had yet to discuss the old man Marcie mentioned seeing during her accident since that night and didn't want to make her keep remembering something that brought her so much pain and anxiety. He'd leave it until she was feeling stronger. Then he could see if she remembered things in the same way. Nathan was looking forward to just lying low for a while, and taking care of Marcie and the Raven Inn. This would allow him to spend more time with her, happily getting to know her all over again.

Mark hadn't been around too much. The Todd Harper case was keeping him busy. He had not turned up more evidence, nor was he able to provide them with any more information about Marcie's accident.

Finally, the ambulance arrived and they got Marcie settled into a bed in the living room, where she could be around Nathan, Maggie and activities of the house. She wanted to be in the middle of everything to ensure things were done to her liking. This way, she could boss Maggie and Nathan around as well. After everyone had gone, Nathan brought Marcie some juice for her medicine. Marcie hated taking pills and Nathan had to coax her each time to get them down.

While Maggie was in the kitchen cleaning, Nathan took a quick opportunity to spend some time alone with Marcie. "Are you comfortable?" he asked.

"Yes, as comfortable as I can be with this huge cast on my leg. I'll be glad to get this thing off so I can get around a little better." Marcie rubbed her hand along the cast as though she were trying to scratch an itch. "This is going to drive me crazy before I get it off."

"Here, I made you a scratcher," said Nathan, handing her a long slim stick that fit perfectly down in her cast. "You can reach most places with that."

"Nathan, you have thought of everything." Marcie pushed the stick down into the cast immediately and started scratching away.

"I broke my leg once, sometime back, and I wouldn't have taken a million dollars for my scratcher."

"How did you break it?"

"Oh, a friend of mine talked me into going skiing. Unfortunately, I wound up rolling down the mountain instead of skiing down. It was really embarrassing. It happened right after we got there. The girl I was with was really impressed. She ended up spending all of her time skiing with my friend, while I was hobbling around on crutches," Nathan laughed.

"Was she pretty?" Marcie asked teasingly.

"Yeah, I guess you could say that."

"Were you two close? I mean, were you serious?"

"We were serious for a while, but I couldn't keep up with her lifestyle. She loved traveling all of the time, staying in expensive places. I'm more of a homebody. It doesn't take much to make me comfortable. After a while, we just realized it wasn't working between us and we just drifted apart." Nathan shrugged his shoulders as if to say it wasn't important to him. "It worked out for the best anyway. The last I heard, she hooked up with a lawyer who was willing to spend all his money on her, so I'm sure she's happy. Besides, I'd rather be here with you." Nathan leaned over and kissed Marcie. He knew this was where he was meant to be. Just as he was about to kiss her again, Maggie bounded into the room armed with a list of chores.

"All right you two, Marcie needs her rest and I have a list of things that need doing right away," Maggie announced, handing the list of jobs to Nathan. "You'd better get started. There's a lot to be done."

"Yes, ma'am," Nathan said, saluting Maggie. "I'm up to the challenge." He winked at Marcie and headed outside to the barn.

"Thanks a lot, Mom. I can see it's going to be fun having you around. Shouldn't you be over at the Raven Inn?"

"No, my friend Velma is filling in for me today. Now you get some sleep and let me get to my house cleaning. I'll try to be quiet about it." Maggie wandered off to her next task.

Marcie sank down in her bed to take a nap, happy that Nathan was here again. She couldn't wait to get well, so they could do things together. As she drifted off to sleep, she could hear the sounds of Nathan chopping wood outside. The sound of Maggie humming an old hymn was coming from the next room as she dusted the furniture. "Now this house is starting to feel like a home," she thought.

# 16

Nathan took a break from his chopping to admire the view from Marcie's house. It was gorgeous. You could see for miles over the mountains. They looked as though they were covered with green carpet as far as the eye could see. Nathan wondered why he ever left this place. He liked the small town life of Fairhaven much better than the maddening pace of a big city. As he reflected, he saw Mark's car coming up the long driveway. Nathan put down his axe and threw up his hand at him.

"So you're staying here now?" Mark asked, getting out of the car.

"Just to help out until Marcie's back on her feet. Maggie's in the house. What brings you up here?"

"Oh, I just wanted to make sure the patient made it home, but I can see she's in good hands." Mark leaned up against the car and lit a cigarette.

Nathan walked over a little closer. "Are you always this interested in Marcie's welfare?" he asked.

"I've known her all my life. Of course I'm interested in what happens to her. She nearly got killed." Mark threw down his cigarette after only a few short puffs. "I've got to quit smoking these nasty things. They're going to be the death of me yet."

Nathan stepped in front of Mark to get his full attention. "Does Gracey know about your great interest in Marcie?"

"What do you mean? Like I said, I've known her for a long time. I'm a good friend, that's all. I'm probably the closet thing she has to a brother. I want to make sure no harm comes to her. Besides, you've been gone a long time, years. I don't know your motives for returning here. Why did you come back anyway?" Mark stood inches from Nathan's face.

Nathan backed away, realizing he may have accused Mark too harshly. "I just wanted to come back home for a while. My life was getting too fast paced and I thought coming here would put things back into perspective for me. Seeing Marcie again has been especially good for me. Maybe she's what I need in my life."

Mark walked up to Nathan and put his hand on his shoulder. "Look, I guess I've been pushing you pretty hard. It's just that, this is a small town. Everybody knows everybody's business, but we're also close, like a family. If something happens to one of us, we get involved. It's not like living in some huge city where nobody wants to know what's going on with anybody else. Then out of the thin, blue sky, after all of these years, you show up. That's going to make people a little uneasy around you for a while. To us, you're just another stranger. That's why I've been sticking a little closer to you than maybe you would like, but then, that's just the sheriff in me. I don't mean any harm."

Nathan pushed Mark's hand off of his shoulder. "I'm in love with Marcie. I would never do anything to harm her."

Mark walked back toward his car. "I can see that. You can see it in her eyes too. What are your plans?"

Nathan paused for a moment, not sure how to take Mark's fatherly questions. "I'm not sure just now. We'll just have to take it slow and see what happens. I don't plan to leave anytime soon. I can do my writing here just as easily as I can somewhere else. Is that okay with you?"

Mark got in his car and started the engine. "Sure, it's fine with me. There's no law against it. Just be careful, though. There's a killer running around here somewhere and we haven't been able to find many clues for the killing of Todd Harper. But, like I said, this is a small town. I've got plenty of time to hunt him down." Mark backed up his car and headed down the driveway toward the road.

Nathan, using his hand to block the sun from his eyes, watched him drive away. For some reason his heart was pumping as though he had been running a race. "I have to talk to Marcie soon," he thought." I have to confide in her about my memories of Robert and the old man." Somehow he felt she could help him unlock the puzzle in his mind. He figured if he could remember everything about Robert, it might lead to some connection between his death and that of Todd Harper. It may be possible that even Marcie's accident is related.

That evening Nathan fixed a big supper for Marcie and Maggie. He wouldn't let Maggie near the kitchen to help him. He wanted it to be a big surprise for both of them. Nathan placed a table in the living room in front of Marcie so they could all three eat together. Marcie couldn't help but be impressed by all of the trouble Nathan was going through. Maggie was fit to be tied. She believed that a woman's place is in the kitchen, but it's the last place you should find a man. However, Nathan was truly enjoying himself. He was used to cooking and actually liked preparing meals for more than one person for a change. Adding the finishing touches to the table, he brought out a beautiful herb roasted chicken with all the trimmings. Marcie and Maggie looked at one another with great surprise. It actually looked edible.

As they sat down to eat, Maggie bowed her head. "We have so much to be grateful for dear Father. Thank you for looking out for Marcie during her accident and for allowing us to bring her home. Thank you for sending Nathan to help us during this time of need and for blessing him with the talent to cook a meal without the fire department showing up. Bless this food that's been prepared for us and keep us safe in your care. In Christ's name we pray. Amen."

Nathan shifted in his seat a little. He had not always remembered to say grace before meals, even though he was brought up to do so. It made him feel at home. "Amen," he repeated after Maggie. "Now, let me serve you some of this wonderful bird."

As Nathan prepared to carve, the doorbell rang. "Were you expecting company tonight?" Nathan asked Marcie.

"No, I wonder who it could be?" Marcie replied, glancing at her watch.

"I'll see who it is." Nathan opened the door and there stood Mark's wife, Gracey.

"Hey, Nathan, honey. I hope I'm not interrupting anything, but I just had to come over and see how Marcie is doing. I haven't had a real chance to visit with you since you got into town." Gracey waved to Maggie from the doorway, "Hi honey. I hope it's not a bad time. I brought one of my tuna casseroles just in case you haven't eaten yet."

"Oh, no, we were just sitting down to eat. Come on in. This casserole will go great with the meal. Let me take your coat. Marcie, look it's Gracey." Nathan took her coat and the tuna casserole. Gracey rushed in, hugging and kissing Marcie and Maggie. "Where's Mark?" Nathan asked, returning to the table.

"Oh, he's out chasing criminals. He's been working a lot of overtime these days, you know, what with the killing of that Harper boy and everything. I just couldn't take sitting in the house all alone tonight, so I thought I'd dash over here and visit for a while."

"I hope you're hungry, because we've got a lot of food here. Do you like chicken?" Marcie asked.

"Oh, honey I eat anything as long as it's not still moving. Oh, this looks scrumptious. You're such a wonderful cook, Maggie."

"I can't take the credit for this. Nathan prepared this meal," Maggie said placing her napkin in her lap. "I say we dig in before it gets cold."

"Nathan, is there anything you can't do? You're a writer and now a cook too. He's a real catch," Gracey whispered to Marcie, who just smiled in agreement.

"Hand me your plate, Gracey, and I'll serve you up some of my masterpiece." Nathan served everyone and then himself.

"This is just simply scrumptious," Gracey announced with the exaggerated tone of someone who had just tasted chicken for the first time. "You must give me your recipe, Nathan." Gracey was the type to flower everything with flattery. Everything is marvelous, wonderful or scrumptious. Nathan knew not to let her compliments go to his head.

"How's Mark coming with the Harper investigation, Gracey?" Marcie asked.

"You know, I've never seen a man work so hard in all of my life. He's either in his office or out in those woods trying to find clues. I bet he's talked to just about everybody in this town that knew that little boy. But so far, I don't believe he's been able to turn up much that can help him. He always looks exasperated when he finally does come home. Sometimes he barely takes time to eat. Of course, if I could cook like this, he'd probably make more of an effort. Most of the time he grabs something at Jordan's and goes on his way." Gracey's face changed to a solemn look. "I wish there was more I could do to help. That poor boy's parents are suffering something terrible through all of this. They loved that boy so. Do you know them, Nathan?"

"Well, I went with Mark to talk with them when it first happened. They seem like really nice people."

"They are the sweetest two folks you'd ever want to meet." Gracey pushed her plate back and took out a pill from her purse. "I need something to calm my nerves," she said, swallowing the pill down with a sip of sweet ice tea. "It makes me think of our son's death, not too many years ago. He would have been Todd's age today. His name was Charles. We called him Charley though. He was my pride and joy." Gracey took her napkin and wiped her eyes.

Nathan gave a puzzled look to Marcie and Maggie. "I didn't know that you and Mark had a child, Gracey."

"Well, I'm ashamed to say that he was born before Mark and I were married. I always felt like he was Mark's son, although I'm ashamed to admit it's possible another man was the father. Anyway, I didn't want to pressure Mark into getting married if he didn't want to, and I figured I could take care of him somehow on my own. But finally, Mark just popped the question and asked me to marry him, just like that. I was so shocked, but I was extremely grateful. He's a good man and a good provider."

"What happened to Charley?" Nathan interrupted.

"He drowned. He was swimming with a bunch of other kids. We were told that he and some of the other boys were playing a game, trying to see who could swim out the farthest from the shore of Brown's Pond. The others gave up, but Charley kept on going and then he just disappeared." Gracey started to sob. "Mark really took it hard. He really loved Charley and blamed the other kids for daring him to swim out past where he should have. I just think they were being kids, you know, and he got in over his head." Gracey paused for a long time and no one knew what to say. "Well, listen to me going on and on about myself when my purpose for coming over here was to visit with you. Forgive me, Marcie." Gracey grabbed Marcie's hand and squeezed it tightly.

"Don't worry yourself about it, Gracey. We're all family here." Just then the phone rang. Maggie got up to answer it in the next room.

"Are you doing pretty good, sugar?" Gracey asked, quickly changing the subject.

"Yes, I'm moving around rather slowly these days, but I'm getting better every day, especially with Maggie and Nathan here to help me." Marcie said, smiling at Nathan.

"You're very fortunate to have so many people who love and care about you. Mark said your hospital room was filled with flowers from your friends and neighbors. I just love flowers, don't you?" asked Gracey.

Maggie returned from the telephone call. "That was Mark. He wanted to let you know he was home. He was wondering where you were. I told him you were just visiting with us for a spell."

"Gracious me, I'd better get home and see if I can get him to take a bite of food. I'm sorry to rush out like this, but I don't want to worry Mark. Lord knows he's got enough to worry about." She rushed to the door, but remembered her coat.

"I have it right here, Gracey." Nathan helped her with her coat and opened the door for her.

"Goodnight, I'll call on you again when I get the chance. Marcie, I'll bring you some of my homemade soup." With that, she left just as quickly as she had arrived.

Nathan stood at the door and watched as she got in her car. "She's a crazy kind of gal, but she has a good heart."

Maggie finished clearing the table. "I remember when her son died. It was a terrible accident."

Nathan sat down beside Marcie. "I never knew that Mark had a son. I guess I've missed a lot being away for so long. I feel really bad for them. It must have been hard to hear their only son was drowned. Maybe I should try to lighten up on him a little, you know, give him some room to do his job. He's just been leaning on me so hard, it's easy to want to take a punch at him."

"He'll let up once he gets to know you better," said Maggie. "He's got a good heart, but he's got a lot of pressure right now, trying to find an answer to Todd Harper's death. I suppose that doesn't make him the friendliest guy in town."

Nathan looked over at Marcie, but she was already asleep. "We'd better let this lady get some rest." He pulled the covers up around her and kissed her lightly on the cheek. So much had happened since he came home, but still, he was glad to go through it all if it meant being with her again. "Oh, I'm pretty beat myself. Goodnight, Maggie. I'm going to bed. It's been a long day."

"Good night, dear." Maggie waved her hand to him and winked. "I'm going to sit up for a spell and read. I'll turn out the lights when I go to bed. I just want to make sure she rests well tonight."

Nathan went upstairs to his room and fell in his bed. He closed his eyes, quickly drifting off to sleep wondering what the days ahead would bring.

# 17

The next morning Nathan was up bright and early. He decided he wanted to go into town to pick up a few things they needed. He also wanted to take the opportunity to stop by and try to make peace with Mark. Perhaps he did have a lot on his mind, chasing down clues while trying to push away bad memories. This was a problem Nathan could relate to. He wanted to try to be more of a help to him, rather than a source of suspicion.

As he arrived in town, he saw Mark's car parked at Jordan's. "He's probably having breakfast," Nathan thought. "Maybe now is as good a time as any." He walked over and went inside. He could see Mark sitting in the back drinking a cup of coffee.

"Can I get you a table?" a young man asked.

"Uh, no thanks. I see someone at the back." Nathan slowly walked toward the table and stood in front of Mark. "Mind if I sit down?"

Mark looked surprised. He lowered his coffee cup and gestured to the empty chair at his table. "Why not?"

Nathan took a seat. "I'll just have some coffee and a piece of toast," he told the waiter. For a few minutes, the two just exchanged uneasy looks.

"So, is the breakfast good here?" Nathan asked, trying to break the tension between them.

"I think so, but you can't really go by me. Jordan's is the only place I ever eat. I'm sure it's not as good as Maggie's cooking over at the Raven Inn, but I feel at home here. It's kind of my home away from home."

The waiter brought Nathan's order and poured another cup of coffee for Mark. "Anything else I can get for you?" he asked.

"No thanks," said Nathan. "I'm fine."

"So, what brings you to town this morning? Surely you didn't come in just to have coffee with me," Mark said sarcastically.

"Actually, I did. I mean, I needed some things from the store too, but I really wanted to come in and have a talk with you." Nathan didn't really know where to begin, but he decided to just get right to the point. "Look Mark, you and I used to be pretty good friends. Now we're like strangers. I think I expected you to just welcome me with open arms when I returned to Fairhaven, even though I've been gone a really long time. Then all of these weird things started happening, like Todd Harper's body being found and Marcie's accident. I don't blame you for being suspicious of me. Maybe I would have reacted the same way."

Mark just stared at Nathan at first, not really sure how to take his attempt to start over again. "I guess I have treated you like a suspect ever since the accident with Marcie. Maybe you've misinterpreted my motives toward her. She's like a sister to me. I may have been interested in her at one time, but she seemed to miss you so much, there was no way anybody else could catch her eye. Anyway, she and I have been friends for too long. We could never be anything more than close friends. I just tend to be over protective of her. She's a very special lady, you know?"

"You've got that right," Nathan said, smiling. "Look Mark, I just want you to know I want to be a help to you if I can, instead of causing you problems." He paused for a moment, measuring his words carefully. "I'd like us to be friends again, if that's all right with you. We could make a pretty good team." Nathan quietly waited for a response from Mark, but he didn't answer. "Gracey came for a visit last night, as you know."

Mark grinned, shaking his head. "Yeah, she's very concerned about Marcie. People here tend to look down on her, but she's got a huge heart. There's room in there for the whole town, but they just think she's an uneducated, flamboyant, loose woman who deserves their pity more than their attention." Mark looked away from Nathan and lit up a cigarette. Taking only a couple of long puffs, he quickly put it out.

"Still trying to quit?" Nathan asked. Mark didn't answer." I think Gracey's a fine lady, Mark. She's different, sure, but that's what makes her so great. You know how people are. If someone's not the same as them, they weed them out like trash. You know that's not true though. It's plain to see she loves you. She worries about you."

"Yeah, she does."

"She told me about your son drowning."

Mark turned back toward Nathan. You could see his face change just at the mention of his son, Charley. "Why would she be talking to you about that?"

"I don't know, out of concern for you, I guess. She was talking about how hard Todd Harper's investigation has been on you, I mean, being the same age as Charley. Anyway, I wanted to tell you I'm sorry. I didn't even know you ever had a son."

"Most people told me I was foolish for marrying Gracey. They all said Charley's father could have been any number of other men. I don't know. I just felt like it was the right thing to do. He needed a father. Besides, I always felt he was mine. He had my eyes." Mark stared into space. "Charley was my son. Those kids shouldn't have dared him to swim out so far. Why do they do that? He was smaller than the rest, but full of spunk. He had to take their dare just to hold his own with them. They were always testing him, always teasing him about who his real father was. I guess he felt like he had to show them he wasn't afraid. I guess he felt he had no choice."

Nathan shifted uncomfortably in his seat. "I didn't mean to bring up such a painful subject, man. I just want to make peace with you. Let me help you find out the mystery behind Todd's death, better still, Robert's death. You and I both have memories that we need to deal with somehow. Maybe we can do it together."

Mark brought his focus back to Nathan. For once, he looked like he believed what he was saying. He slowly reached out his hand to him. "Okay, Nathan. It's a deal. I'm willing to try if you are. Far be it from me to turn down help."

The two finished their coffee, talking about different subjects. A couple of times, they even laughed at some things they did when they were kids. Nathan began to see the friend he once had in Mark.

They both risked vulnerability sitting in Jordan's that morning, but Nathan felt it was a risk well worth taking. After that day they became close friends again. They rediscovered their similarities and differences as friends do in the days that followed.

Nathan welcomed the relationship. Even when he was a young boy, he longed for the closeness of a friend who could share his secrets after Robert died. Yet, he still found it hard to share everything, like Marcie seeing the old man during her accident. He wanted their relationship to be stronger before he shared too much.

# 18

As the days passed, along with several trips to the doctor's office, Marcie slowly regained her strength and was able to get up and around again, first on crutches and then on her own. Nathan moved back into his room at the Raven Inn to give Maggie a hand until Marcie was fully recovered. He enjoyed working around the inn. It was always a special place to him while he was growing up. When he was a boy, Marcie would invite him over for cookies or pie. He would roam from room to room, studying the interesting pictures hanging above the beautiful old furnishings. It was a real pleasure to be around this place again.

One of the many tasks that Nathan had on his to-do list was to drive into town to pick up some items for Maggie, but his mind was everywhere but on the road. Thoughts about his career, Marcie and other things were spinning around and around in his head. He had begun writing again when he could sneak in the time. However, Maggie seemed to always have a list of things for him to do. Still, he would steal away to his room on occasion to work on his book. Quite often he worked on it late into the night while it was quiet, and Maggie wasn't awake to hound him.

He was beginning to feel pretty settled in Fairhaven and was giving a lot of thought to moving back permanently, but Nathan was also beginning to miss the city life, just a little. He wondered whether he could be happy living in a small town like Fairhaven. Everyone knows your business in a small town, sticking their noses in your personal affairs. He decided to put off making any decisions about moving for a while longer, even though Marcie was beginning to bring up the subject in her own subtle way. Nathan knew he wanted to be near her, but he wasn't sure she would be willing to leave her home and Maggie to follow him. After all, she had grown up here and seemed content to remain in Fairhaven. Perhaps that was the reason Marcie's marriage ended before it started.

Arriving in town before he even realized, he wondered how he had managed to make the drive with his mind so far away. As he got out of the car and headed for the store, he ran into Todd Harper's parents, Dan and Elizabeth, on their way out. They didn't seem to notice him at first. They looked straight past him as he held the door for them.

"Mr. and Mrs. Harper?" he asked as they passed. At first they didn't recognize him and only gave him a blank stare as they kept walking. "I'm Nathan. I don't know if you remember me, but I came with Mark Temple to your house to talk to you about your son's death."

"Oh, Nathan. I'm sorry. We're just out running some errands. We didn't even see you standing there. Please, call me Dan." Dan stepped back to shake hands with Nathan. "You remember my wife, Elizabeth."

"Yes, it's nice to see you both again." The three stood and looked at each other in silence for a brief, awkward moment. Not sure what to say to them, Nathan found himself grasping for something general to discuss.

"It's a beautiful day isn't it? It's a good day for running errands. As a matter of fact, that's what I'm doing."

"Yes, well, we won't keep you then." Dan and his wife started down the street toward their car.

"Dan, wait!" Nathan shouted after them. He quickly walked over, feeling like he had to say something more to them.

"I want you to know that Mark is doing everything he can to find out what happened to your son. I know you haven't had any news lately, but he hasn't stopped the investigation."

"We know," answered Dan. "But it doesn't make our lives any easier. We can't rest until we know for sure what happened to Todd. We will find out, even if it means hiring our own private investigator."

"A private investigator? Are you serious?"

"Yes, we are. So far Mark hasn't been able to turn up anything helpful. You understand we can't just forget about it and walk away. Someone has to find out, and if we have to spend every last dollar we have, we'll keep searching for the killer."

"I know it's hard Dan, but sometimes these things take a long time to piece together. Apparently, this person didn't leave a lot of clues lying around. Whoever it was, knew what he was doing."

"Yes and he'll strike again. Someone else is going to suffer the loss of a child if he's not caught. We wouldn't want anyone else to go through what we've been through. Do you expect us to just sit around and wait for Mark to find this monster? There has to be something we can do to help. Anyway, the investigator won't get in Mark's way. He'll be working completely on his own and we'll be paying him. Maybe this way we'll get some straight answers."

"Are you saying you think Mark isn't telling you everything? I know he's talked to everybody in town at least twice. If he had something he could tell you, I'm sure he would. He'd have no reason to hold anything back from you."

"I think Mark's truly interested in finding out what happened to Todd, but I don't believe he's doing everything he can to find his killer."

"What makes you think such a thing? He's been working long hours on this case. He barely eats or sleeps because of it. You just don't understand how difficult a case like this can be—"

"Well, what about the old man that was seen in the woods by my neighbor, Jake. Why doesn't he investigate that more closely? I would think that information could lead to something."

Nathan stepped back in shock. "An old man? What about him?"

"My neighbor saw an old man wandering in the woods close to the time that my Todd was killed. He told me he had mentioned seeing him, but Mark didn't say much about it. Nobody said anything to us about the old man until I confronted Mark about it.

"What did he say?"

"Oh, he just dismissed it. He said he'd already checked into it and it didn't lead to anything. Nobody else saw him, so I guess he thinks Jake is lying."

Nathan could feel his heart begin to pound inside of him. Someone else had actually seen the old man. Marcie had seen him too. He had to be real, not just an illusion he had made up in his own mind.

"Nathan, did you hear what I said?" asked Dan.

"Yes, I heard you Dan. I'm sorry, I'm sure Mark knows what he's doing. I've got to get on with my errands. I'll talk to you later." As he started to walk away, he turned to Dan, "Would you let me know when your private investigator shows up? I'd like to talk with him myself, if that's okay with you."

Dan looked puzzled by Nathan's request. "You want to talk to him?"

"I might be able to give him some general information that would be helpful, since I was with Mark when they found Todd. If you don't mind, give me a call."

"All right, Nathan," Dan said as he and his wife got into their car and drove away.

Nathan stood in front of the store in a daze. His dreams were becoming more real every day. This old man is a real person and he may be a killer. He may be Robert's killer. Who is he? Why didn't Mark mention this to him? He'd asked Mark about the case on a regular basis, but he never mentioned an old man had been seen near the scene of the crime. Maybe he should confide in Mark that he had also seen the old man. Now that he knew for certain that he wasn't a figment of his imagination, he had to let Mark know this was a lead worth following.

# 19

On his way back to the Raven Inn, Nathan stopped by Marcie's to see how she was doing and to make sure that she didn't need anything. As he drove up, he could see her sitting on the front porch in the sunshine. He was glad to see she was resting and taking it slow.

"How's my patient today?" Nathan asked as he stepped out of his car.

"Good morning. I'm holding my own. Did you come to check up on me, to make sure I'm not out plowing the fields or painting the house?"

"I just wanted to make sure you have everything you need. How about some lunch? I can whip us up a couple of sandwiches and a cold drink." Nathan sat beside Marcie on the front porch and kissed her.

"How about we just sit for a while first? I miss you being around the house. What have you been up to?"

"Your mother has been running me ragged. She doesn't let me stand still for very long, but I'm not complaining. I love it."

"Before you know it, I'll be back to relieve you. The doctor says I'm doing fine as long as I take it easy." Marcie could see that something was on Nathan's mind. She could always read his eyes. "What's bothering you? You seem a hundred miles away. Did something happen?"

"I ran into Dan and Elizabeth Harper in town. We had a chance to talk."

"Oh, those poor people, I know this has to be very hard for them. How are they holding up?"

"As good as could be expected, I suppose, but Dan said something to me. Marcie, do you remember while you were in the hospital, I think it was the first night there, you asked me if I was alone when I found you? Do you remember, you mentioned seeing someone else before I arrived?"

Marcie thought for a moment, "Yes, but I figured I must have dreamed it, since you said you were alone. You know, I was pretty out of it at the time. I'm not sure I really saw someone else. It's all still pretty hazy. Why, Nathan? What are you getting at?"

"While I was talking with Dan Harper, he mentioned that his neighbor, Jake, had talked with Mark about seeing an old man walking in the woods right around the place where Todd was found dead."

"An old man?" Marcie sat back in her chair, staring at Nathan. "Did he say what he looked like?"

"No, I didn't ask. I haven't had a chance to talk to Jake myself yet, but I intend to ask him a few questions. I wanted to see if you remembered anything else about what you saw first. Can you recall anything, anything at all about what you saw?"

Marcie closed her eyes, trying to remember that night. She could only remember being in great pain and calling for help. As she sat with her eyes closed for a while longer, she could see herself in the accident with the car turning over and over as it flew over the cliff. Marcie could feel herself being tossed about in the car, hitting her head several times. As the car came to rest at the bottom of the mountain, she recalled how quiet it was while she waited the long hours for someone to rescue her. "I was so cold. I couldn't move a muscle in the car. For a moment I was able to open my eyes, but it was pitch black all around me. I do remember someone calling my name, very softly, like they were afraid someone would hear. It was a man's voice. At first I thought I was hallucinating, but then there was a light. It was moving around above my head. I couldn't see who was behind it. I asked him to please help me, but he just kept shining the light in my face. Then, he dropped the flashlight. For a moment, it was shining back on him. I could see the man was old. He even had white hair. I remember thinking, he'll never be able to get me out of here by himself, but maybe he'll go and get help. Suddenly, he grabbed the light and started to leave. Then, strangely, he stopped and said, 'Goodnight, Marcie.' Nathan, he said my name."

Nathan put his arms around Marcie, shaking her a little to bring her back to reality. "It's okay, Marcie. You're with me now, you're safe."

"How could he have known me?" She pulled back from him a little to look into his face. "Do you think he was the same man that Jake saw in the woods?"

"Maybe, it's possible. The strange thing is Dan said Jake told Mark, but Mark seemed to dismiss it, like it wasn't important."

"I'm sure Mark would have followed up on information like that, Nathan. He's as interested in finding Todd's killer as they are, I'm sure. He works on nothing else lately, you know that."

"I know, but I want to talk to him and find out what he's got to say about it." Nathan thought for a moment, "Marcie, I've seen this old man myself, not in person, but in my dreams, well maybe they weren't all dreams. Somehow he's stored away in my memories about Robert's death. I might have even talked to him on the phone once."

Marcie couldn't believe what she was hearing. "What do you mean you talked with him on the phone? What does he have to do with Robert's death? Nathan, you're not making any sense."

"No, I'm not. Look, I just haven't bothered bringing it up before now because I thought he was just someone I imagined, but every time I think of Robert or remember anything about his death, I end up seeing this old man with white hair smiling back at me. He says my name as though he knows me well. When you had your accident, I climbed into your house, searching for anything that might lead me to you. While I was there, the phone rang. When I picked it up, I didn't even say a word, but he knew it was me. After a minute, I thought I recognized the voice on the other end. Marcie, I believe it was him, the old man. He warned me to stay out of the woods. He even suggested I should go back where I came from, like he was threatening me."

"He's actually someone around here? So the man I saw was real? But how could he be the same man you remember seeing when Robert died? That was more than fifteen years ago. You were just a boy."

"I don't know, but there's got to be a connection. Now, Jake has seen him too. That's more than coincidence. That's why I need to talk to Mark about this, but if you see him first, please don't mention it to him. Let me be the one to talk to him."

Later that evening, Nathan got a chance to sit in his room and do some writing. He had decided to begin a new book, but the words just weren't coming. He had hoped writing another book would be a good distraction for him, but his mind was filled with too many questions. He just couldn't concentrate. Pushing back from his laptop and rubbing his eyes, Nathan was feeling too tired, but he tried to start again. His fingers somehow seemed to be typing all by themselves. His thoughts kept drifting away from the story back to Robert.

The room felt too warm, so Nathan decided to raise the window. Pulling back the curtain, he could see someone standing outside by his car. He raised the window as far as it would go and looked again. This time no one was there. Shrugging his shoulders, he sat back down at his computer and started to read back what he had typed, "The old man killed Robert. The old man killed Robert," he read. These were the only words on the screen. They filled the entire page.

Nathan's mind was racing. "What's happening? Why can't I remember anything?" His anger turned to rage. Grabbing the computer, he threw it across the room. As it smashed up against the wall, he heard a voice.

"Nathan! Nathan, come outside for a while."

He stopped dead and didn't move a muscle. He nearly stopped breathing, as the voice sent a chill up his spine. "Robert? Is that you?" Nathan backed up against the wall, frozen in place.

"Nathan, can't you see me? I'm down here."

Nathan could hear the voice coming from outside his window. As he looked out, he saw a small boy standing in the light shining from his room. Nathan's voice was trembling as he called down to the boy, "Robert?"

"Over here. Come on down. It's a great night for exploring. Let's head for the river. Hurry, before someone sees me."

Nathan instinctively ran down the stairs, pausing for a moment to make sure no one heard him. As he made his way out the front door, it was pitch black and no one was around. Nathan walked around in the direction to where his bedroom window looked out over the meadow.

"Robert, are you there?" Waiting for an answer, the roar of the inn's heating system kicking on was the only sound.

Just as he turned to go back to the other side of the inn, he heard Robert's voice again. "Nathan, I'm over here by the trees. Let's go."

Robert took off toward the woods waving his hands wildly above his head. Suddenly he was out of sight, but Nathan could still hear him calling him.

"Nathan, Nathan, come on, hurry!"

"I'm coming," he shouted back, running toward Robert's voice. As he entered the woods, he stopped to listen." I should have grabbed a flashlight," he thought.

"I'm down here by the river, Nathan. Hurry up, slow poke. Are you afraid?"

"Yeah, I am little. We shouldn't be out here at night. My mom has told me over and over again not to come out here after dark. What if we get caught? She won't ever let me hang around you again."

"Oh, stop worrying. We won't get caught. There's nobody out here. Now stop whining and get down here."

"Okay, okay, I'm coming, but wait for me." Nathan ran down to the river, stopping to look behind him, making sure there were no dragons or monsters around to fight. When he reached the river, he saw Robert sitting on a big rock, looking in the water. He climbed up with him and sat down. "Look how the moon shines down on the water," said Robert, pointing below him. "Isn't it spooky looking?"

"Yeah, really scary. Maybe we should head back."

"No, let's walk down the river on the rocks for a ways. Maybe we'll find a buried treasure or a dragon to fight."

"I don't know, Robert. It's awfully late already."

"Don't worry. We won't go far, just down to the bend in the river there. Come on Nathan. Be brave. What could happen?" Robert took off again and started jumping from rock to rock.

Nathan decided to follow. He didn't want Robert thinking he was scared. After all, if he ran into a dragon, he would never be able to fight him alone. As he jumped on the rocks trying to keep up with him, he thought he heard a scream.

"Nathan, Nathan over here. Help me!"

Nathan's heart nearly stopped at the shrill voice. "I'm coming! Hold on!" He ran as fast as he could, slipping into the water from the wet rocks. As he tried his best to get to Robert, he could hear voices.

"Oh no, you've killed him. Look what you've done."

Nathan looked around, but he couldn't see a thing. Suddenly, he could hear someone behind him, breathing heavily, like they were running. As he turned, the breathless runner whizzed right by him, but Nathan still couldn't see. Then someone moved in the bushes near him.

"Nathan, Nathan," he heard a voice calling.

Was it his mother calling him to come home? He couldn't tell. He ran toward the voice, but it was so dark he couldn't tell which way to go.

"Nathan, over here, I'm hiding over here."

Walking in the direction of the voice, he could see someone crouched low behind a rock. Abruptly, someone jumped out, grabbing him and shoving him to the ground. They rolled around with Nathan fighting as hard as he could. "Let me up!" he cried. "What are you doing, Robert?"

"Shut up and keep quiet. I'm not Robert!"

Nathan fell backwards. He couldn't tell who he was wrestling with, but it was someone his own size. Finally he broke free from his hold. He jumped up to run away, but he ran directly into someone standing behind him. As he looked up, he could see an old man with white hair.

"Nathan, where you going?" the old man asked.

"Who are you?"

"I'm friend. Do you want play?"

Nathan jerked away and ran for his life. He could hear breathing behind him, but he didn't look back. He kept running until he got out of the woods. Then, stopping to catch his breath for a minute, he fell down on the ground behind a tree, gasping for air. He pulled his legs up underneath him and stayed as still as he could. "I'll stay here all night if that's what it takes," he thought.

# 20

The next morning, as Maggie was preparing to serve breakfast, she looked out the back window, as she often did, to catch the view of the mountains and the meadow. There, underneath the big oak tree in the back, she saw someone lying on the ground. She took off her apron and walked out the back door to get a closer look. As she walked a little farther, she stopped dead in her tracks. "Oh, my, Nathan," she said to herself. He was sound asleep underneath a tree. "Nathan, can you hear me?"

Opening his eyes slowly, he could see a blurry figure standing over him.

"Can you say your name, son?"

Nathan wanted to answer, but his mouth wouldn't cooperate. He just shook his head yes, at first, but then managed to mumble his name softly. Then he just blacked out again.

When he opened his eyes again he found himself on a bed. "What happened?" he asked trying to raise himself up.

"We're hoping you can tell us," a voice replied, pushing him back down onto the pillow.

Nathan finally focused his eyes on the doctor standing over him.

"Do you remember anything at all?" the doctor asked while examining Nathan's eyes with a light.

"A little, I guess, but why are you here?"

"Well, it seems you decided to sleep outside in the backyard last night. Maggie here, found you this morning, curled up under a tree, sleeping like a baby. Do you remember going outside?"

"I'm not sure. I'm a little confused myself." Nathan sat up and looked around. "Is Marcie here?"

"No, not yet," answered Maggie. "She's on her way. I asked Mark to stop by and pick her up. How do you feel?"

"Fine, I'm fine." Nathan rubbed his hands over his face as though he was trying to awaken from a bad dream.

The doctor motioned for Maggie to step outside the room with him. "I can't really see anything physically wrong with him. It's probably just a simple case of sleepwalking. A lot of people suffer from it. It's pretty common. I don't think there's anything to be alarmed about. He just needs to rest and stay warm. It was a pretty cool night last night to be sleeping outside. Let me know if he starts showing signs of a cold and I'll get him some medicine. Other than that, he should be fine. I would, however, recommend that he make an appointment with a therapist or psychiatrist to help him with this sleepwalking business. It seems to be serious enough to need attention."

"Thank you, doctor. I'll tell him. Thanks for coming so quickly. Seeing him just threw such a scare into me, I didn't know what to do. He looked so pale, lying underneath that tree. At first, well, I thought he was dead," Maggie's voice broke.

"Don't worry yourself, now. He's going to be just fine. Call me if you need me." The doctor gave Maggie a pat on the shoulder as he was leaving.

Just as the doctor was leaving, Mark drove up with Marcie. She ran into the house and started right in on Maggie. "Is he all right? What happened? What did the doctor say?"

"The doctor says he's going to be just fine. He thinks Nathan suffers from some kind of sleepwalking problem. He said he should get plenty of rest and stay warm. Oh, Marcie, you should have seen him this morning. I thought I would pass out before I could get to him. The doctor and Mr. Holland, he's one of the guests here, had to carry him into the house. He didn't even wake up when they picked him up off the ground."

"I've got to see him, where is he?"

"He's in his room, but he may be sleeping"

Marcie took off up the stairs before Maggie could finish. She flung open the door to his room and started crying just as soon as she saw his face. "Nathan, are you all right? Maggie told me what happened. How do you feel? Do you need anything?"

"Whoa, Marcie, slow down. I'm fine, okay? I'm just a little hazy on what happened last night."

"The doctor says you're a sleepwalker. Has this ever happened to you before?"

"I've never slept outside all night, unless I was camping, if that's what you mean. I don't believe I've ever done any sleepwalking before now."

"Well, what else then? Why would you fall asleep underneath a tree all night? You don't even remember yourself what happened. It must be sleepwalking."

"No Marcie. I do remember bits and pieces. I remember—"

"How's the notorious sleepwalker doing?" asked Mark from the doorway. "They say you prefer to sleep outside these days. Were you feeling pretty rugged last night and just decided to brave the elements?"

"Hi, Mark. Thanks for bringing Marcie over. I don't know for sure what made me go outside last night. Maybe the doc's right. I'm a sleepwalker and I didn't even realize it." Nathan gently took Marcie's hand.

"Well I'm glad to see you're doing better. Stay in bed and rest. Marcie, don't let him wander around outside. I've got to go, but I'll stop by and see you later."

"Bye and thanks again," Nathan said, waving him off.

"I'm going to fix you a cup of hot tea," said Marcie, as she started for the door.

"Wait, don't go just yet."

"I'm not leaving, Nathan. I'm just going downstairs to fix your tea."

"I want to talk to you. You can get the tea later."

Marcie smiled and sat back down on the bed. "Whatever you want."

"Marcie, do you love me?"

"You know I do, honey. Why do you ask me such a question? I'm always telling you I love you. Driving over here with Mark, I thought my heart would burst until I could get to you and make sure you were okay. Of course, I love you."

"Then go away with me. Go back to the city with me. I need to get away from here. I don't know what it is, but I feel like I'm slowly slipping away into my past by staying here."

"Go away? Nathan, I grew up here, and what about Maggie? She doesn't have anybody to look after her." Marcie stood up and started pacing back and forth. "You're just talking crazy because of last night. It's just sleepwalking, that's all. You don't have to run away from it."

"I'm not running away from anything, Marcie, but I can't seem to sort things out here. There's always going to be the memory of Robert's death to haunt me while I'm here."

"Nathan, that was a long time ago. Let it go. You don't have to solve his death. It won't bring him back. We could be so happy here. You said yourself that you liked the pace of a small town and you love my house, or we could build a different house. I want to be with you, but I don't know if I can leave my home and family. Don't ask me to do that, Nathan."

"Marcie, that's what happens when two people fall in love. They leave their former lives behind and move on to a life together. How do you know you couldn't be happy somewhere else? Maggie has friends all around to look out for her. We can hire someone to help her with the Raven Inn. Or better yet, she could come and live with us. We could get married and build a nice big house on the ocean. Maggie could enjoy the life of leisure for a change. Maybe it's time for a change Marcie. I know it is for me."

"I knew this was going to happen. You never intended to stay here. It's just like before when you left. You were running away from something then and you're still running. I don't need a big house on the ocean. Maggie loves this old inn. Do you think she could give it up so easily?"

"Marcie, last night I was a boy again, sneaking out of the house to play with Robert, just like when he was killed. I lost all sense of time, and I could hear his voice calling me, just as clearly as you speaking to me now. We actually ran through the woods together last night, in my mind. I must be acting out my thoughts and memories, but it's much more than sleepwalking. It's something I experienced before I left here, and now that I'm back, it's starting all over again. I don't think I'll ever be able to live here in peace."

"Maybe you can get some professional help, Nathan. You don't have to battle this all alone, you know. There are people who can help you get over this, to help you understand what's happening to you. But if you just run away and hide, it's going to follow you for the rest of your life. Let's get help. Let's go see someone. It doesn't have to be here. Let's go to someone who doesn't know this town or the people here."

Marcie stared at Nathan with her eyes full of tears. Her whole world seemed to be slipping through her fingers in just one day. She desperately wanted to hold on to him, because she knew she would never be able to love anyone else, but she couldn't expect him to stay where he didn't want to be. She was prepared to help him fight through the nightmare for as long as it would take to get him whole again, but she didn't want to leave behind everything she knew and loved. She rested her head on his chest and closed her eyes. "Let's not talk about it right now. Let's just be with each other. Just rest Nathan, please don't talk about it anymore."

# 21

Nathan finally agreed that it would be a good idea to go see a psychiatrist about his dreams of Robert. He wasn't sure it would be much help, as he didn't care to spill his deepest thoughts to a person he had never met before. Nonetheless, he felt it might help his relationship with Marcie.

Nathan and Marcie drove to the next town to see Dr. Seyler. Neither of them knew this doctor, but they did some checking and heard some good things about him. Both were nervous and didn't know quite what to expect, but they did know something had to be done to find some answers for what he had been going through. As they walked in, the receptionist took Nathan's name and asked them to have a seat for a moment. Nonchalantly, he flipped through a magazine, while his leg nervously bounced up and down as though it had a mind of its own. Marcie calmly placed her hand on his leg, but it continued to bounce anyway.

"Nathan Staby, you can come in now," the receptionist announced.

Nathan just stared up at her for a while, making a last minute decision as to whether or not he wanted to go through with it. Marcie prodded him out of the chair. Finally he made his way towards the door.

"Can she come with me?" asked Nathan, pointing to Marcie.

"Well, as you know the sessions are of a confidential nature. If your friend would also like to talk with the doctor separately, to offer additional information, or her own perspective, she may. However, the doctor can't disclose anything about you to her without your written consent."

"It's all right, Nathan. It's better if you go in alone. I'll wait here for you," replied Marcie.

He hesitantly agreed, staring back at her until the receptionist closed the door behind them.

"This way," the receptionist said, leading Nathan into Dr. Seyler's office.

The room was very open and airy with windows all along the back wall. "Maybe this won't be so bad," he thought.

"Come in, Mr. Staby. I'm Dr. Scott Seyler. You may call me Scott if you wish. May I call you Nathan?"

"Yes, Dr. Seyler, I mean, Scott. I'm sorry, I'm a bit nervous. I've never been through anything like this before, even though, I probably shouldn't have waited so long."

"That's quite all right. Most people are shaky when they come in at first. You'll start to relax after we've had a few sessions. Please, have a seat."

"Should I lie down on the couch?"

"Do you want to lie down?"

"Not really. I just thought that's how it's done. You know, I lie down on the couch and you sit beside me and ask me all kinds of questions about my childhood. You nod and say, 'I see,' a lot and I leave somehow feeling better about myself."

"I see."

"What?"

"Never mind, just have a seat in the chair if you don't mind. I save the couch for my own afternoon naps, or when my wife locks me out of the house."

Nathan smiled and sat down. He felt a little more comfortable knowing the doctor had a sense of humor.

"Where would you like to start?"

"I'm not sure. I thought you started it."

"I'm not the one with the problem. Suppose you start by explaining to me what brought you in to see me. You don't mind if I use this recorder do you? I find it much easier to listen if I'm not scribbling down notes. It seems to make the patient more comfortable as well. That way you won't have to spend all of your time wondering what I'm writing about you. Is that all right with you?"

"Sure, you're the doctor here."

"Good, now, why did you come in to see me today?"

"Well, really it was my girlfriend, Marcie, who talked me into coming to see you. She thought it would be helpful."

"So why did she want you to come in?"

Nathan shifted in his seat a little, trying to get the courage up to begin.

"Just pretend I'm not here by talking to the tape recorder. After a while, you'll forget I'm even in the room."

Nathan looked at the tape recorder and turned in his seat to face it directly. He paused for a good while before he began. "When I was a boy, I had a good friend named Robert. We did everything together. He could imagine the best games for us to play. I loved being with him. We fought dragons and monsters together in the woods where I grew up. There wasn't anybody we couldn't defeat, at least, not in the make believe games we played. But one day I was running in the woods, chasing a dragon. I remember battling him with my sword. While I was chasing him I fell down. Right in front of my face, in the leaves, was a small hand. I moved the leaves away from the face. I could see it was Robert. He was dead." Nathan paused for a moment. "Anyway, I told the police where the body was, but I couldn't remember anything else to tell them. The case was never solved. It was a few months after I found Robert when I started seeing him in my dreams, you know, remembering bits and pieces. He always calls me to come out and play with him. I follow him back through the woods, but then, something happens, something that's not clear to me. I can hear voices in the woods, and Robert calling for help. I wrestle with someone, but I can't see his face. At the end, I always see this old man standing in front of me. He's smiling, always smiling. He knows my name. Then, I just run away."

"Do you still have these dreams or thoughts?"

"They stopped for a while when I moved away, but when I came back to Fairhaven, they started again. Now they're more frequent and intense, almost real."

"In what way are they almost real?"

"I find myself acting out the thoughts or the dreams. I woke up a few days ago passed out underneath a tree. The night before, I dreamed I was running behind Robert in the woods. Apparently, I went outside in the middle of the night and actually ran around all night chasing him, or dreaming I was chasing him. A doctor examined me and said it was a simple case of sleepwalking, but I know it's much more."

"What makes you think the doctor is wrong?"

"Do you think it's just sleepwalking too?"

"No, I just want to know why you think it's not. You said it's much more than that. Why do you think it is?"

"Because it's so real. It doesn't just happen to me when I'm sleeping at night. It happens anytime of the day or night, even when I'm wide awake."

"But you said you see Robert in your dreams. Are you awake when you have these dreams?"

"I don't know. Sometimes it's like he invades my thoughts, but then it becomes a dream. I'm not sure. I can't explain it any better than that."

"But this didn't happen to you before you came back home?"

"No, I never had a thought or dream about Robert at all once I moved away."

"Why did you move away?"

"I'm not sure. I think it was because I couldn't stop thinking about Robert. I also needed a change. I didn't want to spend the rest of my life in some small town where everybody knows your business. So the first chance I got, I packed up and left."

"And the dreams stopped?"

"Yes, pretty soon after I left."

"Why did you come back?"

"I guess I wanted to get out of the fast lane of the big city life and my big city friends. Really, I'm not sure why I came back, other than to see Marcie."

"Is Marcie your girlfriend?"

"Yes, I really missed her. I tried dating other girls, but I could never get her out of my mind. I could never get the courage to call her or come back to see her until now."

"What made now a good time?"

"I'm not sure. It just felt like the right time."

"Did your friends act like they were glad to see you after all this time of being away?"

"Yeah, I think so. It took some longer than others. I guess they thought of me as an outsider at first. They were slow to let me back into their lives, especially Mark. He was a friend of mine when I was younger, but when I came back home, he acted as though I was some kind of threat to this town. He treated me with suspicion, right from the beginning."

"Suspicion? Regarding what?"

"About everything. Shortly after I arrived, a boy's body was found in the woods. He had been murdered. Mark just seemed to treat me like a suspect after that, especially after what happened to Marcie."

"What happened to Marcie?"

"She was in an accident. Her car skidded off the road over a cliff one night while she was driving home. I was the one who found her."

"And you think Mark blames you for these incidents?"

"I don't know that he blames me now, but I felt like he did when they first happened. But then, later, we became good friends and actually started hanging out together. Still, I sometimes get the feeling he doesn't trust me."

"Does he have a reason not to trust you?"

"No. None that I know of, except—"

"What?"

"Well, except I think he's jealous of me and Marcie. I think he had a crush on her while I was gone and now I'm back. Maybe that's the threat he feels."

"How does Marcie feel about Mark?"

"She loves me."

"I'm sure she does, but how does she see Mark? Are they friends?"

"Yes, they're friends. I guess you could say more like brother and sister."

"Tell me about the old man you mentioned earlier. The one you always see when you're chasing Robert."

"There's not much more to tell. He's always in the picture, but I'm not sure why. I don't know what he has to do with Robert."

"But you always see him with Robert?"

"Not with him, but in the woods, in the distance. He's always there when Robert's calling for help."

"Why do you think he's always there?"

"Maybe because he killed Robert. I think I saw him kill Robert, but I just can't fit all of the pieces together."

"Have you ever seen this old man before, I mean in person?"

"No, not that I can recall, at least I don't remember ever seeing him until after Robert died. Then he's always in my dreams or thoughts."

"Do you think he's real?"

"Yes. I believe he's a real person, otherwise, why would I keep seeing him? Besides others have seen him as well. Marcie saw him at her accident and I found out that a neighbor of Dan Harper's saw an old man walking in the woods on the day Todd Harper was killed. But nobody seems interested."

"Have you told the sheriff about the old man?"

"He knows about him, but he just doesn't seem to believe he's real."

"Could you have imagined him?"

"Why would you ask that? I just told you others have seen him too."

"I don't know, I'm just asking the question. You say you've never seen this person outside of your dreams. Could he be a part of your imagination? Maybe the others saw someone, but it doesn't mean it's the same old man you saw when you were just a boy. That would be very unlikely, wouldn't it?"

"Why would I make up something like that? Are you saying that you don't believe me?"

"No, Nathan. I'm just trying to explore all the options. It doesn't matter whether or not I believe you. What matters is that you are able to detect what's real from fantasy when you're awake. I'm trying to help you sort through things, so we can decide which is real and which is not. You don't have to convince me of anything, only yourself."

Nathan dropped his head and closed his eyes. "I'm not sure I'll ever be able to decide which is which."

"Let's not go any further today. I think we've done enough for now. How about every Thursday? Does that suit you?"

"Every Thursday?"

"Yes, your appointments will be on Thursdays. Is that all right with you?"

"How long do we have to do this?"

"Until we find the answers we're looking for, or until you terminate the sessions. I'll see you next Thursday at 9 am."

Nathan stood up and headed for the door. He turned toward the doctor for a moment as if to add something.

"Did you want to say something, Nathan?"

"No, no I don't think so. I'll see you Thursday."

"Nathan."

"Yes?"

"Relax, don't think so hard. We'll get to the bottom. We'll fit all of the pieces together. You may not like the picture we see at the end, but we'll put it together. It just takes time."

Nathan nodded and shut the door behind him.

# 22

That night at the Raven Inn, Maggie, Marcie and Nathan had dinner together. It was a quiet night, as there were only a few guests staying over. Maggie prepared a wonderful meal, but Nathan didn't have much of an appetite. He promised Marcie that he wouldn't discuss leaving and going back to the city until after he had completed his sessions with Dr. Seyler. It was hard not to think about it though. He felt it might be the only way to find any peace in his life, but he couldn't bare the thought of Marcie staying behind. How would he live without her now? She had become entwined in his every thought, at least those that weren't taken up by the memory of Robert.

"Don't you like my cooking anymore?" asked Maggie. "You've hardly touched your food. You look like you're playing with it instead of eating."

"I'm sorry. You know your cooking is the best in the county. I'm just not very hungry tonight."

"You're not upset by your visit with Dr. Seyler are you?" asked Marcie.

"No. Well, maybe I am. It's hard to tell a stranger how you're feeling inside, especially, when you're confused about everything and you can't explain any of it."

"Do you like Dr. Seyler? I hear he's a good doctor," said Maggie, picking up Nathan's plate.

"I guess he's all right. He's nice enough. I'm sure he's a fine doctor."

"I had a friend once who had a nervous break down and had to see a psychiatrist once a week for two years. It was a painful thing to see her day after day, struggling to hold on to her sanity," Maggie said, as she shook her head in dismay.

Marcie glared in disbelief. How could she even bring up such a subject in front of Nathan? "But she got all right after the two years didn't she Mother?"

"No, the poor dear finally swallowed a bottle of pills and ended it all right there in her living room. It was such a shame, her paying all that money for treatment and then killing herself like that. You'd think her family would have gotten a refund."

"Mother, please. I don't think Nathan wants to hear any of your stories right now." Marcie placed her hand on Nathan's.

Nathan could see Maggie smiling back at him with a wink. He knew she was only teasing him, trying to lighten things up a bit. "Thanks, Maggie for the encouragement. I think I'll survive." He kissed her on the cheek and gave her a hug. "You're a wicked old lady," he whispered in her ear.

"I know what, let's have some ice cream and coffee in the living room," suggested Maggie. "It's homemade by my very hands."

"I'm in," said Nathan, getting some bowls out of the cabinet.

"Then count me in too," replied Marcie, grabbing spoons.

"There's nothing like ice cream to cheer things up a bit," Maggie said, smiling as she scooped mounds of banana ice cream from a tin canister.

The three sat, laughing like old times in the living room for most of the night. Nathan took the doctor's advice and tried not to think too much about all the mysteries that needed solving. Maggie and Marcie were his family. He could be himself around them without worrying. No matter what happened, he knew he wanted these two to be with him.

"My heavens! Just look at the time. We've been chattering and laughing all night. I need to drag these tired old bones up to bed." Maggie started picking up the cups and bowls.

"Just leave it, Mom. I'll take care of it," said Marcie. "You go on up to bed."

"All right, goodnight then," Maggie called, as she climbed the stairs to her room. "See you two love birds in the morning light."

"Here, let me help you," Nathan offered. He slowly took the cup from Marcie's hand, but as their eyes met, he sat the cup down, took her in his arms and gently kissed her lips, face and neck. He wanted to hold her in his arms forever. "Marcie, I love you so much, I don't think I could ever live without you. Please promise me you'll never leave me."

She took Nathan's face in her hands and kissed him warmly on the lips. "You have me always, babe. I'm not going anywhere. You're the one who wants to leave."

"I don't want to leave you. I want to be with you. I just don't know if I can stay here."

"You promised me you would stay until you finished the sessions with Dr. Seyler."

"I'm going to try, Marcie, I really am. Maybe Dr. Seyler can help me make sense to this long nightmare. But what if he can't, or what if he finds something out that neither of us can live with? What then?"

"You're talking crazy. There's nothing that would make me not want to be with you. Nathan, I love you. I'm going to stand by you through this. I know you don't believe that, but it's true. When this is all over, I'm going to be standing right here beside you, just like I am now. You can rely on that."

"What if I remember things about Robert's death I could have told a long time ago, things that might have prevented Todd Harper's death? How can I live with that?"

"You don't even know if the two deaths are related. You're just assuming the same person killed Robert and Todd. You don't know that for a fact." Marcie fell on the couch exhausted. "We seem to have the same conversations over and over again. You're so obsessed by Robert's death that you can't see anything else beyond it. You can't see our lives together in the future, because you can't get beyond the past. Nathan, you've got to let go. Let Dr. Seyler help you, but then live your life now, in the present. I want to plan for the future. Can't you see how important that is to me, to us?"

"I'm sorry. This is what I've been trying to tell you. Until this puzzle is solved, I can't think beyond the past. I want to, believe me I do, but it's not that simple." Nathan sat beside her and took her hands. "Unless we go away. I know if I can get away from Fairhaven, this torment will stop. I'll find a doctor in the city. There are loads of them there. I can still get help, without having to live in the middle of this nightmare every day. Marcie, please think about it. If I mean anything to you at all, think about it. How do you know you won't be happy unless you try it? If you're not happy after a year, we'll move back here. Please, Marcie, come away with me. I have a big place. We can bring Maggie. I'll make the arrangements for the Raven Inn to be managed properly for her. She can still own it without being here to run it. We can get someone else to do that."

Marcie stared back at Nathan, not knowing what to say. She stood up and grabbed her jacket. "I feel like I'm going to lose you to the past, no matter what happens. Whether we stay here or go away. How did our lives ever get so complicated?" Marcie kissed Nathan softly and left him to ponder her question.

# 23

It had been weeks since Nathan and Marcie had discussed leaving Fairhaven. He had been careful not to bring it up again, as it wasn't Marcie's favorite subject. He didn't want to do anything that would push her away from him. He managed to avoid the subject at all cost when he was with her, even though the desire to escape back to his comfortable life in the city was strong. Life here was getting harder. The mystery of Robert's death could be held at bay for a short while, but then it consumed his every thought.

His visits with Dr. Seyler hadn't uncovered much, but at least he was getting his secrets out on the table, instead of carrying them around inside of him. He liked Dr. Seyler. If he did leave, he wondered whether he would be able to find another doctor who could make him feel as comfortable. Starting over with someone new wouldn't be easy. Maybe staying here would be best for now. He had just about talked himself into staying and sticking it out, at least for a while longer. Marcie would definitely be glad to hear his decision. He could hardly wait to give her the news.

Nathan bounced up the steps to Marcie's house and rang the doorbell. However, it was a while before she answered. When she finally did come to the door, she had a kerchief tied around the top of her head and she was wearing a pair of old torn jeans that looked like they had seen better days.

"What's going on? Are you doing some major spring cleaning or is this your day to really dress down?" Nathan said, laughing at the sight of her.

"Very funny. I'm cleaning, you know, throwing out some things. It's amazing what you accumulate in just a short period of time, but I need a break. I'm glad you stopped by. I'd like to ask you something." Marcie took Nathan by the hand and led him over to the couch. As they sat down, she leaned over and kissed him on the neck.

"Nathan, do you really love me?" she asked.

"More than anything, Marcie. That's why I came over here. I came just to tell you—"

"Just answer my question, please. Do you really love me?"

Nathan was puzzled by Marcie's questions, but decided to play along.

"Yes, with all of my heart."

"Would you always love me, even if I grew fat and walked around the house wearing an old robe, eating chocolate bars?"

"Forever and ever, fat and all."

"If I got desperately sick, would you stay by my bedside day and night and promise to never leave me alone?"

"Marcie, are you sick? Is that what this is about?"

"Nathan, please. I'm not sick. Just answer the question."

"Yes, I will stay by your bedside until life has left your body. Have you been drinking?"

"Nathan, do you want to marry me?"

"Well, uh, of course, one day, but what about all the things we've got to work out before—"

"Nathan!"

"I know, just answer the question. Yes, I do."

"That's good, because if I leave Fairhaven, and go back to the city with you, I want to go as your wife."

"You mean you'll go back with me? You're willing to leave this town? When did you decide this?"

"I've decided I've been selfish. I can't just think about me all the time. If I'm going to be a wife, I have to learn to think of someone else beside myself. Anyway, I think maybe the change would do us both a world of good right now. I'm willing to try something new if it means I'll have you around."

"Marcie, I don't know what to say. You've caught me completely off guard. What does Maggie say about all this?"

"I haven't told her yet. I'm sure she's going to want to stay here for a while longer, until we get settled. Then, perhaps, she would consider your offer to come and live with us, but I have a feeling she'll just stay put right here. She's too set in her ways for changes. A big city can be pretty scary for someone who's not used to it. I can adjust, but she would be a different story. She loves that old inn. I don't know what she would do with herself if she didn't have it to take care of, at least, for a while longer. If she doesn't want to leave, she can come for long visits. I can come back to visit her as often as possible. She'll probably say she doesn't think it's right for two newlyweds to start off their marriage with a mother-in-law living with them or that she'd miss her friends and this little town too much to leave."

"Marcie, are you sure you know what you want, moving away from Maggie and putting up with me and my crazy problems? Have you thought about it? I mean, really thought it through?"

"Yes, I know it will be hard at times, but my love for you is big enough to get through those hard times. I'm ready to build our own lives, our own memories. Look, I'm a big girl. I don't have to live right around the corner from my mother. It's time I did some growing up myself. Maybe I've been hiding out from life here in this little story-book town. I don't even know all I'm capable of, because I've never allowed myself to try anything new. Yes, I want this. Let's get married, raise a family and take care of each other. That's all I want out of life right now. In fact, let's do it right now."

"Now? You mean, get married right now? Don't you want Maggie or any of your friends to be there?"

"No, I had a big wedding planned before when I thought I wanted to marry David. We worked for months on making sure everything would be perfect, but then everything fell apart. It's not the ceremony I want this time, Nathan. It's our love I want to be strong and perfect. Let's just ride to Reed's Gorge and see a Justice of the Peace, get married and begin our lives together. There will be plenty of time for celebration with Maggie when we get back."

Nathan could see that Marcie wanted this very badly. He wanted it too, but he felt like he was stealing her away from those who loved her. They held each other for a long time without saying another word. This was more than he had ever hoped for or dreamed would come true.

"I'll be back to pick you up in an hour. Be ready," said Nathan, as he rushed out the door toward his car.

Marcie watched as he sped away and then she ran upstairs like a schoolgirl going to her first prom. She quickly jumped in the shower and then rummaged through her closet to find something suitable to wear. Her hand came to rest on a cream colored dress with a tiny yellow design and tiny lace around the collar and sleeves. The material looked like new, like it had never been worn. As she lifted it from the rack, she noticed a note attached to the sleeve. "For Marcie, to wear on a special day. Love, Mom." Marcie had admired this dress in a shop, along with Maggie, some time back. She had no idea Maggie had bought it for her. How did she manage to sneak it into the house without her knowing about it? "Oh, Mom," Marcie said through tears. "It's going to be so hard to say goodbye."

# 24

The next morning Maggie decided to get to some of the projects she had been putting off for so long. The morning breakfast was done so she decided to organize the pantry in the kitchen before she did anything else. The plan was to take everything off the shelves, sorting as she went. She was tired of searching forever for things. New shelf paper was also on the agenda. Turning on the light in the pantry, she could see the job was bigger than she thought, but she pulled her apron over her head and started right to work, grabbing cans, boxes and bottles off the large shelves and placing them on the floor. She smiled to herself imagining how pretty it would look when she finished. "Marcie will be so surprised," she thought.

"Mom, hello. Where are you?" Marcie called from the doorway. "Are you here?"

"I'm in the pantry, honey."

Marcie and Nathan walked into the kitchen and pushed open the door to the large pantry area. There stood Maggie surrounded by piles of cans and boxes sitting all over the floor.

"Mom, what on earth are you doing?"

"Surprise! I finally decided to tackle this mess and get it organized so you won't have to fuss so much about it anymore. I know it looks like a mess now, but when I get through, it's going to look so organized, you won't believe it's mine."

"Mom, this is too big a project for you to do by yourself."

"You two want to help?"

"Uh, Mom, Nathan and I have something to tell you."

"Oh, what's that?" Maggie asked, still busily pulling things off the shelves.

"Mom, can you stop for a while? We need to talk to you."

"Dear, can't it wait? I've been putting off this project for so long, if I don't stay with it I'll never get it done."

"No, it can't wait. Please, Mom, would you stop and come into the kitchen for a minute?"

Maggie complied with a frown on her face, wiping her hands on her apron and then taking a seat at the kitchen table. Marcie and Nathan sat down with her, smiling suspiciously.

"What's going on with you two? What's so important that you have to drag me away from my work?" Just then Maggie noticed Marcie was wearing her new dress. "Oh, look at you. I see you found my surprise, but dear, you weren't supposed to wear it for everyday. I wanted you to save it for something special. Oh, it looks so beautiful on you. Stand up and let me see how it looks on you."

Marcie took Nathan's hand in hers as they both looked at one another and smiled. "Mom, we're married."

"You're getting married? Oh, Marcie, that's wonderful. When's the big day? We've got a lot of planning to do. You know, you could have the wedding right here at the Raven Inn. It's perfect. You're right. The pantry job can wait. Oh, this is so exciting! Well, I'm not really surprised, though. I knew it was just a matter of time before you two—"

"Mom, we got married yesterday. We went to a Justice of the Peace. It's done. We just drove up to Reed's Gorge, got married and came home this morning."

Maggie's expression changed from great joy to one of great disappointment. "A Justice of the Peace? Marcie, how could you? You mean, you didn't tell anybody else? Why, Marcie? We could have planned such a beautiful wedding. I just don't believe it." Maggie got up and walked away from the table. She turned her back on both of them, staring out at the garden.

Marcie walked over and put her arms around her. "Oh, Mom, I know you're disappointed about the wedding, but I'm so happy. It was my idea to do it this way. I knew if I told you ahead of time you'd talk me into going all out. You'd never settle for anything less. We just want to be together, that's all. Mom, please understand. I've never been happier in my whole life. Isn't that what's important?"

Maggie took a tissue from her apron pocket and blew her nose. She turned to face Marcie with tears rolling down her cheeks. "It's just, well, I'm an old woman. I need my special moments, because they're so few these days. You're my only daughter. I always imagined your wedding to be like something out of a fairy tale, something folks around here would talk about for years to come. But, I suppose you know what you're doing. Anyway, I can never stay mad at you for very long," she said, throwing her arms around her.

Nathan cleared his throat, "Ahem, remember me?"

Maggie opened her arms wide and began smothering him with hugs and kisses.

"Mom, please, he can't breathe," Marcie said, as she gently pulled her back.

"This calls for a big celebration. We must invite people over. At least let me throw you a party in honor of your marriage," said Maggie, running to grab a pad and a pencil. "Let's see, we have to invite Mark and Gracey and my good friend, Velma."

"Mom, promise me you won't do anything elaborate. Just keep it simple, okay?"

"Yes, dear, don't worry. I'll keep it small."

"Maggie, there's something else we have to tell you, before you rush off to make your party plans," said Nathan, putting his arm around Marcie. "Marcie and I aren't going to be staying here. We're going to move back to my place in the city."

Maggie stopped her scribbling. She looked like a child whose balloon had just burst right in front of her. "You're leaving?"

Marcie knelt down beside Maggie and took hold of her trembling hands. "Mom, Nathan and I talked about this. We both think it's best. Nathan needs to get back to his writing and, well, I need a change too. Of course, I want to be wherever Nathan goes."

"Maggie, we want you to come with us. I have a large apartment in the city that can easily accommodate us, until we can find a house. We're thinking about finding something right on the water. It'll be beautiful. You'll go for walks on the beach, collect shells, help with the house, and—"

"No, no I could never leave Fairhaven. This is my home, my work. I don't want to leave it. Anyway, who wants a tired old woman living with them in the house when they just got married and trying to get used to one another. You certainly don't need a meddling mother-in-law around."

"Mom, we mean it. We want you to come along. You'll love it. You can help me decorate and organize. You know how I need your help cooking and shopping for food. We both love you. We want you with us. You'd never be in the way."

"Marcie, you have a husband to look after now. You need to start your own life. I can take care of myself. My old friends can keep me company. I can call them if I need help. Besides, I have too many roots in this little town. It would break my heart to leave it, but you have your whole life ahead of you, both of you. You'll be starting a family and buying a new home. It's best if I stay here where I belong." Maggie gently touched Marcie's face. "But, if I get sick and I'm not able to take care of myself, I expect you both to come and take me back home with you. I don't want to wind up in one of those homes for loony seniors with someone playing an out of tune piano while we all do aerobics in slow motion."

They all three burst into laughter in the middle of their tears. Marcie put her head on Maggie's shoulder, "You're a stubborn old woman. I promise you'll never have to do senior aerobics."

"Now, you two must have a million things to take care of what with packing and everything. Please, get out of here while I make my party list. I have a lot to do here in a short time," Maggie said, pushing them out of the kitchen.

"All right, we'll be by later for dinner, okay?" called Nathan as they rushed out of the door.

"Fine, fine. See you later," said Maggie, waving goodbye.

As she watched them drive away, she knew her life was about to change. She was so happy for Marcie. "I can do this," she thought. "I'll be just fine." She held a tissue to her cheeks, but it was too small to catch all of her tears. "Goodbye, baby girl," she said softly. "You've got a whole new life in front of you."

# 25

The arrival of the next evening found the Raven Inn greeting various friends and family to celebrate the marriage of Nathan and Marcie. Maggie arranged everything on short notice, since she wasn't sure how long before the new couple would want to leave and head for the city lights. In a small town like Fairhaven, the news of Marcie's secret marriage was a big deal and people wouldn't miss this celebration for anything in the world. Maggie greeted guests at the door with a hug and they were immediately offered a sparkling glass of champagne. The rooms were buzzing with expressions of surprise that the two didn't have a large wedding in town, instead of running off to a Justice of the Peace. Still, others felt it was the most romantic thing they could have done. As they gathered in small groups and debated the issue, Marcie and Nathan, the guests of honor, arrived at the inn.

"The newlyweds are here," shouted Maggie from the hallway. Everyone pushed toward the door to get a look at the new Mr. and Mrs. Nathan Staby. They were greeted by smiles, kisses and best wishes as they made their way into the inn's living room. Maggie even had the room decorated with streamers and balloons in Marcie's favorite colors of yellow, rose and green.

"I can't believe the trouble Mom has gone to for this party," said Marcie, as she looked around the room at the decorations, champagne and the guests. "It's beautiful."

"You knew Maggie wasn't going to let us get away without a big send off. She loves to give a party. Let her have her fun," said Nathan, sipping a glass of champagne. As he spoke, he could see out of the corner of his eye the arrival of Mark and Gracey. He wondered how Mark would react to his marrying Marcie, especially since he wasn't invited to be a part of it.

"Well, there's the sneaky couple at last," shouted Gracey from across the room. She made her way over and threw her arms around both of them. "I just think this is wonderful. You two were meant to be together and I think it's so romantic that you got married with a Justice of the Peace instead of some big fancy ceremony. Can I see the ring?" she asked, grabbing Marcie's hand.

"Congratulations, Nathan," Mark said, shaking his hand. "You're a lucky man. I couldn't believe it when I heard the news. I never thought Marcie would leave her home to run away with you. It must be true love."

"Thanks, Mark. Don't worry, I plan to take good care of her," Nathan replied.

"You'd better or I'll come looking for you." Mark kissed Marcie and wrapped his arms around her. "I'm going to miss you a bunch, little lady. This town won't be the same without you around."

"We won't be that far away. We'll be back for visits. You'd better look out for Maggie. She's going to need you sometimes, so watch out for her for me until I can pry her away to come and stay with us," Marcie whispered back.

"When are you two leaving town to become big city slickers?"

"In a couple of days I hope, just as soon as we can finish packing some things, then we'll be on our way," replied Nathan.

"Make sure you leave us your address so we can keep in touch with you guys," said Gracey. "Do you plan to start a family right away? I think a big family is so special. You should have as many children as you can stand, honey. You'd make such a good mother."

"Whoa, slow down a bit Gracey," said Nathan, holding up his hands. "We need to get used to being married first and then we'll discuss babies. We've got plenty of time."

Marcie smiled at Nathan, "I don't know, a big family sounds all right to me. I'd love to have a house full."

"Stop, you're making me nervous," Nathan said, laughing.

"So you're giving up on your visits with Dr. Seyler?" Mark interrupted.

Nathan looked down at his feet and then back at Mark. "I can see someone back in the city just as good as Dr. Seyler." Nathan was definitely not comfortable discussing this subject with Mark right now.

"I'm sorry, I didn't mean to upset you. It's just that there are no secrets in a town this small and news travels fast. I was glad to hear you were finally trying to get help, but you might be blowing your chances by leaving now."

"Like I said, I can get help somewhere else. It doesn't have to be Dr. Seyler. Now, if you don't mind, I'd rather not discuss it anymore."

"Sure, Nathan. I'm sorry." Mark patted him on the back and left to go talk with some other guests.

Marcie put her arm in Nathan's, "Don't let him get to you. He really does mean well. He's just a bit jealous I think."

"I don't think he's ever going to forgive me for taking you away."

"All right everyone," announced Maggie loudly. "There's a buffet set up in the dining room. Please, help yourselves to food and drink, compliments of the Raven Inn."

"Oh my goodness, she even has a buffet dinner," exclaimed Marcie. "What next, a band?"

The party lasted until late into the night with a beautiful wedding cake and coffee. As the last guests finally left, Marcie and Nathan collapsed on the sofa, while Maggie danced around the room picking up trash, humming to herself. "It was a beautiful party, don't you agree?" asked Maggie.

"It was lovely, Mom. You did a great job and in such a short time. You amaze me," said Marcie, motioning for her to come and sit by them. "Thank you so much. You're the best mother a girl could want. I should buy you one of those t-shirts that say, 'World's Greatest Mom.'"

"Nothing's too good for my baby," said Maggie. "I couldn't let you go without showing you how much your friends and family love you first."

"Mom, I know you love me. I don't need a party to prove that." Marcie pulled Maggie close to her and kissed her on the cheek. "I'm going to miss you more than I can even express. We'll have to call each other every day. What will I do without you?"

Nathan decided to leave the room and allow them some time alone. As he stood at the kitchen door, he could hear soft sobbing and then laughter. He knew this parting was going to be very difficult for both of them. They had never been very far apart and Maggie had depended on Marcie for most things. He wished she would change her mind and come with them, but he knew that would probably never happen.

Later that night, at home, Marcie was very quiet, as she got ready for bed. Nathan walked up behind her as she brushed her hair and wrapped his arms around her tightly, kissing her shoulder. Marcie placed her hands on his and she smiled sweetly at him through the mirror.

"I know this is very hard for you and I want you to know that I'll do everything within my power to make you happy, Mrs. Staby. I promise to cook for you, take out the garbage, and mow the lawn. When you're sick, I'm going to sit beside you and feed you chicken soup until you're well again. I'll never leave your side, unless you send me away. I'm going to protect you from anything that might try to hurt you and make you laugh when you're feeling down. Marcie, I love you more than I've ever loved anyone and I want you to know that you don't have to worry about a thing. I'll always take care of you, because that's all I've ever dreamed of doing."

"Oh, Nathan, I love you so much. I'm so glad you came back for me." With that Nathan lifted her in his arms and laid her across the bed. Tonight, Nathan's mind was at peace and he wasn't afraid of the darkness. He was with the one he loved, and for now, it was just the two of them.

# 26

Nathan taped up the box he had just finished packing and shoved it over with the rest. "This packing is never going to get finished," he thought. "She's going to need three trucks to take along all of these belongings," he laughed to himself. He grabbed another empty box and started looking for the next room to be done. Marcie was downstairs busy packing up the kitchen.

He decided to take a look out back in the barn to see if there was anything they'd want to take with them. Looking around inside, he saw some tools on the shelf that he thought might come in handy later. He brought the box over and began packing them away.

As he grabbed the last tool, he noticed a vinyl bag, stuffed underneath the shelf, behind some wooden crates. He decided he'd best check to see what was in it. Pulling the bag out, he recognized it as his own. "I must have left this here when I was looking after Marcie," he thought. He carried the bag over to the open door so that he could see what was inside. He wrestled with the zipper for a moment and then finally pulled it loose. As he opened the bag, he saw a shirt belonging to him. Underneath the shirt was something folded and neatly tied with a sash. He knelt down and took out the tied object with great curiosity. As he untied the sash, the item unfolded into his hands.

Marcie took the last dish out of the cabinet and was just about to wrap it in newspaper, when she heard a blood-curdling scream from outside. The dish dropped from her hands and shattered on the kitchen floor. Her heart jumped inside of her chest as she raced to the window to look outside, but she couldn't see anything. She ran to the back door and looked around. "Nathan, where are you?" she screamed. "Nathan!"

Suddenly she noticed two legs sticking out of the barn door. She ran to the barn and pushed the door the rest of the way open.

She stepped back in horror. There on the ground lay an old man with white hair. She kicked his foot to see if he was dead, but there was no movement. Then she noticed that the boots looked like Nathan's. "Oh my God, no!" she gasped. Marcie slowly knelt down beside the body and took a closer look. Slowly, she reached out her hand and touched the face of the man. It felt like rubber. He was wearing a rubber mask. Carefully lifting the head of the man, she started pulling the mask from his face. It was Nathan. "No, no. I don't believe it. Nathan, wake up. Can you hear me? Oh, dear God, what should I do?"

Marcie wasn't sure she wanted to call anybody just yet without being able to talk to Nathan first. After all, he was her husband and she wanted to give him a chance to explain to her what was going on. She took the mask and threw it in the bag that was beside him, and then, after looking around, saw a shirt in his right hand. Grabbing the shirt, she held it up in the light. It was covered with bloodstains. Marcie held the shirt close to her and looked behind her to make sure no one was around. "Nathan, can you hear me?" she shouted, but there was no reaction from him.

Marcie's head was spinning in confusion, but she needed to act fast. She crammed the shirt inside the bag with the mask and stuffed it behind a cabinet in the far corner of the barn. She placed some boards all around the cabinet, so that the bag couldn't be easily seen. Racing back to the house, Marcie called the doctor. She told him that Nathan had passed out in the barn, but she didn't know what was wrong with him. Then she just sat beside him, wringing her hands in worry, trying to understand what she had just seen and what Nathan would say when he opened his eyes. He lay very still without moving a muscle, but she could see his chest slowly moving up and down with each breath. "Nathan, please wake up so I can talk to you. The doctor's coming honey. You're going to be all right. Please, open your eyes." There was no response. Marcie just sat and waited for the doctor's arrival. She felt like crying, but she was in such shock that she just sat and stared at him. Who had she married? What had she done?

"Marcie, are you here?" the doctor called from the yard.

"Yes, back here, doc. Please hurry. I don't know what happened. I found him passed out on the ground just like this. He hasn't moved at all, but he's breathing."

"Okay, move back and let me have a look at him now." The doctor pulled up Nathan's eyelids, but they looked lifeless and dark. The doctor listened to his heart and checked his head for bumps. He waved something under his nose to try and bring him around, but nothing seemed to work.

"I'm going to have to call an ambulance. I can't seem to bring him around."

"Can't we try just moving him into the house first?" asked Marcie quickly. "Maybe he'll wake up while we're moving him."

"Marcie, Nathan needs to be in a hospital so we can do some tests to find out what happened to him. Besides, he's too heavy for you to carry."

"Not if you help me. Please, let's try first."

The doctor hesitated, but then agreed and took hold of his legs. Marcie grabbed his arms and together they struggled toward the house. They finally made it to the living room and placed Nathan on the couch, but he still didn't wake up. Marcie ran and got a wet washcloth and dabbed Nathan's forehead and face as sweat poured from him.

"Marcie, we're going to have to call an ambulance. He's not coming around. Where's your phone?"

"Over by that chair," she said, pointing to the corner.

While the doctor placed the call for an ambulance, Marcie put her head on Nathan's chest. "My love, what has happened to you?" she asked quietly. "You promised you'd never leave me. Please, wake up and tell me everything is going to be all right. Please baby." But Nathan only continued breathing without uttering a word. He was some place else and his secret was with him.

The ambulance arrived and Mark drove up behind it.

"Marcie, what happened? Is he okay?" Mark asked, watching them place Nathan inside the ambulance.

Marcie didn't answer at first. She couldn't take her eyes off of Nathan. He almost looked like he was dead with his pale face and still body.

"Marcie, what happened?"

"I'm not sure. He passed out in the barn and that's all we know. I have to go with him in the ambulance. I'll talk to you at the hospital." She jumped in the ambulance and the attendants closed the door behind her. As they drove away, she could see Mark talking to the doctor. "Don't worry, Nathan," she whispered to him. "I'm right here."

The ambulance siren screamed in her ears as they sped to the hospital. Marcie sat in a trance, feeling numb. How could her life change from such joy to complete chaos so quickly? She didn't know what else to do, except to hold on to Nathan's hand and pray. "Please, dear God, don't let it end this way."

# 27

Upon arriving at the hospital, Marcie found herself sitting in a waiting room while the doctors examined Nathan. Her mind was jumping, thought to thought without resting in one place for too long. She thought about their future together and whether or not Nathan would get well. Would he be able to remember anything when he woke up? Even though it seemed too impossible to consider, could Nathan actually be the one who killed her brother, Robert? She refused to believe that the man she loved could instead be a monster stalking children in the woods. Her dream of a life with Nathan had turned into a nightmare. What was taking so long? She wanted desperately to talk to him and find out the truth.

"Mind if I sit with you?" asked Mark from the doorway. He walked over and sat beside Marcie, putting his arm around her. "Have you heard anything yet?"

"No, and it seems like it's been hours. Maybe he's still unconscious, or in shock. Oh, Mark, it's terrible."

"I know, but let's wait until we hear what the doctor has to say before we get too upset. He may pull through and be just fine again. You never know about these things."

"You're right, I'm just so nervous right now I don't even know what I'm saying. I just want to see him." Marcie began to cry into her hands. Mark handed her his handkerchief and continued to hold her close. "It's okay, I'm going to stay right here with you."

Finally, the doctor came into the waiting room and sat across from Marcie. He took her hands away from her face and placed them in her lap. "Marcie, Nathan is still unconscious. He wakes up just for a moment, but then he fades away again. When he's awake, he looks terrified, as though he's seen something horrible. I need your help, here. Do you have any idea what could have happened to him out in the barn? What could he have seen or heard that would send him into shock?"

Marcie wanted to tell him what she had found, but she was too afraid to talk about it. What if they blamed Nathan for Robert's death or the death of Todd Harper? They would lock him away and he might not ever get help. She loved him too much to betray him. She wanted to hold out until she could talk to Nathan herself.

"Marcie," said Mark softly. "Did you hear what the doctor asked you? Is there anything at all that you can remember or that you saw?"

"No, it happened just like I told you. I was in the kitchen and I saw Nathan lying on the ground in the barn. His legs could be seen from the kitchen window. Don't ask me what made him pass out. Maybe he's just been working too hard lately, you know, with the packing and everything. Couldn't it just be something like that?"

"This is more than just exhaustion, Marcie," replied the doctor. "Something happened to trigger this reaction in him, something too shocking for him to handle. I took the liberty of calling Dr. Scott Seyler, the psychiatrist he was seeing."

"How did you know about Dr. Seyler?" asked Marcie.

"Mark and I were talking while you were in the ambulance and he told me that Nathan had been seeing a psychiatrist. It's information that could prove very important to finding out what happened to him."

Marcie stood to her feet in anger. "Mark, you had no right to give out that information about Nathan without talking to me first. I'm his wife and I'm responsible for his well-being now. I'd appreciate it if you wouldn't go around telling everything you know to everyone who asks."

"I'm sorry, Marcie, but the doctor asked me if I knew anything that could help him. We're here to help Nathan, not harm him. I wasn't telling the doctor anything that he shouldn't know. Don't you want him to get well?" Mark walked over to her and stood in front of her. "For heaven's sake Marcie, it wasn't like we were just sharing idle gossip about him. He's never going to get well if everybody keeps trying to protect him from everything. The doctor has a right to know if he's going to treat him." Mark placed his arm around Marcie.

Marcie quickly pulled away and sat back down in front of the doctor. "All right, yes, he was seeing Dr. Seyler, but he'd only been for a few visits and he said he didn't think they were helping him at all."

"So he was seeing a psychiatrist. What finally prompted him to go?" asked the doctor calmly. "Was it the sleepwalking again?"

"He..." Marcie paused, choosing her words carefully. "He doesn't think it's just sleepwalking. It's more than that. He sometimes has dreams about the death of my brother, Robert and he acts them out. They were best friends and Nathan's the one who found him when he was killed. He's never gotten over it. I think he feels like there was more he could have done to protect Robert. He can't remember anything that happened the day Robert died, only bits and pieces. Returning here brought back some of those memories and so he was hoping Dr. Seyler could help him remember something. We were leaving this town and going back to the city, to Nathan's home, and we were going to find another doctor there. He felt like he would be able to remember things there if he wasn't so close to the place where it actually happened. Robert was like a brother to him, so you can understand why his death has been so difficult for him to accept."

"He was also with me when we found Todd Harper's body in the woods," Mark quickly added. "That probably set off a lot of things in his mind too. He probably shouldn't have been with me that day, but he insisted. He felt Robert's death was somehow connected to Todd's murder."

"It sounds as though he may be suffering from what we call Post Traumatic Stress Syndrome," the doctor said, while pouring himself a cup of coffee. "It's when someone sees something so shocking and so horrible that the brain can't contain it all, and so the memory just shuts down. Later bits and pieces of the memories may come back, but sometimes not enough to make a whole picture. Since Nathan found Robert dead, his brain may have hidden this memory away from him."

"That may be true, doc, but what could have caused him to pass out in the barn? What could have triggered such a strong reaction?" Mark asked the doctor.

"Well, it could be any number of things. Maybe a clear and vivid memory of Robert's death came back to him suddenly and it was more than he could handle. Maybe his mind released those locked memories and flooded him with thoughts that overwhelmed his senses. For instance, Nathan could have seen who killed Robert, but has been unable to remember the killer's face all these years because of the shocking experience. But something could have allowed his brain to unlock that picture." The doctor turned back to Marcie. "Has he ever discussed any of this before, Marcie?"

"Very little. Nathan's not one for sharing his thoughts. He mostly keeps things inside," she said carefully. "He's a quiet type of guy, you know, he's not one for sharing his feelings when it comes to his emotions."

"Would it be possible for me to talk to him when he wakes up?" asked Mark quickly. "If Nathan has information that could solve Robert's death or maybe even Todd Harper's, I'd like the opportunity to hear it before he forgets it again."

Marcie jumped to her feet and faced both the doctor and Mark. "Now you listen to me, both of you. That is my husband in there and if anybody is going to talk to him when he wakes up, it's going to be me. I won't allow you to use him as a guinea pig for your own purposes. Mark, how dare you only think about interrogating him, just to try to close a case no one's been able to solve all of these years. He's a sick man and he needs medical attention right now. He doesn't need you asking him a lot of questions that will cause him to stress. And as for you doctor, I will thank you to confine your conversations about Nathan's health to me, if you don't mind. I'll make the decisions as to who will and who will not talk to Nathan, not you or the local sheriff's department."

"Marcie, please, don't you want to know—" Mark began, but Marcie ran out of the waiting room before he could finish.

Mark started to follow her, but the doctor grabbed his arm. "Let her go. She's just very upset right now. Let's give her some time. I think she's right. It may not be a good time for you to talk with Nathan when he wakes up. We need to handle this carefully and slowly. We don't want to cause him more problems than he already has. I'll let you know when he's up to questioning."

# 28

Marcie was standing outside, getting some fresh air as the doctor came up behind her. "Marcie, I only want what's best for Nathan. Don't worry. You'll be the first to talk to him when he wakes up. Come on, I'll take you to his room. Maybe hearing your voice will help him to come round." He took her by the arm and led her to Nathan's room. Then he left her alone.

Nathan looked so calm and still lying there in the bed. He had an IV line running to his arm. There was no color in his face and his beautiful brown eyes were closed tightly.

Marcie sat beside him and remembered the vows she and Nathan had spoken to each other. "Through sickness and in health," she said to herself. "I'm here, Nathan. It's me, Marcie, honey. I don't know if you can hear me, but I'm going to stay right here with you until you wake up. I'm not going to talk to anyone else until I hear from you." She brushed his hair back from his forehead and ran her hand down the side of his face. It was hard to believe that, just the night before, the two had embraced in passionate love and they were able to push the whole world away for a time. Now, that world was crashing in around them, and she wished Nathan would awaken to help her push it away again. She placed her head on his chest and listened to the sounds of his breathing, as she had done the night before, only today, his breathing was a lonely sound.

Closing her eyes Marcie tried to pretend that everything was all right. She couldn't help but feel she should have gone with Nathan sooner. Maybe he wouldn't have ended up in the hospital this way. Yet, in the back of her mind, she couldn't escape the haunting thought that Nathan was a troubled man who could possibly be a murderer. She closed her eyes even more tightly and tried to block it out of her mind. "Everything will be better tomorrow," she thought and drifted off to sleep, her head moving up and down with each breath that Nathan took.

Marcie awoke the next morning to find Nathan was still asleep. The morning nurse came in and kindly offered some breakfast to Marcie. She had remained in Nathan's room all night and had gotten very little sleep. She was too tired and worried to think about eating. After kissing Nathan good morning and staring at him, trying to will his eyes to open, she poured herself a hot cup of coffee and wrapped her fingers around the cup. She held it close to her and the steam from the cup encircled her face. It was morning, but her world hadn't improved overnight. The sun was shining, but in the room with Nathan, it was dark and quiet. As she sipped her coffee, she reached over and touched the wedding band on his hand and then her own. How could she help him?

She made her way into the bathroom and ran warm water over a washcloth, then draped it over her face. It felt as though time was standing still and it would never move past this horrible moment. Marcie couldn't even think about what their future would hold because the past was holding it for ransom. The hands on the clock seemed to crawl around the numbers in slow motion, with no regard for the pain she was feeling. How would she ever get through this? She hung her head over the sink and splashed more water on her face and neck. The room was warm and she began to feel a little nauseous. She sat on the floor and rested her head on her knees for a moment.

Outside of the room she could hear the conversations of the nurses in the hallway. Their general conversations about ordinary, everyday things seemed so far removed from the dramatic events unfolding in her life right now. They laughed at one another's jokes and comments as her heart was breaking inside of her. She wanted so much to be a part of that ordinary world again, where her only worry was whether or not she would get all of her housework done and make it to the market on time or whether or not it was going to rain before she could finish setting out her flowers. That world seemed so far away from her.

As she sat on the floor, she heard a nurse come into the room. "Oh, look at you. You finally decided to wake up and take a look around."

"Where's Marcie?" Nathan asked in a hoarse voice.

Marcie scrambled up off of the floor, glanced in the mirror very quickly and dried her face. She pulled her hair back and wrapped a rubber band around it to hold it in place. She took a deep breath and came back into the room. There was Nathan with his eyes wide opened. He smiled when he saw her.

"I knew you'd be here," Nathan said softly.

"Oh, babe, you know I wouldn't be anywhere else," she answered, kissing his lips and face.

"She was here all night with you, Nathan. She hasn't eaten a bite and barely touched her coffee. You had us all worried there for a while. Can I get you something? How about some ice water or juice?" the nurse asked, as she checked his pulse and blood pressure.

"Water would be good," Nathan replied, never taking his eyes off of Marcie.

The nurse poured Nathan a glass of ice water and put a straw in the glass. "Try to drink as much of this as you can. You're dehydrated a bit, so it's important that you drink plenty of fluids. I'll just go and alert the doctor that you're finally awake. I'm sure he's going to want to examine you as soon as possible. I'll check on you two later." She quietly left the room, looking back over her shoulder until the door was completely closed.

"Nathan, do you remember anything at all? Do you remember passing out in the barn?" asked Marcie nervously. "You don't have to talk about it if you don't want to, but Mark is going to be asking you some questions later, and I thought, maybe you and I should talk first. I wanted to hear from you what happened. Can you talk about it, Nathan?"

Nathan's smile disappeared and his expression was serious and hard. "Marcie, I—," his voice broke away for a moment.

"Just start slowly, Nathan. It's just me here with you. I love you more than anything in the world. I'm going to hold on to you, no matter what you say. Don't be afraid to tell me. Please, you've got to trust someone. Let it be me."

"It's so hard to look at you right now," Nathan said turning away.

"Don't concern yourself about me. I want to know what happened in the barn. You found something didn't you?" Marcie hated to press him to answer her questions, but she knew she had to do it before Mark did.

"Yes, I found a bag, my bag. I must have placed it there in the barn when I was staying in your house. I don't remember putting it there, but I must have. When I opened it up, inside there was one of my shirts." Nathan bit his lip as tears fell from his eyes. "It was my shirt, but it was covered in blood." He covered his face with his hands, but then he slowly lowered them and looked at Marcie. "That's not all. I found a mask. It was a rubber mask that resembled an old man with white hair. It was in my bag with the bloody shirt. Marcie, it was me! I killed Robert and probably Todd Harper. I did it! Oh, my God, what have I done? You need to get away from me. Go far away. I'm a sick man, Marcie. Can't you see? That's why I couldn't remember anything. I did it. That's why the old man was in my dreams all of the time. It was me. I must have used the mask as a disguise. But, I still don't remember any of it. When I saw the mask, I just placed it over my head and screamed as loud as I could. I just screamed and screamed." Nathan began to cry loudly and pounding his face with his hands.

Marcie backed away from him for a moment, but then something rose up inside of her. She grabbed Nathan's hands and shouted at him, "Stop! Stop doing this to yourself! I love you, Nathan. Listen to me!"

Nathan calmed down and looked in Marcie's eyes. "How can you say those things?" he asked. "I'm a killer. I killed your brother. You can't love me. I'm a monster. Please Marcie, I won't let you ruin your life with me. I'm so, so sorry that I've hurt you. I never knew, but now, now you have to tell them the truth. I need to be locked up before I hurt somebody else. Please, Marcie, tell them."

"No, no I won't. Nathan, I don't believe you. You loved Robert. He was your closest friend. You two were like brothers, you were inseparable. How could you have killed him? It's just not in you to do such a thing. You're not a killer."

"But the mask and the shirt are proof enough. Just because I can't remember it doesn't mean I didn't do it."

"Will you please listen to me? I think somebody is trying to get to you. Somebody planted that bag in the barn. It's not yours. I know it's not yours. Now you have to let me help you. You can't tell any of this to Mark. If you do, he'll have you put away for life. Nathan, are you listening to me? You have to let me help you."

Nathan stared back at Marcie, confused and surprised. "Why do you believe I'm innocent? You just don't want to face the facts do you?"

"No! No more talk about this. Let me speak for you. Together we'll figure this out. Now they don't have anything on you right now, as long as you don't go and confess something to them, something that you didn't do. Please Nathan, believe in me, if you can't believe in yourself. Look at me. I love you, and I'm going to help you. You have to believe that there's more to this than you realize. I don't know all of the answers right now, but I know something strange is going on here and someone is trying to hurt you. So far they've done a very good job. They're trying to turn you into a basket case and to confuse you until you don't know what's true and what's not. Trust me on this, Nathan. Let me handle it. When the doctor talks to you, tell him that you just passed out in the barn. Tell him you just remembered something painful about Robert's death, but now you don't know what it was. Tell him anything, but don't tell him about the bag you found. Oh Nathan, baby, don't you see what they're trying to do? I need you to stay with me on this. Try to focus on me. Don't let anything distract you. They're playing with your mind, honey. They want you to think that you did it. Don't you see?"

"I'm so confused, Marcie. Why would someone try to make me think that I did it? Who would do such a thing?"

"The real killer, that's who. They're afraid you're going to remember something, and so they're planting thoughts in your head to throw you off track. Nathan, do you think for a moment, that if I really believed you killed my brother, I would still be able to love you? I know you. I know your thoughts and your intentions and they're not evil. We need to find the answers for Robert and for Todd. Until we know all of the facts, let me help you."

"What are we going to do?"

"Nothing, we're not going to say or do anything different from what we already planned. You'll tell the doctor that you can't remember anything else, and after you're released from the hospital, we'll leave town as scheduled. I think you're right. You'll think more clearly, once we're away from here. I won't feel safe until we get out of this town."

"Are you sure you want to go away with me? Won't you be afraid? Marcie, I couldn't bare it if I did something to hurt you."

"I'm not afraid, because I know you would never hurt me. Now are we agreed on our plan? Will you go along with me on this?"

Nathan just stared at Marcie for a moment. Tears filled his tired eyes. "Okay, we'll try it your way, Marcie." Nathan caressed Marcie's face in his hands and kissed her tenderly.

"Now, I'm going to send for some breakfast for you. I want you healthy and back on your feet. We've got a lot to do."

As Marcie left the room, Nathan wondered if what they were doing was right. He couldn't help but believe Marcie was blinded by her love for him and refused to see the truth. But what if she's wrong? What if he is the real killer?

He sank back into his pillows and pulled the covers up closely around him, feeling scared as his hands began to tremble on their own. He placed them between his knees and turned over on his side. Suddenly, Nathan wasn't sure who he was anymore. As he closed his eyes, he could hear a distant voice calling to him.

"Nathan, Nathan." He recognized the voice as belonging to Robert. Closing his eyes tightly, he tried not to listen, but it continued, "Nathan, did you kill me? Did you Nathan?"

Nathan tried to drown out the voice by thinking about something else. Just then, Marcie stuck her head in the door, "Breakfast is coming, and I'm going to go and call Maggie and let her know you're finally awake. I'll be right back."

He just shook his head and closed his eyes again. The voice was gone for now. "Please, hurry back, Marcie. Please hurry."

# 29

Nathan had been sleeping for hours, when he felt someone pull up one of his eyelids and shine a small light into his eye. He blinked a few times and opened both his eyes to see the doctor leaning over him.

"I'm sorry to wake you, but I didn't think you were going to wake up on your own again any time soon. You've been sleeping for hours," the doctor said, checking Nathan's other eye in the same manner.

"I have? I don't even remember going to sleep. Am I all right?"

"Well, when Marcie came back in to bring you some breakfast, you had your pillow over your head and you kept saying something like, 'make him stop, make him stop.' Do you remember any of that?"

"No, I can't remember anything about what you're telling me. Did I just finally go to sleep?"

"I had the nurse give you a mild sedative to help you rest. You seemed so restless, I wanted you to be able to calm down and rest. You've been asleep ever since. How do you feel now?"

"Kind of groggy I guess, but otherwise, I feel fine. What's wrong with me, doc? Why am I hearing things and seeing things that aren't really there? Am I going crazy?"

"Of course you're not. Is he doctor?" Marcie quickly answered. "You're just confused from a lot of stress right now. You'll be fine. Won't he, doctor?"

"Well, it's a bit more than just stress, Nathan. I believe you're suffering from Post Traumatic Stress Syndrome."

"What? Post what? What does that mean? It certainly doesn't sound good," Nathan replied.

"It means that you've seen something that's too shocking for your brain to contain. So it somehow stores the memories away. You don't have ready access to them, but sometimes they gradually start to creep forward in your mind in bits and pieces, like a puzzle. Nathan, something is hiding in your memory that you want to remember, but it's too horrible for you to visualize. Something must have jogged this secret in your mind the other day just before you passed out in the barn. It must have been sudden or so startling that your brain just shut down right then and there. Think back, can you remember anything, anything at all about that day?"

Marcie started to bite her nails as she stood just behind the doctor. She tried to speak to Nathan with her eyes. "Don't do it, Nathan," she said to herself. "Don't tell them anything."

Nathan was silent as he turned his head away from Marcie and stared out of the hospital window. He wanted to tell them the truth, because he wanted it to be over, even if it meant he would be put away and punished. How much more could he stand? "Robert's voice will never leave me alone," he thought. "I have to get everything out in the open. I'm so tired of hiding things and cowering in the dark." He looked again at Marcie's eyes. She looked as though she was pleading with him without even uttering a word. She was the love of his life and he realized living without her would be as torturous as the secret of Robert's death. What if she was right? What if he was innocent and someone was trying to frame him. He closed his eyes for a moment, and then he looked up at the doctor.

"I don't remember anything. I'm sorry. Everything is a total blank. No matter how hard I try, I just can't remember. Please, leave me alone now. I just want to be with Marcie."

"That's fine, Nathan," said the doctor. "You just relax now. We'll talk again later. Sometimes these things take a lot of time before anything happens. Would you mind if I send Dr. Scott Seyler over to see you again? Since you've talked with him before, maybe it would be a good idea for you to visit with him some more while you're in here. What do you think?"

"I guess so, okay, I'll talk to him again. Now, please, leave me with Marcie for a while."

Everyone left the room except Marcie. She held Nathan in her arms with tears running down her face. "Oh, Nathan, I was so afraid that you were going to tell them. You did the right thing. As soon as you're stronger, we're going to leave this town. Once we're away, you'll see that everything will look much clearer to you. You need to get away, soon." She kissed him and held him in her arms. "No one will be able to hurt you once we leave this place."

"What about Maggie? What does she say about all of this? Does she think I'm crazy?"

"Maggie loves you. You're like a son to her. She's only concerned about your wellbeing. I haven't told her about the bag you found or what was in it. It's better that we not tell anyone about it. Just let it be for now. She just thinks the same as everyone else. After we get settled, we can send for her to come and stay with us for a while. Everything will be all right, you'll see. We'll sort it out between us, just you and me, but while we're here I just don't feel that you're safe. Someone is watching you, Nathan. Maybe it's the killer. We've got to get you out of here."

"Everything is so mixed up. I can't even think straight myself. I'm not sure what's right and what's wrong. Marcie, maybe it would be best if I just left town alone and you stay here with Maggie for a while. I need to get myself straightened out before you run away with me. I...I could be dangerous, you just don't know for sure."

"There will be no more talk like that. I'm going to stay with you. You don't need to be alone. When you start to feel afraid, I'll hold you until the fear passes. I'll protect you and love you. I won't let anyone harm you. You need me with you. I'm so afraid that you'll break down and tell them something that will make them want to put you away forever. I believe in you. Nathan, please don't push me away. Please, don't do this to me." Marcie laid her head on his chest and started to cry. "We have to stay together through this. They're trying to separate us, can't you see? Someone wants to drive you away."

Nathan placed his arms around Marcie and pulled her close to him. When they kissed, Nathan felt such a burning passion that he knew he had to have her with him at all cost. He had never felt anything like this before. His love for her burned inside him. He held her with the intention of never letting her go again. Whether he was right or wrong, he was going to hold on to the one thing he was sure of as long as he possibly could.

"Is it okay for me to say hello for a minute?" asked Mark through the cracked door to Nathan's room. "I promise not to stay too long."

Marcie wiped her eyes and pulled Nathan's face close to hers. "My love will keep you strong," she whispered. "Don't be afraid." With that she pulled herself up off of the bed and smiled at Mark as she went into the bathroom. As she closed the door behind her, her heart beat so loudly, she felt surely that Mark could hear it as she passed him.

"I just wanted to drop by to see how you were doing. I tried to give you some time before I bothered you."

"I'm going to be fine. I just had a little fainting party in the barn, that's all." Nathan swallowed hard as the words left his mouth, but his eyes stared straight ahead at Mark.

"I'm really glad to hear that, because you didn't look so good when they put you in the ambulance." Mark pulled up a chair and sat down beside the bed. "But, I have to say, you do look a little better now. The doctor says you've been resting. That's good, you need lots of rest."

"Mark is there another reason you came to see me today? I don't really think you're interested in my sleeping habits are you?"

"Well, I did ask the doctor if it would be all right if I talked to you for a minute, you know, ask you a few questions. Is that agreeable to you? It won't take too long, and then you can get back to your visit with Marcie. How's she holding up under all this by the way? Is she staying calm? Does she need anything?"

"She's holding up just fine. She's worried about me, of course, but other than that, we're good."

"Good, I'm glad to hear it. If she does need anything, you tell her to let me know. I'll be glad to do whatever I can. Oh, and Gracey sends her love. She was really upset to hear that you had to go to the hospital. She thinks that you two are some romance novel that she reads every day. She wants to know everything that happens to you."

"Tell her we appreciate her concern, but this is only a temporary set back. We'll be leaving town, just like we planned, as soon as I get out of here."

"Oh, so you're still planning on going away. I would have thought you would want to stay here a while longer, to make sure you're back on your feet and maybe continue to talk to Dr. Seyler."

"No, there's no need for me to stay here. I, we, both think it would be best if we just left as we had originally planned. I should be back on my feet soon. Everyone's making a big deal out of me fainting in the barn. A lot of people pass out for one reason or another and I'm no different from them. Once I get into the city, I'll find another doctor and continue my therapy until I find the answers I need. Now what questions did you want to ask me?"

Mark smiled slowly and shook his head. "You know, you act like you already have all of the answers. Tell me, what did you see just before you fainted in the barn, Nathan? What overwhelmed you enough to make you go unconscious for hours?"

"I told the doctor and now I'm telling you. I can't remember anything. If I could remember, then I wouldn't be having so many problems, now would I?"

"No, I guess not, but it must be convenient to be able to selectively forget things whenever you feel it's appropriate."

"Are you suggesting that I'm not telling you something that I do remember? Are you saying that I'm lying to you? Just what is it you think I know, Mark? Why don't you tell me for a change? You seem to be the one with all the answers around here. You tell me what I know."

Mark stood up and walked over to the window. "I'm not sure, Nathan, but it's more than you're willing to share. I'm pretty good at reading people and your eyes don't look as clear to me as they did when you first arrived." Mark walked over closer to Nathan. "Run away if you want to, but the truth will eventually come out and then, you won't have anywhere to hide."

"Are you accusing me of something? If you are, then just come out with it, and stop beating around the bush with these games you keep playing. Do you have some evidence that I need to know about?"

"No, only my gut feeling and those feelings don't lie. You know something, and you're not telling me. I'm not accusing you of anything, but I know you've got more in that memory of yours than you let on. I don't have any more questions for now, but we'll talk again, before you leave. Think again about what you're doing, Nathan. If you change your mind, give me a call. You know how to get in touch with me." Mark walked to the door to leave and then turned around. "Tell Marcie she can come out now. I'm leaving."

Marcie pushed open the bathroom door just as Mark left and looked over at Nathan. "Are you all right?" she asked. "Nathan?"

He didn't answer her. He just kept staring at the door shutting behind Mark. "How could he see through me so clearly? What made him think that I know something more? Maybe my guilt is showing more than I think." Nathan wanted to call Mark back and tell him the truth, but he couldn't. He had become a prisoner to his secrets and to his dreams. As Marcie softly stroked his hair, her lips were moving, but he couldn't hear anything that she was saying. He could only see Robert running through the woods, dancing, skipping and laughing back at him.

# 30

The next morning, Dr. Scott Seyler showed up early. He was very eager to talk to Nathan. He hoped Nathan would be just as enthusiastic.

Nathan was indifferent to his coming and more interested in getting out of the hospital as soon as possible. His doctor promised to release him after his visit with Dr. Seyler. So he was understandably eager to get this visit done and to get on with his life with Marcie.

"I thought I'd catch you early in the day while your thoughts were fresh and, hopefully, after you've had a good night's rest. How are you feeling this morning, Nathan?"

"The same as yesterday, confused as ever, but well rested. I'm climbing the walls in this place."

"I see. So you haven't been able to remember anything about what happened to you in the barn at Marcie's house?"

"Nothing. I keep telling everyone the same thing, but no one seems to want to believe me. Why should you be any different?"

"I believe you, Nathan, I just want to try and help you remember as much as you can. You want to get well don't you?"

"I don't know whether getting well is as important as getting out of town, away from everyone and their prying questions. I think a lot of the questions are just because people are nosey and have nothing to do with trying to get me well again."

"Why do you express such hostility toward those who care about you?"

"Care about me? The only person that cares about me is Marcie. The rest are just leaches, trying to suck me dry."

"I've never heard you sound so negative before," said Dr. Seyler. "The first time I met you I pegged you as a pretty laid-back kind of guy, the kind that doesn't judge people so quickly. Has something happened to suddenly make you change your mind about people?"

"Yeah, you could say that. I feel like I'm the center attraction in a three-ring circus here. Everybody thinks I'm some sort of freak that they can come in and poke at for a while and then go on about their lives. I've got nothing to tell you doctor, you're just wasting your time with me."

"Not so fast, Nathan. There's plenty we have to talk about. We don't have to just discuss what happened to you the other day when you passed out. You've been telling me about your dreams and your thoughts about Robert. Let's talk about that instead."

"Why? So you can find out what deep dark secret is hiding inside of me? What difference does it make anyway? Robert's death happened a long time ago. Why should it affect me now? Nothing I can remember will bring Robert back. Even if I was able to name his killer, Robert would still be dead and I would still miss him. So what's the point in digging anything out of me?"

Dr. Seyler sat and stared at Nathan over his glasses for a moment. He didn't speak at all for a good while and it made Nathan uncomfortable.

"Why are you staring at me? Did I finally say something profound?"

"No, it's just that I usually believe what you tell me. Yet, for some strange reason, I can't buy what you just said. I believe what you can remember about Robert's death makes all of the difference in the world. You're right. It won't bring him back, but this is not about bringing Robert back again and you know that. We're talking about releasing you to live your life without having him constantly running through your dreams and thoughts. Wouldn't you like that? Peace of mind is a valuable treasure. Many people would pay dearly for just a moment of peace in their life. No, I believe you want to get rid of the torture. The dreams are turning to nightmares that frighten you and you want more than ever to rid yourself of this burden that you keep carrying around with you. If you don't allow yourself to find all of the pieces to your puzzle, Robert will be interrupting your life until he consumes it completely."

Nathan looked up at the ceiling, trying to keep the tears that were swimming around in his eyes from running down his face. Dr.

Seyler was right. He wanted so much to share his feelings and to let somebody else carry this weight for him. His lips started to tremble and he gripped the sheets on the bed tightly in his fists.

"Oh, hi, Dr. Seyler, I didn't realize you were here," said Marcie, as she entered the room. She gently kissed Nathan and sat down beside him. "How are you feeling today? You seem to have a bit more color in your face and the nurse said you ate your breakfast this morning. You must be feeling better." Marcie looked back at Dr. Seyler. "Did I interrupt something here?"

"Well, actually—"

"No, we were just finishing when you came in," replied Nathan quickly. "I don't have anything else to tell you doctor. I'm really sorry."

"All right, Nathan. I understand you're still planning to leave town soon."

"Yes, pretty soon in fact. Why?"

"I hope you will make sure you find another doctor to continue your therapy once you're settled. It's very important. If you like, I could give you some recommendations and if you'll let me know whom you decide to see, I'll make sure your records get forwarded from my office to theirs. You have my number, give me a call before you leave, won't you?"

"Sure, I can do that. I'll be in touch with you." As the doctor headed for the door, Nathan suddenly felt over whelmed by panic, "Dr. Seyler."

"Yes?" the doctor asked turning around at the doorway.

Nathan's eyes met Marcie's and he could see the fear in her face. "I...I just wanted to say thanks. You've been a big help to me. I'll make sure I call your office before I leave town."

"You're welcome, Nathan. Let me know if there's anything else that I can do for you. I wish you both all the best."

"Goodbye," said Marcie, as Dr. Seyler left the room. "So what did you two talk about? Anything important?"

"I didn't tell him anything, if that's what you mean." Nathan looked troubled and seemed a little cold toward Marcie.

"Nathan, is there something wrong? You know I'm only trying to protect you from yourself. You're confused and you think you want to tell them what appears to be the truth in your mind, but you must wait until we have all of the pieces to the puzzle. Otherwise, you'll just incriminate yourself. Oh, darling, I only want what's best for you. Now you've just got to trust me and let me help you."

"I know. I know you're probably right, but I feel like I'm going to explode inside. I don't think I can keep carrying all of this inside of me. Maybe when I get to the city, I should do as Dr. Seyler says and find a doctor right away. What do you think?"

"We'll see. Let's just take one day at a time. First we have to get you home, get a good home cooked meal inside of you for a change. Then we'll discuss when we should leave. Here, I brought you some clothes and the doctor says you can check out this afternoon if you feel like it. How about it? Are you ready to go home?"

"I've been ready. A home cooked meal sounds too good to be true."

"Good. Here are your clothes. I'll be gathering up your belongings while you get ready to go. Oh, Nathan, I can hardly wait for us to be alone in the city together. I just think things are going to be so much better there for us. You'll see."

Nathan felt dizzy as he stood up to put on his clothes, but he was glad to be leaving. He felt like a caged animal and was looking forward to some fresh air and a change of scenery. He was also glad to have Marcie looking out for him. If he were on his own, he'd never be able to handle everything that was happening to him. He was also looking forward to going back to the city and the fast-paced life there, where he barely had time to allow his thoughts to wander for more than a moment. Marcie was right. Things were going to be better for both of them there.

Watching her from across the room, Nathan could see she took great care in gathering up his things. She smiled at him as she looked around to make sure they weren't leaving anything behind. "I guess that's everything. Are you ready?"

"You bet. Let's go home."

The nurse arrived with a wheelchair and together they started out of the hospital room and past the nurse's desk. As they waited for the elevator, one of the nurses noticed them there. "Now, there's a couple in love if ever I saw one. You just don't see that these days."

"Yes, must be nice," said another nurse while scribbling on some charts. "They look like they were made for each other."

When the elevator arrived they disappeared inside. As the doors closed in front of them, Nathan caught a glimpse of Mark standing in the hallway.

# 31

Nathan was glad to finally get back home and out of the fish-bowl life at the hospital. Going back to the city sounded better every minute. Just a little more packing to do and they would be on their way. He hoped that nothing else would get in the way of their leaving this time.

Marcie had made a place for him on the sofa to relax while she cooked up something special for him in the kitchen. She enjoyed cooking, now that she had someone special to cook for. Nathan was easy to please and bragged about every meal she prepared for him. She peeped out of the kitchen to see how he was managing on his own, and she could see that he had his head back with his eyes closed. "Good," she thought. "He needs all of the peace and quiet he can find." She continued cooking, trying to be as quiet as possible.

Marcie had carefully hidden the bag Nathan had found in the barn, making sure no one would find it. She planned to take it with her when they left for the city and dispose of it there. She didn't want to leave anything to chance until she could find out the real truth about what happened.

A few minutes later she checked on Nathan again to find him wide awake and reading a book. She came in and sat on the sofa beside him.

"I made some hot tea. Would you like a cup?" she asked.

"Yes, that would be nice," replied Nathan. "You know if this keeps up, I'm going to be so spoiled, you won't be able to stand me after a while."

"I love spoiling you. Besides, I want you to feel comfortable and relaxed. You've been through so much." She handed him a cup of hot tea and watched as he quickly raised it to his lips. "Careful. I just made it. It's very hot."

"It's delicious. You make a fine cup of tea, my lady."

"Thank you, sir," Marcie said laughing. "Dinner's almost ready. I hope you've got an appetite."

"I'm starving. Just sitting here with those wonderful smells coming from the kitchen is more than I can take. All of a sudden I could eat a horse."

"Well, you won't have to suffer much longer." Marcie stood up to go back into the kitchen.

"I thought you might have invited Maggie over for tonight. Did you?"

"Not tonight," Marcie answered from the kitchen. "I wanted it to be just the two of us. Is that okay?"

"Yes, it's just that, we'll be leaving soon and I know you want to spend as much time with her as you can. It's okay if you want to call her to come over."

"No, I'll be able to visit her tomorrow. Let's just have a cozy dinner, just the two of us tonight. I'm sure she understands."

"I'm really going to miss her when we leave. I wish she would change her mind and come with us," said Nathan.

"Well, you know how a person her age hates changes. Maybe we'll be able to convince her later on. She might get lonely enough to change her mind."

Marcie finished setting the table and lit a couple of white candles for the center of the table. "There, doesn't that look romantic?" She went over to the stereo and turned on the switch. Soft jazz flowed from the speakers as the last touch was added to the table.

Nathan walked over and put his arms around Marcie. "This was a good idea," he said softly in her ear. As he kissed her on the neck, Marcie took his arm and led him over to the table. "Will this seat do, sir?"

"It all depends on who will be dining with me," he replied jokingly.

"Oh, the hostess always sits with the best customer." Nathan pulled out the chair for her and then took his seat directly across from her. The light from the candles danced across their faces as they looked at each other. Neither of them could believe they were finally alone together with no one around asking questions. Marcie held out her hand for his plate and began serving the meal as he watched her every move. Everything seemed so perfect.

Just as they were about to eat, the phone rang. Neither Nathan, nor Marcie, made an effort to answer it at first.

"Let's just let it ring. They can leave a message," said Marcie. "I don't want anything to spoil our evening."

As the answering machine switched on, Marcie was startled. "Marcie, this is Mark. Please pick up, I know you're home. It's an emergency. It's about Maggie."

Marcie ran over to the phone and grabbed it, "Mark, what's wrong? What about Maggie?"

"The rescue squad is here at the Raven Inn. I think your mother has just had a heart attack. Please get over here as soon as possible. I'm not sure how bad her condition is right now. Please, hurry."

"Oh, dear God, no! I'll be right there." Marcie hung up the phone and turned to Nathan. "Mom's had a heart attack. I have to go."

"Let me drive you, Marcie. You're too upset to drive."

"No, you don't need this right now. Just stay here. I'll be fine."

"Marcie, don't be crazy. I care about Maggie too. Now I'm going to drive you. Get your coat."

As Marcie was getting her coat, she stopped in the middle of the room and burst into tears. Nathan grabbed hold of her, "Honey, take it easy. We don't know how she is yet. Try not to break down."

"I don't think I could bear anything happening to her. Oh, Nathan, what would I do without her?"

"Let's just get to her as fast as we can. Come on."

As they arrived at the inn, the ambulance was still there and so was Mark's car. They both rushed into the house and were met by Mark at the door.

"She's upstairs, but she doesn't look good," Mark said, walking with them up the stairs. "I heard the rescue squad call come through and rushed right over here."

"Who made the call?" asked Marcie.

"Her friend, Velma was with her. She called from the inn."

As Marcie and Nathan walked into her room, the rescue squad was still there with her. Marcie pushed her way past them and took Maggie's hand. "Mom, it's me, Marcie. I'm right here with you. You're going to be fine, just hold on."

"Maggie opened her eyes and smiled up at her, "Marcie, I love you." She looked across the room and saw Nathan standing at the foot of her bed. Maggie reached out her hand to him and Nathan walked over to the side of the bed.

"Maggie, you're a tough old girl. You're going to make it."

"Not this time, dear. I'm afraid I'm losing this fight." She said squeezing his hand tightly. "Are you doing better?"

"Don't worry about me, you just concentrate on yourself."

Marcie started crying and ran out of the room. Nathan started to follow her, but Maggie held on to his hand. "Listen to me," she said in a strained and weak voice.

Nathan moved closer to Maggie to hear what she was saying.

"Don't go to the city. Stay here a while longer. Promise me."

"Why are you talking about that now? You shouldn't even be trying to talk."

Maggie pulled Nathan closer to her. "Please, do as I say. Stay in town. Don't leave. Will you promise me?"

"Why? Why should I stay here? Maggie, what are you trying to say?"

Maggie coughed and gasped for breath. One of the men from the rescue squad put his hand on Nathan's shoulder. "There's nothing else we can do here. We need to get her to the hospital right away."

"Nathan, stay here for Robert's sake. Will you do it?" Maggie looked as though she was pleading with him.

"Maggie, do you know who killed Robert? Can you answer me?"

She opened her mouth to speak, but all that Nathan could hear was a long gasp of breath. Her eyes flickered a few times and then she died.

Nathan sat holding her hand tightly in his. He couldn't believe she was gone. "Maggie?" he whispered, even though he knew she couldn't hear him.

As he got up from the bed, Marcie was standing in the doorway. "She's gone, baby. She's dead."

Marcie covered her mouth with her hands and sank down to her knees against the doorframe. She wept uncontrollably, calling out her mother's name. "Maggie. No! No!"

Nathan crumpled beside her and put his head against hers. How could he console her in a time like this? He didn't know what to do, except hold her in his arms and cry with her.

Mark stood quietly behind them in the hallway. As the rescue squad prepared to cover Maggie's body, Mark motioned for Marcie and Nathan to come with him downstairs. As Nathan led Marcie downstairs, he felt as though he was in a terrible dream that wouldn't allow him to awaken. He placed Marcie on the sofa in the living room and sat down close to her, trying his best to comfort her as much as he could. As he held her in his arms, he couldn't help but think about what Maggie had said. "Why would she want to make sure I stayed in town?" he thought. "She must have known something about Robert's death that she wanted to tell me, but what?"

"Would you like me to call anybody for you, Marcie?" asked Mark, as he knelt down beside her.

"That won't be necessary," said Nathan. "We'll handle it from here. Thanks anyway."

"All right then, but let me know if there's anything at all that I can do. Call me if you need me. I'll be back to check in on you later."

Nathan sat and rocked Marcie in his arms and held her close to him. "We'll get through this, babe," he said. "Why don't you go in the next room and lie down? I'll take care of the phone calls to the funeral home. Is there a particular place you'd like me to call to handle everything?"

Marcie paused for a moment trying to gather her thoughts. "Um, well, Mom was friendly with the folks that run Howell and Stokes Funeral Home. Call them. They'll do a beautiful job."

Marcie stopped and looked around the room. "I just can't believe she's gone. I can't believe it."

Nathan took her by the hand and led her into the next room. He closed the door behind her quietly and then sat next to the phone to make the call to the funeral home. He paused as he picked up the phone and started to dial. "Did Maggie know something about the deaths of Robert or Todd that she wished she had shared with him?" he wondered. "I may never know now."

# 32

A week after Maggie's funeral Nathan concentrated all his energy into helping Marcie get back on her feet again. Friends and neighbors as well as family came from all over to say goodbye to Maggie. She was well thought of and had many friends and acquaintances continuously dropping by to pay their respects and to offer their condolences to Marcie and Nathan.

He knew Maggie's death was a great shock and it would take a lot of time and special attention to help Marcie through this difficult time. Maggie's death seemed to really send her reeling out of her comfortable world. Nathan tried his best to stay strong for her. He wanted her to lean on him for strength and stability, something he was never sure he would be able to provide.

While Marcie was resting in the next room, Nathan, with some hesitation, started sifting through some of Maggie's belongings. He dreaded having to sort through everything, but he knew that eventually they would have to decide what things they were going to keep and what they would need to give away, or throw away. Decisions would have to be made about the Raven Inn. Nathan found himself in the library, one of his favorite rooms. He could remember spending hours just thumbing through the large collection of books, magazines and newspapers from years gone by.

Nathan sat on the floor and pulled open one of the drawers to a beautiful old antique stand. Inside was a scrapbook, and clippings from various events in the town that Maggie had lovingly cut from the newspapers and saved. It was quite a nice collection of memories from the small town festivities that took place over the years. Nathan flipped each page and read the headlines from many of the articles. She had saved articles on town picnics, parades, parties, etc. They were all set in chronological order with great care. Some of the articles made him smile and made it easy to close his eyes and reminisce about how simple life used to be. "This is definitely a keeper," Nathan thought. "This is a good record of so much history in one place. I've got to have this. Maybe it would be a helpful reference in one of my books." As he continued to slowly look through the book, his heart began to feel very heavy. He realized how much he was going to miss Maggie and how much of the town's memories she had carried with her. She was a wonderful old gal and Nathan knew that her death would leave an empty space in his heart. After his mother had died, Maggie loved him like her own son. She was always easy to talk to and took the time to be very frank with him in their conversations. He could rely on Maggie to tell him when he was doing something wrong or whether he should be cautious about something he was about to do. He sat back for a minute and thought about what Maggie had said to him just before she died. She told him to stay in town. "I wonder why? Was there something here she wanted me to find?" Then a chilling thought crossed his mind. "The bag. She didn't know about the bag that I found," Nathan whispered to himself. "Could it be that she knew about it and wanted me to find it? Could she have known that I was the killer all along, even while she was holding my hand and taking her last breath?"

Nathan shook his head in disbelief, "It just can't be. I know I wouldn't have harmed Robert. There was never a better friend in my life. Maggie must have known that." He wished he had told her about the bag and the mask instead of keeping it a secret. Maybe then she would have shared with him what she knew. She must have been carrying around her own bag of secrets, but why didn't she share them with him? Maybe she was hoping he would just find things out on his own. For the first time, since he found the bag in the barn, Nathan began to have some hope. Perhaps he was innocent. "Maybe Marcie's right. Someone is trying to frame me, but who would do such a thing? Maggie, old gal, I wish you were here right now. I'd tell you everything. We'd have a long talk about Robert." He realized that would never happen now. Maggie was gone and with her, more pieces to the puzzle that he wanted so desperately to put back together. He was just as confused now as he had ever been.

Flipping to the end of the book, his eyes rested on an article from the local newspaper, "Boy Mysteriously Murdered, Body Found in the Woods." The article was about Robert's death. As Nathan continued to read, he saw something unexpected. "Another boy, Jake Foster, witnessed seeing Robert running through the woods just before he was killed and was interviewed by police. He was unable to offer any information that proved to be of any help in finding the killer."

Nathan looked up from the article, "I never knew there had been another witness to Robert's murder." He searched the article again for the boy's name. "Jake Foster." Nathan kept repeating the name to himself. Suddenly he remembered. "Dan Harper mentioned his neighbor, Jake Foster, had seen an old man in the woods on the day that Todd was found dead." Nathan had spoken to him in town. Jake Foster was the boy in the article who saw Robert in the woods that day and now he may also be a witness to seeing the killer again. "I have to talk to him. Why didn't someone tell me this before now? Mark had never mentioned that Jake had been a witness to Robert's death.

Nathan jumped up from the floor with the book under his arm, but then he suddenly stopped in his tracks. "What if Jake did see me in the woods? What if he's known all along that I'm the killer? But if that were so, why would he keep quiet about it? Why would he keep quiet even after his neighbor's son has been found murdered? Maybe there's not a connection, but I have to talk with him. No matter what the outcome is in the end," Nathan decided.

As he headed out of the room and turned the corner, he ran into Marcie standing just outside the doorway. "Whoa, you spooked me."

"I'm sorry, I was wondering where you were and I was just about to look in the library when you came barreling out. Where are you going so fast?"

"No where, I just remembered something I want to do."

"What's that under your arm?"

"It's just a scrapbook I found that belonged to Maggie. I decided I'd like to keep it, since it's got all kinds of history in it about this town. Do you mind?"

"No, not at all. I'm sure there are lots of things we're going to want to keep. We may have to have some of it shipped to the city, rather than trying to carry it all with us."

"Marcie, I need to talk to you about us leaving. Maybe we should postpone our trip for now. I mean, with Maggie's unexpected death and everything that needs to be done, perhaps it would just be better if we stayed here instead, at least for a while longer. Next year might be a better time."

"Next year? Nathan, what are you talking about? I know we have to take care of Maggie's affairs, but that shouldn't take very long. We can put the inn on the market and Arthur Creen, the real estate agent, can handle it from there. He'll contact us if there are any buyers and then we can come back for the closing. Why would you insist that we stay longer? Why do you want to stay for a whole year?"

"I don't know, I just feel it would be best. You know, maybe we could run the Raven Inn for a while instead of just up and selling it. I love this old place and I think we should reconsider selling it so quickly."

"Nathan, you're talking nonsense. Why, all of a sudden, did you have a change of heart about this? I thought it was all settled. What about getting back to the city to clear your mind?"

"I know what I said, and I still want to go back one day, but I think it would be great for us to run the inn for a while before we move away. I figured it would be easier on you. With Maggie's death, you don't want to go through the trauma of moving to another place and making all of these changes in your life do you? Maybe we should just take it slow."

"Has something happened to change your mind? Have you remembered something that makes you want to stay here?"

"I didn't want to worry you with this right now, Marcie. You've got enough on your mind with everything that's happened."

"Nathan, please. No secrets, remember? What did you find?"

"I found an article in this scrapbook written about Robert's murder. In the article they mention a boy who witnessed seeing Robert in the woods just before he was killed."

"A boy? Wasn't that boy you?"

"No. This was another boy. I never remembered there was someone else who saw Robert that day."

"So, you want to go now and try to find this other person?"

"Marcie, the person was Jake Foster. He's Dan Harper's neighbor. He was the witness."

"Well, now that you say his name, I remember the police talked to him that day, but he didn't know anything much, only that he saw Robert. What's so important that you have to talk to him? What's he going to be able to tell you now that he couldn't tell the police back then?"

"Don't you think it's a little peculiar that Jake saw Robert in the woods the day he was killed and now he's also possibly witnessed seeing the murder of another boy found dead in a similar fashion? Don't you see the connection?"

"You think Robert's killer also went after Todd Harper? But why would he? He was no threat to whoever the killer is, because he didn't know anything to tell, unless," Marcie paused and walked across the room. "Unless, maybe Todd got a little too curious for his own good and started poking around where he shouldn't. Maybe Todd overheard something that he wasn't supposed to hear."

"Marcie, I have to talk to Jake. I think he knows something he's not telling us. We have to stay here a while longer. Don't you see? Little by little, the pieces to this puzzle are falling into place. I have to stay a while longer."

Marcie put her arms around him. "Nathan, this is never going to end. I just want to run away from it all. It doesn't concern us anymore."

"How can you say that? I found a bag with my shirt and a mask in it. How do you know, I'm not the real killer? Marcie, I know you don't want to discuss this, but we have to find out the truth, and if it turns out to be me, I have to face up to that fact and turn myself in."

"Nathan, please tell me you won't do anything stupid. Let's find out all of the facts first. I only wanted to get you away from here, so they couldn't take you away from me. You know you're not the killer. You could never hurt anyone." Marcie started to cry and then went limp in Nathan's arms.

"Marcie," said Nathan, trying to shake her awake. She had fainted in his arms. He realized this was not the best timing. It wasn't fair to her. He lifted her in his arms and laid her on the couch. "I'm sorry, baby. I didn't mean to cause so much trouble in your life."

# 33

Nathan waited a few more days before he decided to head out to Jake Foster's house to talk with him. He wanted to wait until Marcie seemed a bit stronger and capable of being left on her own. While she was busy sorting through some of Maggie's belongings, Nathan took advantage of the time to get with Jake and find out what information he might remember about Robert's death. There was no need to mention this visit to Marcie. She had too much stress to deal with as it was. Maybe what she didn't know wouldn't hurt her.

As Nathan knocked on Jake Foster's door, he wasn't sure whether he would even talk to him. What if Jake knew information that could be incriminating for him? "I have to do this no matter what the outcome," Nathan said to himself. "I have to find out whatever I can." Suddenly the door opened and there stood Jake. He was a big man who worked with his hands, but he had a kind face. He looked surprised to see Nathan and was hesitant about opening the screen door.

"What brings you out my way?" Jake asked through the screen.

"If you don't mind, I'd like to talk to you for a while. I promise I won't take up a lot of your time, but if you could just sit with me for a minute, I'd greatly appreciate it."

"I'm kind of busy right now. I'm on my way out to my barn to do a little work. Can you come back another time?"

"How about if I go along with you to the barn? You can work while we talk."

Nathan could see that Jake wasn't crazy about the idea, but he agreed to let him go along. Jake grabbed his hat and the two of them took off to the large old red barn. Neither really talked on the way out, but when they reached the barn door, Jake paused before going inside.

"What's this all about, Nathan? What's on your mind?"

"Robert, Robert Sanding. You remember him, don't you?"

Jake stared at Nathan with a confused look and then twisted his face in an expression of disgust. "Don't tell me you came all the way out here to talk to me about a boy who died when we were kids. I don't have time to walk down that road again. Now if you don't mind, I'd like to get on with my work." Jake walked into the barn and started hammering on a large piece of wood.

"Jake, please, this is important to me. I just found out you were a witness from an old newspaper article I found at the Raven Inn. I was never told that you were involved in anyway. Maybe I was too young to pay attention to what the newspaper had to say, but I need to ask you what you remember about what you saw?"

"Nathan, there's nothing to tell. I don't see the point in rehashing this over again. The police were told what I saw and it was of no use to them at the time, so why would it be of any use today?"

"I know this seems like a waste of time to you Jake, but if you could just indulge me for a moment. Try to remember exactly what you saw on that day. You see, I can't remember much about it at all, and it would be helpful to me to hear it from someone else. Maybe it will trigger something in me that will allow me to recall something that's locked away in my brain."

"This is useless. I don't have anything to tell. Why are you pestering me with this now after all this time? Can't you just let it be?"

Nathan was beginning to wonder if he would ever get Jake to talk to him. If only he could convince him how desperately he needed to learn whatever information he could, no matter how small. He decided to try again to pry into Jake's memory.

"Did Dan ever hire that private investigator to look into his son's death?" asked Nathan.

"No, he decided not to do it. He said he couldn't see that it would do any good."

"But he seemed so determined to do it. What made him change his mind?"

"I just told you, he didn't think it would do much good. Besides, him and his wife don't have lots of money and they just decided not to go through with it. They needed the money for so many other things. It just wasn't practical. It would have been a waste of time."

"What makes you so sure?"

"I just do, all right? You're a nosey 'cuss aren't you? What gives you the right to go prying in other people's business anyway?"

"Because I think, I was with Robert when he died, but I can't remember anything about it. I also saw Dan's son when they found him, and maybe there's some connection between the two incidents."

"There's no connection. I just happened to have seen something a long time ago that turned out to be useless to the police and that's all. Todd's death had nothing to do with that."

"What did you see that day Jake? Please, try to remember. I have to know."

Jake stopped working and went over and sat down on a workbench. He pulled off his hat and dangled it in his hands as he rested his elbows on his knees. Nathan came over and sat down across from him on an old wooden crate, waiting to hear any bit of information he could.

"I didn't see much at all that day, really. I remember playing outside near the woods, and it was getting dark. I didn't feel much like going inside, so I stayed outside for a while longer. I was just hitting an old tin can I'd found with a big stick, you know, knocking it around like a golf ball or something. The can rolled farther into the woods and I ran in after it. Then I hit the tin can again, this time pretty hard, and chased behind it. But I couldn't find it at first, so I just started swinging my stick in the weeds, searching for the can. While I was poking in the grass, I heard some voices, kids' voices. Naturally I was curious, so I sneaked over behind a big tree and watched them playing. One of the boys was Robert and I guess the other one must have been you."

Nathan swallowed hard as he continued to listen carefully to his story. He prepared himself to hear things that he might not want to hear.

"Then Robert ran off and called after the other boy to follow him. He was laughing and jumping over rocks. The other boy, I guess it was you, followed him. I couldn't see you, so I moved a little closer, but Robert kept running, this time along the river. It was now pretty dark and it was kind of hard to see much of anything. I decided it would be best if I headed back home. Just as I turned, I heard a muffled-like scream from one of the boys. I stopped and started to go back to see what happened, but I heard footsteps running toward me. So I ducked down behind some bushes. Then I saw a boy standing in front of me, out of breath. The boy was you. You looked scared and so I reached up and grabbed you to pull you down to where I was hiding. You fought me at first because you were so frightened, but then you thought I was your friend, Robert. I remember telling you, 'I'm not Robert,' but then you were so confused and scared that you fell backwards and ran off. I waited a while, still crouched behind the bushes. Then I ran off home like a scared rabbit. That's all I remember."

"Jake, I remember some of this. I mean, I saw some of this in a dream or something not too long ago. I didn't realize that the boy I wrestled in the bushes was you."

"It was me, but I don't see how that matters, because I can't help you with who actually killed Robert."

"Do you remember seeing anybody else out there, either before or after you heard Robert's screams?"

"No, nobody else."

"What about after I got away from you and started to run away. It seems like I remember running into somebody, a man. Do you remember seeing or hearing anything like that?"

"No, I just remember you running away and then I took off. I was just a boy. I was scared to death. I didn't hang around to see if there was anybody else out there."

"Are you sure there was nobody else there? Think Jake. Please, it's very important."

Just then Jake's wife called out that she needed him to take her to town right away. She had some things she needed to pick up. He jumped to his feet and headed for the barn door. "I'm sorry, I need to go. My wife can't drive herself. I'm sorry. I don't have anything else I can tell you." With that, he walked out the barn door and back to the house.

As Nathan followed behind him, Jake stopped and turned to face him, "I don't want to discuss this any further. I'd appreciate it if you wouldn't come around here anymore."

"Sure, Jake, I understand. Thanks for your time."

As Jake walked away, Nathan called after him, "Jake, wait! One more thing." Nathan ran to catch up to him as Jake waited impatiently.

"I told you, I have to go."

"I know, I know, but just one more thing. With what you can remember, would you say there was any way I could have killed Robert?"

Jake looked shocked at the question. He wiped his face with his handkerchief and turned shaking his head, "I didn't see who did the killing. I just saw what I told you I saw."

"Right, thanks," Nathan replied slowly.

Jake walked away back to his house and Nathan headed off to his car. He wasn't sure if his talk with Jake Foster made him feel better or worse, but he was glad he had done it. At least he knew there was someone else out there that night.

# 34

A few weeks passed and Nathan hadn't talked much about what he and Jake had discussed earlier. He decided to allow Marcie time to mourn the death of Maggie and to sort through some of her treasures. Nathan watched her every day as she roamed through the Raven Inn from room to room and from drawer to drawer, sifting through all of the things Maggie had taken the time to tuck away. They both found themselves pouring over little items that brought back so many memories, smiles and tears. Some of the things made Nathan ponder why Maggie would have even thought to keep them, but he knew she must have had some sort of reason at the time.

In the evenings, Nathan and Maggie would spend their time just sitting on the large wraparound front porch of the Raven Inn. Quietly, they remembered various things brought back by the sounds of the town, the smells of the flowers that surrounded them on the grounds, and in the beautifully shaped vases and old jars around the porch. Sometimes they shared their thoughts, but many times they just sat with their eyes closed, in each other's arms, recalling scenes that drifted in and out of their minds like ghosts. They both missed Maggie. The Raven Inn would never be the same without her, but then, so much of her was present in its rooms.

Nathan's reminiscing was once again interrupted by what Maggie had told him just before she died. Nathan wasn't sure why she would think to make sure that she told him how she felt about his leaving while she was actually dying in front of him. Yet, her reason must have been significant for her to make it her last statement to him.

"Marcie, I've been thinking a lot about our leaving this town."

"I know you have."

"It shows that much?"

"I can see it in your eyes. There's too much for you to let go of here. Maybe there is for me too. I want to go away. Sometimes I want to go as far away as I can, but then other times, like now, I want to just stay where I feel at home."

"Let's stay and run the Raven Inn, Marcie. It's such a beautiful old place, I don't think I can bear to sell it."

"Are you sure that's what you want? What about a house on the ocean? What about leaving behind some of the bad memories this place brings back to you? Are you sure, Nathan?"

"I am. You told me once before to stop running away from things that frighten me. Well, I'm going to stop now. I want to stay here and face whatever is in store for us. Besides, being here and running the Raven will keep us close to Maggie's memory. She would have wanted us to keep this place and to keep it going. It was her whole life and a big part of yours and mine. Would you be disappointed if we stayed?"

Marcie lifted her head from Nathan's shoulder and stared deep into his eyes. Nathan always felt she was searching for something deep inside of him when she stared at him that way. It was as though she could look inside of him and actually see his feelings and thoughts.

"You really do want to stay, don't you?" Marcie asked, while holding his face in her hands.

"Yes, if you'll stay with me."

"Then I'm staying."

They sat quietly for a while longer. "This is the way love is supposed to be between two people," thought Nathan. "I can't ever let this slip away. I have to hold on to it, no matter what else happens to me along the way." Nathan lifted his head toward the starry sky, "We're staying, Maggie," he thought to himself. He knew it would be difficult and that he would have to still pursue his blocked memories of Robert's death, but somehow he felt he could do that better by being close to home for now.

The night air became chilly and so they both went inside for the evening and up to bed. Even though there wasn't much more spoken between them that evening, both knew what the other was feeling and thinking. Nathan held Marcie very close to him throughout that night. Maggie's death made him realize how fragile their lives really are and so he held her tightly, as though it could somehow keep anything that had a mind to, from taking her away from him.

# 35

The next few months were spent fixing up and repairing the inn where it was needed. Nathan enjoyed the work, and put everything that he had into the labor. He always took pride in the fact that he was a pretty decent carpenter and handy man and was glad to have the projects to put his skills to work. He realized he was neglecting his writing more these days, but working at the inn allowed them more time together and that was very important to him right now. He would try to carve out a time for his writing later.

Marcie was looking happier every day. Nathan could see that it was a good decision to stay in town and keep her close to the Raven and to Maggie's belongings. She really seemed to enjoy running the place, but sometimes Nathan would catch her with tears in her eyes, lingering over an old photograph, or something that Maggie had jotted down on an old piece of paper and hid away in a drawer. Nathan would drape his arm over her shoulder and kiss her on the cheek and wipe away her tears with his fingers. Sometimes he would pull her away to see a finished project of his, just to get her mind off of Maggie for a while. They each had their hard moments, but there were many good moments as well, and it was for these times that Nathan was most thankful.

Early the next morning, Nathan and Marcie were awakened by a loud knock on the front door.

"Who in the world would be knocking this hour?" moaned Marcie, half awake.

"I don't know, but I best go see who it is before they wake up the whole house," said Nathan climbing out of bed and grabbing for his sweat pants and t-shirt. The pounding continued as he clumsily made his way down the stairs to the door. "All right, hold on. I'm coming!"

Nathan pulled open the door and there stood Mark and his deputy, Jerry. "Mark, what in the world are you doing banging on the door this early? Are you out of coffee or something?" Nathan said sarcastically, but he noticed that Mark wasn't smiling. "Well, come on in and let me close the door. What's this all about?"

"Nathan," Marked said slowly, while looking down at a bag he held in his hands. "You're under arrest."

"What? Stop joking around, man. It's too early. Come on in the kitchen and I'll get you guys a cup of coffee. I have to start some anyway."

"I'm not joking," Mark replied, as Nathan started for the kitchen. "I've come to arrest you."

Nathan stopped and turned around. "What are you talking about? Are you crazy? Arrest me for what?"

"For the murder of Todd Harper."

Nathan was shocked and didn't know just what to do or say. He grabbed for a nearby chair and sat down quickly. "I'm being arrested for Todd Harper's murder? Mark, why on earth would you arrest me? Based on what?"

"Based on a bag we found on Marcie's grounds, in her barn. It has a shirt that I believe belongs to you and a rubber mask in it. Do you recognize this?" Mark opened the bag in front of Nathan, who fell back in his chair at the sight of it.

"This is crazy. How do you know this belongs to me?"

"It has your initials inside the lining of the bag. Are you saying it doesn't belong to you?"

Nathan didn't answer. He just sat with tears filling in his eyes. "Mark, I—"

"You're not taking him anywhere!" Marcie screamed from the stairs. "What right do you have to be on my property, Mark? You can't just walk out there and start looking around anytime you please."

"We had a search warrant, Marcie. We had a right to look around."

"How dare you barge in here and upset us with this nonsense. You're not taking Nathan anywhere. Now just get out of here."

"Marcie, we have to take him. I can't just ignore this evidence. Now, I know this is hard for you, because it's hard for me too. I don't want to do this, but I don't have a choice right now. I have to take him in. At the hearing you can come down and see if the judge will allow you to post bail for him, but for now, he has to come with me."

Nathan was numb. He was aware that he couldn't feel his hands or arms as they handcuffed him and led him out of the inn. His mind was racing but his thoughts weren't clear. He could see the bag dangling from Mark's hand as they walked out to the car. As he looked up, the guests were staring in shock from their windows, as they placed him in the car. Marcie stood on the porch and screamed at the top of her lungs. Mark's deputy held on to her to keep her away from the car.

Nathan held his head down, not believing the nightmare that surrounded him. As they drove away, he didn't think he would ever be able to forgive himself for all of the pain he had put Marcie through. Just the night before they had been sitting peacefully on that same porch. Today she was being held against her will while they were being ripped apart.

"Nathan, you don't know how hard this is for me," said Mark, as he drove him back to his office. "I'm really sorry it has to be this way."

Nathan didn't answer. He didn't have the words to express how he felt. As they drove on, he could see the river racing by and heading through the woods. People were waking up and walking outside to their cars to go to work or to bring in the newspaper. They were oblivious to the car racing past carrying an accused suspect in a murder case. "What if I am guilty?" thought Nathan. "Maybe I am and deserve to be punished." He closed his eyes and tried to quiet the rage going on inside of him.

As they pulled up outside the office, Mark opened the door for Nathan and escorted him inside without saying a word, still carrying the bag in his hand. He led Nathan to a chair in front of his desk and pushed on his shoulder for him to sit down. Nathan sat in front of him while Mark scribbled on forms and various papers. He then pulled out a fingerprint set and proceeded, very methodically, to take Nathan's prints. After wiping the ink from his fingers, Mark led him to a holding cell. Before he closed the iron door behind him, he tapped Nathan on the shoulder.

"Do you have a lawyer you want me to call for you?"

"I don't know one from around here," Nathan answered quietly.

"I'll get one for you then."

"Wait, in my wallet, there's a card for Douglas Chase. Can I call him? I used him as my lawyer before I came here."

"Sure." Mark handed Nathan a phone and closed the cell door behind him and left him alone to make the call.

Nathan sat on the small cot and stared down at the phone. As he slowly dialed the number he could feel his stomach churning, as though it was rebelling against something. The line on the other end rang several times and then Nathan heard Doug's voice, "Hello, you've reached Douglas Chase and Associates. I'm not able to come to the phone right now, but if you leave your name, phone number and a brief message, I'll get back to you as soon as possible. Thanks." As the beep sounded for Nathan to leave a message, he struggled with his words. "Hi, Doug, this is Nathan Staby. I know we haven't talked for a long time, but I need your help. I've been arrested," Nathan's voice broke for a moment. He paused and started again, "I'm back home in Fairhaven. Please, call me as soon as you get in at," Nathan paused again as he searched for the number on the phone, "555-9692."

Nathan sat the phone down on the floor and lay back on his cot. His stomach was still churning and his head felt like it was about to explode. All he could think about was Marcie. "She must be going out of her mind right now," he thought. He tried to remember exactly what it was that brought him back to Fairhaven in the first place. Maybe it was the truth he'd been searching for. Maybe he knew he was guilty and came back to face up to his crime, or was it just his longing for Marcie that drove him to return.

A couple of hours later Mark came to the cell door. "I think your lawyer is on the phone. You can use the one I left in your cell to talk to him."

Nathan blinked slowly and looked around the cell. He had fallen asleep and had forgotten for a moment where he was and what had happened to him. He reached down to the floor and picked up the phone, "Hello, this is Nathan Staby. Is this Doug?"

"Yeah, Nathan, what's going on there? You said something on your message about being arrested. Have you been jaywalking in that little town?"

"Doug, listen to me. I've been arrested for the murder of a little boy. I need you to come here as soon as possible to help straighten this mess out. Can you come?"

There was silence on the other end of the phone. Finally, Doug's voice came back on the line, "Did you say murder? Nathan, what's happening there? Are you serious?"

"Yes, very serious. Can you come? I need you right away, please."

"Well, you know I'm not a criminal lawyer, Nathan. I handle legal and financial affairs. You need an expert in criminal justice. I'm not your man."

"You're the only person I know to call, Doug. Please, just come for now. Maybe we can work out something when you get here. Just come, all right?"

Doug could hear the strain in Nathan's voice.

"Uh, yeah, sure, I'll try to be there this afternoon. Don't talk to anyone or answer any questions until I get there, all right?"

"Yeah, I won't talk to anybody. Just get here right away." Nathan's voice trailed off as he hung up the phone in a daze. He couldn't believe he was talking to a lawyer about defending him for murder. He felt numb, yet his insides were trembling like jell-o.

"All done?" Mark asked from the cell door.

"Yeah, I'm done."

Mark opened the door and picked up the telephone from the cell. He stopped as he straightened back up and his eyes met Nathan's. They locked into a brief stare as each was trying to tell what the other was thinking at that moment. "Do you want to talk, Nathan?" asked Mark.

"My lawyer says I shouldn't say anything until he gets here. I'll talk when he arrives." Nathan looked up at Mark and tried to see the friend he had once known instead of the sheriff standing in front of him. But it was as if his friend had disappeared and this stranger was left in his place. Nathan didn't want to talk to him or anyone else right now, except Marcie.

"Suit yourself. I'm here if you change your mind. You'll go before the judge tomorrow and he'll decide whether or not to set bail. If he does, then I'm sure Marcie will post it for you and you'll probably be back home with her in no time. But you'll have to stay in town to stand trial."

Nathan didn't respond, except to nod his head that he understood. It was becoming such an effort for him to even speak. He felt tired and his energy was completely exhausted. Everything felt like an effort to him. He put his head back against the wall and closed his eyes again, waiting for the next event to occur. Mark quietly closed the cell door behind him and left Nathan on his own.

# 36

That afternoon, Doug Chase arrived in Mark's office to see Nathan. Mark took him back to Nathan's small cell and left them to discuss their strategy. Nathan hadn't talked with Doug in a long time. He had handled some legal papers for him associated with his books and a few other small things, but this was overwhelming for both of them. They didn't know exactly where to begin. Nathan looked pale and weak and Doug looked nervous and uncertain. The two made a weary pair.

"Well, Nathan," said Doug taking various papers out of his briefcase and a legal pad to write on. "I understand you got married since I last saw you. Who's the lucky girl?" As the words left his mouth, Doug felt he could have better phrased that line.

"I'm not sure she's so lucky anymore. Her name is Marcie Sanding. Well actually, her last name is Staby now. We grew up together here in Fairhaven. I married my childhood sweetheart."

"How in the world did you end up in here charged with murder for heaven's sake? I can't even imagine you being charged with anything. What happened? Suppose we just start from the beginning and you tell me what led up to you landing in jail. First, what's the boy's name that you're accused of killing?"

"His name is Todd Harper. He was found murdered shortly after my arrival here in town. I went with Mark, he's the sheriff, to examine the body."

"Did you know the boy?"

"No, I'd never seen him before that day."

"Did you know his parents?"

"Actually, no, I only met them after the murder. The father's probably around my age. He may be a little older. I also met Jake Foster, who I recently found out was a witness to Robert's death, or at least, he was in the woods that same day."

"I'm not sure I understand. This Jake fellow witnessed the death of another boy? Were you involved in that case?"

"That's a long story. I was with Robert when he was killed, but I've never been able to remember everything about that day. I just found out recently that Jake witnessed part of that scene, and so I went to talk to him, hoping it would jar loose some of my buried memories."

"Would there be any reason for anyone to suspect you in Todd Harper's death?"

"I don't know, but while I was talking to Jake, I asked him if he thought I killed Robert Sanding. Maybe, since I asked that question, he thought I could have something to do with Todd's death, but I'm not sure."

"What evidence do they have against you?"

"Mark found a bag that belonged to me out in Marcie's barn. The bag had one of my shirts in it, covered with blood and a rubber mask."

Doug paused for a moment while he jotted down notes on his legal pad. He was thinking to himself while he was writing, the more he heard, the guiltier Nathan sounded. But he was going to hold his judgment until later. He was here to defend Nathan and he had to get as many of the facts ironed out as he could, as quickly as possible.

"Where's the bag now? Does Mark have it?"

"I suppose he has it locked up some place."

"I'll take a look at it before I leave. Do you remember where you were on the day Todd Harper was killed and what you were doing?"

"I was actually with Mark on the day the body was discovered. We had lunch and then I went back to his office with him."

"Boy, what an alibi. You were with the sheriff. You can't do better than that."

"Well, I was with him when they discovered the body, but they determined that he was killed early that morning. I was at the Raven Inn, in my room alone at that time, sleeping."

"You say this bag that was found was on your wife's property?"

"Yes, she had been in an accident and so I stayed with her for a few months to help her get on her feet again."

"So you were actually living on the property for a while?"

Nathan smiled slightly, "It seems no matter what I say it sounds bad, right?"

"It sure seems to be stacked against you, Nathan. Look, like I said, I'm not a criminal lawyer and that's what you need right now and you need the best. I can go with you to sit before the judge tomorrow for your bail hearing, but then we need to get Steven in here. That's Steven Massie, the best criminal lawyer around these parts. I'll give him a call this evening and see what I can arrange."

"Will you stay as well?"

"Nathan, you won't need me with Steven. He has his own staff he works with. We'd be bumping heads and I'd only be in the way."

"Please, I need someone around that I know right now. I would feel more comfortable. Can't I hire both of you?"

"Yes, I mean, sure you can, but it's not necessary."

"Do you believe I killed Todd Harper?"

Doug didn't answer right away, but then he came over and sat right beside Nathan. "No, I don't believe you're capable. But then, I don't know you all that well. Look, I'm a pretty good judge of character and I don't think you have it in you to do such a thing, especially to a boy. Doug stood up to leave the cell. "We'll talk again tonight. I'll call you and let you know about Steven Massie. Until then, just stay as calm as you can. You may be out tomorrow, if we can get the judge to set bail, but don't count too much on that. He may deem it too big a risk to let someone accused of murdering a boy back out on the streets on bail. He may think it's too risky that you might try to leave town as well. We'll have to wait and see what happens. I'll do my best to get you out tomorrow."

Nathan stood and walked over to Doug and awkwardly stuck out his hand. Doug grabbed his hand tightly, "It's going to be all right. I'll talk to you tonight."

Nathan stepped back and watched Doug walk through the cell door and out of sight. Mark shut the door behind him, and Nathan was alone in his cell once again. He backed up and sat back down on his cot. Life seemed to be moving so quickly right in front of him. It was as though everything had speeded up and all of the scenes were racing in front of him in a blur. He couldn't make sense of anything anymore. The big time writer from the city had been captured by the dragon of his childhood and locked away.

# 37

The next day finally arrived after a restless, and what seemed like, an endless night. Nathan found himself sitting in the old courthouse that he had admired many times from the outside as a boy and as a man. He never really thought about what went on inside of the building. Only that it's magnificent structure and architecture was mesmerizing to the eye. Now that he sat inside of its walls as a charged criminal, he tended to look past the decor and the detailed trim surrounding the walls and instead focused on the eyes of the people in the room. He was trying to read whether or not they thought he could possibly be guilty of such a terrible crime.

As he glanced around the room, he saw Marcie enter the doors. She stopped, looked around and then proceeded to a chair close to the front. As his eyes caught hers, time seemed to slow down for a minute and then pause. He could tell she'd been crying and he wanted to go and comfort her and tell her that everything was going to be all right, but he couldn't do that now. Even if he could, he couldn't promise anything would be all right from here on out. He still wanted to put his arms around her though, even if it was just for a brief moment. He felt he could draw such strength from her touch, but even though the distance between them was short, it might as well have been a thousand miles. She smiled at him briefly and then her face seemed to snap back to the worried expression she was wearing when she came in. Nathan waved his hand slightly, not wanting to draw a lot of attention. Doug Chase, who was sitting beside him, turned to see who he was waving to, and then turned back around and continued to scribble on his pad.

As the judge entered the room, everyone stood until he was seated. Nathan felt like he was in a fog and all he could hear was the Black River rushing by him. The sound seemed to grow louder and louder as he stood there as still as he possibly could manage. He almost felt that, if he stood still and quiet long enough, this would all pass away from him. Then he could just slip out with Marcie and they would be free to go their way.

He could almost feel a cool breeze blowing off of the river rushing by him in his mind. Without realizing it, he closed his eyes and there he was, standing on the banks of the Black River, as it wound its way through trees and over rocks. The sun was shining brightly and he had to squint to see across to the other side. There, on a rock, stood Robert, waving and smiling at him. Nathan looked for a way to cross over to sit with him, but the river was too wide, so he just stood and waved back. Nathan felt so close to him. He never realized how much he missed him and how much he loved him as a friend. They had shared so many long talks, laughter and even tears. As Robert smiled back at him, he realized that he could never, ever harm him. He couldn't even imagine hurting Robert in any fashion. For the first time in his conscience, he felt certain that he could not have killed Robert or Todd Harper. As he stood and watched Robert jump from the rock and run along side the hurried waters of the river, he heard a voice calling his name.

"Nathan, can you hear me? Nathan, are you okay?"

As he opened his eyes, he could see that Doug was staring at him with a concerned look on his face, pointing toward the judge at the front of the courtroom. Nathan's eyes turned and rested on the judge's face as he repeated his question once again,

"How do you plead, guilty or not guilty?"

Nathan paused, closing his eyes again for just a second, to see Robert once more, running along side the river.

"Not guilty, Your Honor," Nathan replied.

The judge decided to set bail for Nathan, based on the fact that there were no previous charges against him and that he had, an otherwise, clean record. Marcie happily posted the bail quickly and another date was set for him to reappear in court.

Doug was talking to him as they left the courtroom, but Nathan couldn't hear a word he was saying. He could only see Marcie's face coming toward him. When she was close enough for him to reach her, he grabbed her in his arms and pulled her to him as tightly as he could. The two of them just stood in the center of the room and held each other for a few minutes, as others passed them, on their way to their other affairs of the day. Doug tapped him on the shoulder and motioned for both of them to follow him outside.

As they reached Marcie's car, Doug took Nathan's arm and pulled him aside, "This doesn't mean you're a free man you know. It just means you don't have to stay in jail while you're waiting for your trial. We still have a lot of work to do before that time and we only have a short period of time to do it."

"I know that, Doug. I'm just so happy to be back with Marcie again. I guess I wasn't listening. I know we have a lot to do. When do we start?"

"You go back to Marcie's house with her and stay put. Let somebody else run the inn for a while, or close it down, or whatever you have to do. I'm going to be meeting Steven Massie in about an hour and we'll drive over to talk with you then."

"Okay, I'll see you in an hour or so." Nathan started to get into Marcie's car, but as he opened the door he saw Mark standing on the courthouse steps talking to Dan Harper. They both looked over in Nathan's direction and then walked the opposite way to Mark's car. He watched as they drove away together.

"Nathan, come on, get in. Let's go home," said Marcie from inside the car.

He got inside and slammed the door behind him, taking Marcie's face in his hands, and kissing her as he had dreamed of doing the night before. "I wasn't sure that I'd get to do that again anytime soon," he said with a big smile.

Marcie stared into Nathan's eyes, "You look so tired, babe. Let's go home and I'll fix you something to eat. You need to get some rest."

"Doug and Steven are coming over in about an hour, so I'd better stay awake. They're going to go over some things about the case with me."

"You need to rest first. You look like you're going to just pass out any minute. They can allow you some time for that, can't they?"

"Marcie, it's very important that we get started right away. Almost everything points to me as Todd's killer. We've got to prove otherwise."

"You sound more confident that it wasn't you. Did you remember something else?"

"No, not really. I just keep seeing Robert's face and I know in my heart, I could never have killed him." Nathan looked out of the window at the scenery, "I loved him. I would never have hurt him, never."

"I believe you. I'm just glad to hear that you believe it too."

As they arrived at the house, Marcie went straight in and ran a hot bath for Nathan. "Rest in a hot tub for a minute at least, before they get here, and then I'll fix you something to eat."

Nathan welcomed the sight of a hot bath and quickly lowered himself into the sudsy water and laid his head back. It was as though his life had become a series of brief resting periods in between explosions of tension and confusion. He cherished the quiet time he had right now and for a second, drifted off to sleep. Suddenly he felt the gentle massaging of shampoo through his hair. He put his hand up and touched Marcie's face. She bent down and kissed him and then continued running her hands through his hair. As he closed his eyes, she poured cups of warm water over his head. She gently wiped away the water from his face and eyes. She then sat beside the tub and gently squeezed a soapy sponge over his chest and arms. With a slow and gentle motion, she rubbed the sponge all over him. Nathan could see tears in her eyes as she took his hands in hers and washed them gently, taking the time to lay them against her face. But then she broke down and started to cry. Nathan leaned forward and pulled her to him and tried to comfort her. They held on to one another, rocking back and forth, with soap and water mixing with their tears. Marcie's cry was so deep that Nathan couldn't actually hear her, but he could feel her shaking in his arms. As the food she had prepared grew cold in the kitchen and as the lawyers were driving to their house, they held each other as long as they could. She later wrapped his robe around him and they lay across the bed in each other's arms, still and shielded from the world outside.

# 38

When Doug and Steven arrived, Marcie held Nathan even tighter, wondering whether it would always be this way, having to steal away moments together. Would they ever be free of it all? Marcie got up and laid some clothes out on the bed for him. "You'd better go ahead and get dressed. I'll let them in. Take your time." She left the room and closed the door behind her. Nathan just lay still on the bed for a moment, hoping to escape this never-ending nightmare. He wanted to lie there forever. He didn't move, but pulled his robe tightly around him. Nathan knew he could not make time stand still. He slowly pulled himself up and got dressed. Leaning near the window, he stared out over the landscape and the breathtaking view below. In a way, he wished Maggie were here to give him some of her homespun advice with her lighthearted ways. There was something that she wanted to share with him, but just couldn't. Why hadn't she taken the time to tell her secret? As he stood a while longer, Marcie opened the door to the room, "Are you ready?" she asked quietly.

"Yes, I guess I am," he answered. Together they left the room and the beautiful view to go downstairs, each holding on to the other one. As they shut the door behind them, they felt as though they were opening another, but they were uncertain where this one would lead them.

Doug introduced Steven Massie to Nathan as the best criminal lawyer that money could buy. Nathan was willing to pay for the best to try and sort through all of the legal mumbo jumbo he had heard since he'd been arrested. Nathan liked Steven and felt comfortable with him. As they sat down to talk, Marcie insisted that Nathan eat something decent. So she served them all sandwiches and hot tea. Then finally, she took a seat beside Nathan. Steven began asking questions to better understand the charges. When he got to the questions concerning the bag, Nathan wasn't much help.

"I know the bag is mine, because I brought it with me on this trip and I also took it with me to Marcie's house while I stayed with her during her accident. But I don't know how my shirt with blood stains or the rubber mask got into the bag or how the bag got stashed in Marcie's barn."

"Could someone else have had access to the bag to place it there?" Steven asked.

"I don't see how. Only Marcie, Maggie and I were staying here at the time. There was no one else around."

"Maggie, who's she?"

"That was Marcie's Mother. She died recently."

"Oh, how did she die?"

"Well, it was a heart attack we were told," replied Marcie.

"What do you mean, that's what you were told? Don't you believe she died from a heart attack?"

"Yes, I mean, that's what the doctor told us," answered Nathan. "But we had no idea that she had any problems with her heart. It was just so sudden. She was always healthy and active. I guess it was just too hard for us to accept that she just gave out. Just before she died, she was trying to tell me something, but she couldn't breathe well and was really struggling to get the words out. I was able to make out that she wanted me to promise her that I would stay in Fairhaven and not try to leave to go back to the city."

"So that's why you changed your mind and wanted to stay here," said Marcie with a surprised look on her face.

"That wasn't the only reason, but that was part of it. I really felt like Maggie knew something she wanted me to find out, and the only way that could happen was for me to stay here in town."

"So you were planning on moving before that?" asked Steven.

"Yes, that was our plan, but then Maggie died and everything changed. So we decided to stay and run the Raven Inn together."

"Then you were arrested?"

"Right."

"Did you kill Todd Harper, Nathan?" Steven asked, leaning back in his chair with his pencil in his mouth.

Nathan was surprised by the question at first, but then he answered, "No, I did not kill him. I had no reason to do it. All they have is my bag as evidence."

"With a blood-covered shirt and a rubber mask," added Steven. "Would you be willing to take a lie detector's test for me?"

"I don't think that's necessary. Why should he?" asked Marcie.

"He needs to do it for me, so I can prepare my case," replied Steven. He leaned forward, "I want to believe you, but it's my job to defend you to the best of my ability. Now in order to do that, I have to have the truth."

"I'm telling you the truth," said Nathan. "I'm telling you everything I know to tell you."

"I'm not doubting you, Nathan. It's normal procedure for your lawyer to ask for a polygraph test. It's not admissible in court as evidence, but I'd like to have it for your case, nonetheless."

"That's just crazy, he—" Marcie started.

"I'll take it," Nathan interrupted. "I'm not afraid to take the test."

"Good, I'll set it up for you then," replied Steven.

"Now, what's the significance of the rubber mask that was found in the bag? Why would that be linked to you in any way?"

"When I was a boy, a close friend of mine, Robert was killed, much in the same manner as Todd Harper. I was with him when he was killed, but I still to this day don't remember much about what happened. But I have dreams about it and I sometimes see an old man with white hair in those dreams. He's always there. I saw him again when we found Todd's body in the woods. The rubber mask resembles the old man I saw."

"You saw an old man walking around in the woods after Todd was killed?"

"Well, I don't know if I actually saw him. Todd's death brought back a lot of memories and right after we examined Todd's body, I thought I could hear Robert calling me. So I followed him through the woods. Then I didn't see him anymore. But I saw the old man at the foot of a waterfall, waving up at me."

Doug and Steven looked at each other while Steven unconsciously tapped his pencil on the legal pad. "You saw a dead kid running around in the woods after you found Todd's body and then you saw an old man waving up at you?" Steven looked down at his feet, "I don't think we want to use this material."

"I know it sounds crazy, but I know I didn't actually see Robert or the old man. It's just that some things bring back pieces of the puzzle from that day, and it just plays in my mind. At the time though, it seems very real. Anyway, what I'm saying is, I think there's a connection between Robert's death and Todd's and maybe that's why the memories come flooding back, only they come in bits and pieces."

"Have you ever told anyone else about this old man that you say you've seen, or dreamed about?"

"Marcie and Dr. Seyler, my psychiatrist."

Steven smiled at Doug, who shrugged his shoulders, as if to say, he wasn't aware of any of this either.

"Yes, I went to see Dr. Seyler to see if he could help me after I was found asleep under a tree in the backyard of the Raven Inn. I had been, what Dr. Seyler calls, sleepwalking, all night supposedly, and acting out a dream I was having about Robert's death. Don't you see? It keeps playing over and over in my mind because I can't see everything clearly? When I go to sleep, or sometimes even if I close my eyes for a moment, that day runs through my thoughts."

"Is that what happened to you in court today?" asked Doug. "When the judge had to keep repeating his question to you? You looked like you were miles away and your eyes were closed."

"Yes, I could see Robert running. He's always running along the river. I could see him as clearly as I see you. At first, when they found the bag in Marcie's barn, I thought that maybe I could have been the one that killed Todd and that's why I couldn't remember anything. Maybe it was too horrible for me to recall. And if I killed Todd, then maybe I could have been the one that killed Robert as well."

"Who else have you told about the old man?" asked Steven with a very curious look on his face.

"No one else. Marcie actually saw him once herself."

"You saw the old man, Marcie?"

"When I was in my accident. I was trapped in the car and someone came and looked inside at me. I could see his face when he accidentally dropped his flashlight. He was an old-looking man with very white hair. He looked like the mask that was found, only it didn't look so much like a mask that night when I saw him."

"Who finally rescued you from the car?"

"Nathan found me," she answered.

"Nathan found you? Was it right after you saw the old man's face?"

"I don't know, I kept blacking out. I'm not sure. I didn't even remember seeing him, until later, in the hospital." Marcie held Nathan's arm tightly in hers.

"What does your doctor say about all of this, Nathan?"

"He says I'm suffering from Post-traumatic Stress Disorder or something like that."

"Would you give me permission to discuss your case with Dr. Seyler and to ask him questions about your condition?"

"I guess so, if it would help you."

"It might not, but I'd like to try and understand as much as I can about his diagnosis."

"Marcie, had you ever seen the bag before the sheriff found it in the barn?"

"Yes, Nathan found it earlier and when he opened the bag its contents frightened him so much that it caused him to pass out in the barn. We had to take him to the hospital and he was unconscious for a long time."

"So you two found the bag, even before the sheriff found it?"

"Yes, but because we had to take Nathan to the hospital, I just stuck it back in the barn, out of sight."

"But you didn't tell anyone about it?"

"No, I know I should have, but I was afraid that they would arrest Nathan and I don't believe that he's guilty. He would never hurt anyone."

"I'm surprised you didn't go back and try to hide the bag or destroy it so that it couldn't be used as evidence," Steven said, shaking his head.

"Actually I did hide it. Later I went back for it, but the bag was already gone. I don't believe that Mark found the bag when he said he did. I think someone took it, knowing that I would try to destroy it."

"Wait a minute, slow down. You're saying that you went back to hide the bag and it was gone? Are you sure? Who else would have known that the bag was there?"

"I don't know, but someone knew because they planted it there."

"You believe someone is trying to frame Nathan for Todd's murder?"

"Yes, but I don't have a clue about who would want to do such a thing. Someone wants Nathan to be blamed for these deaths to clear themselves."

"This is really crazy stuff you're telling me here. You know that, don't you? I mean, all of the evidence points to Nathan. It's his bag, his shirt and there's the rubber mask that only Nathan has talked about with you. I mean, look at it. He's running in the woods, chasing dreams and visions. This doesn't sound very good guys."

"Are you saying you won't take the case?" asked Nathan, standing to his feet. "If that's the bottom line, then you can just leave and Doug will handle the case for me."

"Now wait a minute, Nathan," said Doug. "You need more than what I'm able to—"

"I didn't say I wasn't taking the case," replied Steven. "I'm just saying that everything seems stacked against you. "However, I also know that everything is not always as it appears. Maybe someone is playing a game with you, but this is not going to be easy to prove." Steven paused for a moment. "No, I'll take the case, if you'll pay the bill." Steven said, smiling at Nathan as he put his hand out to close the deal.

Nathan smiled back and shook his hand. "Thanks, Steven."

"Don't thank me yet. Wait until the trial is over and we'll see which side of the bars you're standing on. But let me say this, I don't go down easy." Steven laughed and pulled out a big cigar and started to light it. "You don't mind if I smoke, do you?"

"Yes!" they all three replied at the same time.

Nathan led Steven out to the front porch so he could light up and they talked a while longer. Doug touched Marcie's arm and pointed to Steven, "Don't worry. He's the best."

"You'd better be right, Doug, because the man he's defending is also the best." She walked out to the porch where they were standing, put her arm around Nathan's waist and leaned against him.

# 39

The next morning Steven decided to take Doug along for a visit to Dr. Scott Seyler. He wasn't clear about some of the things Nathan had tried to explain about his condition. He was hoping the doctor could shed some light on the subject by answering some general questions.

"Good morning, Dr. Seyler. We appreciate you seeing us on such short notice, but it is rather urgent that we speak to you," said Steven.

The doctor invited them to have a seat in his office.

"Not at all. I'm glad to be of assistance to you, but I'm not going to be able to discuss the specifics of Nathan's visits here with me. That's confidential, as you know."

"Yes, I'm aware of that, but I did ask Nathan if it would be all right to speak to you. He knows I'm here. I understand your answers must be general in nature. So I'll try to keep my questions simple."

"What would like to know?" asked the doctor.

"As you know, I'm Nathan's defense attorney for his trial regarding the death of Todd Harper. Are you familiar with that case?"

"I'd have to be deaf, dumb and blind not to be aware of it in a small town like this. It's the news on everyone's lips these days," replied Doctor Seyler.

"Right, well, I need to try to understand Nathan's condition, this post-traumatic, something or other."

"Post-traumatic Stress Disorder is the proper term."

"Yes, that's it. Can you tell me a little something about this disorder? For instance, what are some of the symptoms?"

"Well in general terms, the person suffering from such a disorder may have recurring recollections of a traumatic event that happened in their life or recurring distressing dreams in which the event is played out in their mind. It's as though it's happening all over again. The person may even act out the events, behaving as though they are actually experiencing the trauma. These experiences could last anywhere from a few seconds, hours or even days. The person may have trouble falling asleep, or staying asleep. They may avoid thoughts, feelings, or any other reminders of the traumatic event."

"What kind of trauma could bring on this type of disorder in a person?"

"It could be any number of things, such as experiencing a personal violent assault of some sort, or for instance, if a person was taken as a prisoner of war and suffered torture and great fear. Witnessing a violent death of another person or unexpectedly finding a dead body or body parts could also bring it on. Whatever the event, it is something that causes the person grave fear and a feeling of helplessness, especially if such an experience occurs in a child."

"So you're saying that if someone experienced one of these terrible events in their life, they could actually keep reliving it over and over again?"

"Yes, that's right."

"Would the person have any blocked memories of the traumatic experience? I mean to say, would they suffer some sort of amnesia attack on their memory?"

"Well, yes, the person could suffer a type of amnesia in that they avoid anything associated with the event that triggered the disorder. Therefore, they have actually managed to block it from their memory. They may be able to see only bits and pieces of the experience with the horrible, or important parts blocked out."

"How would you treat such a person?"

"By having them come in for counseling and hopefully, after some time, and a lot of talking, the person will be able to remember or recognize what's causing the symptoms in their life. They need to realize it is an experience that they need to let go of or resolve as something that happened in the past and is no longer a part of their life. I try to find out what part of the experience is causing the most fear and anxiety. I try to help them remember." The doctor leaned forward in his chair. "This type of counseling can take quite a long time before you see any results. It just depends on the person."

"Could a person suffering from this Post-traumatic Stress Disorder, as you call it, actually harm someone else if they were going through one of these dreams or reliving the event and playing out the part again?"

"It's possible, I guess, yes. A person who's experiencing the event through a dream feels their experience is real, you see. So they aren't aware of reality. They are only acting out something that happened to them. So it's possible they could, unknowingly, do harm to someone else, or even to themselves for that matter, and perhaps not even remember what they've done."

"I see. Well, this has been very helpful, doctor," said Steven, scribbling on his notepad.

"I'm sorry, but um, I do have patients waiting to see me at this point. Would you mind if we continued this discussion another time perhaps?"

"Certainly, doctor. We understand. Thank you again for your help. Do you have a card I could have in case I need to get in touch with you again?" asked Steven.

The doctor handed him a business card and stood up to walk them out of the office.

"Would you be available if I needed your expert testimony in court about the things we discussed here today, Dr. Seyler?"

"Well, um, of course. I'd be glad to offer any help I can."

"Again, thank you doctor for your time. I'll be in touch with you later. Goodbye."

"Goodbye," replied Doctor Seyler, as he closed the door behind him.

Steven and Doug stepped outside and Steven immediately lit up a cigar. He took a long puff from it and held his head back and looked up at the sun.

"This is going to be a tough case, Doug. I don't like the way it's adding up."

"Yeah, I know what you mean. How are we going to prove that he didn't just crack up and kill Todd Harper while he was under the influence of one of his wild dreams?"

"We've definitely got our work cut out for us. Who's next for us to talk to on the list?"

"Dan Harper's next in line."

"Let's go and pay him a visit then, but first, how about you and I stopping in over at Jordan's and having a bite to eat. I skipped breakfast this morning and I could use some food before we head off to another interview. Is that all right with you?" Steven asked, walking toward Jordan's.

"Well, I guess so. I had breakfast, but I could use something to drink."

"Good, let's go then. Doesn't the sheriff like to eat in Jordan's too?"

"I don't know. Does he?"

"Yes, last night I believe Nathan mentioned that it was one of his favorite hangouts. Maybe we'll get lucky and run into him."

"Why not just go to his office if you want to talk to him?"

"No, I like to talk to people where they feel the most comfortable. You know, where they're most likely to let their guard down a bit. When they're sitting in their office behind some big desk, they're reminded too much about the role they're playing and so they act out their part really well. They're not likely to slip up or say something unexpected. But when they're relaxed and unwinding, then they might just talk about anything. They forget they're the sheriff, or a doctor, for a moment. They're just themselves and they let their guard fall for a minute. It's in those conversations that you find out the things you most want to know."

"You know, I'm starting to be very impressed with you."

"Stick with me, kid. You ain't seen nothing yet."

Steven and Doug walked over to Jordan's and took a seat at the counter. While they were going over the menu, Gracey, Mark's wife, walked in the door.

"Harvey, have you seen Mark today? I've been looking all over for him. I called his office, but no one seems to be able to find him," she said, as she plopped herself down on one of the bar stools at the counter. Steven's attention turned toward her as she spoke. The strong overpowering scent from her perfume made him want to slide down a few more seats away from her, but instead he stayed planted close by. He grabbed Doug's arm as tried to fan the scent away from him. Steven motioned for him to stop, even though tears were starting to form in Doug's eyes from the unpleasant fragrance surrounding them both.

"Pardon me," said Steven in his most polite tone, "but what is that lovely scent you're wearing? Forgive me for being so bold as to ask, but I must know the name of that scent so that I can get it for my wife. Would you mind sharing its name?"

Doug looked at him like he was out of his mind, but Steven kicked him under the counter to keep him quiet. Doug rubbed his leg and continued to read his menu, trying to stifle the desire to cough.

"Why, I'm flattered that you asked. It's actually a combination that I made up myself."

"Oh, really?" Doug said sarcastically under his breath. He jumped when Steven kicked him again under the counter. "I bruise easily," he muttered to Steven.

"Yes, I collect different perfumes and sometimes I mix them to see if I can come up with another scent all together. It's kind of a hobby of mine. Do you really like it?" Gracey asked, moving a little closer.

"Oh, it arouses the senses like nothing else I've ever smelled. Maybe you could share the secret recipe with me sometime."

"I'm sorry, but I don't believe I know you, do I? I mean, Fairhaven's such a small town. I usually know most people, but I don't believe I've ever seen you two here before."

"No, that's right, you haven't. My name is Steven Massie and this is my most capable associate, Doug Chase."

"My name's Gracey Temple. Oh, I remember Doug from the trial the other day. You're Nathan's lawyers, right?"

"That's right. We're lawyers for the defense. Your husband's the sheriff in this town, is that right?"

"Yes, he is, but I tell you he's a hard man to find these days. He stays so busy I hardly have the time to talk to him anymore," Gracey answered with a frown.

"Oh, does his job keep him going a lot?"

"Oh Lord, yes, you know with the trial coming up and everything. Anyway, that's his job, so I just have to accept it. My, I bet it's interesting being a lawyer. I suppose you see a little bit of everything don't you? My husband's told me some wild stories, but I bet you guys have some to tell too."

"Yes, wild is just part of our jobs I'm afraid. What do you do?" asked Steven.

"Oh, me? I'm just a housewife. I stay at home. I'd like to work, but Mark says a woman's place is in the home. He's kind of old fashioned when it comes to those kinds of things, you know. I'd like to work. I've always dreamed of owning my own dress shop and making my own clothes. I love experimenting with different materials and making my own outfits. I think I'd be good at it, but I guess that's just a dream for now." Gracey pulled out a compact and began playing with her hair as she talked. "Mark's so fussy, you know he likes having his supper ready when he comes home and he likes me to stick close by the house. Sometimes I just have to get outside and see what's going on, you know, be kind of adventurous. I love Mark, don't get me wrong, but he doesn't want me to do much of anything outside of the house."

"Why is that?" asked Steven.

"I don't know. Really, I think it's because he's kind of jealous of me. You know, he doesn't want me to be around other men, I guess. I think he just feels more comfortable knowing I'm at home, safe and sound. He'd really be upset if he knew I was here talking to you now," Gracey smiled at Steven.

"What would he do?" asked Steven.

"Oh, Lord knows he would be so mad. He'd have some kind of fit or something. He does go on sometimes. But I know it's because he loves me and all."

"I'm sure he does," Steven answered. "Since you stay at home most of the time, does your husband talk to you a lot about the cases he's working on?"

"No, he don't like to talk too much about his work. He keeps that to himself mostly. He says it's not something I need to know about. He's afraid it might upset me if he told me what goes on every day. I guess he tries to keep me sheltered from his work."

"But you did go to the trial the other day, didn't you?" Steven pressed.

"You mean Nathan's trial?" Gracey's expression changed quickly. "Yes, I did manage to sneak into that. I just can't believe that poor boy is charged with murder. He's the kindest and sweetest man you'd ever want to meet. He's just a perfect gentleman. I was shocked to hear he had been arrested. He and Marcie have been through so much lately with the loss of her dear mama, Maggie. My heart just goes out to them."

"So you don't think he's guilty then?" Steven asked quietly.

"Nathan? Oh, no. He couldn't have done such a terrible thing. I don't think Nathan would hurt a butterfly. Although, they did have to take him to the hospital because of some dream he had. He slept outside all night long. Poor baby, he must have almost froze to death." She leaned over closer to Doug and Steven and began to whisper, "He's been going to see a psychiatrist, you know. Everybody knows that, it's not just gossip. So he does have some problems, but then, don't we all? I mean, why should he get blamed, just cause he's brave enough to admit that he's a little crazy and needs help? Some people in this town think I'm a little crazy too."

"Well, they did find the bag in the barn with the bloody shirt in it, don't forget," Steven reminded her.

Gracey sipped her drink while looking at Steven out of the corner of her eye. "Well you can buy those bags anywhere you know."

"Yes, but this one had his initials inside of it and a bloody shirt. That's kind of hard to explain, don't you think?" Steven stared at Gracey, waiting for her reply.

"Yes, I guess it is. But I tell you there are people who would do anything to blame somebody else and to keep themselves out of trouble. You just never know. Shoot, you can buy those bags practically anywhere. Why, I even had one just like it at one time." Gracey laughed out loud, "Hey, maybe I'm the killer."

Steven laughed politely while Doug stared at Gracey over top of his soda. She was suddenly quiet and then she quickly got up to pay the bill at the end of the counter.

"I'm sorry to run off in the middle of our conversation, but I'd better get back home in case Mark comes in. He may be hungry for some lunch or something. If you see him, tell him I was looking for him, but I'll talk to him tonight if I don't see him sooner. It was really nice talking to you both," she said, shaking their hands. She slipped white gloves on her hands and checked out her hair in the mirror behind the counter. She took out a tissue and wiped away some of the mascara from under her eyes and then waved goodbye to Harvey.

Steven shook his head as he watched her leave. He took another sip of his drink and scribbled something down on a piece of paper.

"Whew, I'm glad she's gone. Now I can breathe again." Doug noticed Steven was scribbling away. "She's an odd one, don't you think?" asked Doug.

"Yeah, she is a bit different, but her heart is like an open book. We may want to talk to her some more a little later. Write her name down. I bet she knows more about what really goes on in this town than most people give her credit for."

# 40

It was the middle of the night and Nathan found himself wide-awake again. He was unable to go to sleep, no matter what gimmick he tried. So he quietly slipped out of bed, being careful not to wake Marcie, who was sound asleep. So many things were going on inside his head. He couldn't even keep his eyes closed. So he slipped on his jeans and sneakers and walked downstairs to have something to drink, hoping that would help him drift off to sleep. Staring inside the open refrigerator door, Nathan didn't see anything that interested him. Instead of something to drink, he decided what he needed was a breath of fresh air and a walk all by himself.

As he stepped outside, he could feel the air was cool and breezy. So he stepped back inside and grabbed his jacket out of the closet. Zipping it up, he headed out to no particular destination in mind. He just started walking slowly with his hands stuffed in his pockets and his collar turned up against the wind. Nathan tried hard to think about something other than the trial, but it was impossible. He found himself walking out to the road and, after pausing for a moment, taking a right turn. He started walking up the road, which wound through the mountains. He just wanted to be on his own for a while. He needed time to think. The wind blew at his back, pushing him along as if it was driving him in a particular direction.

Nathan pondered his future and what the future would bring for him and Marcie. He longed for those mornings when he used to wake up knowing what the day held for him. His life was routine and everything was pretty ordinary. Now, he woke up to anxiety attacks and a fear of what might happen at any given moment. Things can change so quickly and there's no way to predict what lies around the corner. No amount of planning can deter some things from happening to you. For the first time in a long while, he had a feeling of total helplessness. His future was in the hands of people he barely knew, Steven, Doug and a jury of strangers.

Sometimes he wished he had been the one who was killed instead of Robert. He wished someone else had been left to fret over this confused haze of clues instead of him. He even felt angry with Robert for doing this to him. It was his idea to go out into the woods when they should have been at home, safe in their rooms and close by their mothers. Nathan found himself walking faster. His pace quickened with every step. With every thought about Robert, along with all the confusion he left behind, he became more and more angry.

"I was just a boy. How could they let something so horrible happen to me? They should have protected me and watched over me more carefully. Didn't they know I wasn't in my room? Why didn't they come looking for me sooner? Then maybe Robert would be alive today and none of this would be happening. I called out for you to come and help me, Mom. I tried to run back to you. Why didn't you hear me? Why weren't you watching? I ran as fast as I could, but I couldn't find my way back to you. Robert was screaming for help and I couldn't do anything. I was just a frightened little boy. All I knew to do was run as fast as I could. I just ran and ran until I reached home. Someone should have been watching me."

By this time Nathan was running up the road as fast as he could, running from something that happened to him when he was just a child, but to him it was happening all over again. He ran without stopping with tears streaming down his face. Suddenly, there was heavy breathing behind him. Looking over his shoulder, he could see there was no one there. Nathan continued to run even faster now, looking from side to side for someone to help him. In his mind he was pleading for someone to come along and stop him, to rescue him from his past. He could hear the heavy breathing behind him now. No matter how fast he ran, the breathing seemed to catch up to him. He turned around and looked over his shoulder again, and there, behind him, was the old man with his white hair blowing in the breeze. He was wearing a strange smile as he effortlessly ran behind Nathan.

"Who are you?" screamed Nathan as he tried to keep running. "Why are you chasing me?"

But the old man didn't answer.

Nathan decided to cut through the woods. Maybe then he would lose the old man. How could he keep up with him so easily? Nathan quickly dashed off to the side and started running through the woods. He didn't see anyone behind him now, but he was afraid to stop running. His heart felt as though it was going to burst if he didn't stop. As he ran, he could hear the rushing Black River running along beside him.

Finally, because he could run no farther, he stopped and rested on a rock beside the dark waters. He kept a watch through the woods from every angle while he struggled to catch his breath. There was no one in sight, at least, not that he could see. Nathan started to laugh and cry at the same time. It was a very strange feeling, but both flowed out of him as he propped himself up on the rock. "I'm losing my mind," he thought. "I'm slowly, but surely, going out of my mind here."

As he strained to make sure there was no one there, he turned to look at the river. It was always the same, no matter what mysteries took place around it, nothing got in its way. Always hurrying on its way to some other place. It never took the time to notice what was going on around it. Only the river knows what happened here years ago. The Black River carried its secrets with it like the broken limbs and fallen leaves that drifted and swirled in the waters and then dumped them at the end of the journey into the ocean. Nathan began to wonder where the river ended and how simple it would be to just float along in it until it reached its destination. He stood up and watched it rush by the rocks and trees.

"Take me with you," he whispered to the river. "I don't want to be here anymore. It's too hard. I'm no good to Marcie. I only cause her pain and tears anyway. She deserves much better than me. I could never give her what she deserves in this life. I've put her through so much already. Maybe it's time that it ended. I'm tired of searching for answers. I'd be better off if I were dead, like Robert." As he weaved back and forth on the rock, he felt himself leaning forward toward the water. "It would be so easy to do it this way," he thought.

Suddenly he felt a strong hand on his shoulder. He snapped around, but lost his balance on the rock and, in slow motion, he started falling toward the rushing sounds of the river. As he fell, his eyes fixed on an old man sitting on the rock with his hand stretched out to him. As Nathan hit the cold icy water, his head and body submerged into complete darkness. The river picked him up and began carrying him along with it as though he was just another piece of debris from the woods. Nathan desperately tried to grab hold of something, as the water carried him past trees, bushes and huge rocks, but everything was just out of reach. While he was fighting to stay alive, he realized that only moments ago he wanted to die. Now he was thrashing about in the roar of the river trying to save his own life.

As he was carried father downstream, the waters threw him against everything in its path, churning him round and round like clothes in a washing machine. He was completely exhausted. He didn't even have the strength to lift his arms. He drifted in the water like a frail leaf, bouncing up and down at the mercy of the bold river. At one point, his body was caught in a swirling motion, like he was about to be sucked down into some kind of never-ending drain. Then the Black River slammed his head against a rock and everything suddenly went blank.

# 41

When Nathan finally opened his eyes again, he found himself lying up on the banks of the river with a handkerchief tied around his head. He was bleeding. Nathan quickly lifted his head, but a sharp pain shot across his forehead. He could see the sun was just coming up enough to bring some light into the woods, but there was no one around. He was completely alone.

Nathan touched his head and he could feel the blood trickling down his face. Pain was pulsating in various parts of his body, as he slowly lifted himself up to a sitting position. He rested his head on his knees, waiting for the pain to subside so he could try to get to his feet again. He grabbed hold of a nearby limb, using it to pull himself up. He staggered backwards a few steps, but was able to steady himself against a tree. While standing there, Nathan looked back at the river still swirling and pushing itself on to its destination.

"How did I get out of the water?" he wondered. He pulled the handkerchief from around his head to take a look at it. It was a plain white cotton handkerchief that could have been carried by anyone. He held it up against his head and pointed himself in the direction of the road. Struggling up the hillside, he pulled himself up by anything he could grab hold of until he finally reached the road. Nathan carefully looked up and down to make sure no one was coming. He didn't know how he would explain it, because he couldn't even understand it. However, he knew he would have to think of a way to explain it to Marcie.

His legs were weak and unsteady, but he managed to begin walking back toward Marcie's house. In the back of his mind he kept calling her name, "Marcie, Marcie, please help me. Come and find me, please. Come and look for me." He kept walking, stopping every few steps to keep his balance. Just then, he saw a car coming over the hill. He stepped to the side, not sure whether to hide or flag them down. When the car got closer, he dropped to his knees in complete exhaustion. The car belonged to Marcie.

As she jumped out and ran over to him, he just fell into her arms.

"You came for me," he said in a hoarse cry. "You came looking for me."

Marcie held him in her arms, not sure why or how he had gotten there. She rocked him and touched his face with her hand. Then she helped him to his feet and carefully placed him in the car.

Nathan could see Marcie's lips moving as she drove him back home, but all he could think about was that she came for him. Someone rescued him from his strange dream.

When Nathan opened his eyes again, Marcie was sitting beside him on the bed, rubbing a cold, wet cloth across his forehead with short, soft strokes. He reached up and took hold of her hand and kissed it. "I love you," he said in a weak voice.

"You should, because anybody else would run as far away as they could possibly go. Nathan, what happened to you? I woke up and you were gone. I searched the whole house and the yard, but you were nowhere to be found. There was nothing left for me to do but hop in the jeep and take off down the road looking for you. I just had a hunch you might have headed toward the Raven. Then, there you were, staggering up the road like a half-drowned, lost wanderer. Were you sleepwalking again?"

"No, I mean, at least, I think I was awake. It sure felt like I was awake. I couldn't sleep, so I got up to have some warm milk, but then I decided to take a walk outside. I headed out to the road and just started walking."

"But you were soaking wet. How did you manage to get soaked to the skin just by walking along the road?"

"I fell into the river, I think, or did I jump?"

"Nathan, you're talking crazy now. Try to remember what happened to you?"

"Someone was chasing me, or maybe I was dreaming that someone was chasing me. I'm not sure, but I headed into the woods to try to get away from him. I wound up perched on a rock just above the river. I remember swaying back and forth a little, while I was looking at the water, but then I felt something on my shoulder, like a hand. I turned around to see who was there, but someone pushed me, or maybe I just lost my balance, and I fell in the river. Marcie, I—" Nathan stopped for a moment to decide whether or not to tell her what he'd seen. He didn't want her to think he was completely crazy. "I must have fallen. I guess I was just scared."

"Tomorrow I want you to go and see Dr. Seyler again. You haven't been to see him on a regular basis like you planned. Maybe it's time you get back on schedule, now that we're staying in town for a while longer. I'll call him and make an appointment for you."

"Marcie, I'm really scared. I don't seem to have any control over my thoughts, or my actions for that matter. It's as though something heavy comes over me and I just drift away into another world, only waking up to find myself limping down a road or lying under a tree. I'm so afraid of what I don't know. I just want the torture to stop. I just want it to go away."

Marcie held Nathan tightly and tried her best to comfort him. It was difficult for her because she didn't really understand what he was going through. She wanted it all to stop too. A normal life together is what she wanted now. They would raise children and worry about ordinary, everyday problems, instead of the endless nightmare that neither of them could control. It seemed too impossible to even dream about that life, but she did, every day and every night. Without that hope, that somehow, it would eventually get better, she felt she would just collapse into a dark depression. The love that she felt for Nathan kept her strong enough to endure everything they'd been through so far. Marcie prayed it would keep her strong enough to face what might be coming.

# 42

Steven and Doug arrived at Mark's office in town to ask him some questions and get his side of the story. His plan to catch Mark outside of his office in another environment hadn't worked out. As they went inside, they were both surprised to find him there. Mark was very cooperative and offered them a cup of coffee while they talked. To Steven, Mark looked like the wholesome small-town sheriff, who everyone knew and trusted. He had a very pleasant face and a warm, friendly smile.

"I appreciate you taking the time to talk with us today. I promise you we won't keep you too long. I know you're very busy," said Steven. "This is my associate, Doug Chase and my name is Steven Massie. We're representing Nathan Staby in the charges that have been recently brought against him concerning the death of Todd Harper."

"You don't have to be formal here, Mr. Massie. In small towns like this, we just speak plainly and in simple terms so everybody's on the same page."

"Sure, Mark," replied Steven. "Oh, may I call you Mark?"

"Everybody does. Is it okay if I call you Steven instead of Mr. Massie?"

"Yes, please do. We, that is, Doug and I, just wanted to ask you a few questions, examine the bag and then we'll be on our way." Steven pulled out a notepad and a pen. "Have you known Nathan for a long time?"

"Yes, we grew up together. I don't remember not knowing him."

"So you're good friends."

"I guess you could say that. We were closer before he left town and moved to the city, but we're still friends."

"It must have been tough for you to arrest him."

"Yes, it was tough, but I had no choice. Once we found the bag, we had to put him in jail. I don't always like my job, but I still have to do it. You understand that, right? I mean, I'm sure you have to do things you don't like to do with your job too." Mark smiled back at Steven.

"Have you known Marcie for a long time as well?"

"Yes, we all grew up here together. She's like a sister to me, really. I have to say I'm sorry she's had to go through so much with Nathan, you know, him being arrested and losing her mother recently. She's a fine woman and she deserves better."

"What made you decide to search Marcie's barn?"

"I knew that Nathan had been staying there and we had been suspicious of him early on. Todd Harper was killed shortly after Nathan arrived in town and he had been acting kind of strange. When he passed out in Marcie's barn, the doctor said he must have seen something traumatic. That's what sent him into a state of shock. Well, we put two and two together and decided it was time for us to take a look around for ourselves."

"The reasons don't seem to be strong enough to make you want to search her property, Mark."

"We had other reasons too. Pretty soon after Todd's death, a handkerchief was found near the scene. It had Nathan's initials on it. We held on to it without saying anything because I didn't want to make any accusations until I had more proof. Like I said, he's a friend, so I took it real slow. I couldn't believe he would be involved in something like this. I still have a hard time accepting that he's guilty, but I have an obligation to the people of this town and especially to Dan Harper."

"Yes," replied Steven. "Well, speaking of Dan Harper, Nathan told me that he had a chat with his neighbor, Jake Foster recently. Did he tell you anything about that?"

"Yes, Jake told me about it."

"Did Jake tell you that the conversation had more to do with Robert's death than with Todd's? You know who Robert Sanding is, don't you?"

"Of course. He was Nathan's best friend when we were growing up together. He was murdered and left in the woods, similar to Todd Harper's death. Nathan found his body and collapsed into some kind of memory loss afterwards. He found out that Jake Foster had been a witness to the murder when he was a boy. So he probably decided to see if Jake could fill in some of the blank spaces for him, but Jake couldn't help him much. Interestingly enough though, Nathan did ask Jake whether or not he thought he could have killed Robert."

"Do you think that scared Jake? Maybe enough for him to share his conversation with Dan Harper and steer the Harpers into thinking Nathan could have possibly killed Todd as well? I mean, if he could have killed one boy, then why wouldn't he be guilty of killing another? Right? That was the logic, wasn't it, Mark?"

Mark got up from his desk and walked behind Steven and Doug to get another cup of coffee. Steven just sat and tapped his pencil on the pad of paper, waiting for Mark to respond to his question.

"You're right. Dan was scared. His son has been murdered and along comes Nathan, sneaking around, talking to his neighbor about another boy who was killed years ago. It's obvious he wanted to clear his guilty conscience about the death of Robert. So he asks quietly, when there's no one else around. Jake had already told him he didn't see who actually killed Robert. He just happened to be in the wrong place at the wrong time. But then later he started thinking about Nathan's questions. So he called me and told me about the conversation. Of course, I thought it was pretty peculiar, especially after I found his bag in the barn with a bloody shirt and a rubber mask. I thought it was very peculiar. So I told Dan Harper about it"

"May I see the bag that you're talking about please?"

"Sure, this way." Mark took Steven and Doug to the back of the office where the evidence was being held in a locked room. Unlocking the door, he led them to a shelf where various items in clear plastic bags sat waiting for their day in court. He took down a large plastic bag from the top shelf containing the black bag found in Marcie's barn. Opening it up, he sat it in front of Steven. "Put on these gloves and you can have a look see."

Steven put on a pair of plastic gloves and began examining the bag. He pulled out the bloodstained shirt and studied the initials on the pocket. "It says N.S., all right," he pointed out to Doug.

"Pretty stitching too," replied Doug.

"Yes, it's very nice." Steven continued examining the bag. "Where's the mask that I'm told was found inside the bag as well?" Steven asked Mark.

"It's still at the lab being tested. Since we're a small town, we have to send this stuff out to the lab in the next town for testing. I haven't been called to pick it up yet."

"What do you think was the purpose of the mask?" asked Steven.

"Some sort of disguise, I guess," replied Mark.

"Yes, I'm sure it was some sort of disguise," repeated Steven. "Have you had the bag and shirt tested for prints or bits of hair and the like?"

"Yes, we found Nathan's prints on the bag and bits of his hair on the shirt. The bloodstains match the blood belonging to Todd Harper."

"Pretty convincing stuff. Wouldn't you say so, Doug?" Steven asked, as he examined the initials on the bag more closely.

"I'd say so, yes," replied Doug, scribbling on his pad of paper.

"Thank you, Mark. I think we've seen enough for now. You'll let me know when you get the results from the rubber mask, won't you?" Steven and Doug headed for the door. "We'll be on our way now. Don't worry, we can find our way out." Then Steven stopped and turned around, "When did you say you found the bag?"

"I didn't say exactly when I found it. What difference does it make?" Mark asked.

"None maybe, but I was just curious when the bag was actually found."

"A few days before Nathan's arrest. We held off waiting for tests on the bag to come back in, to be sure."

"I see. Well, thanks again for your time." Steven and Doug left the sheriff's office.

Once outside, Steven paused in front of his car and flipped back through his notes.

"What do you think?" asked Doug.

"I don't know, but this case is just too nice and neat for my liking. Everything just fits into place too well, or maybe it's just that our guy, Nathan, is really guilty."

"Yeah, it's hard for me to believe though," replied Doug. "I can't believe he would kill a kid."

"That's what everybody keeps telling me, but all of the evidence says he did, maybe even two kids. Let's go back to see Nathan. I have some more questions I want to ask him."

# 43

By the time Steven arrived to see Nathan he had taken a hot shower and eaten some lunch. He was feeling much better, but was still pretty dazed by his experience. His head had a huge bump from his fall in the river, but otherwise, he was fine. Nathan heard Steven's voice at the front door as Marcie let him inside. He took a deep breath, walked into the living room and sat down on the sofa. He poured himself some juice and carefully touched the bump on his head. It was pretty visible, so he knew he would have to explain what happened to him.

"Good morning, Nathan, I see you're a late riser," said Steven, sitting down beside him.

"Not really, I've just had a rough start to my day. Where have you been?"

"Oh, Doug and I went to pay a visit to Mark's office. I just wanted to have a chance to examine the bag he was holding and to ask him a few questions." Steven stopped and stared at Nathan's head. "Wow, that's quite a knot there. What happened? You two haven't been fighting have you?"

"No, I fell in the river and hit my head on a rock or something I think."

"You fell into the river? When? Today?" Steven asked in a confused tone.

"This morning; early this morning. It's a long story, but I'm fine, really."

"Were you fishing or something, Nathan?" asked Doug, looking just as puzzled as Steven.

"No, I went for a walk before sun up and I ended up in the woods by the river."

"He said someone was chasing him," interrupted Marcie. "He thinks he may have been pushed into that river. Maybe somebody's trying to kill him. The real killer could be stalking him."

"Is that right, Nathan? You think someone pushed you in the water? Steven asked. "Tell me what happened,"

"I don't know that someone was actually chasing me. I could have been dreaming," replied Nathan.

"Look, Nathan, please explain to me exactly what happened. I need to understand what's going on in your life if I'm going to defend you."

Nathan reluctantly explained that morning's event in as much detail as he could remember. He watched Steven's eyes as he told the story, but he couldn't tell whether or not he thought he was crazy. He did, however, see his face change a bit when he told him that the man chasing him was the old white-haired man he had told him about before.

"You say the old man was chasing you? The one that looks like the rubber mask in the bag?" asked Steven.

"Yes, but remember, I dream these things and then sometimes I act them out. I mean, I think they're really happening to me, so there could have really been no one chasing me through the woods. It could have been me just reliving a dream or a memory. I don't know. It's all mixed up."

"But you said that someone actually reached out and touched you on the shoulder, didn't you? And then, that's when you fell into the water?" Steven asked carefully.

"Well, it felt like someone touched me. It all seemed so real. I'm not sure what's real and what's not anymore. I just know something startled me enough to send me reeling into the water. But the really strange part is that I woke up on the banks of the river with a handkerchief around my head. Somebody rescued me and pulled me out. So there had to be somebody there. I couldn't have gotten out on my own. I was being tossed around like a paper doll," Nathan explained.

"You didn't see anybody afterwards? Did you look around?" asked Steven.

"Yes, there was no one around," replied Nathan.

"How'd you get home then?" asked Doug.

"Marcie came looking for me with the car. By then I was walking back down the road to the house. She picked me up and carried me home."

"Marcie, did you see anybody around at all?" asked Steven.

"No, I really didn't pay that much attention. I was too busy trying to get Nathan in the car and back home. He looked terrified."

Steven got up and paced around the room a bit. "This is all so very strange. I just don't know what to make of it. We're dealing with reality and dreams all at the same time. We need to sort out what's really happening to you and what's only occurring in your dreams."

"How do we do that?" asked Doug. "Keep him under surveillance?"

"Not a bad idea, Doug. Maybe we can," Steven said with excitement.

"You mean have somebody watch me for 24 hours?" asked Nathan. "No thanks. I don't want to play."

"We need to see what's going on with you when you have these dreams. We also need to see whether or not some of the things you're seeing are real or only fantasy."

"That's the craziest thing I ever heard of and I don't want any part of it," replied Nathan. "I don't want somebody watching me in my sleep or following me around every time I take a walk. You're my lawyer, not my doctor, Steven."

"Well then, go to your doctor and see what he says about it. At least, consider it. It's the only way to find out what's really happening to you, otherwise, you may never find out the truth."

Nathan was silent as he stared back at Steven, "You think I'm guilty, don't you? You think I killed Todd and Robert. You believe I'm nothing more than a lunatic murderer who roams the woods to kill innocent boys for absolutely no reason. How are you going to defend me if you don't even believe what I tell you? I'm not crazy! I'm just confused by something I saw a long time ago and it scared the memory right out of me. Look, I'm not a killer. I just won't accept that. I would have never done anything to hurt Robert. He was like my brother, for God's sake. Can't you understand that?"

Marcie took hold of Nathan's arm and pulled him toward her. "I believe you," she said softly. "You're telling the truth."

"Look, I'm not here to decide your guilt or innocence," said Steven. "I am here to defend you to the best of my ability. I admit that these stories sound bizarre to me, but that doesn't mean that I automatically assume you're guilty. We've just got to find some answers for some of your actions, or a jury of your peers will find you guilty. I'm talking about separating the facts from the dreams here, Nathan, and right now, I don't think you know what is real and what isn't. That's why you're confused. I'm trying to help you stay out of jail. That's my job!" Steven paced up and down in front of Nathan. "Now, you may not like some of the things that I have to ask you to do, but if we're going to beat this charge of murder, you're going to have to jump through some hoops, my friend. If not, then you might as well find yourself another lawyer who will pat you on the back and say 'don't you worry, son, it's going to be all right.' Meanwhile you'll find yourself sitting in some cell for the next 25 years of your life or longer."

"I'm sorry," said Nathan with a different tone in his voice. "I'll do whatever it takes. I just want to get out of this mess and find out what really happened to Robert. I'll do whatever you ask."

Steven walked over to Nathan and sat on the edge of the table in front of him. "I'm just going to have someone keep an eye on you, especially if you get up in the middle of the night. Who knows, maybe somebody is trying to kill you and this may be our only way of finding out who that person is. I have a good friend back home and I trust him. He's on my staff. I'll give him a call and ask him to come here for a spell. In the meantime, go see your doctor and see what suggestions he has on the subject. He might be a big help in this experiment." Steven got up and gathered his things to leave. "Oh, by the way, I've been meaning to ask you. Do you have a habit of sewing your initials in most of your clothes and bags or do you have someone do it for you?"

"I did have my initials sewn into my bag so I would know it's mine at airports, since so many bags look alike, but not my clothes."

"What about handkerchiefs? Do you own a set of handkerchiefs with your initials on them? Maybe you received them as a gift or something?" asked Steven.

"Not that I recall. I usually buy my own handkerchiefs, but I never had my initials placed on them," replied Nathan, "Why do you ask?"

"Mark tells me they found a handkerchief near the Harper kid's crime scene and it had your initials on it. The shirt in the bag also had your initials stitched on the pocket. I figured you just had a habit of identifying your property that way."

"No, the shirt looked like one of mine, but I know it didn't have my initials on it."

"Do you think it's possible you're suffering from any short-term memory loss as well as the long-term memory loss? For instance, is it possible you can't remember having received a set of handkerchiefs with your initials on them or on your shirt?"

"No, I would remember having my initials placed on my clothes or receiving handkerchiefs as a gift. What's going on here, Steven?" Nathan asked impatiently.

"I don't know, but somebody wants to make sure that all of the evidence leads to you. Somebody's playing a smart game with you, unless you're lying to me, but I don't think that you are."

"Did you ever get back the results from my polygraph test I took?" asked Nathan.

"Yes, it was a little strange. Sometimes, when you answered the same question twice, the test would show you were telling the truth and other times it showed that you were not. I talked to the expert who was reading the results and he said it could be your memory loss causing you to respond in different ways to the same question. So the test wasn't very helpful, except to confirm that you don't remember everything and you're confused about your own innocence sometimes."

Steven and Doug said goodbye and headed back to their hotel to do some more work on the case. Nathan knew that no matter how much he tried to convince others of his innocence, there was sometimes a question in his own mind about what missing pieces of the big puzzle held for him. Maybe that's why he still doubted himself. He couldn't go by what he knew to be true and what he could remember, but only by his feelings and what he thought he was or was not capable of doing.

# 44

A few days later, Nathan found himself at Dr. Scott Seyler's office again, at the request and constant prodding of Marcie and Steven. He wasn't sure the doctor was going to ever be able to unlock his mind long enough for him to remember anything, but he didn't have any other alternatives right now.

As Nathan waited in the doctor's office for his appointment, he picked up a magazine and started to flip the pages. Pictures of people, places and things waved in front of him. He saw pictures of exotic, far-away places, and smiling faces of people having a normal and happy life. Ads offering a better way of doing business and an easier road to walk unfolded in front of him. Everything on the pages seemed so out of reach. The people in the pictures didn't really look happy to him. Behind their smiles Nathan could sense a world of disillusionment and disappointment. "The magazine wants you to think this is the way life really is, and this is how people really look most of the time, but I know better," he thought to himself. "Oh, great. Now I'm talking to a magazine. I must be closer to jumping off the edge than I realized."

Nathan quietly continued to turn the pages of the magazine just to pass the time while he waited. Then he started to focus on a picture of an old, white-framed house. The magazine article was showing before and after pictures of some remodeling a couple had done, but there was something familiar about the house in the before picture. It somehow brought back a memory. He had seen a similar house somewhere in his childhood, but he couldn't get a clear picture. He sat and stared at the picture of the house as he waited.

"Nathan Staby. How are you today? The doctor is ready to see you now," said the nurse at the front desk.

Before getting up from his seat, Nathan carefully ripped the page out of the magazine, folded it and put it in his pocket. "You know, you really are starting to do weird things," he thought to himself. He placed the page in his pocket anyway and followed the nurse into Dr. Seyler's office.

"Have a seat. He'll be right in." The nurse closed the door behind her, leaving Nathan sitting alone in the office.

Nathan reached into his pocket and took out the magazine page once again and unfolded it. As he took another look at it, he could almost see flashbacks of himself sneaking around in the front yard of this house. He could see a person standing on the front porch, but he couldn't make out the face. He closed his eyes and tried very hard to get a clear picture of the person on the porch, but he just couldn't bring the face into focus. He imagined walking a little closer to the front porch, ducking and hiding behind bushes and trees. There was a woman standing on the porch, but he still couldn't quite make out her face. Who was she? He moved closer still. Now he could almost see her face.

"Well, sorry to keep you waiting, Nathan. I'm glad to see you again," said Doctor Seyler. "I was afraid you had given up on coming back to see me. How have you been holding up, considering your arrest and the charges that have been brought against you?"

Nathan quickly folded the picture and put it back into his pocket. "Fine, I guess. Well, actually, not really fine at all. I came back to see you because nothing seems to be getting any better. I still seem to be acting out these crazy dreams of someone chasing me, or running after Robert. Maybe you and I can try to find some answers that will be helpful in my case. Everybody seems to think I'm crazy, or at least, it seems that way. If only I could remember something, anything at all. Even though it's Todd Harper's murder I'm charged with, if I can remember things about Robert's death, maybe it will answer some questions about Todd's death too."

"Well it's going to take some time. I hope we can make enough progress to uncover some things before your trial, but I can't make any promises you know."

"I've read about people being hypnotized and going back into their childhood, remembering things. Is that really possible? I mean, can you do that for me? Do you think it would work?"

"Some people are able to remember things through hypnosis, but it doesn't always work. It depends on how deeply the memories are buried."

"I want to try it," said Nathan. "I'm ready to try anything that might help me find out what happened. Nothing else seems to work."

"You know, you really haven't given just talking about your experience a fair shot," replied Doctor Seyler. "You've only been to see me a few times. It takes a long while to sort through everything before you get to the underlying cause of the problem. If you're looking for a quick fix, I'm afraid you're going to be disappointed, Nathan."

"I just feel like everything is sitting there right on the tip of my brain, but I can't shake it loose," replied Nathan. "It doesn't feel like it's buried very deep. It's like I'm walking closer and closer to the picture, but then once I get close enough to see something, it begins to fade."

"Tell me about your most recent dream," Doctor Seyler requested.

"What about the hypnosis?" Nathan asked impatiently. "Can you do it or not?"

"I've never done it myself, but I've seen it done," replied Doctor Seyler. "I know someone who specializes in hypnosis, but I think we ought to see how far we can get without it first."

"Dr. Seyler, I don't have a lot of time here," said Nathan. "When the trial starts, things could move along pretty fast. I may end up locked away somewhere. It's too late to try to fix things by going the long way around. I need to try and find out whatever I can now, as soon as possible. My life depends on it."

"All right, Nathan," replied Doctor Seyler. "You're the patient. I'll try to set something up this week, if possible. I'll call and let you know when. But for right now, is there anything you want to talk about?"

"Nothing new really, except," Nathan paused. "I suddenly remembered something about an old white house. I recall sneaking around in the front yard as a boy. I don't know if it has any significance, but it feels very familiar to me. There's this person, a woman, on the front porch of the house, but I can't make out who she is. I don't know what it means, or even if it has any meaning at all, but it's a piece of my childhood that I don't remember for some reason."

"What does the house look like?" asked Doctor Seyler.

"It's just a plain, white wood-framed house out in the country. It has a big wrap-around porch on the front with a swing hanging from a tree," said Nathan, closing his eyes.

"How do you feel when you see this house?"

"Um, afraid I guess. I get the sense that I'm sneaking up on them without them knowing, like on a dare or something."

Nathan sat for a moment with his eyes still closed, trying harder to conjure up a picture of the house and the woman he saw there. As his eyes moved across the house and the yard, they came to rest on a big tree with a wooden swing hanging from it. As he strained to look a little closer, he could see someone sitting in the swing, but again, he couldn't see beyond the outline of the figure. The swing was twirling round and round. The person had their head back and their legs stuck out in front, like a child would do while the swing twisted, first one way and then slowly stopped and started to unwind. Nathan tried to move closer to the swing, but his legs were too heavy. He felt like he was frozen in place. The house and the two people around it were way off in the distance. No matter how hard he tried he couldn't bring himself closer to them. Feeling frustrated, he closed his eyes even tighter, hoping it would help to make the vision more clear, but it didn't work. He finally opened his eyes, and found the doctor sitting almost right in front of him.

"I believe you're getting closer, Nathan," he said reaching out and putting his hand on his shoulder. "It's going to come to you, when you're not trying so hard to remember. I'll call you and let you know when I have an appointment set up for the hypnosis. Just don't get your hopes up too high that it's going to be the answer to everything. Sometimes it works, but sometimes it doesn't help at all."

Nathan left Dr. Seyler's office feeling helpless, but maybe a little closer to seeing a part of his childhood that, for whatever reason, he had locked away.

# 45

Driving home from Doctor Seyler's office, Nathan saw Gracey Temple walking down the street. She was wearing a hot-pink suit with matching pink shoes with heels so high, he wondered how she could actually walk down the street. She was carrying a vase with flowers in it and a large bow was wrapped around the front of it. He pulled up beside her and slowed down a bit, "Hey, Gracey, where are you off to?"

"Nathan, why how in the world are you, darlin'? I've wanted to come over and see you, but I just haven't had the chance. Well, I don't think Mark would let me anyway, you know, with you being, well, you know, arrested and everything. Where's Marcie?" asked Gracey.

"She's at home. I've just come into town on an errand. You're looking pretty, all dressed up in that pink suit. Are you heading any-where special?" asked Nathan.

"Well, this is kind of awkward, but I'm walking out to take some flowers to Maggie's grave. I wanted to look nice for her, so I decided to put on my Sunday best," Gracey said with a huge smile.

"Why don't you let me drive you? It's a pretty good walk from here."

"Well, I don't know. I don't think Mark would like it too much. Maybe I'd better just walk," answered Gracey.

"I understand," replied Nathan. "Maybe I'll get to see you later." Nathan waved and started to pull away.

"Nathan, wait!" Gracey said, running back up to the car. "I don't really care what Mark thinks. I would really like it if you gave me a ride. It's really warm today, and I might just be dripping wet by the time I walk out to the cemetery. Besides, we're good friends, right?"

"Right," Nathan replied, getting out of the car. "Let me get the door for you." Nathan got out and opened the passenger side door for Gracey. As he was getting back in the car, he saw Mark coming out of his office. He quickly put the car in gear and sped off toward the cemetery. He didn't want to get Gracey in any kind of trouble.

"So, how have you been?" asked Gracey. "I know you've been under a lot of pressure, what with everything going on. You look like you've lost a little weight to me. Are you eating right?"

Gracey was the type to ask a lot of questions, but she didn't always wait for the answers. Nathan just smiled and kept on driving.

"I know how Maggie always loved flowers. So I wanted to bring some fresh ones to put on her grave. Do you like them?"

"They're beautiful, Gracey," replied Nathan. "I'm sure Maggie would have thought so too."

"She always had such a green thumb when it came to growing things," said Gracey, touching the flowers. "I always admired how she was able to grow such gorgeous flowers from nothing but seeds. Her garden was always a nice place to visit. I used to love to just walk around the grounds of the Raven Inn and pick me a bouquet of flowers. Now mind you, I didn't pick many, just enough to take home and put on the table for dinnertime. The smell of fresh flowers on a table at dinner is so lovely. Don't you think so, Nathan?"

Nathan just smiled.

"It just adds so much to the dinner table. Maggie knew I was picking her flowers, but I don't think she ever minded too much. At least, she never said so to me anyway. Don't you just miss her so much?" asked Gracey.

Nathan glanced over at her and he could see a tear flowing down her cheek. "Yes, I miss her a lot. She was a lovely lady."

As they pulled up to the cemetery, Gracey got out before Nathan could open the door for her. She quickly walked over to Maggie's gravesite and knelt down beside it. Very carefully, she removed the withered flowers and replaced them with the fresh ones. She took great care to fuss over the arrangement. Gracey carefully brushed away some of the dirt and debris from the grave itself. Nathan stood behind her, not wanting to disturb this quiet moment for Gracey. He could see that she loved Maggie a lot and placing the flowers there was her way of showing it.

As Gracey knelt there on the ground, she began to hum a tune. It was an old hymn that was soft and sweet. Nathan stood silently beside her and listened. The tune seemed to transport him to another place and time. He felt a great sense of peace inside. The song was, 'Amazing Grace.' It somehow brought him great comfort, hearing it again. He remembered sitting with his mother in the small Grace Baptist church on Sunday mornings and watching her get all teary-eyed whenever they would sing that old song. Suddenly, he was a child running through a field of yellow wild flowers, dancing and jumping outside the church.

His mother always cooked up a batch of fried chicken and cornbread on Sundays. They would go off on a picnic near the Black River. He loved it there. He would run and play to his heart's content until his mother would call him to come and eat. Then she'd make him lie down for a spell and put his head in her lap. She'd read to him until he fell asleep with the faint sounds of the river rushing by in the background.

His mother would softly stroke his hair, while she hummed that sweet tune to him. He remembered wishing he could stay like that forever. It was so peaceful there, in his mother's lap. He was never ready to leave.

Suddenly he could hear someone faintly calling his name, "Nathan, Nathan, wake up." He didn't want to wake up. He just wanted to go on sleeping and listening to the sweet music, but then he felt someone shaking him.

"Nathan," called Gracey. "Wake up, darlin'. Did you pass out or something? Are you okay? Nathan?"

His eyes opened to find Gracey looking down at him. His head was in her lap. He quickly jumped to his feet, but he felt dizzy.

"Careful dear, you're going to pass out again," said Gracey, holding to his arm. "Do you want me to drive you to the doctor?"

Nathan staggered around a bit. Gracey kept holding to his arm. "I've got you honey. You're just tired I bet. Here, let me help you walk back to the car. I guess with everything that's been going on lately, you're just overwhelmed by it all. You need to get some rest and slow down now, you hear me?" Gracey walked Nathan back to his car and started to open the passenger side door for him.

"I'm fine now, Gracey," said Nathan, taking his arm away. "I think I can drive okay."

"Are you sure, Nathan?" asked Gracey. "You look all flushed in the face. I think I'd better drive you."

"No, really, I'm okay now, maybe just a little dizzy, that's all. I skipped breakfast this morning. I guess I'm starting to feel it now."

Nathan held the door of the car for Gracey to get in on the passenger's side. "Don't worry, I'm steady now."

Gracey reluctantly got in the car, looking a little unsure.

Nathan slowly walked around the back of the car, pausing for a moment to look around at his surroundings. His dreams were so real, he couldn't imagine how he could be one place first, and then so vividly be in another place all at the same time.

"Are you sure you don't want me to drive?" Gracey called with her head stuck out of the car window.

"No, I'm coming. I just wanted to get a little more fresh air." Nathan got into the car and Gracey stared at him with great curiosity. "Is that why you've been going to the psychiatrist, because you just pass out in some places?" asked Gracey.

Nathan didn't answer.

"I don't think that means you're crazy, darlin'," said Gracey. "I think you just need some rest. What does the doctor say about it?"

"He thinks I need some rest too," Nathan looked over at Gracey again. "I really miss my mama sometimes. That old song made me think of her just now, I guess."

"Yeah, my mama used to sing that to me when I was just a baby. If I couldn't sleep or if I was crying, she would scoop me up in her arms and hum that tune to me. I didn't even know if it had any words for a long time, because she only used to hum the melody to me. I always felt so safe and warm when she sang to me. Silly, but I guess I've never forgotten it. I used to hum it to Charley, my son, when he was a baby."

"I haven't heard it in a long time," replied Nathan. "Gracey, I'm sorry if I scared you back there. You don't have to mention what happened to Mark. I don't think he'd understand."

"Don't worry, darlin'," replied Gracey. "I don't plan to trouble Mark with it. He doesn't tell me everything. So I guess I don't have to tell him everything either. We'll just keep it between us friends."

"Thanks, Gracey. You know, you're really something special to me. You're quite a lady," said Nathan.

Gracey smiled and grabbed Nathan's hand. "I know you're not guilty, Nathan." Everything's going to work out fine at the trial, you'll see. The truth will come out. A man like you just doesn't get his life taken away from him like that. You've got a lot of things to write about and Marcie has to have your children. You two are going to be just fine. I pray for it every night. I believe that."

Nathan gently touched Gracey's cheek. "Thanks, I'll hold on to that."

After dropping Gracey off, Nathan headed back to town. As he drove past Maggie's grave again, he could see the fresh yellow flowers waving in the gentle breeze.

"Maybe everything was going to be okay, just like Gracey said," Nathan thought to himself.

# 46

Marcie sat on the front porch, enjoying the view and the quiet that surrounded her. She sipped hot tea from one of her favorite cups Maggie had given her for her birthday, wishing she could find a way to make time stand still, if only for a short while. At this time of the day she painfully missed Maggie. She recalled how they would sit together and talk about anything and everything, changing from subject to subject without so much as a blink. Marcie would tell Maggie about problems she was trying to work through and she would always offer her best advice. They were very close, and it was that closeness that now left a void in her life.

Marcie sighed and looked out over the mountains that seemed more like green cushions floating up and down as far as the eye could see. Maggie had loved the mountains so much, especially when the colors changed in the fall. She always said there was never a picture painted that could capture the true colors of the leaves when they were all blended together in the mountains. The spring flowers were just as breathtaking. In fact, just about anytime of the year was beautiful in Fairhaven. She missed taking long walks through the gardens with her mother, discussing each flower and its name. Maggie poured over each one, as though they were her children. No one could have put more love into their garden than she did, fretting over the cold winds and the damage that could be brought to her delicate flowers. Maggie never missed watching the weather on television. Like a farmer, she would listen religiously, straining to hear what help the good Lord was going to send her way. "She used to say, 'there's nothing that can take the place of a good hard rain sent from the Lord Himself,'" Marcie remembered.

Suddenly the tears started to flow. "I miss you, Mom," Marcie said softly. She put her head down on her arms and once again, felt that familiar pain deep inside of her. It was hard to believe that time would eventually take some of the pain away, because it was so unbearable. Then, just as quickly as the tears started, the pain subsided and she felt calm. Her emotions were on some kind of rollercoaster over which she had little or no control. She wished Nathan was home and sitting beside her.

She sat for a while longer with her head down until she almost drifted off to sleep. Suddenly she was awakened by the sound of a car driving up the road. As she reluctantly lifted her head, she saw Steven waving at her from the car. He walked up onto the porch and pulled up one of the chairs to sit down in front of her.

"Are you feeling all right? You look as though you've been crying," said Steven.

"I'm okay, I guess. Some days are harder than others I suppose," Marcie answered.

"Is now a bad time to stop by?"

"No, it's fine, but Nathan's not home right now. He went in to see Dr. Seyler. He should be along in a minute or so. Would you like some hot tea?"

"No thanks, I just had something. Do you mind if I wait a while for him?"

"No."

"While I'm waiting, can I ask you a couple of questions?"

"What do you want to ask?"

"Do you truly believe that Nathan is innocent?"

Marcie looked startled and stared back at Steven in silence for a moment. "What? Are you crazy? Boy, you really get right to the point, don't you? Do you think I would actually be sticking by him like this if I really thought that he was capable of killing two young boys, one of them being my brother? I know he didn't do it."

"Why are you so sure?"

"I just know him, that's all," Marcie shot back. "He could never harm anyone. Besides, I think there's some kind of conspiracy going on here to frame him for the death of Todd and Robert."

"In what way?" Steven asked.

"Well, for instance, I don't believe my accident was really an accident at all. I think someone tried to run me off the road that night.

Someone wanted me out of the way because they knew I would fight to the end to protect Nathan. They also were planning on framing him for my death, most likely."

"What happened that night, Marcie?" asked Steven.

"I can only remember a car pulling out from nowhere, right in front of me. It wasn't coming head on, as a car would come from the other direction, but it seemed to dash out from the side of the road."

"And could you see the driver?"

"No, no I couldn't. It all happened so fast," answered Marcie. "I only remember waking up in the car and realizing I was trapped inside."

"Did you tell the sheriff that you thought someone was trying to kill you?"

"No, I wasn't sure enough to prove it and I didn't trust anyone at the time, other than Nathan and my mother. I guess I was afraid to tell Mark."

"So you just let it go?" asked Steven.

"I didn't know what else to do. We were planning on leaving town, but we never made it."

"This all seems so crazy. It's hard to believe someone would go through all of the trouble to frame Nathan. I mean, what would be their motive?"

"I'm not sure, but I believe it has something to do with Nathan's memory. Maybe someone is afraid he will eventually remember what really happened to Robert and they don't want that to happen. I believe Todd and Robert's deaths are some how strangely connected. It's like we're trying to find our way through a giant maze, and it seems we'll never find the end of it."

"Tell me some more about the old man you saw while you were trapped in the car. Do you believe you really saw him?" asked Steven.

"Well, at first I wasn't sure, but then I heard Nathan talking about seeing an old man chasing him. I guess I just started believing that he's a real person. I mean, we wouldn't both be having the same dreams and hallucinations."

"Did he look like the mask that was found in Nathan's bag, in your barn?"

"Yes, he did, I think," Marcie paused. "I'm not sure. I only saw him briefly when his flashlight fell and then I blacked out. You're not still suggesting that Nathan is the old man, are you?"

Steven stared back at Marcie. "No, I'm just trying to piece some things together here. You say the old man looked into the car, but then he left. Do you think he left to go and get help?"

"I don't know. Maybe he left me to die or maybe he thought I was already dead," answered Marcie.

"Then Nathan came and rescued you from the car some time after that, but you don't remember how long after, is that right?"

"Like I said before, Steven, I must have blacked out. I can't say for how long."

"Have you seen this old man since then?"

"No, I haven't," answered Marcie softly.

Just then Nathan arrived and joined them on the porch. "What's this, a secret meeting?" Nathan asked.

"No, nothing like that. I was just talking to Marcie while I was waiting for you to come home," replied Steven.

"Oh, I see," said Nathan.

"We were discussing the old man that Marcie saw in her accident. Do you remember what time it was when you arrived at the car and started to help Marcie out?"

"No, but it was getting dark or was pretty dark already. I had to use a flashlight. Maybe it was somewhere around six or six thirty."

"Nathan, why didn't you tell Mark about the old man Marcie saw looking in the car?" asked Steven with a more serious tone.

"I don't know," answered Nathan. "Mark seems pretty suspicious of everything I do or say. I didn't really trust him enough to tell him much. I thought maybe we could find more clues before we confronted him with our suspicions about the accident, but everything just moved so quickly, we haven't been able to do that."

"I don't know whether or not I'll be able to convince a jury that the old man really exists other than in your memory or dreams," said Steven, walking across the porch. "Marcie says she saw him, but she was fading in and out of consciousness. She's not really capable of describing him to a jury."

"But you can't just dismiss that she saw him. Someone was there," replied Nathan.

"What I don't want is to give the jury any room to decide that the old man could have been you wearing a disguise, like the rubber mask that was found in your bag," said Steven quietly.

Nathan sat back in his chair. "Why would I want to kill Marcie? Why would I have left her to die out in the middle of nowhere? I love her."

"But Nathan, you are also seeing a psychiatrist because you're reliving some past events in your life," Steven answered quickly. "The jury could just see you as a poor helpless psychotic man who can't remember what he does when he's reliving these terrible moments. I'm just trying to second guess what they might assume."

"What about Jake Foster, Dan's neighbor?" Nathan asked. "He told Dan Harper he saw an old man walking around in the woods just before Todd was killed. Dan told Mark, but nothing ever came of it."

"I'll have to pay this Jake person a visit," said Steven. "Are you sure you can't remember anything else?"

"Steven, my mind is going ninety miles an hour. I've been charged with murder and I'm struggling to remember bits and pieces of things that happened to me when I was just a boy. It's not like I don't want to remember anything," Nathan said standing to his feet.

"I understand that, Nathan, but do you want to spend the rest of your life behind bars? If there's anything else that you haven't told me I need to know it. Everything is important, Nathan," said Steven loudly.

"I'm sorry, my mind isn't dealing straight with me right now," replied Nathan, staring down at his feet.

"Look, I know this is very hard, for both of you," said Steven. "I don't mean to yell at you because I'm angry. It's because I want to have every bit of information you can give me to put this case together. Do you understand that I'm trying to help you?" Steven got up and walked to the other side of the porch and lit up a cigar. "How did the visit with Dr. Seyler go today?"

"He's going to try to arrange for me to be hypnotized to see if it will release some of my childhood memories," answered Nathan. "He said it might help or it might not, but I figure it's worth a shot. I'm ready to try anything right now."

"I talked with my friend, you know the one I was telling you about? He's the one who is going to keep an eye on you. His name is James, James Carwood. He's going to be here tomorrow. Will you have a place for him to stay? I want him around you as much as possible, at least for a while. Is that still all right with you?"

"I'm not looking forward to it," replied Nathan. "But I suppose I can put up with it."

"Well, I'm going to head back to the office and see how Doug is doing," said Steven, walking toward his car. Maybe I will see if we can catch up to our friend Jake. I'll talk to you guys later." Steven started for his car and paused before getting in, "Nathan, would you mind if I sat in on your hypnosis session when you do it? Do you think the doctor will allow it?"

"I don't mind. I'll have to touch base with him," answered Nathan. "I'll let you know when."

"Thanks," said Steven.

Marcie and Nathan stood on the porch and watched Steven drive out of sight. Even though it was just the two of them, the quiet had some how been disturbed and they were left with too many thoughts to enjoy the view or the sounds around them. Nathan went inside the house and Marcie sat back down on the porch and continued sipping her tea.

# 47

Steven and Doug wound their way around a twisting, narrow country road that led them through the mountains, to Jake Foster's house. Around every bend they anticipated seeing the house, but it seemed that the road would go on forever. It was a beautiful, warm day, so neither of them minded the long drive.

"I think I could live out in the country like this sometimes, but I'm afraid I'd miss the city too much," said Steven.

"Well, this guy must not miss the rest of the world. He's really secluded back here. Are you sure we're going in the right direction?" asked Doug, as he nervously played with the map.

"We should be coming up on it shortly," replied Steven. "Relax and enjoy the scenery. It's beautiful out here. I can see how someone would leave everything behind and move out to a place like this. It's quiet and peaceful and—"

"And away from everything I love," interrupted Doug.

"Such as?"

"Well, such as pizza at 1 A.M. and the movie rental store and—"

"Never mind," said Steven smiling. "I can see you're a real nature lover. Don't you ever get a longing to just throw everything aside, find some secluded place, stretch out and listen to the sound of the birds singing from the trees and the wind rustling through the leaves?" asked Steven.

"No," said Doug staring out the window. "I'm more of a honking-horn-barking-dog-crying-baby-kind-of-guy, I guess. I just love the city, man. The only way I could sleep out here would be with a loaded shotgun lying across my chest."

"Hey look," said Steven pointing. "I think this is it."

Steven and Doug sat in the car for a moment, looking around.

"Wow, there's not another house around for miles," said Steven. "I sure hope he's home. Nobody answered the phone when I tried to call earlier."

As they looked around it appeared no one was there. It was quiet and still.

"Well, we might as well try the front door," said Steven. "Come on."

Steven started out of the car when Doug grabbed his arm, "Wait, I think I see somebody at the window, and if I'm not mistaken, it looks like he might be aiming a rifle at us."

Steven looked closely at the window where Doug was pointing. Just behind the lace curtains, you could see the image of a man with a rifle in his hands, pointed straight at them. Steven honked the horn and waved his hand.

Doug nearly jumped out of his skin, "What in the world are you doing? Do you want to get us killed, or something? It's obvious he's not in a talking mood, so let's just get out of here before mountain pappy decides to blow us away. He could bury us and nobody would ever find us way out here."

"Just wait a second," said Steven quietly. "Calm down. He's not about to shoot us." He slowly opened the car door and stepped outside, holding his hands in the air so the man in the window could see he was unarmed.

"It's okay," shouted Steven. "I'm a lawyer for Nathan Staby. I'm here to speak to Jake Foster. Is that you, sir?"

There was no answer from the house.

"I promise not to take much of your time if you could just tell me where to find Jake, please?" said Steven with his hands in the air. "Is he around somewhere?"

Still, there was no answer.

"Steven, let's just go," Doug shouted. "He doesn't seem to want visitors right now."

Just then the man lowered his gun and disappeared from the window. Steven stayed by the car just in case the man was coming to get a closer aim at him. Suddenly, he saw the front door open and a woman stepped out on the porch.

"Jake said he don't want to see nobody right now," said the woman loudly. "Please just get back in your car and go away."

"Ma'am, we just want to ask a few questions about the day Todd Harper was killed. You see, I'm Nathan's defense lawyer and I understand Jake may have seen an old man walking around in the woods that day. It could be a big help to us if he would just let me talk to him. I'll stay by the car if it would make him more comfortable," shouted Steven.

The woman stepped back toward the door of the house, as though she was conferring with someone, but then she stepped back out on the porch alone.

"He said to go away! He don't want to be involved with any of this killing business. We just want to be left alone, that's all. Now you just better go on away from here."

"I understand, ma'am, but this is very important," answered Steven nervously. "You see a man's life is at stake here. Can't he at least answer yes or no to whether or not he actually saw someone in the woods that day?" Steven persisted.

"Steven, please, don't push him," Doug yelled from a crouching position by the car. "These people will shoot you and then hide your body so nobody will ever find it. Let's go like she says, before you get us both shot."

Then a man stepped out of the house and onto the porch. He was carrying a rifle, "I said, get off my property mister. I don't care who you are or what you need. I ain't talking to you, or nobody else about anything. Now get out!" The man stood with the rifle aimed precisely at him, but Steven boldly stood his ground.

"Mr. Foster, I know you don't want to be involved, but if I have to, I can make you testify at Nathan's trial," Steven shouted back. "Now, please, just cooperate, Mr. Foster. You're not in any trouble, but you can be if you withhold information that's needed in this case."

"You do what you got to do, but I'm not talking to nobody today," Jake answered. "Now this is your last warning." Jake raised the gun to his shoulder and took aim at Steven.

"If you change your mind, here's my card. I'll just leave it here for you on the ground," said Steven.

He carefully took out one of his business cards and placed it down on the ground where Jake could see it. Then he and Doug slowly got back into their car and backed onto the road. Meanwhile, Jake was still aiming the rifle at them. Steven sped away from the house as quickly as he could go.

"I can't believe you!" shouted Doug, holding his head in his hands. "You almost got us shot back there. Are you crazy? These people back in these mountains don't care whether you're a lawyer or a doctor or anybody else. They'll shoot you for just looking at them wrong. What's the matter with you?" asked Doug, looking back over his shoulder.

"He wasn't looking to shoot us, Doug," Steven said. "He just wanted me to leave him alone. He's a man who knows something that he's not being allowed to tell. Somebody got to him before we did and gave him a good scare. Now we only need to know what he's hiding and who shut him up."

"Oh, is that all?" Doug said sarcastically. "Well, I think we have an open and shut case then. Wouldn't you say so?" Doug folded his arms with a smirk on his face.

"Well, at least we know there's more to this story than Nathan being the killer. There's more to know, Dougie boy, and I'm going to find out what it is."

"In a small town like this, it's almost impossible to get neighbors to rat on each other," replied Doug. "They would just about rather die first."

"We'll see about that," answered Steven. "Let's get back and go over our notes one more time. Maybe there's a piece to the puzzle dangling right in front of our faces that we've somehow missed. I want us to go over every written statement and every piece of paper we have on this case. Let's make sure we're not overlooking anything here. Nathan deserves our best defense."

"What do you think Jake is hiding from us?" asked Doug. "Why would someone be trying to keep him quiet? Do you think he really did see the killer? The killer could be living right here in this town, and maybe he's threatening Jake somehow." Doug paused for a moment. "This is getting really weird, Steven. The killer could be watching our every move." Doug looked back over his shoulder again to make sure nobody was following them. "I'm starting to get a creepy feeling about all this."

"Don't fold on me now, son," said Steven. "I'm going to need all the help I can get on this. I just hope Nathan doesn't flip out before we're able to solve this mystery. He seems to be dangling on the edge more and more these days. If somebody is trying to tip him over, they're doing a real good job of it."

Steven began driving a little faster as he headed back to his office. He was beginning to sense the urgency in Nathan's situation.

As they wound their way back to town, Doug couldn't help but look back over his shoulder at least one more time.

Meanwhile, back at Marcie's house, a tall slim young man rang the doorbell and waited outside. Nathan glanced through the window at him before answering the door. He had never seen him before.

"Yes, may I help you?" Nathan asked cautiously.

"Hi, my name is James Carwood. I'm a friend of Steven Massie. I believe he said you would be expecting me."

Nathan just stared at him with a puzzled look on his face at first. Then he realized he was the one Steven wanted to come and watch over him for a while.

"Oh, yeah, Steven did tell me about you," Nathan replied. "I'm sorry. Come on in, James."

James stepped inside with his bag and then scratched his head. "This is very awkward for me. I suppose Steven explained to you why I'm here, right?"

"Yeah, he did." Nathan laughed. "You're going to make sure I don't do anything strange in my sleep, right?"

"Well, Steven said that you're a sleepwalker," replied James. He wants me to observe your actions if you start to roam around while you're supposed to be sleeping. I guess I'll have to do my sleeping during the day."

"Look, this is probably not necessary," said Nathan. "I'll just tell Steven this is too strange. We'll forget the whole deal."

"No, actually it sounds like a good idea," said James. "He said you sometimes have problems remembering what you do or where you go when you're sleepwalking. At least I can make sure you don't get hurt and help you to remember what happens to you." James paused awkwardly for a moment. "It sounds pretty exciting to me. Maybe we should give it a try, just to see what happens. Aren't you a little bit curious about what happens when you go out for a nightly stroll?"

"I'm curious in some ways, but on the other hand, I might be better off not knowing," said Nathan, shaking his head. "It's a little scary for me. Aren't you a little uneasy about having to follow me around? I've been charged with murder, you know. Steven did tell you that, right?"

"Yeah, he did actually," replied James. "He's asked me to do stranger things, believe me. I'm comfortable with it if you are. Look, I know Steven has your best interest at heart. He's a great lawyer. You're very lucky to have him representing you. He may seem a little crazy, but he'll do anything to get at the truth. That's what's so good about him. He's not afraid to push the limits."

"Great, I'm half crazy and now I find out my lawyer may be crazy too," said Nathan with a smile. "We make a good pair. Come on, let me show you where you'll be staying." Nathan started up the stairs to the bedroom where James would be sleeping during the day. "I have to tell you, I'm not really wild about having a stranger in the house, much less having you follow me around, but I guess if you're a friend of Steven's, you're all right."

"Steven and I have been friends for a long time," said James. "We go way back. Believe me, you're in good hands."

Nathan smiled and continued up the stairs. "Yeah, I'm starting to feel better already," he said quietly.

# 48

The time for Nathan's trial was fast approaching and he was feeling less confident now about his chances of being found innocent than ever before. In his opinion, Steven and Doug had not been able to uncover anything that might help his case, even though they had been working long hours with little sleep. Marcie seemed to be getting more depressed as each day passed and Nathan was afraid that he was going to lose her if they weren't able to get on with some sort of normal life soon. Living moment to moment, not being able to plan their future was hard for both of them. They didn't really even dare dream beyond the present day and time. Each day was more difficult than the other as the trial grew closer. Nathan spent long hours just thinking, trying to remember something useful, but nothing new was coming.

Finally, Dr. Seyler set up a session with the hypnotist, as he had promised. Nathan was scared, but also anxious to see if any results would come from it. He had envisioned all of his memories spilling out, and with them, the answers to the deaths of Todd and Robert. He tried not to get his hopes up too high, for fear of great disappointment if the hypnosis didn't work. Feeling desperate, Nathan knew it may be his last hope of discovering the truth.

Nathan had told Steven he could sit in on the session. They both arrived at Dr. Seyler's office that day with great anticipation. Marcie decided to stay home and wait for any news that the session had been a success. She felt her presence there in the office might inhibit Nathan in some way. She didn't want to interfere with his ability to remember something significant.

Dr. Seyler greeted both Nathan and Steven and then introduced them to Dr. Thomas Gresser, a psychiatrist and an expert in the field of hypnosis. As they all took a seat in Dr. Seyler's office, Nathan wanted to take off running, as far away as possible, but he knew he had to stay and face his past, whatever the consequences. Dr. Gresser seemed pleasant enough. So Nathan tried to calm himself into being brave enough to go through with the experiment. Maybe something important would come out of it after all.

"Nathan, you can call me Tom if you like," said Dr. Gresser. "I want you to feel as comfortable as possible. Now, before we begin, I want you to know there's a possibility that the hypnosis won't help you to remember any more than you're able to remember right now. Sometimes it's a useful tool in unlocking deep memories that have long been forgotten or blocked out, but often these memories remain locked away and even with hypnosis we're unable to bring them to light. There may be any number of reasons for this and I won't go into all of them with you now. I just want you to be aware so that you won't be too disappointed if nothing happens here today," explained Dr. Gresser. "Do you understand?"

"Yes, I understand," answered Nathan, taking a deep breath. "But you will try your best to make me remember, won't you?"

"It's not up to me. It's up to you," replied Dr. Gresser. "You are the one who is holding your memories somewhere far away from everyone. You're the only one who can allow them to be reached and brought out in the open. I'll try to guide you to different areas that will help you remember various things in your life, but then it's up to you to go deeper." Dr. Gresser paused for a moment looking at Nathan. "Are you nervous?"

"Yeah, you could say that," replied Nathan. "I'm shaking like a leaf, but I want to do this. I'll be fine. Let's get on with this thing."

"Is it okay if I take notes?" asked Steven.

"Who are you?" asked Dr. Gresser, looking over his glasses at Steven.

"It's okay," replied Dr. Seyler. "He's Nathan's lawyer and he has been given permission by him to be present during this session. Steven, why don't you sit over there in the corner out of sight? That way, Nathan will forget you're even here."

Steven took a chair in the corner and took out his pen and pad of paper, ready to write. "Is it all right if I use this mini tape recorder as well?"

"Yes, it's okay by me, that is, if Nathan doesn't mind," replied Dr. Seyler.

"I don't mind," replied Nathan. "I would like to hear the tape myself when it's all over. Hopefully there will be something worth recording."

Nathan took another deep breath and tried his best to settle into what was about to take place. He wasn't even sure if he was capable of being hypnotized. He used to scoff at the very mention of such a thing. He always doubted that it would be possible for someone to take control of his thoughts.

Dr. Gresser dimmed the lights in the room, "This is just to make you feel more relaxed, Nathan. Now, are you comfortable?"

"Yeah, as comfortable as I'm going to feel, I suppose."

"Good, now I want you to listen to the sound of my voice. Just close your eyes and listen only to my voice. Can you hear me?"

"Yes, I hear you," replied Nathan softly. The room was very quiet and he felt as though he could drift off to sleep at any minute.

"Now, I want you to keep your eyes closed and imagine yourself lying in the middle of a beautiful meadow. It's peaceful and there's a warm breeze blowing around you. You're very tired and you've laid down for a rest. There's not another soul around, but you can hear the sounds of a nearby creek babbling past as you begin to drift off to sleep. You feel safe here. You're totally relaxed with no worries. You can still hear the sound of my voice. Are you starting to feel sleepy, Nathan?"

"Yes, I'm very tired," replied Nathan.

"Wow, that's amazing," interrupted Steven, without meaning to speak out loud.

"Please, you must remain silent!" Dr. Gresser cautioned Steven in a loud whisper. "Do not interrupt again. If you do, I will have to ask you to leave the room."

"I'm sorry. I've just never seen this done before," replied Steven with a tone of excitement in his voice. "I won't make another sound." Steven sat down and covered his mouth to ensure he kept quiet.

"As you fall asleep, Nathan, you will begin to dream," continued Dr. Gresser. "You're dreaming of your childhood. You're just a young boy. I want you to describe your dream to me as we go along. Just tell me whatever it is you see."

Nathan's eyes were closed and his whole body was limp in the chair. Dr. Gresser could see his eyes moving back and forth under his eyelids, like someone who was in a deep sleep and having a very vivid dream.

"What do you see, Nathan?" asked Dr. Gresser.

"I'm in a big field with some kids. We're hiding behind some bushes near an old white house. They're daring me to go closer to the house by myself. I'm afraid, but I don't want them to know. So I'm taking on the dare."

"Whose house is it, Nathan?" asked Dr. Gresser.

"It looks like there's a woman on the porch, but I'm not sure who she is," he replied.

"Nathan, I want you to keep trying to see the face of the person on the porch. Try to run closer to her. Try very hard, Nathan," encouraged Dr. Gresser.

"I'm trying, but it just gets farther away."

"Run as fast as you can, Nathan. Use all of your energy to get closer. Now, what do you see?"

"I'm running, but it's too far," replied Nathan. "I'm tired and I have to rest."

"No, you must keep trying," said Dr. Gresser. "You're not tired, Nathan. You're young and full of life. You can run forever. Now get going. Run as fast as you can to the porch, Nathan. Go ahead, you can do it."

Nathan's head jerked back and forth as he forced himself to run. He began to sweat and turn red in the face.

"Tell me what you see," insisted Dr. Gresser. "Are you on the porch?"

"I'm hiding behind an old tree stump near the porch," Nathan said quietly. "There's a woman sitting on a chair, snapping green beans. She's talking to another person, but I can't see them."

"Do you recognize the voice?" asked Dr. Gresser.

"It's a woman's voice, but I don't recognize it," replied Nathan. "It's not my mother's voice, but it sounds familiar to me."

"Can you understand what she's saying?"

"No, not really," answered Nathan. "Wait, she's slowly turning around."

Nathan's heart was racing, but he strained to see her face. Just as he's about to get a closer glimpse, another person runs up onto the porch and the woman's arms reach out for him.

Nathan gets closer. "It looks like a man, but he's crying. The woman is holding him tightly in her arms and rocking him back and forth."

Suddenly, Nathan sees the woman's face clearly. "Old lady Radcliff! I mean, it's Betsy Radcliff!" he shouted. "We use to tease her when we were boys, and throw rocks at her house. The place is all run down, like a haunted house. They dared me to run close to Betsy Radcliff's house without her seeing me."

"Nathan, please stay calm. I don't want you to wake up just yet," Dr. Gresser said softly. "Try to stay there for a while longer. You've opened a door that's been closed for a long time. Now, try to see the other person she's rocking. Who do you see?"

"I'm not sure," moaned Nathan. "The face is hidden. I can't make out who it is. Oh no, the kids are throwing rocks at the house. She's upset. She's screaming at them. I'm scared! I'm running away as fast as I can."

Nathan pauses for a moment. "I, I can't see him anymore."

"That's okay, Nathan," said Dr. Gresser very softly, "Let's move on to another time. Now you're older. You're playing in the woods with your best friend, Robert. This is the day that Robert was killed, Nathan. Try to tell me what you see now. Where are you?"

"We're running in the woods along side the Black River. It's starting to get dark. I know I should be getting home, but Robert still wants to play. He says I'm too scared to stay out in the woods while it's dark. So I'm staying to show him I'm not afraid."

"That's good, Nathan," said Dr. Gresser. "What else?"

"Robert is jumping from rock to rock along the river. He's yelling for me to follow him. We're having a great time. It's like we're on our own and there's nobody around to tell us what to do. We're king of the woods. We're pretending to be chased by a dragon. So we quickly make swords out of big tree branches on the ground." Nathan smiles. "Robert can run so much faster than I can. He keeps running way ahead of me, out of sight. Now I can't see him. I can only hear his voice. He keeps calling for me to follow him."

Suddenly Nathan seems startled.

"Nathan, what's wrong?" asked Dr. Gresser. "Did something happen to Robert?"

"I hear him screaming," said Nathan. Sweat is forming on his forehead now. "Robert's calling for help, but his voice sounds different to me. He's not pretending anymore. It's for real. He really needs my help. I'm running as fast as I can. I'm trying to get to him. Wait! Now I hear another voice. This time it's not Robert's voice. I can't see what's going on, but I'm scared. I want to run away, but somebody grabs me and wrestles me down into the bushes. I know it's not Robert."

"Listen carefully, Nathan," said Dr. Gresser. "Can you hear any other voices in the woods?"

"Yes, I hear talking, but I can't really make out what they're saying. I'm really scared. I bolt out of the bushes and start running for home. I'm running and running, but I keep thinking of Robert. There's, heavy breathing behind me. Someone's chasing me. I'm running faster, but the breathing seems to be all around me now. It's so close. It feels like it's going right through me."

Nathan jumped a bit, like something or someone had hold of him.

"Nathan, what's happening?" asked Dr. Gresser.

"Someone just ran past me in the dark, but I can't see them. I'm hiding behind a big tree for a little while to make sure it's clear. I'm afraid to move."

Nathan pauses for a while. He starts to shake uncontrollably.

"Nathan, try to go home," said Dr. Gresser. "You'll be safe there."

Nathan keeps shaking. "I'm back home. My mom is fussing over me about eating before she has to go to work, but I can't eat. I just go to my room. I'm shaking so hard I pull the covers up around me, but I can't stop shaking. It won't stop!"

"Nathan, listen to the sound of my voice," said Dr. Gresser quietly and calmly. "You're safe now. No one can harm you. Just relax."

After a while Nathan stops shaking and becomes very still.

"Nathan, when do you find Robert?" asked Dr. Gresser in a low voice. "Do you find him later?"

"Yes, the next morning. I'm back out into the woods early. I find him buried in a shallow grave of colored leaves. His hand is sticking out of the leaves, all pale and cold."

"Do you see anything else?"

"I'm scared again. I start to run back out of the woods to get the police, but someone else is standing there, an old man with white hair and a sash. He, he almost looks like an angel, but his face looks strange and old. He speaks to me. He knows my name, but I don't know who he is. I just run away again. I can see him waving at me as I look back."

"Do you recognize him at all? Try very hard."

Nathan tries his best to stare back at the old man, but for some reason, he can't look at him for very long. "No, I don't know who he is. I can't see clearly. I'm so afraid, please, please take me away from here." Nathan started to cry. "Robert! Robert, I'm sorry I couldn't help you. Oh, dear God, I should have been there to help you."

"Nathan, I want you to wake up now," said Dr. Gresser in a loud voice. "You're no longer tired and you're ready to awaken from your dream. When I count to three, you'll wake up from your sleep. One, two, three, wake up Nathan."

Nathan slowly opened his eyes, blinking several times before he is fully conscious.

"How do you feel?" asked Dr. Gresser. "Are you all right?"

"Yes, I'm okay I guess." Nathan stood up from his chair and walked across the room to the window. He stood quietly for a while, "I remember Betsy Radcliff. I saw her in my dream. Why would I remember anything about her?" Nathan stopped and leaned against the wall next to the window.

"You were able to remember at least that much, but not very much about Robert's death that you don't already remember," said Dr. Seyler.

"But you do remember that Robert was killed by someone else, and not you. That's what's important," said Steven. "Dr. Gresser, why didn't you ask him about Todd Harper? That's who he's accused of killing, not Robert Sanding."

"We'll have to do it a bit later. We can't expose the patient to too much at once, or his whole memory may shut down. It's too much of a shock to the system. Do you want to try again tomorrow, Nathan?" asked Dr. Gresser.

"No, it's no use doctor. I'm never going to remember anything this way. If I can't remember anything more about Robert's death, then I'm certainly not going to remember anything new about Todd's death. I know I didn't do it, but this is not the way to prove it. Now, if you don't mind, I'm going home. I've got to sort through some things on my own." He left the office and Steven followed closely behind him.

"Nathan, wait, we need to talk."

"Not now, Steven. Please, just give me some time. I need to be alone right now."

Nathan got in his car and drove away. His mind was going over and over again the picture of Betsy Radcliff reaching out to the man on the porch. What did it mean? He felt more confused than ever now. He felt as though everything he tried made matters worse instead of better. His trial was just around the corner and he had nothing to offer in his defense.

# 49

Nathan walked into the Raven Inn late in the afternoon. As he walked in, he looked around like it was his first time there. It was very strange, but everything that had been familiar to him now felt strange and distant. He walked into the library and began thumbing through some of Maggie's old books and magazines. He knelt down and slid open one of the mahogany panel doors. There were more books and envelopes stuffed with various papers inside. Nathan's fingers moved across each item before coming to rest on an old photo album that was covered with dust. He carefully lifted it from the shelf and sat on the floor to examine it. Maggie had taken great pains to place each photograph in a book, but he didn't recall ever seeing this particular one. She had so many memories sealed away. It was no wonder he couldn't remember seeing this one.

As Nathan turned the pages, he saw photos that he may have seen in the past without actually taking notice of the faces, but now they curiously took on more significance than before. Nathan studied each photograph. He had no idea what he was hoping to find. The people in the pictures all looked alike to him. They were just old, yellow pictures of people, most since passed on, but apparently each one held a special place in Maggie's heart. She had carefully placed each one side by side in these books, taking the time to place handwritten notes beside a lot of them.

Nathan turned the pages slowly as he walked through a time before he was born and while he was a young boy. A picture of two young girls caught his eye. They were both dressed in frilly clothes and lace bonnets. Underneath the picture Maggie had scribbled something. Nathan got up and took it over to the window for a better light. The note read, "Me and my sister, Betsy, on Easter Sunday before church."

Maggie had never mentioned her sister around him that he remembered. "Betsy," he said to himself. As he turned to the next page, there was a wedding picture. The young man was smiling and wearing a black tuxedo and a hat. Beside the photo Maggie had written, "My sister's wedding day." Nathan looked closely at the faces in the picture. The woman looked familiar to him. It was the woman he had seen while under hypnosis.

"It's Betsy Radcliff," Nathan mumbled to himself in disbelief. "Wait, she and Maggie were sisters? But she never mentioned her, not even when we told stories about Betsy's house being haunted. I told her about how we dared each other to ride our bikes in front of her broken-down-white house."

Nathan looked out of the window, just staring into space. "An old white house," he thought. "Could it be the same house I remembered under hypnosis?"

Nathan took a seat by the window, balancing the book on his lap. "Maybe this is what Maggie wanted me to find out," he thought. "This is why she wanted me to stay here. But I wonder what all this could have to do with Robert's death? Why didn't Maggie just tell me this herself?"

He suddenly felt like he had been cut loose from everything he had been tied to in his past. His childhood memories all drifted away from him.

"Are you okay in there?" Marcie called from the doorway. She stepped into the room and she could see Nathan was a thousand miles away. She lifted the book from his lap and took his hand. "Nathan, I've been worried about you. I called the doctor's office and they said you left a while ago. I figured you might have come here. How did it go? Did it help at all?"

Nathan squeezed her hand tightly and pulled her to him. He held her tightly. "Don't ever go away, Marcie. Promise me you'll stay with me until they won't let you stay."

"Nathan, what are you saying?" said Marcie, pulling away from Nathan. "What's wrong with you? You look pale and your hands are cold. Are you getting sick?"

"No, no I'm not getting sick. I'm slowly, but surely, finding out about the past. Some of it's hard to swallow though. I keep saying I want to remember things, but when I find out something, I find myself wishing I never looked."

"Why? What did you find?" asked Marcie. "Can you tell me?"

"Marcie, did you know your mother had a sister named Betsy? Did she ever mention her to you?"

"I suppose she did, but she didn't mention her often. She told me that her sister died when she was young. Why do you ask such a thing? What's that got to do with—."

"Her sister was Betsy Radcliff," interrupted Nathan. "I guess Maggie figured if I stayed here long enough I would find out."

Marcie stood up and took her hand from Nathan's. "You're being silly, Nathan. How could my mother's sister have been Betsy Radcliff? Why, she was a wretched old woman that everybody hated. What a terrible thing to say. How dare you!"

Nathan slowly handed the photograph of Betsy's wedding to Marcie.

"I don't believe it!" Marcie said with her hand over her mouth.

"Listen to me, Marcie. I've been seeing this white wood-framed house in my dreams, or my imagination or whatever it is. I didn't know what it meant, but while I was undergoing hypnosis, I saw the white house again, and a woman was sitting on the front porch. Marcie, I saw her face. It was Betsy Radcliff. She was holding and rocking someone. I couldn't see the face. Marcie, all of this must have some meaning or a connection in some way. Something happened between Betsy and Maggie, something that caused Maggie to tell people her sister was dead."

"Nathan, this is just so much to take in. I mean old lady Radcliff was a mean, ugly old woman. All of the kids used to throw rocks at her house and call her names. I can't believe she's my mother's sister. Why would she lie about a thing like that? Mom never even went to visit her or talk about her around us. This is just too hard!" Marcie stormed out of the room and outside to the car, then stopping and putting her hands to her head, she was beginning to feel faint. Marcie couldn't take much more of this. Every day something changed in her life, spinning her in circles.

Nathan walked up behind her and put his arms around her to steady her. "Are you all right? I'm sorry Marcie, I know it seems strange and it's hard to believe that it's true, but it is. I don't know what that has to do with anything else that's happened here, but little by little I'm finding out the truth. Please stay with me through this, baby." Nathan turned her toward him and pulled her close. "There may come a time, very soon, when they separate us and we won't be together again for a long time, maybe forever. Let's not waste what time we have together now."

"Nathan, please don't talk that way. I can't even think about us being apart or surviving without you in my life now and I don't want to even try." Marcie kissed him and hugged him as tightly as she could. "Let's run away. Let's just pack up and leave town in the middle of the night where nobody can find us. Please, Nathan, let's do it. I don't think I can bear much more of this. Let's just be together, with no one else around asking questions and poking into our lives. Forget about your past. It doesn't matter now. What does matter is our future together. We have to protect that."

Nathan stared deeply into Marcie's eyes. He could see she was being sincere. He knew now that she truly loved him. Running away was very tempting. If they could find some place where no one would ever find them and they could spend the rest of their days in each other's arms, he would be tempted to try it. But Nathan knew he had to continue to find out the truth about himself and about who killed Robert and Todd. There was no way he could put that behind him now. He had gone too far into his past to run away from it now.

"No, Marcie. We have to stay here. Don't you see?" said Nathan. "If we run, they will definitely believe I'm guilty. We've got to stay here and fight this. Our future depends on it. I want us to live without having to look over our shoulders at every turn and without the past hanging over our heads. We have to stay here."

Marcie buried her head in Nathan's chest. She knew it was true, but running away just seemed the easier thing to do right now. She just wanted everything to disappear around them and allow them to lead everyday, normal lives again. But that felt more like a fantasy, than a reality.

# 50

The first day of the trial had finally arrived and Steven and Doug knew that their case was too weak to convince a jury of Nathan's innocence. Still, they didn't have a choice but to go in with what they had and pray for a miracle. As they sat at the front table, Steven could see that Nathan was very nervous. He reached over and put his hand on his shoulder.

"We're going to give it all we've got. I promise you I'll do my best," said Steven reassuringly.

"I know you will," replied Nathan with a half smile on his tense face. Yet he continued to wring his hands and to shake his leg under the table. His eyes ran across the jurors' faces. They looked like ordinary-down-to-earth folks who could easily reason anything out. He wanted them to believe his side of the story so badly. He wanted to just go over to each one and explain everything to them, but he knew that wasn't possible.

As the judge entered the courtroom, everyone stood to their feet, including Nathan. He was feeling wobbly and a bit dizzy as he stood. He couldn't bring himself to believe this was actually happening and that it wasn't one of his dreams. He almost jumped out of his skin when the judge slammed his gavel down to begin the session. Again, Steven took his arm and tried to comfort him as best he could.

Nathan looked back over his shoulder and gave a quick smile to Marcie. She looked pale and tired, but she managed to send a smile back to him. "Maybe running away wasn't such a bad idea," Nathan thought. He mouthed the words, "I love you" to Marcie. She smiled as she fought back tears.

"Is the attorney for the defense ready to make his opening statement?" asked the judge in a loud voice.

"Yes, I'm ready, Your Honor," replied Steven.

"Then proceed, if you will."

The room had high ceilings and the judge's voice echoed throughout the courtroom. As Steven stood and walked toward the jury, you could easily hear each step on the wooden floor.

Steven approached the jury box and just stood in front of them for a few moments, as though he was trying to remember what it was he wanted to say.

"You did say you were ready, didn't you, Counselor?" asked the judge with a stern look on his face.

Nathan was really starting to get nervous now. Doug was busy chewing on the end of his pen and staring at Steven. He wanted to go over and slap him on the back to give him a jumpstart.

Finally Steven began to speak. "I just wanted to take a moment to look over the good people that are serving on the jury for this case. I have to say that each of you looks to be intelligent and reasonable. I'm sure each of you is capable of hearing a case and realizing that all is not as it seems on the surface. Sometimes there are circumstances in a case that can't necessarily be seen at first glance. So you have to look and listen very carefully. This is just such a case."

"Great," Nathan whispered to Doug. "He's already telling them we don't have any proof of my innocence."

Doug just stared back at Nathan as he continued to chew on the end of his pen.

Nathan hung his head for a moment. "We're in deep here and there's no way out," he thought to himself.

"The person you see before you today grew up right here in Fairhaven and knows a lot of the people around here," began Steven. "He's a successful writer and a responsible and concerned citizen of this town. Although he did move away for a while, he later returned here. Nathan has always loved and cherished this town and its people, just like most of you. This trial today begins a horrible chapter in his life. He's been charged with the murder of Todd Harper, a young boy who also lived in this town. But I submit to you that he's been charged out of desperation and with no real proof and it's my intent to prove that to you here in this courtroom."

Steven walked back and forth in front of the jury as he spoke. "All I ask of you, ladies and gentlemen of the jury, is to keep your ears and your eyes open at all times. Listen carefully to what is said and how it's said, because the prosecutor is going to rattle off a lot of information that will, at first glance, seem to point to the guilt of my client, but there's definitely more here than what you'll see in front of you. This case has to do with the past, the present and the future. It has little to do with what the prosecutor will dangle in front of your eyes and everything to do with intangible things, such as feelings and thoughts. I just ask you to listen carefully and not to make any decisions until you've heard everything."

Nathan scribbled nervously on the pad of paper in front of him. He couldn't bring himself to look at anyone while Steven was talking. He felt like the whole room was glaring at him. Who knew what they were thinking of him?

Steven paused for a moment and leaned on the bar in front of the jury. "I tell you that the man sitting in front of you today is innocent of all charges. He's only here because he was a convenient target and he's here because the sheriff's office felt pressured to find someone to blame for this senseless murder. Yes, the murder was terrible and someone has to pay, but the man sitting here is not the killer. There are some secrets in this town, but we're going to try our best to uncover them, and by doing so, we hope to expose the real killer to you."

Steven walked back to his desk. "Don't be afraid to hold out for justice and to do the right thing. Don't be pressured to make this a quick fix, because if you do, and the wrong man is put away, that means the killer is still out there and your children are not safe. Think about it. Take the time to get it right. Thank you."

Steven sat next to Nathan and began scribbling on his legal pad.

Nathan was beginning to feel a little more at ease now. If nothing else, at least Steven had the passion he needed to win this case. Doug was still unconsciously chewing on the end of his pen like he was witnessing a nightmare right in front of his eyes.

Steven leaned over to Doug, "Stop looking so worried. The jury can see your face too, you know. Try to look a bit more confident." Doug slowly shook his head and removed the pen from his mouth, wondering what their next step would be.

"Is the attorney for the prosecution ready?" asked the judge in a monotone voice.

"Yes, Your Honor," replied attorney, Pete Jacobsen.

"Then you may begin."

"Thank you, Your Honor," began Pete. Pete was a tall man with a thunderous voice. As he spoke, he definitely held the attention of the jury. They watched his every move and their eyes shifted over to Nathan as he spoke of the rubber mask, the bag with Nathan's initials and the bloody shirt. You could actually see their eyebrows go up as the prosecutor described Nathan as a disturbed man who was undergoing psychotherapy. He described Nathan as a scared man, running from his past. It seemed as though Pete's opening statement wiped out everything from the jury's mind that Steven had previously stated. You could see their faces change and some were wiping away tears as he described how the murdered boy was found in the woods and how Nathan had been on the scene as well that day.

As the prosecutor closed his statement and headed back to his seat, Steven slumped down in his seat a little and rubbed his face with his hands. "This is going to be a long day," he said under his breath.

# 51

After two days of sitting and listening to the prosecutor present his damaging evidence, everything seemed hopeless. At the end of the second day Nathan found himself completely drained of emotions and energy. He pretended to eat the supper that Marcie cooked for him that evening, but even food had no pleasure for him. Nathan felt like a walking-shell-of-a man. After sitting and listening for two days to people describing him as a disturbed, distant stranger, who obviously was capable of murder, Nathan was starting to believe it too. All he wanted to do that night was crawl into bed and pull the covers up over his head. Sleep became his refuge from all his attackers and everyone else who tried to probe him with question after question. Nathan found himself even trying to escape from Marcie sometimes. He thought because the situation was so lost that he might as well get used to not being around her, assuming it would be less painful for both of them.

Marcie could feel him starting to drift away from her, but she held on as tightly as she could. Even though he would sit for hours and not talk, she would still put her head in his lap or take his hand in hers and hold on as much as he would allow. She did everything in her power to keep him with her. In her heart she knew there was a good possibility the jury could find him guilty and lock him away from her. She tried hard not to think of that. She just tried to stay as close to him as she could, while there was still a chance.

That night Nathan fell asleep just as soon as his head hit the pillow. Marcie had hoped this would be the night they could talk about what was going on, but sleep seemed to be the only thing that brought any peace to Nathan these days. So she let him rest, staring at him as he drifted away into his world of darkness and dreams. She pushed his hair out of his face and touched his lips with her fingers, missing him already. Her dream of a peaceful life with Nathan had turned into an unending nightmare. Nathan was all she had ever really wanted in her life. Even though they had exhausted all of their resources to find the truth, they weren't able to uncover anything more than confusion.

Marcie sat up in bed while Nathan slept, thinking about Maggie having a sister named Betsy. She wondered why her mom never told her about Betsy. They were always able to talk about everything. Maggie was such a caring, thoughtful person. Marcie couldn't begin to imagine her mother being so ashamed that she actually disowned her sister, her own flesh and blood. Perhaps there was some sort of link there. "Why did Maggie never talk about her?" Marcie wondered. "What could Betsy have done? What could drive the sisters apart?" Marcie knew Maggie had always lived her life strictly according to her convictions. She had little patience for those who didn't do the same. Her mother was a loving woman, but she also had high expectations for those she loved.

Marcie pulled her legs up to her chest and wrapped her arms around them. She remembered, right after she had married Nathan, Maggie telling her she should remain loyal to him, no matter what happened between them. Maggie was a firm believer that marriage was a lifetime commitment that shouldn't be broken apart over just anything and everything that came along. What was it that made Maggie ashamed of Betsy? Perhaps she hadn't been faithful to her husband. Marcie looked down at Nathan, who was sound asleep, wondering what possible connection there could be? Whatever it was, it was bad enough that Maggie and Betsy were never able to mend things between them again.

All of this seemed too impossible to be true, but it somehow made sense the more she thought about it. Knowing she wasn't going to get much sleep, she quietly made her way downstairs and fixed herself a glass of milk and a piece of chocolate cake. While she was eating, the phone rang. Marcie couldn't believe someone would be calling so late. A phone call in the middle of the night never brought good news. She quickly grabbed the phone before it rang again to keep it from waking Nathan.

"Hello," Marcie answered in a whispering voice.

"Marcie, hi honey, it's me, Gracey. I'm sorry to be calling you so late, but I just had to do it. Will you forgive me?" she asked in a very quiet, muffled tone.

"Uh, yes, I forgive you Gracey, but what on earth is the matter? You scared me half to death."

"I, I just had to call you. You and Nathan have been through so much, I just feel so sorry for you both. Anyway, the reason I called is, a while back, Nathan picked me up in town and gave me a ride to the cemetery. I was on my way there to visit Maggie's grave. I know you miss her something awful. Let me tell you, I miss her too. Sometimes I sit up nights and cry just thinking about her being gone and how much that must hurt you."

"Gracey, I don't understand. Did you call to tell me you miss Maggie?" asked Marcie, now totally confused.

"No, I mean, I do want you to know that I miss her, but the reason I'm calling is—"

"Gracey? Are you still there?"

"Yes, I just thought I heard Mark up and I didn't want him to know I'm on the phone at this late hour. He'd have my head. I think he's still asleep though."

"Gracey, please. Did you call to tell me something?"

"I'm sorry, honey. It's just that, Mark can't find out I'm on the phone." She began to speak in even more of a whisper, "You see, while we were at the cemetery, Nathan kind of passed out or something. I couldn't wake him up, so I just put his head in my lap and waited for him to open his eyes. When he did wake up, we talked about an old hymn I'd been humming, 'Amazing Grace'. He said it was one of his favorites. Anyway, it meant so much to him that it got me to thinking when I got home and I went searching for an old hymnal I had in my dresser. I couldn't remember all of the verses you see, and I wanted to refresh my memory."

"Gracey, I'm so sorry, but none of this makes any sense to me. Why would you call and tell me all of this now? I don't understand."

"Well, while I was looking for the book, I found something else. I just couldn't believe it. Marcie, I love you both very much and I would never lie to either of you about anything. You know that, don't you? Oh, no, I hear Mark coming, so I better hang up now. I love you. Please ask him to forgive me. I've got to go now. Bye."

Marcie stood holding the phone in her hand. She didn't understand anything that Gracey said. "She's such a strange creature," Marcie said as she held the phone. She could hear the dial tone buzzing in her ear, so she finally hung up and sat back down at the kitchen table.

Suddenly, she heard someone calling her from the stairs. It was James Carwood. "Marcie, please come quick. Have you seen Nathan? He's not in his room. Is he down there with you?"

Marcie shot up from the table and ran up the stairs, past James, to her room. Nathan was gone.

"I thought you were going to follow him when he walked around in his sleep!" screamed Marcie.

"I didn't know he was up. I thought I heard something, but I checked on him and he was gone. Marcie, I was sitting in the hallway. He couldn't have gotten past me. I saw you head downstairs to the kitchen by yourself, and assumed Nathan was still asleep in his room."

"We can't fight over this now. We've got to go and find him. He could get killed. Go after him, please. I'll call Steven," said Marcie, rushing to the phone.

James ran downstairs and started looking around outside. There were no cars missing, so he knew that Nathan had to be on foot. He ran out to the road and looked both ways, but there was no sign of Nathan. Just as he was about to turn around and head back to the house, he saw someone run into the woods down the road a ways. "Nathan!" called James, but no one answered. He turned on his flashlight and pointed it toward the trees, but he still couldn't see anything. "Nathan, please answer me," he shouted again.

James started running down the road to the woods where he thought he had seen someone duck into the trees. He stopped and flashed the light all around him and noticed footprints in the mud alongside a ditch. There was no choice but to follow the footsteps. He was shaking like a leaf, but decided to go anyway.

It was so dark that James couldn't see much, even with his flashlight. He didn't know what he was going to walk into, but kept walking slowly, calling out Nathan's name. Something moved over to his right and he headed in that direction, trying to follow his light. "There could be snakes in here," he kept thinking. "Nathan, please, it's James. Let me help you. Wake up. You're sleepwalking again. It's all right, man. I'm here with you. Can you hear me, Nathan?" Suddenly out of the corner of his eye, he saw someone move, so he ran in that direction, shining his flashlight ahead of him. "Nathan, please stop moving. I can't see a thing."

As he pointed the flashlight through the darkness, he saw someone duck behind a tree. James stood quietly to see if he could see them move again, but nothing happened. He cautiously moved toward the tree, hoping that Nathan would be passed out by now and he could get him back home. As James stepped very carefully, he could see someone was still standing behind the tree. "Nathan, is that you?" he called again.

Just as he reached the tree he was relieved to see that Nathan hadn't moved. He was still standing in the same place. "It's so dark out here I don't think I could have followed you much farther." There was no answer. James put his flashlight up to the person's face, and suddenly, a man jumped out from behind the tree.

"Boo! I scared you! Boo! I scared you!"

James stumbled backwards, but managed to hold the flashlight in his hands. When the light hit the face of the man behind the tree, he could see that he was an old man with thin white hair.

James could hardly breathe. He just stayed still on the ground holding the flashlight on the face of the strange-looking man. The old man laughed and ran away into the woods, but James was too afraid to follow him. He jumped up and headed back to the road. Tree branches and vines kept hitting him in the face and scraping his arms, but he didn't slow down. He ran until he found the road again and then he swung around and held the flashlight on the woods. There was no one there. No one had followed him out.

He ran backwards for a little ways and then turned around and made a full sprint toward the house. As he hit the front door, he saw Marcie and Steven sitting in the living room.

"Marcie, Steven, you won't believe what I just saw," James said as he gasped for air. "I'm not sure if I believe it."

Just then Nathan stepped from the kitchen door holding a cup of coffee in his hand, "What did you see?"

"Nathan, you're here," James said in a frightened voice.

"He was sitting on the back patio all along. I didn't find him until I had already called Steven," said Marcie. "I went to look for you, but you were no where to be found. So we just waited for you to come back. Are you all right? You look like you've seen a ghost or something."

James sat back on the couch and just shook his head. "This was no ghost. I'm not sure what it was. I'm just glad Nathan's here, safe and sound. That's all that matters." James took a cup and poured himself some hot coffee. He took a big gulp and then turned toward Nathan. "I think I saw the old man. He was running in the woods."

Nathan sat in front of James and grabbed his arms, spilling coffee all over the floor and James. "You saw him? Just now?"

"Yes, I was eyeball to eyeball with him for just a few seconds and then he ran off into the woods. I thought I was chasing you. I'm glad I was wrong."

Nathan sat back in his chair and closed his eyes. "He does exist," he kept saying to himself. Steven and Marcie just looked at each other in disbelief. Now all they had to do was to find him.

# 52

The next day in court the prosecutor had Mark on the stand as a witness for his case. Mark answered questions concerning the evidence presented against Nathan. They discussed the black bag found in Marcie's barn that held the bloody shirt with Nathan's initials on it, as well as the rubber mask. They also discussed the incriminating handkerchief found in the woods near the place where Todd Harper was found dead. The handkerchief also had Nathan's initials stitched on it and members of the jury were seeing Nathan in a different light with every piece of evidence presented to them. It clearly looked as though Nathan was guilty based on everything that the prosecutor presented to the jury.

When it came time for Steven to cross-examine Mark, he took his time in glancing over his notes. The judge, who was growing impatient while waiting for Steven to start asking questions, cleared his throat loudly and raised his eyebrows. Doug nervously punched Steven under the table, "He's waiting," Doug whispered.

"Yes, I know he is," answered Steven. "I'm ready, Your Honor," he said, as he slowly walked toward Mark.

"I'm glad you've decided to begin Counselor," snapped the judge. "We wouldn't want to rush you. We're not going too fast for you are we?" the judge asked sarcastically.

"Well, actually," Steven started to answer, but he was interrupted.

"Please begin your questioning, Counselor, or your time for cross-examining will be expired. Do you understand?"

"Yes, Your Honor, I do. I'm sorry. It's just that not everything the witness has stated makes a lot of sense to me and I'm thinking that the jury may be a little confused as well." Steven walked over closer to Mark and leaned on the oak rail that separated the two men. "Now, did I understand you to say, Mr. Temple, that you found a black bag in the barn?

"Yes, that's right."

"And it contained a bloody shirt and a rubber mask? Is that correct?"

"That's right," answered Mark.

"What made you search the barn for the bag in the first place?" asked Steven. "Why did you look for anything on that property?"

"We found a handkerchief in the woods with Nathan's initials on it, near where we discovered Todd Harper's body. So we had reason to be suspicious of Nathan. He had been staying on the property at the time."

"Did you search the house as well?"

"We started in the barn, found the bag and figured we had enough evidence for a conviction at that time. I wanted to get everything checked out by the lab as soon as possible. So no, we didn't get to search the house," Mark explained.

"But you picked the barn as the first place to look?" asked Steven. "I mean, after all, Mr. Staby had been staying in the house at the time and not the barn. What was it about the barn that attracted your attention rather than the house where Mr. Staby's things would have been kept?"

"Nathan passed out in the barn a few days prior to our finding the bag. The doctor said that something traumatic must have happened there to cause him to be unconscious for a good spell. We picked the barn as the first place to look for that reason. I figured that there had to be something in there that upset him."

"Now, did you go into the barn right away after Nathan's fainting spell and start searching or did you wait a few days?" pressed Steven.

"We waited to get the search warrant processed."

"So you did have a proper search warrant?"

"Yes."

"So was it three days, two days or how long after Nathan Staby passed out in the barn and was put into the hospital that you actually searched the premises?" asked Steven.

"It was a couple of days after he went into the hospital," Mark answered.

"So you didn't get to search the barn right away. I mean, not as soon as they took Nathan away?"

"No because we needed a search warrant."

"And when you found the bag, did you arrest the suspect right away?"

"No, I waited for some lab tests before I arrested him."

"And how long did it take to get the lab results back?"

"A few days."

"By a few days, do you mean three?"

"Yes, three days."

"Why did it take so long to get the results back? Aren't these types of things normally processed fairly quickly, especially when you're waiting to arrest a suspect based on the information the lab gives you?" asked Steven, leaning on the rail in front of Mark.

"We don't have a lab here in town, so it had to be taken to Reed's Gorge and dropped off," answered Mark. "They were a little backed up, so it took three days."

"Weren't you sweating bullets because it was taking so long?"

"Not really."

"But isn't it true Nathan and Marcie were planning to leave town after they were married?"

Mark didn't answer.

"Mr. Temple, are you saying you didn't see any urgency to the situation?"

"Well, I wanted the information back as soon as I could get it, but I had to wait for it. I knew I wanted to be sure and not rush things, just so we could make an arrest in the case. This was someone I had known for a lot of years, and I wasn't interested in getting things wrong. I wanted to have all of the facts in front of me before I accused Nathan Staby of anything."

"How would you describe your relationship with the accused?"

"We grew up together. We were friends."

"Close friends?"

"Sure, you could say that."

"And are you still close friends, at least prior to your arresting him for murder?"

"Yes, we were for a while."

"Mr. Temple, you stated you grew up with Nathan. Would you describe him as the sort of person who would kill someone?"

"I'm not sure," Mark answered cautiously. "He was always a quiet kind of guy and easy going, but you just never know about people. You never really know what they might be capable of doing."

"Let's get back to the black bag for a moment," said Steven. "You say you obtained a search warrant before looking for evidence on the property?"

"That's right."

"Mr. Temple, isn't it true that you did not, in fact, wait for the warrant, but went directly back to the barn that night to search it?"

"No, that's not true," insisted Mark. "We waited for the warrant."

"Your Honor, I object. Unless the defense has proof of such an accusation, I don't see why the witness has to keep answering the same question over and over again," Pete pointed out.

"Sustained," replied the judge. "Counselor, unless you're able to produce evidence to the contrary, I suggest you move on."

"All right, Your Honor. We'll come back to this issue later on. How well do you know Nathan's wife, Marcie Staby?" asked Steven abruptly.

"What?"

"Objection!" shouted Pete. "What does this line of questioning have to do with anything?"

"Counselor, are you going somewhere with this or are you on a fishing expedition?" asked the judge, growing more impatient.

"Your Honor," answered Steven. "I'm just trying to establish the various relationships involved with this case. I do believe you'll see the relevance to my question."

"I'd better be able to see it soon, because right now it doesn't look like you know what you're trying to establish," replied the judge. "The objection from the prosecution is over ruled, for now. Continue Counselor, but you'd better get somewhere fast with this."

"Thank you, Your Honor," said Steven." I'll repeat the question for you, Mr. Temple. How well do you know Marcie Staby?"

"I've known her all my life. We grew up together as well. She's like a sister to me. I'm very fond of her in that way."

"You're fond of her only as a sister?"

"Yes, we've always been good friends."

"Isn't it true that you once had a crush on her and would have been interested in dating her, before Nathan Staby returned to town?"

"Objection! Your Honor, must we listen to childhood love stories this afternoon? Pete asked. "Mr. Temple is not on trial here and I don't see the relevance to whether or not he ever had a crush on someone that he grew up with."

"Over ruled. I'll allow it for now. Please answer the question, Mr. Temple," replied the judge.

"I considered asking her out a few times, sure. Nathan moved away and was gone for a long time. It's a small town and we were around each other a lot. She and I were both single. Yes, I guess I would have dated her then, but I'm a happily married man now. That was a long time ago."

"Isn't it a fact that you were upset when Nathan Staby moved back to town and you felt that your relationship with Marcie was then threatened by him?" asked Steven. "Isn't it true that you would like to put him behind bars just to get him out of the way so you can work out a relationship with Marcie, his wife?"

"Objection! Your Honor," shouted Pete once again. "The Counselor hasn't established that there even was a relationship to be threatened between the witness and the suspect's wife. These questions are way out of line and do not relate to this case or have any purpose at all, other than to confuse the jury with a bunch of nonsense."

"Sustained. Would the attorneys please approach the bench?"

While Steven and Pete approached the judge's bench, the pencil Doug was chewing on broke in half. Nathan buried his face in his hands. Who had he really picked as his lawyer? Steven seemed to be stabbing at anything and everything, but he didn't seem to have a real plan of attack.

"Listen to me," the judge growled at Steven. "You have been wasting this court's time and money with a bunch of random questions that are leading nowhere. It appears that you are only stalling. Now I suggest you start defending your client with something more than the sheriff may have had a crush on the defendant's wife and stop playing these games in my courtroom. Is that understood?" The judge's face was blood red and a vein began to pop out on his neck.

"Your Honor, please, I do have a purpose in my questions," pleaded Steven. "It's just that things are not as clear cut as they appear to be. So I have to ask some questions that may seem, on the surface, to have no relevance, but later you'll see that they do. I only ask that the judge be a little more tolerant and I will try to be a little more specific with my questions."

"All right, but you'd better get yourself on some sort of a track and stay there," answered the judge in an angry tone.

"Yes, Your Honor," answered Steven. "Thank you."

As Steven turned back around, he could see both Doug and Nathan staring back at him with very worried expressions on their faces. Steven smiled back at them and quickly picked up his legal pad of notes and began questioning Mark again.

"Do you recall the night that Marcie Staby lost control of her car and crashed it over the side of a mountain, not too far from her home?"

"Yes, I went to see her in the hospital," answered Mark.

"Did you think there was anything suspicious about that accident? I mean, did you believe it was an accident?"

"Well, to tell the truth," said Mark. "I knew that she had just left Nathan Staby's room at the Raven Inn. I figured they had argued or something. I knew Marcie had driven that road a million times. There would be no reason for her to run the car off of the road. I assumed she was upset and crying. Maybe she didn't see the turn in the road."

"Where were you the night of the accident?" asked Steven.

"I was at home with my wife," answered Mark.

"Isn't it true that you were so furious with Marcie for getting back with Nathan Staby that you intentionally tried to run her off of the road that night?" accused Steven. "Isn't it true that if you couldn't have her, you didn't want anyone else to have her either?"

"Objection!" shouted Pete. "The defense is accusing my client of having something to do with an accident that doesn't even relate to this case. Your Honor, may I suggest—"

"Sustained!" interrupted the judge. "Need I remind you, Counselor, of our little conversation that we had not two minutes ago? Is this the track you intend to pursue or do you not have a track at all?"

"Your Honor, I'm merely trying to show the jury that Mr. Temple had personal interests in Marcie's relationship with Nathan Staby," answered Steven in a calm, low voice. "He was a jealous man who would stop at nothing to keep them apart, even if it meant killing the person that he wanted more than anything. He would even go so far as accusing Nathan of murder to get him behind bars and out of the way. The jury needs to know this is not a simple case of who done it, but a matter of jealousy and deceitfulness. Mr. Temple is hiding something from this court and he knows it. There is more to this case than just the death of Todd Harper, Your Honor."

"Objection!" shouted Pete. "I insist that the witness not be badgered with false accusations that have not been proven and that the attorney for the defense end this line of questioning immediately!"

"Objection sustained," answered the judge. "Counselor, your questions for this witness are out of line and you have been warned not to make accusations that you can't back up with proof in this courtroom."

Steven closed his notes and walked back to his seat. "That's all the questions I have for Mr. Temple at this time, Your Honor."

"You may step down, Mr. Temple," said the judge. "This court is recessed until 9 A.M. Monday morning."

"Steven, what in the world were you doing up there? You were all over the place with him. The jury is going to think you don't have a defense at all," said Doug nervously.

"No, they'll remember more than you think," answered Steven with a smile. "I'm trying to establish some measure of suspicion regarding the sheriff's character. I know it doesn't make much sense from here, but the jury will recall bits and pieces enough to make them have some doubt about whether or not Mr. Temple is really the true-blue boy scout he pretends to be. I have a gut feeling about this one, guys. Besides, I believe he's hiding something."

"You're the boss, but I've got to tell you, I'm getting a little worried," replied Doug, shaking his head as he headed out of the doorway.

Steven walked over to Nathan and sat beside him. Nathan had his head down on the table. "It doesn't look good, does it?" he asked without picking up his head.

"Trust me, Nathan," answered Steven. "I know what I'm doing here. I know we don't have any hard evidence, but for now I have to raise some reasonable amount of suspicion with the jury. I want them to start to see that everything may not be as it appears in this case. They bought more of it than you realize. Now come on, I'll take you home. You look washed out."

As Steven led Nathan out of the courtroom, he watched him take Marcie's hand, knowing that time was growing shorter and something had to be done quickly. He would have to take more definitive steps toward proving Nathan's innocence. There really wasn't anything concrete to offer, unless someone was willing to speak out. Someone who was not afraid to tell the truth about what happened to Todd Harper. He just had no clue who that someone would be. Someone had clamped down hard on Jake and others that might know something more. Steven would just have to push a little harder to get someone to talk.

# 53

On Saturday morning Steven sat with Marcie and Nathan around their kitchen table having coffee. At least they had the weekend to ponder the evidence in the case and to try to come up with more answers. It was quiet in the kitchen, only the sounds of them sipping coffee could be heard.

"Maybe you should put James on the stand to testify about seeing the old man in the woods," suggested Marcie. "After all, he did see him and Nathan has been saying all along that he remembers an old man being involved somehow. Maybe you could actually convince Jake to testify to what he saw around the time that Todd Harper was killed."

"But we don't have any proof that the old man did anything other than the fact that Nathan sees him in his dreams or memory," replied Steven. "Besides, I don't think I'll ever be able to convince Jake to talk. Somebody's got him gagged and bound with fear, but he knows something all right."

Suddenly, Nathan got up from his chair and put his coffee cup in the sink. "I have to go out for a while. I just need to get some fresh air. After all, I don't know how much longer I'll be able to do that," Nathan said, pausing by the door. "I'm going for a drive."

"I'll go with you," interrupted Steven. He stood up and grabbed a jacket and a cap.

"No, that's not necessary," answered Nathan. "I'd just really like to be alone. I promise I'll be fine."

"The only problem is that every time you go off alone something happens," said Steven. "Come on, let me go with you."

Marcie walked over to Nathan and kissed him on the cheek, "Please don't go out alone. I'd feel so much better if you were with someone. I'd really feel a lot better if you would just stay here with me, but I know you want to just get away for a few moments. Please, let Steven go with you," Marcie pleaded quietly.

"No, really, I'll be all right. I just want to go for a drive for a little while to clear my head," answered Nathan. "Besides I love the river and I just want to enjoy it for a bit by myself." As he started to leave, he turned back around and grabbed Marcie in his arms, "Don't ever think that I've stopped loving you. That could never happen. They may separate us, but I'll always love you." They kissed each other and just held on to one another for a long while. Steven quietly stepped out of the room to give them some privacy.

Nathan found it hard to let go of Marcie, but he finally left her and jumped into his car. He just started driving with no idea where he was going. As he drove through the mountains, he felt like he was on some kind of a mission, but he had no idea what kind or for what purpose. Driving down the twisting, winding roads, he couldn't help but notice how beautiful the trees were, bending in the gentle winds that blew through the mountains. This was such a peaceful place. At least, it had been before he arrived. It was hard for him to imagine this nightmare could be happening to him there, of all places. He kept driving, almost in a trance, without a destination.

The rushing sound of the Black River seemingly wrapped itself around the trees, rocks and mountains that Nathan loved so dearly. He slowed down to listen to the sound and then stopped the car along side the road. Nathan got out and walked around a bit, just stretching his legs, but at the same time he felt as though he was walking with a sense of purpose rather than just rambling through the woods. The river was moving quickly as it pushed its way through the trees and around the huge rocks that had fallen in its pathway. Perching himself on top of one of the rocks, he stared down at the waters rushing past him. The sounds of the river drowned out everything. That's what he wanted right now. He closed his eyes and listened to the water's music. Mixed in with the roaring river sounds were the sweet chirps of the birds in the treetops above him. "I remember listening to this symphony," he thought. It was as though they had all gathered in one place for one last song for him. Their singing echoed throughout the woods and then was lost in the bellowing cry of the river.

While Nathan quietly listened, he heard a twig snap loudly close by him. He turned quickly to look, but he didn't see anyone. "Hey Steven, is that you?" he yelled out, figuring Steven had decided to follow him after all. But there was no answer. Nathan looked all around, but there wasn't a sign of Steven or anyone else.

Jumping down from the rock, Nathan started to cross the waters by jumping from one rock to another, just like he and Robert had done when he was younger. While jumping from rock to rock, he began to feel like a boy again. Nathan wondered what it would have been like if Robert had lived and they had grown up together. He wondered if they would they still be friends. Would he be glad that he and Marcie were married? But now he would never know. It was funny how, after all of these years, he still missed him like it had happened only yesterday.

Just as he was about to jump to the next rock, he saw something move out of the corner of his eye. He stopped and stood very still. "Steven? Are you following me?" he called out again. "How did you get to the other side so quickly?" There was no response. As he looked closely, he thought he could see something standing near one of the trees, on the other side of the river. He strained to get a closer look, but he was too far away to tell what it was. While he was trying very hard to get a better view, his foot slipped off of the wet rocks and he landed on his back, with the water racing over him. "Not again," he thought. As he struggled to get back onto his feet, he saw a hand stretched out in front of him. He assumed it was Steven and grabbed hold of it tightly. But as he swung himself back up to his feet and spun around to thank him, there, in front of him, stood the mysterious old man.

Nathan was startled and stumbled backwards a bit, but the old man pulled him up on the banks of the river. His hair was white and his face was rough and leathery looking. The old man didn't move, but just stood in front of him. Nathan was very still, not really knowing what to do. His first notion was to run, but he had to find out who this person was and what he wanted with him. He could feel himself trembling inside, but he just stayed still, staring at him.

Slowly, the man knelt down in front of him and put his face close to Nathan. "Boo! I scare you!" he said laughing.

Nathan leaned back away from him as far as he could.

"You Nathan," the old man said, but in a voice that didn't seem to match the age on his face. "You Nathan," he said again.

"How do you know my name?" Nathan asked, looking around him for a weapon in case he needed it.

"I know you, Nathan," he answered.

As he looked more closely, he realized that the old face he was staring at didn't look real. It looked like a rubber mask. He started to reach up and touch it, but the man backed away. "Don't touch me," he yelled.

"I'm sorry," answered Nathan. "Um, who are you? Why are you wearing that mask?"

"I'm an angel. I live in heaven. Have you ever been there?" the man asked.

Nathan didn't know what to answer. This person was obviously missing some marbles, but he didn't want to upset him or make him run away. "No, I've never been. What's it like there?"

"Come with me. I show you, Nathan," he said, running away through the woods.

Suddenly the man disappeared through the trees. "Wait, not so fast! Where'd you go?"

"This way, Nathan," he replied. "Come this way to heaven."

Nathan ran behind him as the man in front of him dodged tree limbs and jumped over rocks. "Wait, I'm trying to keep up. Not so fast," he called out.

"I show you, Nathan. Keep running, keep running," the man yelled back.

Nathan remembered following Robert through the woods in the same way on the day he was killed. He couldn't believe he was running behind the person that had haunted his thoughts and dreams since he was a child. This just couldn't be real. Maybe he was having another one of his mysterious dreams, but this time he was almost certain that he was awake. Nathan looked back several times to see if there was any sign of Steven. He hoped he would somehow show up and see the old man for himself. Maybe then the whole town wouldn't think he was losing his mind. Maybe he could even convince himself.

The old man was pretty far ahead of him, but he could still see him, ducking in and out of sight, like a child, playing hide and seek. As Nathan drew closer, he could see a clearing up ahead, through the trees. His pace began to slow a little bit. There was something vaguely familiar about the place. He pushed branches and vines away from his path and continued to walk toward the clearing. The old man had disappeared, but he had a feeling he was somewhere close by.

With great anticipation, Nathan pushed past the bushes and tree limbs. He didn't understand why, but for the first time in a long while, he was beginning to have the feeling something from the past was waiting for him. There in the clearing he could see an old, broken down, white house. It was the one he saw in his dream, only it looked like it was about to collapse now. The old man stuck his head out of one of the windows and yelled at him, "Nathan, come in. Come inside and see."

Nathan walked toward the house with his heart pounding in his chest. He was afraid his heart might just stop beating altogether. He struggled against the weakness in his legs. He was afraid of what waited inside for him. He turned around once more to look for Steven, but he was alone, except for the strange man hanging out of one of the broken windows of the house.

"Nathan, this way. Don't be scared. It's okay."

Being careful not to step through any of the rotted wood, Nathan stepped up onto the porch. Just standing there sent a chill down his back.

"Nathan, come inside. You can see better in here. Come in," called the old man from the darkness of the house. "Don't be afraid. Nothing can hurt you here."

Nathan slowly walked through the doorway, trying to peep inside first to make sure it was safe. Flowered wallpaper was peeling from the walls and naked wires were strung from the ceiling to rusted light fixtures barely hanging on. Dirty yellow lace curtains hung on one of the windows.

"Come up here, Nathan," cried the old man with great joy in his voice. "Come upstairs to loft. You can see everything." The old man darted back up the stairs just as quickly as he had appeared.

Nathan turned around and around in the room. He remembered sneaking around this house, but never daring to come inside. Betsy Radcliff would have shot him on sight, but here he was standing inside. His thoughts were interrupted once again by the excited strange man on the stairs begging him to come up.

Climbing the stairs, he kept staring over his shoulder to make sure there was no one else around. Nathan ran his fingers along the wall where pictures used to hang. Now the wall was empty, except for a few nails.

At the top of the stairs he could see what apparently used to be a baby's room. The walls were light blue and a plastic moon still hung from the ceiling by a wire, swinging back and forth from the breeze coming in through the broken glass in the windows. Nathan reached up and touched it.

"Nathan, come see. This my room. It very nice. Come see, Nathan. You like it. I know you like it." The odd man disappeared into the room he wanted Nathan to see so badly. He cautiously walked down the hall and into the room where there was a small broken bed with blankets piled together in a corner. The old man rolled down on his home made bed and looked up at the ceiling. "Look up at heaven, Nathan," the man said, as he pointed up at the ceiling. "You can see heaven." Nathan sat on the floor and looked up at the ceiling. Someone had painted an angel with stars all around her on the cracked ceiling. Nathan looked over at the old man. His fear had subsided and he was more curious than anything else now.

"Who are you? What's your name?" asked Nathan.

The man didn't answer. He just kept staring up at the ceiling.

"How do you know my name?" asked Nathan. There was still no response.

"See angel. I want to be angel too."

"Is that why you're wearing that mask? Are you trying to look like an angel?" asked Nathan.

"I want to do good like angels. Mama said they help people. They don't hurt nobody."

Nathan looked up at the ceiling, "Did you paint that picture?"

"No, I did!" shouted an old woman. "What are you doing in my house?" She ran over and stood in front of the man as if to guard him.

Nathan quickly jumped to his feet. "Who are you?"

"That's none of your business. Who do you think you are sneaking around in my house? It's bad enough they sneak around outside, but you have the boldness to just walk right in! Now get out, before I get my gun and shoot you."

Nathan realized he was talking to Betsy Radcliff herself. He didn't even know she was still alive. She was frail and bent over slightly in her posture. Her dress was worn and dirty with a shabby apron over top of it. He could hardly swallow. All of his saliva was gone and his tongue was sticking to the roof of his mouth.

"I'm sorry. I was invited in by, uh, this man here," Nathan said, pointing over to the man lying on the bed.

"Well, he don't know no better. He'd let anybody in that had a mind to come in. But this is my property and my house and I'm telling you to get out."

"He just showed up in the woods and told me to come with him. He brought me to this house."

"Samuel, run and get my gun. This man don't want to leave on his own, so I'll help him along. Hurry up, now!"

"Wait, please don't go. I'd really like to talk to, uh, Samuel. Please, it's very important."

"No! You're not taking my boy anywhere. He didn't do nothing. He just stays here with me being no trouble to nobody. So you just back away. Samuel, I said get me my gun."

Samuel ran out of the room and scrambled down the stairs. He returned moments later with a shotgun that was bigger than the old woman. She held it up and aimed it right at Nathan's face.

"Please, Betsy, I mean, Mrs. Radcliff. Be careful with that thing. I'm not here to hurt anybody. But I need desperately to talk to your son. He is your son, right?" asked Nathan.

"He's not allowed to talk to any strangers. How do you know my name? They sent you, didn't they? You come here to take my boy, but you ain't going to touch him. Now you better be leaving while you can."

"Can I just ask you why he wears that mask? It's very important for me to know. I think I've seen him somewhere before, or maybe I dreamed him, but I know I've seen him before. Can I see him without the mask for a second?" Nathan asked, reaching toward the man.

"No! Don't you touch my boy. He ain't never hurt nobody and you've got no right coming in here to take him away from me. I know the truth. He never killed that boy. It's all lies, every bit of it! Just because he's not like everybody else don't mean that he'd kill somebody. It's all lies they made up about him. You ain't taking him nowhere. Get back before I blow your sorry head off! Just leave us be! Why can't people just leave us be?" The old woman sat on the bed beside Samuel and started to cry. She pulled him close to her, "I'm sorry, Samuel. It's just no use no more. They'll come for you for sure, now, unless I shoot this man. Then they'll come and take me away and you won't have nobody to look out for you. I just can't hold on to you no more."

Nathan slowly leaned down near her, not knowing whether or not he should touch her. "Betsy, what do you mean, Samuel didn't kill anybody? What do you know? Maybe I can help you protect Samuel if you tell me the truth. Are you talking about Todd Harper's murder?"

"I've been a terrible mother. I tried my best to provide for my boy and bring him up by myself. But it don't matter no more. I'm going to lose him no matter what I do now."

"Are you Maggie Sanding's sister, Betsy?" Nathan asked.

"Shut up! Don't say that name to me," shouted the woman. "That woman caused me nothing but pain. She was an evil woman. Because of her I lost the man I loved more than anything else in this world. All of this is her fault. She was always so much better than me, or so she thought. She had a good life, but she didn't want me to have nothing."

"What happened between you two?" asked Nathan. "What drove you apart?"

Betsy didn't answer, but got up and walked down the stairs and out onto the front porch. Samuel ran past her and out into the yard.

Before Nathan stepped out of the room, he stared up at the angel painted on the roof. He bowed his head and said a quiet prayer in hopes that this would be the day that he would finally learn the truth about a lot of things.

# 54

Standing on the front porch, the old white house seemed so much smaller somehow. As a child, he would run up to the house on a dare, touch it and then run for his life. Now, here he was, standing on the front porch. Nathan couldn't stand waiting much longer for Betsy to talk to him. Not wanting to press her, he decided to wait and see if she talked on her own, but the silence was too much for him.

"Where's Samuel? Did he run away?" asked Nathan, looking all around.

"He's over there on the swing," said Betsy, pointing to an old oak tree some distance from the house.

Nathan walked over to the edge of the porch and saw Samuel twirling round and round in an old swing hanging from a sturdy tree limb. He watched closely as he swung around in a circle, laughing to himself, like a child. The swing looked as though it would break any minute under his weight, but Samuel didn't seem to notice. Nathan turned around and Betsy was standing behind him, her eyes red from crying.

"Betsy, please tell me about Samuel. I've been seeing him in my dreams for most of my life now," said Nathan, feeling desperate. "I'm not leaving here without finding out about him. I promise, I'll try to help you in any way I can, but you have to talk to me. You've got to trust somebody."

"Samuel is my son," Betsy began. "He's really a man in a child's body. In age he's 35 years old, but in his mind he's only about seven or eight. I have to do everything for him, tie his shoes, bathe him, cut up his food, everything. He was born with a damaged brain." Betsy paused for a moment, looking out at nothing in particular.

Nathan quietly sat in one of the chairs on the porch. He didn't want to do anything to distract Betsy. He hung on her every word, sometimes reminding himself to breathe.

"My first husband beat me while I was pregnant," continued Betsy. "He pushed me down the stairs and knocked me around something awful. I never forgave myself, or him, for how our boy turned out, but I tried to give him the best care I could."

"Sounds like there's nothing good to say about Samuel's father," Nathan said.

"Well, the only good thing that ever came from that man was that he had quite a bit of money. He died from a fight he got into one night while he was drunk. It just happened that he pushed the wrong person and they pulled a knife on him and killed him dead in the streets. When he died, I inherited his money, cause he didn't leave no will saying otherwise. It was more than enough to take care of us and to provide a way for me to raise Samuel without having to beg someone else for help. But not too long after, I met a gentle, kind man and fell in love with him. We were married soon after and I got pregnant again. I was so hoping that I'd have another boy, because of the way Samuel turned out. I felt like it was my fault this time. I wanted to make sure I took good care of myself. I didn't drink or touch anything that I thought would harm the baby or myself. When the baby was born, he was healthy and normal. I was so proud, and my husband was so happy with the son I had given him. Even Samuel helped take care of the baby, rocking him to sleep sometimes and rubbing his head. I would rock the baby and sing to him every night. He was my pride and joy. I was so glad to be happy again after all the hell we suffered from my first husband."

Nathan listened carefully, not wanting to miss a word. Samuel was still playing on the swing, oblivious to the world around him. He was still wearing the rubber mask.

"Where's your other son now?" asked Nathan.

"My second husband, David, was his name, he was away a lot of the time because of his job. He chased construction work all over the country back then. I had money, but he was so proud, he would let me use very little of it. He had to make a living for the family." Betsy slowly sat down on the porch. She hesitated for a while, as though she was going over all of the regret in her life.

Nathan waited patiently, knowing how hard it was for Betsy to go back over the painful memories of her past.

"You see, I got lonely with him gone all of the time. So I started going into town and drinking again. I would leave Samuel with the baby, and I'd be gone until late. I know'd it won't right, but I was just so lonely, I didn't know what to do with myself. When David was home, I was a whole different woman. I just wanted him here with me, but soon he'd be off again to another job in another state, sometimes for months at a time." Betsy paused for a moment and wrinkled up her brow as if she was in pain.

Nathan wanted to take her hand, but he didn't think Betsy would like it too much.

"My sister, Maggie, would come over and try to talk to me about my drinking. She'd make sure the children were all right, but I wouldn't listen to her. She didn't know what I was feeling. I was hurting bad, but she couldn't see it. She only wanted to lecture me. I know'd she was ashamed of me. We would have terrible fights. Maggie would leave and I would cry way into the night. I was like a lost little girl. But then one day, David came home and said he found work in town for a while. I was glad to have him back and started to be my old self again, singing to the baby, while I rocked him to sleep and cooking decent meals for the family. Then I found out I was pregnant again."

Nathan was startled when Samuel let out a loud scream of laughter from the homemade swing. He seemed to be having the time of his life.

Betsy smiled briefly and then continued her talk. "At first, David was excited about the new baby, but one morning he went into town and had breakfast with Maggie. Old high and mighty took it on herself to tell him about my drinking and going into town alone at all hours while he was away. Maggie was a very strict woman of firm principles. She thought my life was way out of control. I know'd she was thinking of what was best for the children when she told him all that. She was hoping David could turn me around if he know'd the truth, but instead it turned into a great big ugly mess."

Nathan could sense a lot of bitterness coming from Betsy. There was so much hurt, but no forgiveness. It was apparent in her words and on her weathered face.

"Maggie didn't know I was pregnant at the time. When she told David about me drinking, he just assumed the baby wasn't his and came home in a rage." Betsy wiped away tears from her face. "I swore I hadn't been with another man. I tried to tell him I only went into town to get away from the house for a while and to be with people, but he wouldn't listen. He couldn't stand the possibility of the baby not being his. David was a proud man. He grabbed our baby from my arms, and just took off and left us behind. I ran behind him like a scared little girl, screaming and pleading with him, but he wouldn't listen."

Nathan stared back at Betsy as she turned to look at him. She looked like an empty shell. There was nothing left inside of her, except her love for Samuel. That was clear.

"Me and Samuel, we never saw him again, except in town once in a while, but he never sat foot in this house again. I know'd I wouldn't be able to win against him and get custody of the baby in a court of law. I also didn't want my name spread all around town, calling me an unfit mother and a drunkard. So I just gave up. I felt like I let him down and I'd already caused him so much pain. David married again and that was that. He moved away somewhere and I ain't seen him since."

"What happened to the baby you were carrying when he left?" asked Nathan.

"I was in such a state when he left. I just drank myself into a coma almost, losing the baby one night while I was too drunk to know anything. So it was just me and Samuel left to take care of ourselves. I turned into a bitter old woman in a broken-down old house. I can't even bother fixing it up no more. Why should I? I just don't care no more, but I always cared about Samuel. He's my only joy in life. He stays with me all of the time."

"Betsy, why does Samuel always wear that rubber mask? Has he always worn it?"

"Some kids came sneaking round our place one Halloween night," Betsy said. "Samuel came out of the house before I know'd it and started chasing them away. One of the kids got so scared they dropped the mask and Samuel found it. He put it on in his room and said it made him feel like he was special, someone that nobody could hurt. I guess he wanted to protect me, like an angel. He's always loved pictures and stories about angels for some reason. So I used to tell him that he looked like an angel when he wore the mask. It made him happy. Sometimes he would even throw an old white bed sheet around him and use one of my sashes to tie it up so he'd look like the angels in the pictures. I even painted one on the ceiling of his room because the pictures had a calming affect on him. It was a small thing, but it gave him a lot of pleasure."

"What did you mean before when you said that Samuel never killed anybody?" Nathan asked cautiously. He knew any minute that Betsy could jump up and stop talking. "Do you know anything about Maggie's son, Robert, being killed or Todd Harper's death? It's important that I know everything. I don't know if you realize it, but I'm on trial for the death of the boy they recently found out there in the woods. There are still unanswered questions swimming around in my head, like why I remember Samuel in my dreams. I never understood who Samuel was. If you know something you've been afraid to tell, I really need to hear it. I know you're trying to protect Samuel, but from what? Did he do something wrong? Did Samuel kill Robert or Todd?"

Betsy dropped her head, but then she stood to her feet, pointing her finger in Nathan's face. "He didn't kill nobody. I know the truth now. Nobody's going to take my only son away from me, not again. No!" She walked to the edge of the porch and then spun around with her eyes wide open. "The day Robert was killed Samuel was in the woods playing by himself. The next thing I know'd, a boy comes up to my house yelling that he just saw Samuel kill a boy and that I'd better come quick. I couldn't believe it. Samuel would never hurt nobody. I followed the boy to the woods and saw Robert's body lying there on the ground. I called for Samuel, but he was gone."

"So the old man I saw in the woods that day was Samuel?" asked Nathan.

"Yes," replied Betsy. "The boy told me that Samuel was chasing behind you. I knew he didn't mean you no harm. Samuel knew you because Maggie sometimes brought you along to my house when you were much younger. He won't never gonna hurt you. He just wanted to play with you. He chased you for a ways. I ran behind you through the woods calling your name because I was afraid you would go and tell Maggie what happened. I didn't know what to do. I just walked back to where Robert's body was lying there in the leaves. We just stood there, staring at the body. I grabbed the boy and begged him not to tell nobody. I told him if he told they would come and take Samuel away from me. To make sure that he didn't talk, I offered him some money to keep him quiet. He agreed to keep his mouth shut. Then he helped me cover up the body with the dirty wet leaves. Samuel finally came back. I just grabbed him and ran back to the house."

"I remember hearing someone call my name over and over again," said Nathan. "I was so confused I didn't know which way to turn. It must have been you."

Betsy just nodded.

"I didn't actually find the body until the next day. It was like I was living that moment again. The next morning I headed back out to the woods, walking along the river, just as Robert and I had done. When I found Robert's body, I guess I went into some kind of shock. I saw his hand sticking up out of the leaves and it was blue and cold."

Betsy stared out at Samuel playing on the swing. She seemed far away while Nathan put the pieces of the puzzle together.

"I remember that all I could tell the police was that I found the body," said Nathan. "I couldn't remember much of anything else. It was all blocked out. I kept reliving the event over and over in my mind and I always ended up seeing an old man with white hair waving at me from the woods or chasing me through the trees. It was real. I saw Samuel."

"But my boy didn't killed nobody," Betsy said firmly.

"But you just said—"

"No, somebody else was in the woods that day and saw who done it," replied Betsy. "He came and told me years later. He told me the truth about that day. Samuel didn't kill that boy."

"Was it Jake Foster?" asked Nathan, leaning forward in his chair. "Was he the one that told you what really happened?"

"I ain't saying who. But I know the truth."

"Then who killed Robert if it wasn't Samuel?" Nathan asked. "If you know the truth, why won't you tell somebody?"

"I've tossed and turned over this most every night since it happened," said Betsy. "I know'd if I tried to tell the truth, nobody would believe me against the real killer. I'd end up losing Samuel for sure and I ain't about to risk that."

"What about Todd Harper?" Nathan asked. "Do you know anything about that? Are the deaths connected in some way?"

Betsy just sat silently.

"Betsy, please, my life is on the line here. I know you don't care anything about me, but if you tell the truth, my lawyer will make sure that Samuel is protected. You've got to trust somebody. You can't just keep on living like you don't exist. Samuel needs proper care and there are people who can help you with that. How can you let the real killer walk around free?"

Betsy looked all around the field in front of her, as though she was looking for someone specific who might be standing or hiding nearby.

"Betsy, please tell me. I have to know. We'll make sure nothing happens to you. Don't be afraid to tell me."

Betsy shook her head and stepped inside the house. "I ain't saying no more. I done said too much already. Samuel needs me. He's all I got left now." She called for her son to come inside with her and closed the door behind them.

Nathan stepped slowly off the porch, then turned facing the house, "Betsy, if I have to, I'll tell them about Samuel. You can only protect him by telling them the truth. I'll make sure nobody hurts you or Samuel. Please, for Samuel's sake, you've got to do it."

There was no response. Nathan walked across the field, back through the woods to his car. He sat there beside the road for a while and thought about everything Betsy told him. He wondered whether Maggie ever knew the truth about what happened to Robert. "Maybe she was suspicious that Betsy knew something all along and that's why she wanted me to stay in town," he thought. He slowly drove away, feeling as though he was leaving behind the only people that could free him from his nightmare.

# 55

On Monday morning Nathan again found himself seated in the old courthouse, but today his heart was pounding in his chest. Everything Betsy told him was swimming around in his head. He had shared with Marcie and Steven about his encounter with Betsy Radcliff. He didn't know what Steven could do with the information without Betsy's testimony to back it up. It all worried him to no end. For some strange reason, even though his life depended on Betsy's knowledge, Nathan felt an obligation to protect her and Samuel. Yet, he wasn't sure if he was really prepared to go that far. He prayed silently that God would somehow convince Betsy to come forward and rescue him, even though he wondered what that would mean for Samuel. He didn't expect anything good to happen.

As the judge entered the room, everyone stood to their feet and waited for him to take his seat. The pounding of his gavel brought the murmurs in the courtroom to a hush and the day's proceedings began.

"Is the Defense ready to begin?" asked the judge.

"Yes, Your Honor. I would like to finish my questioning of Mark Temple if it pleases the court." Steven's voice bellowed through the courtroom as he took great confidence in what he was about to do. Nathan wondered what Steven had up his sleeve, hoping that he wasn't bluffing this time.

Mark again took the witness stand and was reminded that he was still under oath. Steven stood and stared at Mark for a while before he began questioning him.

"Your Honor, may I approach the witness?"

"You may."

Steven walked over to Mark and leaned almost right into his face and whispered, "It's over." Mark shifted in his seat a little, but kept a stone expression on his face just the same.

He pounded Mark with question after question about the deaths of Robert and Todd, but Mark remained firm in his answers. Objections from the prosecutor were screamed out, one after the other, but the judge seemed more interested in hearing Mark's answers than did the prosecution. Steven never let up, but kept throwing question after question at Mark, as though he was trying to break him down, but Mark met each of the questions with an answer and never flinched.

"Tell me again about how you came to find Todd's body in the woods," asked Steven.

"I didn't find it, some men on my staff found it and called me. I immediately went to the location of the body and started my investigation."

"And where had you been previous to that phone call?"

"To lunch and then my house and back to the office," answered Mark.

"Who were you with at the time?"

"I had lunch with my wife, Gracey and then Nathan showed up and joined us. I dropped my wife back at the house and then Nathan and I went back to the office together."

"You and Nathan?"

"Yes, I asked him to come along and meet my deputy and to spend a little more time with me. I hadn't seen him for a long while, so I figured it would be good to get to know each other again."

"Had you seen Todd Harper that day at all prior to his death?"

"No."

"When was the last time you saw Todd Harper before he was found murdered?"

"I hadn't seen him in weeks or maybe even months," answered Mark. "I don't recall exactly when I saw him last."

"Do you know anybody by the name of Samuel?"

Mark hesitated for a moment, but then quickly answered, "No, I don't believe I do."

"Are you sure?" asked Steven, leaning forward a bit. "Do you need to think about it for a while?"

"I meet a lot of people in my line of work, but I don't recall meeting anybody by that name."

"This is such a small town, to be sure you would know someone by that name if they lived around here. Is that right?"

Mark shifted again in his seat, but again answered, "No, I don't know of anyone by that name that lives around here. That doesn't mean that there couldn't be someone by that name. Maybe I just never met him."

"Fine, we'll come back to that later then," said Steven, quickly changing the subject. "Is it true that Jake Foster told Todd's father, Dan Harper, that he had seen an old man in the woods just prior to his son's death and that Dan Harper reported that information to you?"

"Yes, that's true," replied Mark. "I did follow up on that, but I never could find any leads to support it. I had to just let it drop after a while because nobody else saw him and I couldn't find any trace of evidence of him being in the woods."

"So you just dismissed it then," said Steven. "Is that correct?"

"I kept the information in the file, but I never was able to do anything with it."

"A boy is dead, and a neighbor reports seeing a strange man in the woods just around that time and you just stick it in the file and you don't do anything with it?" Steven said, facing the jury.

"No, I did try to find out who the man was, but nobody else saw anything," Mark quickly explained. "This is a rural area and people can come and go pretty easily without anybody else ever seeing them. He could have been some bum living in the woods or just passing through to the next town. I see that happen every day, but there was no name or a way for me to trace him down, even if there was anyone by that description in the woods."

"So you think Jake just made that up?"

"No, no, not at all," said Mark. "I'm just saying that I couldn't do a lot with the information he gave me. There was no one by that description around this area that I could find."

"You know, I went out to Jake's house and paid him a visit the other day. We had a short talk," said Steven smiling.

"I bet it was really short."

"What do you mean by that?" asked Steven.

"People in these parts don't like talking to strangers," replied Mark sharply. "That's all I meant."

"No, you're right. He didn't want to talk at all. As a matter of fact, he ran me off of his property with a shotgun aimed at my head."

Moans went up from the jury.

"People around here just want to protect their property and be left alone," said Mark. "He wouldn't have shot you. He just wanted to scare you off."

"Oh, but he seemed really scared for some reason," answered Steven. "It wasn't just his property that he was trying to protect. It seemed to me that he was afraid for his life. He wasn't afraid of me, because I didn't have a weapon. All I had were some questions and a business card, but he was very afraid of me being there. Why do you suppose that was?"

"Like I said, people around here don't like talking to strangers, especially lawyers." Mark replied with a smirk and then smiled at the jury. The jury laughed along a bit at Mark's comment.

"Oh, I see. It was because I'm a lawyer that he was afraid and not because you were the sheriff and threatened him if he didn't keep quiet about what he saw."

Mark glared back at Steven. "You don't know anything—"

"Objection, Your Honor," shouted the prosecutor. "There's no evidence that the sheriff would have any reason to threaten Jake Foster's life."

"Sustained. Counselor," said the judge. He looked at Steven and spoke firmly. "I'm not sure exactly where you're heading with all of this, but you'd better start stating your case very quickly now."

"Just a few more questions, Your Honor," replied Steven. "I promise not to take too much more time."

Just then, at the back of the courtroom, Gracey walked in, looking for a seat. Mark saw her come in, but continued answering Steven's questions as he watched her take a seat near the front of the room.

"Excuse me, Mr. Temple, I don't believe you finished what you were saying," said Steven. "Could you start again for the jury?" asked Steven with a slight smile on his face.

Nathan watched as Mark's face changed a little. He looked a little surprised to see Gracey in the courtroom.

"Mr. Temple, since you don't seem to want to finish what you were saying, let me go back to a question I asked you before. Do you know anybody by the name of Samuel?"

"No, I told you that before," answered Mark. "Why do you keep asking me that? Are you deaf or something?"

"I don't believe I have any more questions for Mr. Temple, Your Honor," said Steven, returning to his seat.

"The witness may step down," stated the judge.

"For my next witness, I'd like to call Betsy Radcliff."

Nathan turned in his seat in shock to see the doors fly open in the back of the courtroom. In walked Betsy Radcliff in an old, but clean print dress. She held Samuel's hand as she slowly made her way to the witness stand. Samuel wasn't wearing his mask, but he was carrying it in his hand. His eyes wandered all around the room as his face changed from a look of great curiosity to a broad, quick grin and then back again. An officer took his hand and helped him to a seat on the front row, while Betsy continued ever so slowly to the witness stand. The same officer took her hand and helped her to climb the two steps up to the chair. She looked nervous and pale as she stared around the room. Nathan looked at Mark to see his reaction. He sat with his eyes fixed on the old woman, gripping the seat in front of him as she swore an oath to tell nothing but the truth.

Steven smiled broadly at her and then, in a loud voice, making sure she understood every word, he began to question her." Could you state your name for the court please?"

"My name is Betsy Radcliff," Betsy said nervously.

"And do you live here in Fairhaven, Mrs. Radcliff?" asked Steven.

"Yes, I've lived here all my life."

"Do you live alone?"

"No, my son, Samuel lives with me."

"Could you point out your son for the jury, please?" asked Steven.

Reluctantly, Betsy pointed in the direction of Samuel.

"My name is Samuel!" Samuel shouted loudly, as he jumped up from his seat. The people in the courtroom laughed nervously, while the officer coaxed him to take his seat again and to stay quiet.

"He ain't never been in no courtroom before. So he's jumpy, like a bug in a jar," said Betsy.

"Betsy, what do you know about the death of Robert Sanding, the young boy that was found dead years ago here in Fairhaven?" asked Steven.

"Objection!" shouted Pete. "This trial is not about Robert Sanding. We're here to find out who killed Todd Harper."

"Your honor," Steven said firmly. "I just want to establish some important background information that this court may not be aware of at this time."

The judge stared back at Steven for a brief moment. "Over ruled! Let's wait and see where this is going."

Betsy hung her head and then looked over at Nathan before she spoke. He gave her a slight nod of encouragement. Betsy slowly repeated the story she had told him earlier.

"Mrs. Radcliff, you say you paid off a boy to keep quiet about the murder of Robert Sanding. Did your son, Samuel, kill Robert?"

"No, he wouldn't hurt nobody," Betsy answered emphatically. "I found out years later, from somebody else who was in the woods that day. I know the real killer."

"And who was that killer, Mrs. Radcliff?" asked Steven in a loud voice.

"It was the boy that I paid the money to keep quiet," Betsy said with tears in her eyes. "He killed Robert and then blamed it on my Samuel. I paid money to protect my boy, but all along it was that devil that blackmailed me."

"Can you recall this boy's name today?"

"Yes I can. His name is Mark Temple, our high and mighty sheriff."

The courtroom erupted into chaos.

Mark jumped up from his seat, "You crazy old woman! I ought to throw your boy in jail right now. Who do you expect to believe such a wild story? Your Honor, this woman is obviously an insane hermit who's been housing a murderer all of these years. Look at him, he's crazy as a bat and she's just as crazy. I saw him kill that boy with my own eyes."

"Quiet!" the judge screamed, slamming his gavel several times on the desk. "Mr. Temple, I'm going to have you removed from this courtroom if there's one more outburst from you. This witness will be heard if I have to dismiss this entire courtroom. Is that understood? Now everybody best settle down right now! I'll not have this nonsense in my courtroom. Now, continue with your questions, Counselor."

"Thank you, Your Honor," said Steven. "Now Mrs. Radcliff, can you tell us who witnessed the murder of Robert Sanding and later told you the truth about what happened?"

"I don't want to say who it was. He didn't want to cause no trouble. He just wanted me to know the truth about what happened. I don't want to cause him no trouble."

"It was me who told her," Jake Foster said, standing from his seat. "I told her the truth cause I witnessed the whole thing. Mark Temple killed that boy and blamed Samuel for it. He's the real killer, Your Honor, not Samuel."

"Objection, Your Honor. Nathan Staby is the one on trial here, not Samuel or Mark Temple," Pete demanded. "What does all this have to do with the murder of Todd Harper?"

By now, there's total chaos in the courtroom again.

"Mr. Foster, please take your seat now," demanded the judge. "We'll deal with you later."

"Your Honor, what about my objection?" asks the prosecutor.

"Would the Counselors please approach the bench?" requested the judge. The judge rubbed his face with his hands as he tried to maintain some order in the room.

Steven and Pete approached the bench and stood before the judge.

"Steven, you're turning this courtroom into some kind of a circus. Do you have an explanation for all this?"

"Your Honor, my questions are leading up to Todd Harper's death, but there's more background here than just the present murder that we have before us. Please, allow me to continue and you'll see the relevance of her testimony."

"I don't know what you're up to, but you'd better make this mess make some sense real fast or I'm going to dismiss this witness and her testimony. Do you understand me?"

"Yes, Your Honor."

Steven walked back toward Betsy and faced the jury. "Now, Mrs. Radcliff," Steven continued, "did you ever give money to Mark Temple after that first time?"

"Yes, he threatened me several times over the years to have my boy taken from me if I didn't give him money to keep quiet. He's held that secret over my head for many years, but the worst of it is that Samuel never done anything wrong in the first place. Mark Temple know'd nobody would believe me over him, but I ain't afraid of him no more. I got to protect my boy, Samuel. It's him I got to think about now and I want everybody to know the truth. I'm tired of hiding."

"And what is the truth, Mrs. Radcliff?" asked Steven, still looking at the jury.

"Mark Temple is a murderer. He killed Robert Sanding and Todd Harper too. He's a blackmailer and he's a liar!"

Loud mumbling echoed throughout the courtroom. "Quiet!" said the judge, slamming his gavel down once again. "Keep this room quiet!"

Steven continued his questioning. "And how do you know that he killed Todd Harper as well?"

"Because Samuel saw him do it and he told me the truth. He may not be smart, but he's not a liar. He saw the whole thing, he saw Mark kill that poor boy. Mark Temple threatened to have Samuel taken away from me if I tried to make any trouble. He made out like he was protecting me and Samuel, but I know'd better."

"So, why didn't you tell somebody the truth, Mrs. Radcliff?" asked Steven.

"Cause I know'd that I was a nobody and as soon as they took one look at my boy, they'd never believe me against Mark Temple. But then I decided that I had to take a stand for what's right and put a stop to this nonsense. Samuel's a loving, sweet boy. It ain't right that he don't have a life without having this shame hanging over him. I had to come and tell the truth for his sake. I just had to trust that these good folks would believe me."

"Your Honor, I don't have any more questions for Mrs. Radcliff," said Steven returning to his seat.

"Does the prosecutor want to cross examine the witness?" asked the judge.

"Just one, Your Honor," said Pete walking toward Betsy. "Why should this jury believe your story over the testimony of Mark Temple, the sheriff of this town and a model citizen? Isn't it true you're just looking to get your boy off the hook and protect him?"

"No, I ain't just protecting my boy!" shouted Betsy. "I know the truth and I want the rest of this town to know it too. I ain't afraid to stand up for what's right no more." Betsy turned toward the jury for a moment. "I know I ain't nobody to you folks. Most of you wouldn't give me the time of day, I'm sure. I live in a run down house out in the middle of the woods. Why should you believe someone like me? But I'm here to tell you my boy ain't no killer. He may be different from your boys, but that don't make him no killer."

"No more questions, Your Honor," said Pete.

"Very well, then, you may step down Mrs. Radcliff."

Slowly, Betsy slid off of the seat and shuffled her way across the courtroom and took a seat next to Samuel, clasping his hand tightly in hers, like she was holding on to it for dear life. Samuel smiled back at her as though all was right with the world.

"Your Honor, for my next witness, I'd like to call Gracey Temple," stated Steven.

Mark turned quickly, staring in disbelief. "What's going on here? Gracey, what are you doing?"

Gracey got up quickly without looking over at Mark. She took her seat on the witness stand, keeping her head slightly bowed so that her hair hid her face and eyes. She was wearing her best Sunday outfit, a light pink suit with a matching bow in her hair. After taking the oath, she nervously reached for a glass of water and took small sips to quench her dry throat.

"Would you please state your name for the court?" asked Steven.

"My name is Gracey Temple."

"And what relation are you to Mark Temple?"

"He's my husband." She glanced back at Mark briefly and then looked down again.

"Can you tell the court what you found this past Saturday night in your home?"

"Well, I was looking for something, going through our dresser at home, when I found an envelope," Gracey answered.

"What made you pay attention to just a plain envelope?" Steven asked.

"On the outside it had a name written over and over again. The name was Marcie Staby, Nathan's wife. I recognized Mark's hand-writing. So I picked it up and looked inside."

"And what did you find?"

"There was a scribbled note that said, 'Betsy, pay the money by tomorrow or I'll have to tell who really killed Todd. You'll never see Samuel again.' It was signed by my husband, Mark. I knew he'd been getting extra money from some place, but I didn't know from where, until I found this note. I just couldn't believe that he would do such a thing." Gracey started to cry and then she suddenly raised her head and looked over at her husband. "Mark, I'm so sorry, but you don't care about me anymore. I can't lie for you. I just can't let an innocent man go to jail. Please forgive me."

Mark jumped to his feet, "Gracey, I'm sorry. I never wanted you to be hurt. Everything just got so mixed up. I did once love Marcie, from the start, but she would never have me. I wasn't good enough for her. She only wanted Nathan. I tried to get rid of her, by running her car off the road, but when she survived, I knew it was Nathan I had to get out of the way. The money was for you, baby, to take care of you. I did it for you. I wanted you to have things that I couldn't give you. Can't you see, Gracey? I did it for you."

"Mark Temple, you killed Robert Sanding, didn't you?" Steven shouted.

"Yes, I killed Robert, but it was an accident. I always wanted to be good friends with Nathan, but Robert was always in the way. He wouldn't let me hang around with them that day, even though I followed them all the way out into the woods. I just wanted to join in, but Robert told me to get lost. I pushed him down and I hit him with a big stick several times. I guess I hit him pretty hard, but I didn't mean to kill him."

"What about Todd Harper?" Steven screamed. "Did you kill him too?"

Mark hung his head and tears streamed down his cheeks. "I was in the woods looking for Samuel. I lied about not knowing him. I've known him for years. He was supposed to stay close to home, but he was always sneaking out there to play. When I found him, Todd Harper was there, teasing him. I told him to get away from Samuel and go home, but he just kept on teasing Samuel. Then he made a remark about my son, Charley. He said, "Samuel's a loser just like Charley was a loser." He had no right to say anything about my poor Charley. I just wanted to scare Todd, but before I knew it, I grabbed him and slung him up against a rock. I was so angry, but I didn't mean to do it. He must have hit his head or something and he died right in front of me. I only meant to scare him, not kill him. Can't you see it was an accident? I was scared. So I told Betsy that Samuel killed Todd and I threatened to tell if she made any trouble. I didn't know what else to do! It's all messed up. I never meant to hurt anybody. Gracey, please forgive me. I love you."

"What about the black bag and the bloody shirt? Where did those things come from?" asked Steven.

Mark took a deep breath before speaking. "I planted them there so that it would look like Nathan was the killer." Mark paused and looked at Nathan. "He almost believed he was the killer himself. I even called him once when he was in Marcie's house and threatened him to stay out of the woods. I played on his fears so he would believe he could have killed Todd Harper and even Robert. For a while it seemed like everything would be all right. He was a stranger in town to most people. I knew they would believe he was the killer." Mark broke down and started sobbing. "I'm sorry, Nathan. I'm really, really sorry."

"Your Honor, I request that the charges against my client, Nathan Staby, be dismissed and that charges be brought against Mark Temple instead," said Steven.

As the judge dismissed the charges and ordered Mark to be taken into custody, you could hear Mark's voice echoing throughout the courtroom, "I'm not a loser. My son wasn't a loser. People always treated me like dirt, like they're better than me, but they're not. I won't be treated like a crazy person, like that old lady Radcliff. As the sheriff of this town, I demand your respect. I'm not a murderer!"

Nathan watched Gracey's face as she sat and listened to her husband confess to his crimes, knowing that she was going to lose him now for good, but she was finally free of a life of lies and secrets. The jury looked on in shock at all they had heard. The whole courtroom looked stunned at the confession they were hearing. After all, this was a man they had known and trusted for years.

The prosecutor and his team were desperately trying to figure out what had just happened. Everyone was in an uproar. Everyone had assumed Gracey was just a stupid, gaudy girl. Yet now, she appeared to be a woman of grace and dignity. She had done the right thing, bringing to light an awful secret. She seemed to breathe a sigh of relief, as tears continued to fall.

Betsy held Samuel's hand throughout the ordeal and for probably the first time in his life, he sat quietly staring at everything going on around him. He somehow seemed to understand what was happening.

Nathan sat in a daze, not able to grasp that Mark could have been such an evil person. In the middle of all of the commotion, he felt a hand on his shoulder. When he looked up, there in front of him stood Jake Foster and his wife. Tears were rolling down his face. "I did tell Betsy that Mark killed Robert Sanding. I had to tell someone or I couldn't live with myself. I'm sorry I didn't do more to help you, Nathan. I'm real glad everything worked out the way it did." Then he turned and left without saying anything else.

As Nathan stood to his feet, Steven grabbed his hand and slapped him on the back. "I think it's over my friend." As Steven gave him a hug, Nathan caught a glimpse of Samuel sitting across from him. As Samuel turned and caught his eye, he smiled, pulled the mask over his head and yelled back at Nathan, "Don't be afraid, I'm an angel, Nathan."

"You'll always be an angel to me, Samuel." Nathan said softly.

Betsy slowly looked up at Nathan without smiling. She wasn't sure what all of this meant for her and Samuel.

"Don't worry, Betsy," said Nathan, taking her hand. "I'll make sure you get all the help you need for you and Samuel. It's the least I can do for you."

Betsy smiled and grabbed Samuel's hand. They slowly walked out of the courtroom, hand in hand. Samuel kept glancing back at Nathan and waving. "Goodbye, Nathan."

Nathan waved goodbye to Samuel. Then he turned, grabbed Marcie and pulled her as close to him as possible. "Let's go home, Mrs. Staby."

Marcie burst into tears. Their life together was finally beginning. She only wished Maggie was here to enjoy it with them, but somehow she was sure Maggie was witnessing everything.

# 56

That night, back at home, Nathan sat on the front porch and quietly whispered a prayer for Gracey, hoping one day she would finally find the happiness she so richly deserved. He looked forward to a night of sleeping without chasing angels or Robert through his dreams. No one would be calling his name tonight. Yet still, off in the distance, he thought he could hear the sound of the Black River racing around in the mountains that haunted his thoughts and dreams for so long. "All things good and all things bad happen around this Black River, but it just keeps moving, paying no mind to what's going on around it," he remembered Robert saying. Nathan closed his eyes and rested, knowing that the dragon he and Robert had so fiercely struggled to fight all those years ago had finally been slain for good this time.

Nathan leaned back in his chair and scanned the beautiful view of the woods in front of him. It was quiet now. He felt, for the first time, completely relaxed and hopeful about his future with Marcie. It was a brand new start for them in so many ways. He could now focus on the present and the future instead of being consumed with his past. Breathing a sigh of relief, Nathan closed his eyes to drink in the moment. He had been waiting for this season to arrive for most of his life and now it was finally here.

Suddenly he was startled by a voice he had heard many times before, "Goodnight, Nathan, goodnight!"

Nathan quickly opened his eyes and leaned forward in his chair. He stared out at the woods. The voice sounded as if it was coming from that direction. He stared without blinking for a long while. Then he heard it once more, the same voice, "Goodnight Nathan."

Squinting his eyes, Nathan focused his full attention on the trees in front of him. He couldn't believe he was still hearing the voice that haunted him for so long. As he continued to stare, he thought he saw something moving in the trees. He couldn't clearly see what it was, but as he continued to watch he saw it again. It was like a white mist, but at the same time it looked like the shape of a man. Nathan stood to his feet and moved as close as possible to the edge of the porch. He couldn't believe his eyes. Something or someone was waving to him from the woods. Was it Samuel? Nathan wiped his eyes and stared once more out through the trees. He was barely breathing now because he wanted to be sure of what he was seeing. There it was again. It seemed to move freely from tree to tree without any effort.

Nathan began to shake a little, but he tried to maintain his composure as he continued to stare at the trees moving ever so slightly in the breeze. Was it his imagination playing tricks on him again? Suddenly he heard that voice yet again. "I see you, Nathan."

Nathan quickly sat back down in his chair. Perhaps Samuel was watching him from the woods. Then a strange thought dawned on him. Or, perhaps, Samuel had been imitating something he had seen himself in the woods many times before. Could it be that Samuel wasn't the only angel he had been chasing?

"Nathan, are you out there?" Marcie called from the house. "Come inside and let's have some dinner. Are you hungry at all?"

Nathan looked out once more toward the woods, but he couldn't see a thing. He turned to go inside and slowly closed the door behind him. He took one more glance out of the window toward the trees. "Goodnight," said Nathan under his breath, lingering at the door a little longer. There was no answer, just the clinking of the glasses as Marcie set the table.

## THE END

# ABOUT THE AUTHOR

Polly Boyette is a writer and an inspirational speaker. Even though "Chasing Angels" is her first mystery novel, Polly has also written two inspirational books, *"Life is a Buffet So Save Room for Dessert,"* and *"Life is a Buffet So What's On Your Plate?"* These books use humor and real life experiences to encourage and inspire women in their everyday lives and to remind them of the joy in serving Christ. Her friends will tell you she has a very strong sense of humor and a gift for telling stories.

Polly was born and raised in Portsmouth, VA and currently lives in Virginia Beach, VA. She previously worked for 28 years as a Human Resources Advisor before deciding to take an early retirement to follow her passion for writing.

www.ingramcontent.com/pod-product-compliance
Lightning Source LLC
Chambersburg PA
CBHW062116170626
46813CB00002B/466